My Friend the Chauffeur

A. M. Williamson and
C. N. Williamson

Illustrated by Frederic Lowenheim

MY FRIEND
The CHAUFFEUR

C.N.&A.M.WILLIAMSON

She was only a tall white girl simply dressed

MY FRIEND THE CHAUFFEUR

By C. N. and A. M. WILLIAMSON

Authors of "Lady Betty Across the Water," "The Princess Virginia,"
"The Lightning Conductor," etc., etc.

With Illustrations
BY FREDERIC LOWENHEIM

A. L. BURT COMPANY, PUBLISHERS

NEW YORK

Published September, 1905

TO

THE OTHER BEECHY

CONTENTS

LIST OF ILLUSTRATIONS.

PART I

TOLD BY RALPH MORAY

I

A CHAPTER OF SURPRISES

"WANTED, LADIES, TO CONDUCT. An amateur automobilist (English, titled) who drives his own motor-car accommodating five persons, offers to conduct two or three ladies, Americans preferred, to any picturesque centres in Europe which they may desire to visit. Car has capacity for carrying small luggage, and is of best type. Journeys of about 100 miles a day. Novel and delightful way of travelling; owner of car well up in history, art, and architecture of different countries. Inclusive terms five guineas a day each, or slight reduction made for extensive trip. Address—"

When Terry had read aloud thus far, I hastily interrupted him. I wasn't quite ready yet for him to see that address. The thing needed a little leading up to; and by way of getting him quickly and safely on to a side rack I burst into a shout of laughter, so loud and so sudden that he looked up from the little pink Riviera newspaper of which I was the proud proprietor, to stare at me.

"What's the matter?" he asked.

I subsided. "The idea struck me so forcibly," said I. "Jolly clever, isn't it?"

"It's a fake, of course," said Terry. "No fellow would be ass enough to advertise himself like that in earnest. Probably the thing's been put in for a bet, or else it's a practical joke."

I had been aware that this, or something like it, would come, but now that the crisis was at hand I felt qualmish. Terry —known to strangers as Lord Terence Barrymore—is the best and most delightful chap in the world, as well as one of the best looking, but like several other Irishmen he is, to put it mildly, rather hard to manage, especially when you want to do him a good turn. I had been trying to do him one without his knowing it, and in such a way that he couldn't escape when he did know. But the success of my scheme was now being dandled on the knees of the gods, and at any instant it might fall off to break like an egg.

"I believe it's genuine," I began gingerly, almost wishing that I hadn't purposely put the pink paper where Terry would be sure to pick it up. "And I don't see why you should call the advertiser in my paper an ass. If you were hard up, and had a motor-car—"

"I am hard up, and I have a motor-car."

"What I was going to say is this: wouldn't it be much better to turn your car into the means of making an honest living, and at the same time having some rattling good fun, rather than sell the thing for less than half cost, and not only get no fun at all, but not know how to get out of the scrape in which you've landed yourself?"

It was Terry's turn to laugh now, which he did, though not uproariously, as I had. "One would think the ass was a friend of yours, by your enthusiasm in defending him," said he.

"I'm only putting the case to you in the way I thought you'd see it most clearly," I persisted mildly. "But, as a matter of fact, the 'ass' as you call him, is my friend, a very intimate friend indeed."

"Didn't know you had any intimate friends but me, anyhow owners of motor-cars, you old owl," remarked Terry. "I must say in your defence, though, it isn't like you to have friends who advertise themselves as titled couriers."

"If you're obliged to start a shop I suppose it's legitimate to put your best goods in the windows, and arrange them as attractively as you can to appeal to the public," I argued. "This is the same thing. Besides, my friend isn't advertising himself. Somebody is 'running

2

him'—doing it for him; wants him to get on, you know—just as I do you."

Terry gave me a quick glance; but my face (which is blond and said to be singularly youthful for a man of twenty-nine) was, I flatter myself, as innocent as that of a choir-boy who has just delivered himself of a high soprano note. Nevertheless, the end was coming. I felt it in the electric tingle of the air.

"Do you mind telling me your friend's name, or is he a secret?"

"Perhaps the address at the end of the advertisement will be enlightening."

Terry had dropped the paper on the grass by the side of his *chaise longue*, but now he picked it up again, and began searching for the place which he had lost. I, in my *chaise longue* under the same magnolia tree, gazed at him from under my tilted Panama. Terry is tall and dark. Stretched out in the basket chair, he looked very big and rather formidable. Beside him, I felt a small and reedy person. I really hoped he would not give me much trouble. The day was too hot to cope with troublesome people, especially if you were fond of them, for then you were the more likely to lose your head.

But the beginning was not encouraging. Terry proceeded to read the end of the advertisement aloud. "Address X. Y. Z., Châlet des Pins, Cap Martin." Then he said something which did not go at all with the weather. Why is it that so many bad words begin with D or H? One almost gets to think that they are letters for respectable people to avoid.

"Hang it all, Ralph," he went on, after the explosion, "I must say I don't like your taste in jokes. This is a bit too steep."

I sat up straight, with a leg on each side of the chair, and looked reproaches. "I thought," I said slowly, "that when your brother behaved like such a—well, we won't specify what—you asked, I might even say begged, for my advice, and promised in a midnight conversation under this very tree to take it, no matter how disagreeable it might prove."

"I did; but—"

"There's no such word as 'but.' Last year I advised you not to put your money into West Africans. You put it in. What was the consequence? You regretted it, and as your brother showed no very keen interest in your career, you decided that you couldn't afford to stop in the Guards, so you cut the Army. This year I advised you not to play that system of yours and Raleigh's at Monte Carlo, or if you must have a go at it, to stick to roulette and five franc stakes. Instead of listening to me, you listened to him. What were the consequences?"

"For goodness sake don't moralize. I know well enough what they were. Ruin. And it doesn't gild the pill to remember that I deserved to swallow it."

"If only you'd swallowed the advice instead! It would have slipped down more easily, poor old boy. But you swore to bolt the next dose without a groan. I said I'd try and think of a better plan than selling your Panhard, and going out to help work an African farm on the proceeds. Well, I *have* thought of a plan, and there you have the proof of my combined solicitude and ingenuity, in my own paper."

"Don't shoot off big words at me."

"I'm a journalist; my father before me was a journalist, and got his silly old baronetcy by being a journalist. *I'm* one still, and have saved up quite a little competency on big words and potted phrases. I've collected a great many practical ideas in my experience. I want to make you a present of some of them, if only you'll have them."

"Do you call this advertisement a practical idea? You can't for a minute suppose that I'd be found dead carting a lot of American or other women whom I don't know about Europe in my car, and taking their beastly money?"

"If you drove properly, you wouldn't be found dead; and you would know them," I had begun, when there was a ring at the gate bell, and the high wall of the garden abruptly opened to admit a tidal wave of chiffon and muslin.

Terry and I were both so taken aback at this unexpected inundation that for a moment we lay still in our chairs and stared, with our hats tipped over our eyes and our pipes in our mouths. We were not accustomed to afternoon calls or any other time-of-day calls from chiffon and muslin at the Châlet des Pins, therefore our first impression was that the tidal wave had overflowed through my gate by mistake, and would promptly retire in disorder at sight of us. But not at all. It swept up the path, in pink, pale green, and white billows, frothing at the edges with lace.

There was a lot of it—a bewildering lot. It was all train, and big, flowery hats, and wonderful transparent parasols, which you felt you ought to see through, and couldn't. Before it was upon us, Terry and I had sprung up in self-defence, our pipes burning holes in our pockets, our Panamas in our hands.

Now the inundation divided itself into separate wavelets, the last lagging behind, crested by a foaming parasol, which hid all details, except a general white muslin filminess. But Terry and I had not much chance to observe the third billow. Our attention was caught by the first glittering rush of pink and emerald spray.

Out of it a voice spoke—an American voice; and then, with a lacy whirl, a parasol rose like a stage curtain. The green wave was a lady; a marvellous lady. The pink wave was a child with a brown face, two long brown plaits, and pink silk legs, also pink shoes.

"We've come in answer to X. Y. Z.'s advertisement in this morning's *Riviera Sun*. Now which of you two gentlemen put it in?" began the lady, with gay coquetry which played over each of us in turn. Oh yes, she was wonderful. She had hair of the brightest auburn that ever crowned a human head. It was done in undulations, with a fat ring in the middle of her forehead, between two beautifully arched black eyebrows. Her skin was very white, her cheeks were very pink, and her lips were very coralline. Everything about her was "very." Out of a plump face, with a small nose that turned up and a chin which was over-round, looked a pair of big, good-natured, nondescript-coloured eyes, and flashed a pair of pleasant dimples. At first glance you said "a stout girl of twenty-five." At the second, you were not sure that the lady wasn't ten years older. But her waist

5

was so slender that she panted a little in coming up the path, though the path was by no means steep, and her heels were so high that there was a suspicion of limp in her walk.

Even to me the lady and her announcement gave a shock, which must have doubled its effect upon Terry. I was collecting my forces for a reply when the little brown girl giggled, and I lost myself again. It was only for an instant, but Terry basely took advantage of that instant in a way of which I would not have believed him capable.

"You must address yourself to my friend, Sir Ralph Moray," said the wretched fellow glibly. "His are the car and the title mentioned in the advertisement of *The Riviera Sun*, which he owns."

My title indeed! A baronetical crumb flung to my father because of a service to his political party. It had never done anything for me, except to add ten per cent to my bills at hotels. Now, before I could speak a word of contradiction, Terry went on. "I am only Mr. Barrymore," said he, and he grinned a malicious grin, which said as plainly as words, "Aha, my boy, I think *that* rips your little scheme to smithereens, eh?"

But my presence of mind doesn't often fail for long. "It's Mr. Barrymore who drives my car for me," I explained. "He's cleverer at it than I, and he comes cheaper than a professional."

The wonderful white and pink and auburn lady had been looking at Terry with open admiration; but now the light of interest faded from the good-natured face under the girlish hat. "O-oh," she commented in a tone of ingenuous disappointment, "you're only the—the chawffur, then." I didn't want Terry to sink too low in these possible clients' estimation, for my canny Scotch mind was working round the fact that they were probably American heiresses, and an heiress of some sort was a necessity for the younger brother of that meanest of bachelor peers, the Marquis of Innisfallen. "He's an amateur chauffeur," I hastened to explain. "He only does it for me because we're friends, you know; but," I added, with a stern and meaning glance at Terry, "I'm unable to undertake any tours without his assistance. So if we—er—arrange anything, *Mr. Barrymore* will be of our party."

"Unfortunately I have an engagement in South Af—" began Terry, when the parasol of the third member of the party (the one who had lagged behind, stopping to examine, or seeming to examine a rose-bush) was laid back upon her white muslin shoulders.

Somehow Terry forgot to finish his sentence, and I forgot to wonder what the end was to be.

She was only a tall, white girl, simply dressed; yet suddenly the little garden of the Châlet des Pins, with its high wall draped with crimson bougainvilla, became a setting for a picture.

The new vision was built on too grand a scale for me, because I stand only five foot eight in my boots, while she was five foot seven if she was an inch, but she might have been made expressly for Terry, and he for her. There was something of the sweet, youthful dignity of Giovanni Bellini's Madonnas of the Trees about the girl's bearing and the pose of the white throat; but the face was almost childlike in the candour and virginal innocence of its large brown eyes. The pure forehead had a halo of yellow-brown hair, burnished gold where the sun touched it; the lips were red, with an adorable droop in the corners, and the skin had that flower-fairness of youth which makes older women's faces look either sallow or artificial. If we—Terry and I—had not already divined that the auburn lady got her complexion out of bottles and boxes, we would have known it with the lifting of that white girl's parasol.

Can a saintly virgin on a golden panel look sulky? I'm not sure, but this virgin gave the effect of having been reluctantly torn from such a background, and she looked distinctly sulky, even angelically cross. She had not wanted to come into my garden, that was plain; and she lagged behind the others to gaze at a rose-bush, by way of a protest against the whole expedition. What she saw to disapprove of in me I was at a loss to guess, but that she did disapprove was evident. The dazzling brown eyes, with the afternoon sun glinting between their thick dark fringes, hated me for something;—was it my existence, or my advertisement? Then they wandered to Terry, and pitied, rather than spurned. "You poor, handsome, big fellow," they seemed so say, "so you are that miserable little man's chauffeur! You must be very unfortunate, or you would have found a better career. I'm so sorry for you."

"Do sit down, please," I said, lest after all it should occur to Terry to finish that broken sentence of his. "These chairs will be more comfortable if I straighten their backs up a little. And this seat round the tree isn't bad. I—I'll tell my servant to send out tea—we were going to have it soon—and we can talk things over. It will be pleasanter."

"What a *lovely* idea!" exclaimed the auburn lady. "Why, of course we will. Beechy, you take one of those steamer-chairs. I like a high seat myself. Come, Maida; the gentlemen have asked us to stay to tea, and we're going to."

Beechy—the little brown girl—subsided with a babyish meekness that contradicted a wicked laughing imp in her eyes, into one of the *chaises longues* which I had brought up from its knees to a sort of "stand and deliver" attitude. But the tall white girl (the name of "Maida" suited her singularly well) did not stir an inch. "I think I'll go on if you don't mind, Aunt Ka—I mean, Kittie," she said in a soft voice that was as American in its way as the auburn lady's, but a hundred and fifty times sweeter. I rather fancied that it must have been grown somewhere in the South, where the sun was warm, and the flowers as luxuriant as our Riviera blossoms.

"You will do nothing of the kind," retorted her relative peremptorily. "You'll just stay here with Beechy and me, till we've done our business."

"But I haven't anything to do with—"

"You're going with us on the trip, anyhow, if we go. Now, come along and don't make a fuss."

For a moment "Maida" hesitated, then she did come along, and as obediently as the brown child, though not so willingly, sat down in the *chaise longue*, carefully arranged for her reception by Terry.

"Evidently a poor relation, or she wouldn't submit to being ordered about like that," I thought. "Of course, any one might see that she's too pretty to be an heiress. They don't make them like that. Such beauties never have a penny to bless themselves with. Just Terry's luck if he falls in love with her, after all I've done for him, too! But if this tour does come off, I must try to block *that* game."

"I expect I'd better introduce myself and my little thirteen-year-old daughter, and my niece," said the auburn lady, putting down her parasol, and opening a microscopic fan. "I'm Mrs. Kathryn Stanley Kidder, of Denver, Colorado. My little girl, here—she's all I've got in the world since Mr. Kidder died—is Beatrice, but we call her Beechy for short. We used to spell it B-i-c-e, which Mr. Kidder said was Italian; but people *would* pronounce it to rhyme with mice, so now we make it just like the tree, and then there can't be any mistake. Miss Madeleine Destrey is the daughter of my dead sister, who was *ever* so much older than I am of course; and the way she happened to come over with Beechy and me is quite a romance; but I guess you'll think I've told you enough about ourselves."

"It's like the people in old comic pictures who have kind of balloon things coming out of their mouths, with a verse thoroughly explaining who they are, isn't it?" remarked Miss Beechy in a little soft, childish voice, and at least a dozen imps looking out of her eyes all at once. "Mamma's balloon never collapses."

To break the awkward silence following upon this frank comparison, I bustled away with hospitable murmurs concerning tea. But, my back once turned upon the visitors, the pink, white, and green glamour of their presence floated away from before my eyes like a radiant mist, and I saw plain fact instead.

By plain fact I mean to denote Félicité, my French cook-housekeeper, my all of domesticity in the Châlet des Pins.

Félicité might be considered plain by strangers, and thank heaven she is a fact, or life at my little villa on the Riviera would be a hundred times less pleasant than it is; but she is nevertheless as near to being an angel as a fat, elderly, golden-hearted, sweet-natured, profane-speaking, hot-tempered peasant woman of Provence can possibly be. Whatever the greatest geniuses of the kitchen can do, Félicité can and will do, and she has a loyal affection for her undeserving master, which leads her to attempt miracles and almost invariably to accomplish them.

There are, however, things which even Félicité cannot do; and it had suddenly struck me coldly in the sunshine that to produce proper cakes and rich cream at ten minutes' notice in a creamless and cakeless bachelor villa, miles from anywhere in particular, might be beyond even her genius.

I found her in the back garden, forcibly separating the family pet, a somewhat moth-eaten duck, from the yellow cat whose mouse he had just annexed by violence.

With language which told me that a considerable quantity of pepper had got into her disposition (as it does with most cooks, according to my theory) she was admonishing the delinquent, whom she mercilessly threatened to behead and cook for dinner that evening. "You have been spared too long; the best place for you is on the table," I heard her lecturing the evil cannibal, "though the saints know that you are as tough as you are wicked, and all the sauce in the Alpes Maritimes would not make of you a pleasant morsel, especially since you have taken to eating the cat's mice."

"Félicité," I broke in upon her flood of eloquence, in my most winning tones. "Something has happened. Three ladies have come unexpectedly to tea."

The round body straightened itself and stood erect. "Monsieur well knows that there is no tea; neither he nor the other milord ever take anything but coffee and whisk—"

"Never mind," said I hastily. "There must be tea, because I asked the ladies to have some, and they have said yes. There must also be lettuce sandwiches, and cakes, and cream—plenty, lots, heaps, for five people."

"As well ask that serpent of wickedness, your duck, to lay you five eggs in as many minutes."

"He isn't my duck; he's yours. You won him in a raffle and adopted him. I suspect it's a physical impossibility for him to lay eggs; but look here, Félicité, dear, kind, good Félicité, don't go back on me. Man and boy I've known you these eighteen months, and you've never failed me yet. Don't fail me now. I depend on you, you know, and you *must* do something—anything—for the honour of the house."

"Does Monsieur think I can command tea, cakes, and cream from the tiles of the kitchen floor?"

"No; but I firmly believe you can evolve them out of your inner consciousness. You wouldn't have me lose faith in you?"

"No," said Félicité, whose eyes suddenly brightened with the rapt look of one inspired. "No; I would not have Monsieur lose faith. I will do what I can, as Monsieur says, for the honour of the house. Let him go now to his friends, and make his mind easy. In a quarter of an hour, or twenty minutes at most, he shall have a feef o'clocky for which he need not blush."

"Angel!" I ejaculated fervently, patting the substantial shoulder, so much to be depended upon. Then with a buoyant step I hastened round the house to rejoin the party in the front garden, where, I anxiously realized, the tables might have been completely turned during my absence.

Ready to hurl myself into the breach, if there were one, I came round the corner of the villa, to meet the unexpected. I had left Terry with three ladies; I found him with seven.

Evidently he had gone into the drawing-room and fetched chairs, for they were all sitting down, but they were not being sociable. Mrs. Kidder's round chin was in the air, and she wore an "I'm as good as you are, if not better" expression. The imps in Beechy's eyes were critically cataloguing each detail of the strangers' costumes, and Miss

Destrey was interested in the yellow cat, who had come to tell her the tragic tale of the stolen mouse.

The new arrivals were English. I can't explain exactly how I knew that, the moment I clapped eyes on them, but I did; and I felt sure their nearest male relative must have made money in beer, pickles, or it might have been corsets or soap. They were that kind; and they had a great many teeth, especially the daughters, who all three looked exactly thirty, no more and no less, and were apparently pleasantly conscious of superlative virtue.

I could see the house they lived in, in England. It would be in Surbiton, of course, with "extensive grounds." There would be a Debrett's "Peerage," and a Burke's "Landed Gentry," and a volume of "Etiquette of Smart Society" on the library shelves, if there was nothing else; and in the basket on the hall table the visiting cards of any titled beings of the family's acquaintance would invariably rise to the top like cream.

"I understand from your friend that it is your advertisement which appears in *The Riviera Sun* to-day," began the Mother, whose aspect demanded a capital M. "You are Sir Ralph Moray, I believe?"

I acknowledged my identity, and the lady continued: "I am Mrs. Fox-Porston. You will have heard of my husband, no doubt, and I daresay we know a great many of the same People at Home." (This with a dust-brush glance which swept the Americans out of the field.) "I think it is a very excellent idea of yours, Sir Ralph, to travel about the Continent on your motor-car with a few congenial companions, and I have brought my daughters with me to-day in the hope that we may arrange a delightful little tour which—"

"Ting-a-ling" at the gate bell robbed us of Mrs. Fox-Porston's remaining hope, and gave us two more visitors.

Little had I known what the consequences of one small, pink advertisement would be! Apparently it bade fair to let loose upon us, not the dogs of war, but the whole floating feminine population of the French Riviera. Something must be done, and done promptly, to stem the rising tide of ladies, or the Châlet des Pins and Terry and I with it, would be swamped.

I looked at Terry, he looked at me, as we rose like mechanical figures to indicate our hosthood to the new arrivals.

They were Americans; I could tell by their chins. They had no complexions and no particular age; they wore blue tissue veils, and little jingling bags on their belts, which showed that they were not married, because if they had been, their husbands would have ordered the little jingling bags into limbo, wherever that may be.

"Good-afternoon," said the leading Blue Veil. "I am Miss Carrie Hood Woodall, the lady lawyer from Hoboken, who had such a nice little paragraph in *The Riviera Sun*, close to your advertisement; and this is my chaperone, Mrs. Elizabeth Boat Cully. We're touring Europe, and we want to take a trip with you in your automobile, if— "

"Unfortunately, ladies," said I, "the services of—er—my car are already engaged to Mrs. Kidder, of Colorado, and her party. Isn't it so, Barrymore?"

"Yes," replied Terry stoutly. And that "yes" even if inadvertent, was equivalent I considered, to sign and seal.

Mrs. Kidder beamed like an understudy for *The Riviera Sun*. Beechy twinkled demurely, and tossed her plaits over her shoulder. Even Miss Destrey, the white goddess, deigned to smile, straight at Terry and no other.

At this moment Félicité appeared with a tray. Whipped cream frothed over the brow of a brown jug like a white wig on the forehead of a judge; lettuce showed pale green through filmy sandwiches; small round cakes were piled, crisp and appetizing, on a cracked Sèvres dish; early strawberries glowed red among their own leaves. Talk of the marengo trick! It was nothing to this. The miracle had been duly performed; but—there were only five cups.

Mrs. Fox-Porston and her daughters, Miss Carrie Hood Woodall and her chaperone, took the hint and their leave; and the companions of the future were left alone together to talk over their plans.

"Lock the gate, Félicité," said I. "Do make haste!" And she did. Dear Félicité!

II

A CHAPTER OF PLANS

So it is that Fate calmly arranges our lives in spite of us. Although no details of the coming trip were settled during what remained of our new employers' visit, that was their fault and the fault of a singularly premature sunset, rather than mine, or even Terry's; and we both felt that it came to the same thing. We were in honour bound to "personally conduct" Mrs. Kidder, Miss Beechy Kidder, and Miss Destrey towards whatever point of the compass a guiding finger of theirs should signify.

It has always been my motto to take Father Time by the fore-lock, for fear he should cut it off, or get away, or play some other trick upon me, which the cantankerous old chap (no parent of mine!) is fond of doing. Therefore, if I could, I would have had terms, destination, day and hour of starting definitely arranged before that miraculously-produced tea of Félicité's had turned to tannin. But man may not walk through a solid wall, or strive against such conversational gifts as those of Mrs. Kidder.

She could and would keep to anything except the point. That, whatever its nature, she avoided as she would an indelicacy.

"Well, now, Mrs. Kidder," I began, "if you really want us to organize this tour, don't you think we'd better discuss —"

"Of *course* we want you to!" she broke in. "We all think it's just awfully good of you to bother with us when you must have so many friends who want you to take them — English people in your own set. By the way, do you know the Duchess of Carborough?"

"I know very few duchesses or other Americans," I replied. Whereupon Miss Kidder's imp laughed, though her mother remained grave, and even looked mildly disappointed.

"That's a funny way of putting it," said Beechy. "One would think it was quite an American habit, being a Duchess."

"So it is, isn't it?" I asked. "The only reason we needn't fear its growing like the Yellow Peril is because there aren't enough dukes. I've always thought the American nation the most favoured in the world. Aren't all your girls brought up to expect to be duchesses, and your men presidents?"

"*I* wasn't," snapped Beechy. "If there was a duke anywhere around, Mamma would take him, if she had to snatch him out of my mouth. What are English girls brought up to expect?"

"Hope for, not expect," I corrected her. "Any leavings there are in the way of marquesses or earls; or if none, a mere bishop or a C. B."

"What's a C. B.?" asked Mrs. Kidder anxiously.

"A Companion of the Bath."

"My goodness! Whose bath?"

"The Bath of Royalty. We say it with a capital B."

"My! How awkward for your King. And what was done about it when you had only a Queen on the throne?"

"You must inquire of the chamberlains," I replied. "But about that trip of ours. The—er—my car is in a garage not far away, and it can be ready when—"

"Oh, I hope it's a *red* car, with your coat of arms on it. I do so admire red for an automobile. We could all fix ourselves up in red cloaks and hats to match, and make ourselves look awfully swell—"

"Everybody'd call us 'The Crimson Ramblers,' or 'The Scarlet Runners,' or something else horrid," tittered that precocious child Beechy.

"It isn't red, it's grey," Terry managed hastily to interpolate; which settled one burning question, the first which had been settled or seemed likely to be settled at our present rate of progress.

16

"If you are keen on starting—" I essayed again, hope triumphing over experience.

"Yes, I'm just looking forward to that start," Mrs. Kidder caught me up. "We *shall* make a sensation. We're neighbours of yours, you know. We're at the Cap Martin Hotel. Isn't it perfectly lovely there, with that big garden, the woods and all? When we were coming to the Riviera, I told the man at Cook's that we wanted to go to the grandest hotel there was, where we could feel we were getting our money's worth; and he said all the kings and princes, and queens and princesses went to the Cap Martin, so—"

"We thought it might be good enough for us," capped Beechy.

"It's as full of royalties, as—as—"

"As a pack of cards," I suggested.

"And some of them have splendid automobiles. I've been envying them; and only this morning I was saying to my little girl, what a lot of nice things there are that women and children can't do, travelling alone—automobiling for one. Then, when I came on that advertisement of yours, I just *screamed*. It did seem as if the Hand of Providence must have been pointing it out. And it was so funny your home being on the Cap, too, within ten minutes' walk of our hotel. I'm sure it was *meant*, aren't you?"

"Absolutely certain," I responded, with a glance at Terry, who was not showing himself off to any advantage in this scene although he ought to have been the leading actor. He did nothing but raise his eyebrows when he thought that no one was looking, or tug at his moustache most imprudently when somebody was. Or else he handed the cakes to Miss Destrey, and forgot to offer them to her far more important relatives. "I'm so sure of it," I went on, "that I think we had better arrange—"

"Yes, indeed. Of course your ch—Mr. Barrymore (or did I hear you say Terrymore?) is a very experienced driver? We've never been in an automobile yet, any of us, and I'm afraid, though it will be perfectly lovely as soon as we're used to it, that we may be a little scary at first. So it would be nice to know for sure that the driver understood how to act in any emergency. I should *hate* to be killed in an automobile. It would be such—such an *untidy* death to die, judging from what you read in the papers sometimes."

"I should prefer it, myself," I said, "but that's a matter of taste, and you may trust Terry—Mr. Barrymore. What he doesn't know about a motor-car and its inner and outer workings isn't worth knowing. So when we go—"

"Aunt K—I mean Kittie, don't you think we ought to go home to the hotel?" asked Miss Destrey, who had scarcely spoken until now, except to answer a question or two of Terry's, whom she apparently chose to consider in the Martyr's Boat, with herself. "We've been here for *hours*, and it's getting dark."

"Why, so it is!" exclaimed Mrs. Kidder, rising hurriedly. "I'm quite ashamed of myself for staying so long. What will you think of us? But we had such a lot of things to arrange, hadn't we?"

We had had; and we had them still. But that was a detail.

"We *must* go," she went on. "Well, we've decided nearly everything" (this was news to me). "But there are one or two things yet we'll have to talk over, I suppose."

"Quite so," said I.

"Could you and Mr. Terrymore come and dine with us to-night? Then we can fix *everything* up."

"Speaking for myself, I'm afraid I can't, thanks very much," Terry said, hastily.

"What about you, Sir Ralph? I may call you Sir Ralph, may I not?"

"Please. It's my name."

"Yes, I know it. But it sounds so familiar, from a stranger. I was wondering if one ought to say 'Sir Ralph Moray,' till one had been acquainted a little longer. Well, anyway, if you could dine with us, without your friend—"

I also thanked her and said that matters would arrange themselves more easily if Barrymore and I were together.

"Then can you both lunch with us to-morrow at one o'clock?"

Quickly, before Terry could find time to object if he meditated doing so, I accepted with enthusiasm.

Farewells were exchanged, and we had walked to the gate with the ladies—I heading the procession with Mrs. Kidder, Terry bringing up the rear with the two girls—when my companion stopped suddenly. "Oh, there's just one thing I ought to mention before you come to see us at the hotel," she said, with a little catch of the breath. Evidently she was embarrassed. "I introduced myself to you as Mrs. Kidder, because I'm used to that name, and it comes more natural. I keep forgetting always, but—but perhaps you'd better ask at the hotel for the Countess Dalmar. I guess you're rather surprised, though you're too polite to say so, my being an American and having that title."

"Not at all," I assured her. "So many charming Americans marry titled foreigners, that one is almost more surprised—"

"But I haven't married a foreigner. Didn't I tell you that I'm a widow? No, the only husband I ever had was Simon P. Kidder. But—but I've bought an estate, and the title goes with it, so it would seem like a kind of waste of money not to use it, you see."

"It's the estate that goes with the title, for you, Mamma," said Beechy (she invariably pronounces her parent "Momma"). "You know you just love being a Countess. You're happier than I ever was with a new doll that opened and shut its eyes."

"Don't be silly, Beechy. Little girls should be seen and not heard. As I was saying, I thought it better to use the title. That was the advice of Prince Dalmar-Kalm, of whom I've bought this estate in some part of Austria, or I think, Dalmatia—I'm not quite sure about the exact situation yet, as it's all so recent. But to get used to bearing the title, it seemed best to begin right away, so I registered as the Countess Dalmar when we came to the Cap Martin Hotel a week ago."

"Quite sensible, Countess," I said without looking at Beechy-of-the-Attendant-Imps. "I know Prince Dalmar-Kalm well by reputation, though I've never happened to meet him. He's a very familiar figure on the Riviera." (I might have added, "especially in the Casino at Monte Carlo," but I refrained, as I had not yet learned the Countess's opinion of gambling as an occupation.) "Did you meet him here for the first time?"

"No; I met him in Paris, where we stopped for a while after we crossed, before we came here. I was so surprised when I saw him at our hotel the very day after we arrived! It seemed such a coincidence, that our only acquaintance over on this side should arrive at the same place when we did."

"When is a coincidence not a coincidence?" pertly inquired Miss Beechy. "Can you guess that conundrum, Cousin Maida?"

"You naughty girl!" exclaimed her mother.

"Well, you like me to be childish, don't you? And it's childish to be naughty."

"Come, we'll go home at once," said the Countess, uneasily; and followed by the tall girl and the little one, she tottered away, sweeping yards of chiffon.

"I do hope she won't wear things like that when she's in—ahem!— *our* motor-car," I remarked *sotto voce*, as Terry and I stood at the gate, watching, if not speeding, our parting guests.

"I doubt very much if she'll ever be there," prophesied Terry, looking handsome and thoroughly Celtic, wrapped in his panoply of gloom.

"Come away in, while I see if I can find you 'The harp that once through Tara's halls,' to play your own funeral dirge on," said I. "You look as if it would be the only thing to do you any good."

"It would certainly relieve my feelings," replied Terry, "but I could do that just as well by punching your head, which would be simpler. Of all the infernal—"

"Now don't be brutal!" I implored. "You were quite pleasant before the ladies. Don't be a whited sepulchre the minute their backs are turned. Think what I've gone through since I was alone with you last, you great hulking animal."

"Animal yourself!" Terry had the ingratitude to retort. "What have *I* gone through, I should like to ask?"

"I don't know what you've gone through, but I know how you behaved," I returned, as we walked back to the magnolia tree. "Like a sulky barber's block—I mean a barber's sulky block. No, I—but it doesn't signify. Hullo, there's the universal provider, carrying off the tray. Félicité, *mon ange*, say how you summoned that tea and those cakes and cream from the vasty deep?"

"What Monsieur is pleased to mean, I know not," my fourteen-stone angel replied. "I visited with haste a friend of mine at the hotel, and I came back with the things—that is all. It was an inspiration," and she sailed away, her head in the air.

Terry and I went into the house, for the sun had left the high-walled garden, and besides, the talk we were going to have was more suitable to that practical region, my smoking-room-study-den, than to the romantic shade of a magnolia tree.

We unpocketed our pipes, and smoked for several minutes before we spoke. I vowed that Terry should begin; but as he went on puffing until I had counted sixty-nine slowly, I thought it simpler to unvow the vow before it had had time to harden.

"A penny for your thoughts, Paddy," was the sum I offered with engaging lightness. "Which is generous of me, as I know them already. You are thinking of Her."

Teddy forgot to misunderstand, which was a bad sign.

"If it weren't for Her, I'd have got out of the scrape at any price," said he, bold as brass. "But I'm sorry for that beautiful creature. She must lead a beastly life, between a silly, overdressed woman and a pert minx. Poor child, she's evidently as hard up as I am, or she wouldn't stand it. She's miserable with them, I could see."

21

"So you consented to fall into my web, rather than leave her to their mercy."

"Not exactly that, but—well, I can't explain it. The die's cast, anyhow. I'm pledged to join the menagerie. But look here, Ralph, do you understand what you've let me in for?"

"For the society of three charming Americans, two of whom are no doubt worth their weight in gold."

"It's precisely their weight that's on my mind at this moment. You may know one or two little things, my dear boy, but among them motoring is not, otherwise when you were putting that mad advertisement into your pink rag, you would have stopped to reflect that a twelve-horse power car is not expected to carry five grown persons up airy mountains and down rushy glens. Europe isn't perfectly flat, remember."

"Only four of us are grown up. Beechy's an Infant Phenomenon."

"Infant be hanged. She's sixteen if she's a day."

"Her mother ought to know."

"She doesn't want any one else to know. Anyway, I'm big enough to make up the difference. And besides, my car's not a new one. I paid a thumping price for her, but that was two years ago. There have been improvements in the make since."

"Do you mean to tell me that car of yours can't carry five people half across the world if necessary?"

"She can, but not at an exciting speed; and Americans want excitement. Not only that, but you saw for yourself that they expect a handsome car of the latest make, shining with brass and varnish. Amateurs always do. What will they say when my world-worn old veteran bursts, or rather bumbles, into view?"

I felt slightly crestfallen, for the first time. When one is an editor, one doesn't like to think one has been caught napping. "You said you ought to get two hundred pounds for your Panhard, if you sold it," I reminded him. "That's a good deal of money. Naturally I thought the motor must be a fairly decent one, to command that price after several seasons' wear and tear."

Terry fired up instantly, as I had hoped he would; for his car is the immediate jewel of his soul. "Decent!" he echoed. "I should rather think she is. But just as there's a limit to your intelligence, so is there a limit to her power, and I don't want it to come to that. However, the thing's gone too far for me to draw back. It must depend upon the ladies. If they don't back out when they see my car, I won't."

"To all intents and purposes it's my car now," said I. "You made her over to me before witnesses, and I think I shall have her smartened up with a bit of red paint and a crest."

"If you try on anything like that, you can drive her yourself, for I won't. I like her old grey dress. I wouldn't feel at home with her in any other. And she sha'n't be trimmed with crests to make an American holiday. She goes as she is, or not at all, my boy."

"You are the hardest chap to do anything for I ever saw," I groaned, with the justifiable annoyance of a martyr who has failed to convert a pagan hero. "As if you hadn't made things difficult enough already by 'Mistering' yourself. At any moment you may be found out— though, on second thoughts, it won't matter a rap if you are. If you're a mere Mister, you are often obliged to appear before an unsympathetic police magistrate for pretending to be a Lord. But I never heard of a Lord's falling foul of the law for pretending to be a Mister."

"If you behave yourself, there isn't much danger of my being found out by any of the people most concerned, during a few weeks' motoring on the Continent; but it's to be hoped they won't select England, Scotland, or Ireland for their tour."

"We can tell them that conditions are less favourable for motoring at home—which is quite true, judging from the complaints I hear from motor-men."

"But look here; you let me in for this. What I did was on the spur of the moment, and in self-defence. I didn't dream then that I should be, first cornered by you, then led on by circumstances into engaging as chauffeur, to drive my own car on such a wild-goose chase."

"It's a wild goose that will lay golden eggs. Fifteen guineas a day, my son; that's the size of the egg which that beneficent bird will drop into your palm every twenty-four hours. Deduct the ladies' hotel expenses—say three guineas a day; expenses for yourself and car we'll call two guineas more (of course I pay my own way), that leaves you as profit ten guineas daily; seventy guineas a week, or at the rate of three thousand five hundred guineas per annum. Before you'd spent your little patrimony, and been refused an—er— fratrimony, you weren't half as well off as that. You might do worse than pass your whole life as a Personal Conductor on those terms. And instead of thanking the wise friend who has caught this goose for you, and is willing to leave his own peaceful duck for your sake, with no remuneration, you abuse him."

"My dear fellow, I'm not exactly abusing you, for I know you meant well. But you've swept me off my feet, and I'm not at home yet in mid air."

"You can lie on your back and roll in gold in the intervals of driving the car. I promise not to give you away. Still, it's a pity you wouldn't consent to trading a little on your title, which Heaven must have given you for some good purpose. As it is, you've made my tuppenny-ha'penny baronetcy the only bait, and that's no catch at all for an American millionairess, fishing for something big in Aristocracy Pond. Why, when that Prince of hers discovers what is doing, he will persuade the fair Countess Dalmar that she's paying a high price for a Nobody—a Nobody-at-All."

"What makes you think he doesn't know already, as he evidently followed the party here, and must be constantly dangling about?"

"My detective instinct, which two seasons of pink journalism has developed. Mrs. Kidder saw the advertisement this morning, and was caught by it. May Sherlock Holmes cut me in the street if Prince Dalmar-Kalm hasn't been away for the day, doubtless at Monte Carlo where he has lost most of his own money, and will send the Countess's to find it, if she gives him the chance."

"I never saw the fellow, or heard of him, so far as I can remember," said Terry thoughtfully. "What's he like? Middle-aged, stout?"

"He looks thirty, so he is probably forty; for if you look your age, you are probably ten years past it—though that sounds a bit more Irish than Scotch, eh? And he's far from being stout. From a woman's point of view, I should say he might be very attractive. Tall; thin; melancholy; enormous eyes; moustache waxed; scar on forehead; successful effect of dashing soldier, but not much under the effect, I should say, except inordinate self-esteem, and a masterly selfishness which would take what it wanted at almost any cost to others. There's a portrait of Prince Dalmar-Kalm for you."

"Evidently not the sort of man who ought to be allowed to hang about young girls."

"Young girls with money. Don't worry about the vestal virgin. He won't have time in this game to bother with poor relations, no matter how pretty they may happen to be."

Terry still looked thoughtful. "Well, if we are going in for this queer business, we'd better get off as soon as possible," said he.

I smiled in my sleeve. "St. George in a stew to get the Princess out of the dragon's claws," I thought; but I refrained from speaking the thought aloud. Whatever the motive, the wish was to be encouraged. The sooner the wild goose laid the first golden egg the better. Fortunately for my private interests, the season was waning and the coming week would see the setting of my *Riviera Sun* until next November. I could therefore get away, leaving what remained of the work to be done by my "sub"; and I determined that, Prince or no Prince, luncheon to-morrow should not pass without a business arrangement being completed between the parties.

III

A CHAPTER OF REVENGES

Mrs. Kidder, alias the Countess Dalmar, either had a fondness for lavish hospitality or else she considered us exceptionally distinguished guests. Our feast was not laid in a private dining-room (what is the good of having distinguished guests if nobody is to know you've got them?); nevertheless, it was a feast. The small round table, close to one of the huge windows of the restaurant, was a condensed flower-show. Our plates and glasses (there were many of the latter) peeped at us from a bower of roses, and bosky dells of greenery. The Countess and the Infant were dressed as for a royal garden party, and Terry and I would have felt like moulting sparrows had not Miss Destrey's plain white cotton kept us in countenance.

Mrs. Kidder had evidently not been comfortably certain whether we ought not to march into the restaurant arm in arm, but the penniless goddess (who had perhaps been brought to Europe as a subtle combination of etiquette-mistress and ladies'-maid) cut the Gordian knot with a quick glance, to our intense relief; and we filed in anyhow, places being indicated to Terry and me on either hand of our hostess.

A painted satin menu, with a list of dishes as long as Terry's tailor's bills, lay beside each plate. We were to be provided with all the luxuries which were not in season; those which were would have been far too common for an American millionairess, such as I began to be more and more convinced that our hostess was. It was the kind of luncheon which calls for rare and varied wines, just as certain poetical recitations call for a musical accompaniment; therefore the Countess's first words on sitting down at the table came as a shock.

"Now, Sir Ralph," said she, "you must just order any kind of wine you and Mr. Ter—Barrymore like. Mr. Kidder never would have alcohol in the house, except for sickness, and we three drink only water, so I don't know anything about it; but I want that you gentlemen should suit your own taste. Do make the waiter bring you something *real* nice."

My sparkling visions of Steinberger Cabinet, Cos d'Estournel, or an "Extra Sec" of '92, burst like a rainbow bubble. Here was one of life's little tragedies.

Neither Terry nor I are addicted to looking too lovingly on wine when it is red, or even pale golden; still, at this moment I had a sharp pang of sympathy for Tantalus. To be sure, that hint as to "something real nice" grudged no expense; but I must have been blest with more cool, unadulterated "cheek" than two seasons of journalism had given me, to order anything appropriate while our hostess drowned her generous impulses in iced water.

With a wooden expression of countenance, I asked Terry what he would have.

"Water, thanks," he replied airily, and if, instead of gazing at the ceiling with elaborate interest, he had allowed his eye to meet mine at that instant, a giggle might have burst over that luncheon-table, out of a clear sky. Perforce, I felt obliged to follow his lead, for only a guzzling brute could have bibbed alone, surrounded by four teetotallers; but, deprived of even an innocent glass of Riviera beer, my soul thirsted for a revenge which could not be quenched with iced water; and I took it without waiting for repentance to set in.

"You see, Barrymore is a chauffeur," I carefully explained "and it's *en regle* for him, even though an amateur, to drink nothing stronger than cold water. You will notice during our trip, Countess, how conscientious he is in sticking to this pledge."

I felt that Terry's eye launched a dagger; but it was now my turn to be interested in the ceiling.

"Oh, how *good* of him!" exclaimed our hostess. "I do *admire* that in you, Mr. Tarrymore." (I couldn't help wondering incidentally whether the Countess would have had such frequent lapses of memory regarding Terry's name, if she knew that he was the brother of a marquis; but it may be that I wronged her.) "We shall feel as safe as if we were in a house when you are driving, now we know what kind of a man you are, shan't we, girls?"

Poor Terry, irrevocably pledged to blue ribbonism for the term of his natural chauffeurdom! I could have found it in my heart to pity him, had not the iced water come jingling ironically round at that moment. Let it then be upon his own head, with ice or without.

And this came of lunching with the widow of a Simon Pure Kidder! for I had no longer the slightest doubt as to the middle name of the deceased. With a brain almost cruelly clear and cold, I entered the lists with the lady's conversational gifts, and after a spirited but brief tourney, conquered with flying colours. My aim was to pin her down to something definite ... like an impaled butterfly: hers was to flutter over a vast garden of irrelevances; but she did not long evade the spike. I tipped its point with the subtly poisonous suggestion that all arrangements must be made in the hour, otherwise complications might arise. There seemed to be so many people who had been attracted by that simple little advertisement of mine, and really, I must be able to say that I and my car were engaged for such and such a date—preferably a near one—or I should have difficulty in evading requests for an intermediate trip with others.

The butterfly wriggled no more. Indeed, it hastened to assure the executioner that it was only too anxious to be comfortably pinned into place.

"When could *you* go, Sir Ralph?" the Countess asked.

"Day after to-morrow," I answered boldly. "Could you?"

She looked rather taken aback.

"We—er—haven't motor things yet," she demurred.

"You can get 'every requisite' (isn't that the word?) in the Nice or Monte Carlo shops, if that's your only reason for delay."

Still the lady hesitated.

"Mamma's new crown isn't painted on all her baggage yet," said Beechy, living up, with a wicked delight, to her *rôle* of *enfante terrible*.

"It's being done, but it wasn't promised till the end of the week. Say, Sir Ralph, don't you think she's mean not to give me even so much as *half* a crown?"

What I really thought was, that she deserved a slap; but Terry spared the Countess a blush and me the brain fag of a repartee conciliatory alike to parent and child.

"I think we ought to warn you," he said, "that the car hasn't precisely the carrying capacity of a luggage van. Perhaps when you find that there's no room for Paris frocks and hats, you'll repent your bargain."

"Can't we take a small trunk and a satchel apiece?" asked the Countess. "I don't see how we could do with less."

"I'm afraid you'll have to, if you go in—er—my friend's car," Terry went on ruthlessly. "A small box between the three of you, and a good-sized dressing-bag each, is all that the car can possibly manage, though, of course Moray and I will reduce our luggage to the minimum amount."

Mrs. Kidder looked grave, and at this instant, just as I felt that Terry's future was wavering in the balance, outweighed probably by a bonnet-box, there was a slight stir in the restaurant, behind our backs. Involuntarily I turned my head, and saw Prince Dalmar-Kalm hurrying towards us, his very moustache a thunder-cloud. He could not have appeared at a less convenient time for us.

I was sure that he had not been consulted in regard to the automobile trip; that perhaps even now he was in ignorance of the plan; and that, when he came to hear of it as he must within the next five minutes, he would certainly try (as Beechy would have put it) to snatch the American ladies out of our mouths. It was like Terry's luck, I said to myself, that this evil genius should arrive at the moment when Mrs. Kidder had been mercilessly deprived of her wardrobe by a mere chauffeur. Terry had stupidly given her an opening if she chose to take it, by suggesting that she might "repent her bargain," and I was sure it wouldn't be Dalmar-Kalm's fault if she didn't take it.

A second later he had reached our table, was bending low over Mrs. Kidder's hand, smiling with engaging wickedness at Beechy, and sending a dark look of melancholy yearning to catch Miss Destrey's sympathies.

"Why, Prince," the Countess exclaimed in a loud tone, calculated to reach the ears of any neighbouring royalties, and let them see that she was as good as they were. "Why, Prince, if you're not always surprising people! I thought you were staying another day with the Duke of Messina, in Monte Carlo."

"Told you so!" my eyebrows—such as they are—telegraphed to Terry. "He *has* been away; only just back; pantomime demon act."

"I found myself homesick for Cap Martin," returned the Prince, with an emphasis and a sweeping glance which made a present of the compliment to the woman, the girl, and the child.

"Humph," I sneered into the iced water; "lost all he'd got with him, and the money-lenders turned crusty; that's when the homesickness came on."

"Well, now you're here, do sit down and have lunch with us," said Mrs. Kidder, "unless"—archly—"your homesickness has destroyed your appetite."

"If it had, the pleasure of seeing you again would restore it;" and once more the Austrian's gaze assured each one of the three that she alone was the "you" referred to.

A nod and a gesture whisked a couple of attentive waiters to the table, and in the twinkling of an eye—even an American eye—a place was laid for the Prince, with duplicates of all our abortive wine glasses.

"Aha, my fine fellow, *you* are no friend of cold water," I said to myself in savage glee, as I acknowledged with a bow Mrs. Kidder's elaborate introduction. "You will suffer even more than we have suffered." But I reckoned without a full knowledge of the princely character.

History repeated itself with an invitation to the new guest to choose what he liked from the wine card. I looked for a courteous refusal, accompanied by some such gallant speech as, that he would drink to the ladies only with his eyes; but nothing of the kind happened. He searched the list for a moment with the absorption of a connoisseur, then unblushingly ordered a bottle of Romanée Conti, which wine, he carelessly announced, he preferred to champagne, as being "less obvious." The price, however, would be pretty obvious on Mrs. Kidder's bill, I reflected; seventy francs a bottle, if it were a penny. But did this coming event cast a shadow on the Prince's contentment? On the contrary, it probably spangled its fabric with sequins. He sniffed the wine as if it had been an American Beauty rose, and quaffed it ecstatically, while Terry and I gulped down our iced water and our indignation.

"You are just in time, Prince," said Mrs. Kidder, "to advise us about our journey. Oh, I forgot, you don't know anything about it yet. But we are going a tour in Sir Ralph Moray's automobile. Won't it be fun?"

"Indeed?" the Prince ejaculated hastily; and I had the satisfaction of knowing that one swallow of the Romanée Conti was spoiled for him. "No; I had not heard. I did not know that Sir Ralph Moray was one of your friends. Has not this been suddenly arranged?"

"It was only *decided* yesterday," replied the Countess; and it was revealed to me that the plump lady was not without feminine guile.

"What is your car?" inquired the Prince, turning abruptly to me.

"A Panhard," I answered, with a gaze as mild as milk. I knew that my answer would disappoint him, as he could pick no flaws in the make of the machine.

"What horse-power?" he continued his catechism.

"Something under twenty," I conservatively replied.

"Twelve," corrected Terry, with a brutal bluntness unworthy of a Celt. He can be very irritating sometimes; but at this moment he was looking so extremely handsome and devil-may-care, that my desire to punch his head dissolved as I glared at him. Could any woman in her senses throw over even a titleless Terry and twelve horses worth of motor for a hat box or two and an Austrian Prince?

"A twelve-horse-power car, and you propose to take with you on tour three ladies, their maid, and all their luggage?" demanded Dalmar-Kalm in his too excellent English. "But it is not possible."

I felt suddenly as if Terry and I were little snub-nosed boys, trafficking with a go-cart.

"They won't need their maid, Prince," said Miss Destrey. "I know how to do Aunt Kathryn's hair; and the dear Sisters have taught me how to mend beautifully."

This was the first time she had opened her lips during luncheon, except to eat with an almost nun-like abstemiousness; and now she broke silence to rescue a scheme which yesterday had excited her active disapproval. The girl, always interesting because of her unusual type of beauty, gained a new value in my eyes. She excited my curiosity, although her words were a practical revelation of her place in the trio. Why did she break a lance in our defence? and had she been torn from a convent to serve her rich relatives, that she should mention the "Sisters" in that familiar and tender tone? Had her beautiful white sails veered with a new wind, and did she *want* to go with us, after all? Did she wish to tell the Prince in a sentence, how poor she really was? These were a few of the hundred and one questions which the Fair Maid of Destrey's charming and somewhat baffling personality set going in my mind by a word or two.

I thought that the Prince's face fell, but Mrs. Kidder's contribution to the defence distracted my attention.

"We don't expect to take *all* our luggage," she said. "I suppose some things could be sent by rail from place to place to meet us, couldn't they?"

"Of course," I assured her, before Dalmar-Kalm could enlarge upon the uncertainties of such an arrangement. "That's what is always done. And your maid could travel by rail too."

"She is a Parisienne," exclaimed Mrs. Kidder, "and she's always saying she wouldn't leave France for twice the wages I pay."

"Try her with three times," suggested Beechy. But Miss Destrey was speaking again. "As I said, it doesn't matter about Agnes. Aunt Kathryn and Beechy shan't miss her; and she never does anything for me."

"What a pity," complained the Prince, "that my automobile is at the moment laid up for repairs. Otherwise I should have been only too delighted to take you three ladies to the world's end, if you had the wish. *It* is not 'something less than twenty,' as Sir Ralph Moray describes his twelve-horse-power car, but is something *more* than twenty, with a magnificently roomy Roi de Belge tonneau and accommodation for any amount of luggage on the roof. By the way, yours has at least a cover, I make no doubt, Sir Ralph?"

"No," I was obliged to admit, my mouth somewhat dry—owing perhaps to the iced water.

"No cover? How, then, do you propose to protect these ladies from the rain?" This with virtuous indignation flashing from his fierce eyes, and a gesture which defended three helpless feminine things from the unscrupulous machinations of a pair of villains.

My ignorance of motor lore bereft me of a weapon with which to parry the attack, but Terry whipped out his sword at last.

"The ladies will be protected by their motor coats and our rugs. I'm sure they're too plucky to sacrifice the best pleasures of motoring to a little personal comfort when it may happen to rain," said he. "A roof gives no protection against rain except with curtains, and even when without them it curtails the view."

"Ah, it is cruel that I cannot get my car for you from Paris," sighed the Prince. "Perhaps, Countess, if you would wait a little time—a week or ten days, I might—"

"But we're going day after to-morrow, aren't we, Kittie?" quickly broke in Miss Destrey.

"I suppose so," replied Mrs. Kidder, who invariably frowned when addressed as "Cousin Kathryn," and brightened faintly if spontaneously Kittied. "We've been here more than a week, and seen all the Nice and Monte Carlo sights, thanks to the Prince. There's nothing to keep us, although it will be about all we can do to get off so soon."

"Why be hurried, Countess?" with a shrug of the shoulder half-turned from me.

"Well, I don't know." Her eyes wandered to mine. "But it suits Sir Ralph to leave then. I guess we can manage it."

"Where will you go?" inquired Dalmar-Kalm. "I might be able to join you somewhere *en route*."

"Well, that's one of the things we haven't quite settled yet," replied Mrs. Kidder. "Almost anywhere will suit me. We can just potter around. It's the automobiling we want. You know, this is our first time in Europe, and so long as we're in pretty places, it's much the same to us."

"Speak for yourself, Mamma," said Beechy. "Maida and I want to see the Lake of Como, where Claude Melnotte had his palace."

"Oh, my, yes! In 'the Lady of Lyons.' I do think that's a perfectly sweet play. Could we go there, Sir Ralph?"

"I must consult my chauffeur," said I, cautiously. "He knows more about geography than I do. He ought to; he spends enough money on road-maps to keep a wife. Eh, Terry?"

"There are two ways of driving to the lakes from here," he said, with a confidence which pleased me. "One can go coasting > along the Italian Riviera to Genoa, and so direct to Milan; or one can go through the Roya Valley, either by Turin, or a short cut which brings one eventually to Milan."

"Milan!" exclaimed Miss Destrey, with a rapt look. "Why, that's not very far from Verona, is it? And if it's not far from Verona, it can't be so far from Venice. Oh, Beechy, think of seeing Venice!"

"It would be easy to go there," Terry said, showing too much eagerness to fall in with a whim of the poor relation's; at least such was my opinion until, with a glint of mischief in his eyes, he added, "If we went to Venice, Countess, it would be very easy to run on if you liked, into Dalmatia and see the new estate which you told us you thought of buying, before you actually made up your mind to have it."

It was all I could do to strangle a chuckle at birth. Good old Terry! Even he was not above taking a neat revenge; and the Prince's face showed *how* neat it was. Could it be possible that the estate in Dalmatia which carried with it a title, had any resemblance to Claude Melnotte's in that "sweet" play, "The Lady of Lyons?" I could scarcely believe that, much as I would have liked to; but it was clear he would have preferred to have the American millionairess take the beauties of her new possessions for granted.

"Oh, I have made up my mind already. I made it up before we arrived here," said the Countess.

"She made it up in the train coming from Paris," corrected Beechy, "because she had to decide what name to register, and whether she'd have the crown put on her handkerchiefs and her baggage. But she had to cable to our lawyer in Denver before she could get money enough to pay what the Prince wanted in advance, and the answer only came back this morning."

"And what does the lawyer say?" asked the Prince, flushing, and with a strained playfulness contradicted by the eager light in his eyes.

"Just guess," said Beechy, all her imps in high glee.

"Lawyers are such dry-as-dust persons," remarked His Highness, hastily lifting his glass to toss off the last of the Romanée Conti. "If he is a wise man who studies his client's interests, he could not advise Madame against taking a step by which she ascends to a height so advantageous, but—"

"Oh, he said yes," cried Mrs. Kidder, clinging to her Countesshood.

"And he put after it, 'If you will be a fool,'" added Beechy. "But he'll have to pay for that part of the cable himself."

"He is my late husband's cousin," explained Mrs. Kidder, "and he takes liberties sometimes, as he thinks Simon would not have approved of everything I do. But you needn't tell *everything*, Beechy."

"Let's talk about Venice," said Miss Destrey with a lovely smile, which seemed all the more admirable as she had given us so few. "I have always longed to see Venice."

"But you didn't want to come abroad, you can't say you did," remarked Beechy the irrepressible, resenting her cousin's interference, as a naughty boy resents being torn from the cat to whose tail he has been tying a tin can. "And I know *why* you didn't!" She too had a taste for revenge!

Miss Destrey blushed—I wondered why; and so, no doubt, did Terry wonder. (Had she by chance been sent abroad to forget an unfortunate attachment?)

"You wanted to stay with the Sisters," Beechy took advantage of the other's embarrassed silence to go on. "And you hardly enjoyed Paris at all, although everybody turned to look after you in the streets."

"Well, now that I have come, I should enjoy seeing the places I've cared most to read about in history or poetry," said Miss Destrey quickly, "and Venice is one of them."

"Maida has lived more in books than she has in real life," remarked Miss Beechy with scorn. "I know a lot more about the world than she does, although I am only—only—"

"Thirteen," finished the Countess. "Beechy darling, would you like to have some more of those *marrons glacés*? They aren't good for you, but just this once you may, if you want to. And oh, Sir Ralph, I should love to see my new estate. It's a very old estate really, you know, though new to me; so old that the castle is almost a ruin; but if I saw it and took a great fancy to the place, I might have it restored and made perfectly elegant, to live in sometimes, mightn't I? Just where *is* Schloss (she pronounced it 'Slosh') what-you-may-call-it? I never *can* say it properly?"

"Schloss Hrvoya is very far down in Dalmatia—almost as far east as Montenegro," replied the Prince. "The roads are extremely bad, too. I do not think they would be feasible for an automobile, especially for Sir Ralph Moray's little twelve-horse-power car carrying five persons."

"I differ from you there, Prince." Terry argued, looking obstinate. "I have never driven in Dalmatia, although I've been to Fiume and Abbazzia; but I have a friend who went with his car, and he had no adventures which ladies would not have enjoyed. Our principal difficulty would be about petrol; but we could carry a lot, and have supplies sent to us along the route. I'll engage to manage that—and the car."

"Then it's settled that we go," exclaimed Mrs. Kidder, clapping two dimpled hands covered with rings. "What a wonderful trip it will be."

I could see that the Prince would have liked to call Terry out, but he was too wise to dispute the question further; and a dawning plan of some kind was slowly lightening his clouded eye.

My wish was granted at last; something was settled. And later, strolling on the terrace, I contrived to put all that was left upon a business basis.

Never had man a better friend than Terence Barrymore has in me; and my whole attention on the way home was given to making him acknowledge it.

IV

A CHAPTER OF HUMILIATIONS

After all, we did not start on the day after to-morrow. Our luncheon had been on Tuesday. On Wednesday a note came, sent by hand from Mrs. Kidder, to say that she could not possibly be ready until Friday, and that as Friday was an unlucky day to begin any enterprise, we had better put off starting until Saturday. But I must not "think her changeable, as she really had a very good reason"; and she was mine "Cordially, Kathryn Stanley Kidder-Dalmar."

Having first stated that she could not be ready, and then added her reason was good, I naturally imagined there was more in the delay than met the eye. My fancy showed me the hand of Prince Dalmar-Kalm, and I firmly believed that each finger of that hand to say nothing of the thumb, was busily working against us.

All Thursday and Friday I expected at any moment to receive an intimation that, owing to unforseen circumstances (which might not be explained) the Countess and her party were unable to carry out the arrangement they had entered into with us. But Thursday passed, and nothing happened. Friday wore on towards evening, and the constant strain upon my nerves had made me irritable. Terry, who was calmly getting ready for the start as if there were no cause for uncertainty, chaffed me on my state of mind, and I rounded upon him viciously, for was not all my scheming for his sake?

I was in the act of pointing out several of his most prominent defects, and shedding cigarette ashes into his suit-case as he packed, when Félicité appeared with a letter.

"It's from her!" I gasped. "And—she's got her coronet. It's on the envelope, as large as life."

"Which means that she's ready," said the future chauffeur, examining a suit of overalls.

"Don't be so cocksure," said I, opening the letter. "Hum — ha — well, yes, it does seem to be all right, if you can ever judge a woman's intentions by what she says. She wants to know whether the arrangement stands, that we're to call for them at ten o'clock to-morrow morning, and whether we're to go rain or shine. I'll scratch off a line in answer, and say yes — yes — yes, to everything."

I did so with a trembling hand, and then gave myself up to the weakness of reaction. Upon Félicité fell the task of doing my packing, which consisted in cramming a suit of flannels, my evening things, and all the linen it would hold without bursting asunder, into a large, fitted suit-case. Terry had a suit-case too, five times better than mine (Irishmen in debt always do have things superior to those of every one else); we had motor-coats, and enough guide-books and road-maps to stock a small library; and when these were collected we were ready for the Great Adventure.

When Terry visits me at the Châlet des Pins, he keeps his car at a garage in Mentone. His habit has been to put up his chauffeur close by this garage, and telephone when he wants to use the car; but the chauffeur was paid off and sent away ten days ago, at about the time when Terry decided that the automobile must be sold. He had not been in spirits for a drive since, until the fateful day of the advertisement, but immediately after our luncheon with the Countess he had walked down to the garage and stayed until dinner-time. What he had been doing there he did not deign to state; but I had a dim idea that when you went to call on a motor-car in its den, you spent hours on your back bolting nuts, or accelerating silencers, or putting the crank head (and incidentally your own) into an oil bath; and I supposed that Terry had been doing these things. When he returned on Wednesday, Thursday, and Friday, spending several hours on each occasion, I went on supposing the same; but when at nine o'clock on Saturday morning he drove up to the garden gate after another trip to Mentone, I had a surprise.

Terry had almost bitten off my head when I had innocently proposed to have his car smartened up to suit the taste of the Countess; but, without saying a word to me, he had been at work improving its appearance.

"She" (as he invariably calls his beloved vehicle) was dressed in grey as before, but it was fresh, glossy grey, still smelling of turpentine. The tyres were new, and white, and a pair of spare ones were tied onto the motor's bonnet, which looked quite jaunty now in its clean lead-coloured paint.

The shabby cushions of the driver's seat and tonneau had been re-covered also with grey, and wherever a bit of brass was visible it glittered like pure gold.

At the sound of the Panhard's sob at the gate, Félicité and I hurried down the path, armed with the two coats and suit-cases, there to be surprised by the rejuvenated car, and dumbfounded by a transformed Terry.

"Mon Dieu, comme il est beau, comme ça," cried my domestic miracle worker, lost in admiration of a tall, slim, yet athletic figure, clad from head to foot in black leather. "Mais—mais ce n'est pas comme il faut pour un Milord."

"Why, Terry," exclaimed I, "I never thought—I never expected—I'm hanged if you're not a real professional. It's awfully smart, and very becoming—never saw you look better in your life. But it's—er—a kind of masquerade, you know. I'm not sure you ought to do it. If Innisfallen saw you like that, he'd cross you out of his will."

"He's dead certain to have done that already. When I engaged as your chauffeur I engaged as your chauffeur and I intend to look the part as well as act it. I want this car to be as smart as it can, which unfortunately isn't saying much, and towards that end I've been doing my best these last three or four days. She isn't bad, is she?"

"From being positively plain, if not ugly, she has become almost a beauty," I replied. But I thought you were determined to preserve her from the sin of vanity? Why this change of mind?"

"Well, I couldn't stand Dalmar-Kalm running her down," Terry confessed rather sheepishly. "There was so little time, that half the work on her I've done myself."

"That accounts, then, for your long and mysterious absences."

"Only partly. I've been working like a navvy, at a mechanic's shop, fagging up a lot of things I knew how to do on principle, but had seldom or never done with my own hands. I was always a lazy beggar, I'm afraid, and it was better fun to smoke and watch my man Collet making or fitting in a new part than to bother with it myself. This will be my first long trip 'on my own,' you see, and I don't want to be a duffer, especially as I myself proposed going down into Dalmatia, where we may get into no end of scrapes."

"By Jove!" I exclaimed, gazing with a new respect at my leather-clad friend and his car. "You've got some good stuff in you, Terry. I didn't quite realize what a responsibility I was throwing on you, old chap, when I named you as my chauffeur. Except for my drives with you, I suppose I haven't been in a motor half a dozen times in my life, now I come to think of it and it always seemed to me that, if a man knew how to drive his own car, he must know how to do everything else that was necessary."

"Very few do, even expert drivers, among amateurs. A man ought to be able not only to take his car entirely to pieces and put it together again, but to go into a mechanic's shop and make a new one. I don't say that I can do that, but I can come a bit nearer to it than I could five days ago. I don't think that the poor old car will be such a shock to the ladies now, even after some of the fine ones they must have seen, do you?"

He was so ingenuously proud of his achievements, had toiled so hard, and sacrificed so much of his personal vanity in providing his employers with a suitable chauffeur, that I did not stint my commendation of him and his car. Félicité, too, was prolific in compliments. The duck, who had waddled out to the gate to see what was doing, quacked flattery; the yellow cat mewed praise; and Terry, pleased as Punch with everything and everybody, whistled as he stowed away our suit-cases.

The moment of departure had come. With some emotion I bade farewell to my family, which I should not see again until I returned to the Riviera to open the autumn season with the first number of the *Sun*. Then one last look at the little place which had become dear to me, and we were off with a bound for the Cap Martin Hotel.

Terry, when in a frank and modest mood, had sometimes said to me that, with all the virtues of strength, faithfulness, and getting-thereness, his car was not to be called a fast car. Thirty miles an hour was its speed at best, and this pace it seemed had been far surpassed by newer cars of the same make, though of no higher power, since Terry's had been built. This fact I took for granted, as I had heard it from Terry's own lips more than once; but as we flew over the wooded road which divided the Châlet des Pins from the Cap Martin Hotel, I would have sworn that we were going at the rate of sixty miles per hour.

"Good Heavens!" I gasped. "Have you been doing anything to this car, to make her faster than she was? Help! I can't breathe."

"Nonsense," said Terry, with soothing calm. "It's only because you haven't motored for a long time that you imagine we're going fast. The motor's working well, that's all. We're crawling along at a miserable twenty miles an hour."

"Well, I'm glad that worms and other reptiles can't crawl at this pace, anyhow, or life wouldn't be worth living for the rest of creation," I retorted, cramming on my cap and wishing I had covered my tearful eyes with the motor-goggles which lay in my pocket. "If our millionairesses don't respect this pace, I'll eat my hat when I have time, or—"

But Terry was not destined to hear the end of that boast—which perhaps was just as well for me in the end, as things were to turn out. We spun down the avenue of pines, and in less than a lazy man's breathing space were at the door of the Cap Martin Hotel.

Quite a crowd of smart-looking people was assembled there, and for one fond second I dreamed that they were waiting to witness our arrival. But that pleasant delusion died almost as soon as born. As the group divided at our approach we saw that they had been collected round a large motor-car—a motor-car so resplendent that beside it our poor rejuvenated thing looked like a little, made-up, old Quaker lady.

In colour this hated rival was a rich, ripe scarlet, with cushions to match in her luxurious tonneau. Her bonnet was like a helmet of gold for the goddess Minerva, and wherever there was space, or chance, for something to sparkle with jewelled effect, that something availed itself, with brilliance, of the opportunity.

The long scarlet body of the creature was shaded with a canopy of canvas, white as the breast of a gull, and finished daintily all round with a curly fringe. The poles which held it were apparently of glittering gold, and the railing designed to hold luggage on the top, if not of the same precious metal, was as polished as the letters of Lord Chesterfield to his long-suffering son.

One jealous glance was enough to paint this glowing picture upon our retinas, and there it remained, like a sun-spot, even when a later one was stamped upon it. Three figures in long, grey motor-coats, exactly alike, and motor-caps, held on with shirred chiffon veils came forward, two advancing more quickly than the third.

"How *do* you do, Sir Ralph? Good morning, Mr. Barrymore," Mrs. Kidder and Beechy were saying. "We're all ready," went on the former, excitedly. "We've been admiring the Prince's car, which came last night. Isn't it a perfect beauty? Just *look* at the sweet poppy- colour, and his crest in black and gold. I never saw anything so pretty, did you?"

"I like Sir Ralph's car," said Miss Destrey. "It's such a cool grey, and even in wind or dust it will always look neat. We shall match it very well with our grey coats and veils."

I could have kissed her; while as for Terry, standing cap in hand, he looked grateful enough to have grovelled at our fair champion's feet. Nevertheless, we could not help knowing in our hearts that no normal girl could help preferring that celestial peacock to our grey hen, and that Miss Destrey's wish to be kind must have outstripped her obligation to be truthful. This knowledge was turning a screw round in our vitals, when His Highness himself appeared to give it a still sharper twist.

He had been standing at a short distance, talking with a small chauffeur of a peculiarly solemn cast of countenance. Now he turned and joined the ladies with a brisk step and an air of proprietorship.

The fact that he was wearing a long motor-coat, of a smart cut, and a peaked cap which became him excellently, struck me as ominous. Had he caught the birds—our birds—after all, at the last moment, and had they been too cowardly to let us know?

"Oh, good morning, Sir Ralph," said he. "So that is the famous car. Mine is a giant beside it, is it not? No doubt you and your friend are clever men, but you will need all your cleverness to provide comfortable accommodation for these ladies' luggage as well as themselves. I would not mind betting you ten to one that you will fail to do it to their satisfaction."

"I'll take the bet if the ladies don't mind," responded Terry promptly, those lazy Irish eyes of his very bright and dark.

"What—a bet? Why, that will be real fun," laughed the Countess, showing her dimples. "What is it to be?"

A slightly anxious expression hardened the lines of the Prince's face when he found himself taken in earnest. "A thousand francs against a hundred of yours shall it be, Monsieur? I don't wish to plunge my hand into your pockets," said he, shrewdly making a virtue of his caution.

"As you like," Terry assented. "Now for the test. Your luggage has come down, Countess?"

"Yes; here it all is," said Mrs. Kidder, guiltily indicating three stout hotel porters who stood in the background heavily laden. "Dear me, it *does* look as if it was going to be a mighty tight squeeze, doesn't it?"

In response to a gesture, the porters advanced in line, like the Three Graces; and counting rapidly, I made out that their load consisted of one good-sized "Innovation" cabin box, two enormous alligator-skin dressing bags, one small bag, and two capacious hold-alls, umbrellas, parasols, and a tea-basket.

I began to tremble for more than Terry's five pounds. I now saw all the Prince's guile. He had somehow managed to produce his car, and had, no doubt, used all his eloquence to persuade Mrs. Kidder that she would be justified in changing her mind at the last moment. That he had failed was owing either to her sense of honour or her liking for the English-speaking races over foreigners, even princely ones. But refusing to abandon hope, His Highness had pinned his last fluttering rag of faith upon the chance that our car would fail to fulfil its contract. With this chance, and this alone still to depend upon, he had probably kept his melancholy chauffeur up all night, sponging and polishing. If the Panhard refused to absorb the ladies' luggage, there would be his radiant chariot waiting to console them in the bitter hour of their disappointment.

As Terry stood measuring each piece of luggage with his eye, silently apportioning it a place in the car, I felt as I had felt at "Monte" when, at roulette, as many as three of my hard-won five franc pieces might easily go "bang," like the sixpence of another canny Scot. Will it be *rouge*; will it be *noir*?... I could never look; and I could not look now.

Turning to Beechy, who stood at my shoulder eagerly watching, I flung myself into conversation. "What are you laughing at?" I asked.

"At all of you," said the Infant. "But especially the Prince."

"Why especially the Prince?" I was growing interested.

"I should think you'd know."

"How could I know?"

"Because I guess you're pretty bright. Sometimes I look at you, and you seem to be thinking the same things I am. I don't know whether that makes me like you or hate you, but anyway it makes me give you credit for good wit. I'm not exactly *stupid*."

"I've noticed that. But about the Prince?"

"Can't you guess how he got his automobile just in the nick of time?"

"Yes, I can guess; but maybe it wouldn't be right."

45

"And maybe it would. Let's see."

"Well, the Countess heard favourably from her lawyer in Denver on Tuesday, and paid down something in advance for the Dalmatian estate."

"*And* the title. Right first time. The 'something' was eight thousand dollars."

"Phew!"

"That's just the word for it. When she's seen the place, she'll pay the rest—eight thousand more. Quite a lot for those gold crowns on the luggage; but we all have our dolls with eyes to open or shut, and poor Mamma hasn't had any chance to play dolls till just lately. She's busy now having heaps of fun, and I'm having a little, too, in my simple childish way. Well, so long as we don't interfere with each other!... The Prince sees that Mamma can afford to buy dolls, so he would like to play with her, and me, and—"

"And he doesn't want Barrymore and me in the playroom."

"I *thought* you were bright! It made him just sick to think of you two walking off with us from under his nose. *There* was his automobile in Paris, and there was he *here*, perfectly useless, because I'm sure he'd lent the auto to his uncle."

"To his uncle?" I echoed.

"Don't you say that in England, or Scotland, or wherever you come from? 'Put it up the Spout'—pawned it; and he couldn't move one way or the other till he'd got Mamma's money. The minute that was in his pocket he began to plan. The first thing he did was to tell Mamma that he had a surprise for her, which he'd been getting ready for several days, and it would be spoiled if we all went off with you and that awfully good-looking chauffeur of yours on Thursday. He said he *must* have till Saturday morning, and Mamma was so curious to know what the mystery was, and so afraid of hurting a real live Prince's feelings, that she was finally persuaded to wait."

46

"Oh, that is the explanation of her letter to me."

"Yes. I suspected what was going on, but she didn't; having dimples makes people so soft and good-natured. I don't *know* what the Prince did after she'd given her word to stay, but I guessed."

"He wired money to his chauffeur in Paris or somewhere, had the car got out of the clutches of that relative you referred to, and brought on here at top speed."

"But not its own speed. When it arrived here last night, it was just as spick and span as it is now."

"Then it must have come by train."

"That's what I think. I bet the Prince was too much afraid some accident might happen to it on the way, and upset all his plans, to trust to having the thing driven down here by road."

"You must be careful not to let your brain develop too fast," I pleaded, "or when you grow up, you—"

"That's such a long time off, I don't need to worry yet," Miss Kidder remarked demurely. "Do you think I look more than my age?"

"No, but you *talk* more," said I.

"How can you judge? What do you know about little girls like me?"

"I don't know anything about little girls like you, because all the rest got broken; but if you'll teach me, I'll do my best to learn."

"The Prince is doing his best too, I guess. I wonder which will learn faster?"

"That depends partly on you. But I should have thought all his time was taken up with your mother."

"Oh my! no. He wants *her* to think that. But you see, he's got more time than anything else, so he has plenty to spare for me, and Maida too. Do you know what he called us to a friend of his in this hotel? The friend's wife told her maid, and she passed it on to our Agnes, who repeated it to me because we were sending her away. 'Kid,

Kidder, Kiddest.' I'm Kiddest, of course; that's easy enough; but it would save the Prince lots of trouble and brain-fag if he only knew which was 'Rich,' which 'Richer,' and which 'Richest.'"

"Heavens!" I ejaculated. "If you have got together all this mass of worldly wisdom at thirteen, what will you have accumulated at twenty?"

"It all depends on when Mamma allows me to be twenty," retorted the little wretch. And what lengths this indecently frank conversation might have reached between us I dare not think, had not an exclamation from Terry cut it short.

"What do you say to that, Countess, and Miss Destrey? Have I won the bet?" he was demanding, his hands in the pockets of his leather jacket, as he stood to survey his work.

If I had not infinite belief in Terry's true Irish ingenuity, I would have considered the day and the bet both lost before the test had been essayed. But he had justified my faith, and there on the almost obliterated lines of the motor-car, behold a place for everything, and everything in its place.

On one step the "Innovation" cabin-box reared itself on end like a dwarfish obelisk; a fat hold-all adorned each mud-guard, where it lay like an underdone suet pudding; the two huge dressing-bags had been pushed under the corner seats of the tonneau, which fortunately was of generous dimensions, while the third and smallest one (no doubt Miss Destrey's) was so placed that it could be used as a footstool, or pushed to the front out of the way. Umbrellas and parasols stood upright in a hanging-basket especially designed for them; books and maps had disappeared into a box, which was also a shelf on the back of the driver's seat, and the tea-basket had been lashed on top of this.

The Prince's voice responded to Terry's question with ribald mirth before it could be answered by the ladies.

"Ha, ha, ha!" cried he, shouting with laughter at the appearance of the car; and even my lips twitched, though I would have vowed it was St. Vitus's dance if anyone had accused me of a smile. "Ha, ha, the automobile looks like nothing so much as a market-woman going home with the family provisions for a month. But will she ever *get* home?" Here he became spasmodic, and as he had made a present of his picturesque smile to all the lookers-on as well as to those whom it most concerned, a grin rippled over the faces of the various groups as a breeze ruffles the surface of a pond.

If I could have done His Highness Prince Dalmar-Kalm a mischief at this moment, without imperilling my whole future, I would have stuck at nothing; but there is capital punishment in France, and, besides, there were no weapons handy except the ladies' hatpins. Still, it was useless denying it, the car looked, if not like a market- woman, at least like a disreputable old tramp of the motor world, with its wreaths of luggage looped on anyhow, as if it were a string of giant sausages; and I hated the Prince not only for his impertinent pleasure in our plight, but for the proud magnificence of his car, which gained new lustre in the disgrace of ours.

"You have more, what do you call it in English—cheek, is it not?— than most of your countrymen, to ask the ladies whether they can be satisfied with *that*," he went on, between his mirthful explosions. "*Chère* Countess, do not let your kind heart run away with you. Let me tell Sir Ralph Moray that it is impossible for you to tour with him under such conditions, which are surely not what you had a right to expect. If you will go with me, *that*"—pointing a derisive finger at the Panhard—"can follow with the luggage."

Mrs. Kidder shook her auburn head, though her dimples were obscured, and a pinkness of complexion for which she had not paid betrayed the fact that her *amour propre* was writhing under this ordeal. Poor little woman, I really pitied her, for even with my slight knowledge of her character, I guessed that she had dreamed of the sensation the departure *en automobile* of a party so distinguished would create at the hotel. She had confidingly judged the charms of the advertised car from those of the advertisers, and this was her reward. Could we blame her if, in the bitterness of mortification, she yielded to the allurement of that glittering car which was our detractor's best argument? But she was loyal on the rack.

"No," she said, "I never backed out of anything yet, and I'm not going to now. Besides, we don't want to, do we, girls? Sir Ralph's automobile is just as nice as it can be, and it's our fault, not his, or Mr. Barrymore's, if we've got a little more luggage than we were told we ought to take. I guess we'll get along all right as soon as we're used to it, and we shall have *the* time of our lives."

"Mamma, you're a brick, and I'm glad Papa married you," was Beechy's pæan of praise.

"And I think the way our things are arranged looks really *graceful*," said Miss Destrey. "Mr. Barrymore has won that bet easily, hasn't he, Kitty and Beechy?"

"Yes," came faintly from the Countess and cordially from the child. And I whistled "Hail, the Conquering Hero" *sotto voce*, as Dalmar-Kalm, with a smile like a dose of asafœtida, counted out the amount of his lost wager.

"Well," he said, squaring his shoulders to make the best of a bad bargain, "you are three brave ladies to trust yourselves in a machine without room, speed, or power to cross the Alps."

"You can go to the Cathedral at Monaco and pray for us to Saint Joseph, who, Agnes told me, looks after travellers," said Beechy. "But I do think a more modern saint ought to be invented for motorists."

"I shall do better than that. I shall be your protecting saint. I shall go with you as a surgeon attends a company of soldiers," returned the Prince, with his air of *grand seigneur*. "That is, I shall keep as near you as a twenty-horse-power car with a light load can possibly keep to a twelve, with three times the load it's fitted to carry."

"You're not very complimentary to Mamma," glibly remarked the Irrepressible.

"I fancy, in spite of our load," said Terry with undaunted cheerfulness, "we shall find room to stow away a coil of rope which may prove useful for towing the Prince's car over some of those Alps he seems to think so formidable, in case he decides to—er—follow us. If I'm not mistaken, Prince, your motor is a Festa, made in Vienna, isn't it?"

"Certainly; the most successful in Austria. And mine is the handsomest car the company has yet turned out. It was a special order."

"There's an old proverb which says, 'all isn't gold that glitters.' I don't know whether it's apropos to anything that concerns us or not, but we shall perhaps remember it sooner or later. Now, ladies, I think everything is shipshape, and there's nothing to keep us any longer. How would you like to sit? Some people think the best place beside the driver, but—"

"Oh, *I* wouldn't sit there for worlds with no horse in front to fall out on in case anything happened!" exclaimed Mrs. Kidder; "and I couldn't let Beechy either. Maida is her own mistress, and can do as she likes."

"If that girl is going to get in the habit of sitting by Terry day after day," I hurriedly told myself, "I might far better have let him sell his car and grow ostriches or something in South Africa. *That* idea shall be nipped before it is a bud."

"I fear I should take up too much room in the tonneau," I suggested with feigned meekness. "You ladies had better have it all to yourselves, and then you can be comfortable. Terry and I, on the driver's seat, will act as a kind of screen for you against the wind."

"But you really don't take up nearly as much room as Maida does in her thick motor-coat," said Mrs. Kidder. "If she's not *afraid*—"

"Of course I'm not afraid!" cut in Maida.

"Well, then, I think it would be nicer if Sir Ralph sat with us, Beechy," went on Mrs. Kidder, "unless it would bore him."

Naturally I had to protest that, on the contrary, such an arrangement would be what I most desired, had I dared to consult my own selfish wishes. And I had to see the Vestal Virgin (looking incredibly interesting with her pure face and dark eyes framed with the motor-hood) helped to seat herself in fatal proximity to my unfortunate friend. Talk of a powder magazine and a lighted match! — well, there you have the situation as I felt it, though I was powerless for the moment to avert a catastrophe.

V

A CHAPTER OF ADVENTURES

The Prince let us take the lead. He could start twenty minutes later and still easily pass us before the frontier, he said. He had two or three telegrams to send, and one or two little affairs to settle; but he would not be long in catching us up, and after that the ladies might count upon his services in any—er—any emergency.

"He might better have gone on ahead and polished up that old castle of his a bit before Mrs. Kidder sees it," Terry murmured to me; but we had no right to object to the Prince's companionship, if it were agreeable to our employers, and we uttered no audible word of dissent to his plan.

Beechy and her mother had the two corner seats in the roomy tonneau, and I settled myself on the flap which lets down when the door is closed. In doing this, I was not unconscious of the fact that if the fastening of the door gave way owing to vibration or any other cause, I should indubitably go swinging out into space; also, that if this disagreeable accident did occur, it would be my luck to have it happen when the back of the car was hanging over a precipice. Nevertheless I kept a calm face. These things usually befall some one else rather than one's self; the kind of some one else you read of over your morning coffee, murmuring, "Dear me, how horrid!" before you take another sip.

Terry started the car, and though it carried five persons and enough luggage for ten (I speak of men, not women), we shot away along the perfect road, like an arrow from the bow.

At our first fine panther bound, Mrs. Kidder half rose in her seat and seized my right arm, while Beechy's little hand clutched anxiously at my left knee.

"Oh, mercy!" the Countess exclaimed. "Tell him not to go so fast— oh, quick! we'll be killed."

"No, we won't, Don't be frightened; it's all right," I answered soothingly, primed by my late experience in leaving the Châlet des Pins. "Why, we're going slowly—*crawling* at the rate of twenty—"

"Fifteen!" laughed our chauffeur over his shoulder.

"Fifteen miles an hour," I amended my sentence wondering in what way the shock of surprise had affected the Vestal Virgin. Somehow I couldn't fancy her clawing weakly at any part of Terry's person. "You wouldn't have us go slower, would you? The Prince is sure to be watching."

"Oh, I don't *know*," wailed Mrs. Kidder. "I didn't think it would be like this. Isn't it awful?"

"I believe I—I'm going to like it by-and-by," gasped Beechy, her eyes as round as half-crowns, and as big. "Maida, have you *fainted*?"

Miss Destrey looked back into the tonneau, her face pale, but radiant. "I wouldn't waste time fainting," said she. "I'm buckling on my wings."

"Wish she were a coward!" I thought. "Terry hates 'em like poison, and would never forgive her if she didn't worship motoring at the first go-off." As for me, I have always found a certain piquant charm in a timid woman. There is a subtle flattery in her almost unconscious appeal to superior courage in man which is perhaps especially sweet to an undersized chap like me; and I had never felt more kindly to the Countess and her daughter than I did at this moment.

As Lothair with his Corisande, I "soothed and sustained their agitated frames" so successfully, that the appealing hands stole back to their respective laps, but not to rest in peace for long. The car breasted the small hill at the top of the Cap, sturdily, and we sped on towards Mentone, which, with its twin, sickle bays, was suddenly disclosed like a scene on the stage when the curtains have been noiselessly drawn aside. The picture of the beautiful little town, with its background of clear-cut mountains, called forth quavering exclamations from our reviving passengers; but a few minutes later when we were in the long, straight street of Mentone, weaving our swift way between coming and going electric trams, all the good work I had accomplished had to be done over again.

"I can't stand it," moaned Mrs. Kidder, looking, in her misery, like a frost-bitten apple. "Oh, can't the man *see* that street car's going to run us down? And now there's another, coming from behind. They'll crush us between them. Mr. Terrymore, stop—stop! I'll give you a thousand dollars to take me back to Cap Martin. Oh, he doesn't hear! Sir Ralph—why you're *laughing*!"

"Mamma, you'd send a mummied cat into hysterics," giggled Beechy. "I guess together we'd make the fortune of a dime museum, if they could show us now. But the cars *didn't* run over us, did they?"

"No, but the next ones will—and oh, this cart! Mr. Terrymore's the queerest man, he's steering right for it. No, we've missed it *this* time."

"We'll miss it every time, you'll see," I reassured her. "Barrymore is a magnificent driver; and look, Miss Destrey isn't nervous at all."

"She hasn't got as much to live for as Mamma and I have," said Beechy, trying to hide the fact that she was holding on to the side of the car. "You might almost as well be smashed in an automobile as end your days in a convent."

Here was a revelation, but before I had time to question the speaker further, she and her mother were clinging to me again as if I were a Last Straw or a Forlorn Hope.

This sort of thing lasted for four or five minutes, which doubtless appeared long to them, but they were not in the least tedious for me. I was quite enjoying myself as a Refuge for Shipwrecked Mariners, and I was rather sorry than otherwise when the mariners began to find their own bearings. They saw that, though their escapes seemed to be by the breadth of a hair, they always were escapes, and that no one was anxious except themselves. They probably remembered, also, that we were not pioneers in the sport of motoring; that some thousands of other people had done what we were doing now, if not worse, and still lived to tell the tale—with exaggerations.

Presently the strained look left their faces; their bodies became less rigid; and when they began to take an interest in the shops and villas I knew that the worst was over. My arm and knee felt lonely and deserted, as if their mission in life had been accomplished, and they were now mere obstacles, occupying unnecessary space in the tonneau.

As for Terry, I could see by the set of his shoulders and the way he held his head that he was pleased with life, for he is one of those persons who shows his feelings in his back. He had fought against the idea of this trip, but now that the idea was crystallizing into fact he was happy in spite of himself. After all, what could he ask for that he had not at this moment? The steering wheel of his beloved motor (preserved for him by my cunning) under his hand; beside him a plucky and beautiful girl; behind him a devoted friend; in front, the fairest country in the world, and a road which would lead him to the Alps and to Piedmont; to stately Milan and to the blue, rapturous reaches of Como; a road that would beckon him on and on, past villages sleeping under cypresses on sunny hillsides to Verona, the city of the "star-crossed lovers;" to Giotto's Padua, and by peerless Venice to strange Dalmatia, where Christian and Moslem look distrustfully into one anothers' eyes.

What all this would be to Terry I knew, even though he was playing a part distasteful to him; for if he had missed being born an Irishman, and had reconciled it to his sense of humour to be born at all, he would certainly have been born an Italian. He loves Italy; he breathes the air as the air of home, drawn gratefully into the lungs after a long absence. He learned to speak Italian as easily as he learned to walk, and he could pour out liquid line after line of old Italian poetry, if he had not all a British male's self-conscious fear of making an ass of himself. History was the only thing except cricket and rowing, in which he distinguished himself at Oxford, and Italian history was to him what novels are to most boys, though had it occurred to him at the time that he was "improving his mind" by reading it, he would probably have shut up the book in disgust.

He was not a stranger in the country to which we were going, though he had never entered it by this gate, and most of his motoring had been done in France; but I knew that he would revel in visiting once more the places he loved, in his own car.

"Have you ever been in Italy?" I asked the Countess, but she was evilly fascinated by a dog which seemed bent on committing suicide under our car, and it was Beechy who answered.

"We've never been *anywhere* before, any of us," she said. "Mamma and I only had our machinery set running a few months ago, but now we *are* wound up, goodness knows how far we'll get. As for Maida—she's no mechanical doll like us. But do you know the play about the statue that came to life?"

"Galatea?" I suggested.

"Yes, that's the name. Maida's like that; and I suppose she'll go back as soon as she can, and ask to be turned into a statue again."

"What do you mean?" I ventured to inquire; for these hints of the child's about her cousin were gradually consuming me to a grey ash with curiosity.

"I can't tell you what *I* mean, because I promised I wouldn't. But that's what *Maida* means."

"What she means?"

"Yes, to go back and be turned into a statue, forever and ever."

I ought to have been glad that the girl destined herself for a colder fate than a union with a happy-go-lucky Irishman as poor as herself, but somehow I was not glad. Watching the light glint on a tendril of spun gold which had blown out from the motor-hood, I could not wish her young heart to be turned to marble in that mysterious future to which Beechy Kidder hinted she was self-destined.

"Perhaps I'd better make love to her myself," was the suggestion that flashed into my mind; but innate canniness sturdily pushed it out again. With my seven hundred a year, and *The Riviera Sun* only just beginning to shed a few golden beams, I could not afford to take a penniless beauty off Terry's hands, even to save him from a disastrous marriage or her from the fate of Galatea.

Yet what a day it was in which to live and love, and motor over perfect roads through that radiant summer-land which the Ligurians loved, the Romans conquered, and the modern world comes from afar to see.

Though it was early in April, with Easter but a few days behind us, the sky, the air, the flowers, belonged to June—a rare, rich June to praise in poetry or song. Billows of roses surged over old pink and yellow stucco walls, or a soaring flame of scarlet geranium ran along their tops devouring trails of ivy with a hundred fiery tongues. White villas were draped with gorgeous panoply of purple-red bougainvillea; the breeze in our faces was sweet with the scent of lemon blossoms and a heavier under-tone of white-belled datura. Far away, over that polished floor of lapis-lazuli which was the sea, summer rain-clouds boiled up above the horizon, blue with the soft grey-blue of violets; and in the valleys, between horned or pointed mountains, we saw spurts of golden rain glittering in the morning sun.

What a world! How good to be in it, to be "in the picture" because one had youth, and was not hideous to look upon. How good to be in a motor-car. This last thought made the chorus at the end of each verse for me. I was very glad I had put that advertisement in *The Riviera Sun*, and that "Kid, Kidder, and Kiddest" had been before any one else in answering it.

I could hear Terry telling Miss Destrey things, and I knew that if they listened the others could hear him too. This was well, because an unfailing flow of information was included in the five guineas a day, and I should have been embarrassed had I, as the supposed owner of the car, been called upon to supply it.

I listened with a lazy sense of proprietorship in the man, as my chauffeur related the pretty legend of St. Agnes's ruined castle and the handsome Pagan who had loved the Christian maiden; while he described the exquisite walks to be found up hidden valleys among the serrated mountains behind Mentone; and enlarged upon the charms of picnics with donkeys and lunch-baskets under canopies of olives or pines, with a carpet of violets and primroses.

58

He seemed well up in the history of the Grimaldis and that exciting period when Mentone and legend-crusted Roquebrune had been under the rule of tyrannical princes of that name, as well as Hercules's rock, Monaco, still their own. He knew, or pretended to know, the precise date when Napoleon III. filched Nice and Savoy from reluctant Italy as the price of help against the hated Austrians. Altogether, I was so pleased with the way in which he was beginning, that I should have been tempted to raise his wages had he been my paid chauffeur.

We skimmed past Englishmen and English or American girls in Panama hats, on their way to bathe or play tennis; on all hands we heard the English tongue. Skirting the Old Town, piled high upon its narrow nose of land, we entered the East Bay, and so climbed up to the French side of the Pont St. Louis.

"Now for some red tape," explained Terry. "When I came to the Riviera this season I had no idea of going further, and I'm sorry to say I left my papers in London, where apparently they've disappeared. But as the Countess doesn't care to come back into France, I hope it won't matter much."

As he spoke, a *douanier* lounged out of his little whitewashed lair, and asked for that which Terry had just said he had not.

"I have no papers," Terry informed him, with a smile so agreeable that one hoped it might take away the sting.

"But you intend to return to France?" persisted the official, who evidently gave even a foreigner credit for wishing to rush back to the best country on earth with as little delay as possible.

"No," said Terry apologetically. "We are on our way to Italy and Austria, and may go eventually to England by the Hook of Holland."

The *douanier* gave us up as hopeless, with a resigned shrug of his shoulders. He vanished into his lair, consulted a superior officer, and after a long delay returned with the news that we must pay ten centimes, probably as a penance for our mulish stupidity in leaving France.

As he spoke a douanier lounged out of his little whitewashed lair

I dropped a penny into his palm.

"Will you have a receipt for this sum?" he asked.

"No, thanks," I smiled. "I have infinite trust in your integrity."

"Perhaps we'd better get the receipt all the same," said Terry. "I've never been paperless before, and there may be some fuss or other."

"It took them twenty minutes to decide about their silly ten centimes," said the Countess "and it will take them twenty more at least to make out a receipt for it. Do let's go on, if he'll let us. I'm dying to see what's on the other side of this bridge. We haven't been over into Italy before; there was so much to do in Nice and Monte Carlo."

"All right, we'll risk it, then, as you wish it," Terry agreed; and our prophetic souls did not even turn over in their sleep.

On we went, up the steep hill which, with our load, we were obliged to climb so slowly that Terry and I were ashamed for the car, and tried diplomatically to make it appear that, had we liked, we could have flown up with undiminished speed.

Terry pointed out objects of interest here and there. I questioned him rapidly and he, playing into my hand, answered as quickly, so that, if our wheels lagged, our tongues gave the effect of keeping up a rattling pace.

"Don't you think there's something particularly interesting and romantic about frontiers?" asked Terry of the company in general. "Only a fictitious and arbitrary dividing line, one would say, and yet what a difference on either side, one from the other! Different languages, different customs, prejudices so different that people living within ten yards of each other are ready to go to war over them. Here, for instance, though the first thing one thinks of in crossing the bridge is the splendid view, the second thought that comes must be, how bare the Italian country looks compared to the luxuriant cultivation we're leaving behind. We're turning our backs now on cosy comfort, well-kept roads, tidy houses, tidy people; and we're on our way to meet beggars, shabbiness, and rags, poverty everywhere staring us in the face. Yet much as I admire France, it's to Italy I give my love."

"Talking of frontiers," I flung back the ball to him, "I've often asked myself why it is that a whole people should with one accord worship coffin-beds, six inches too short for a normal human being, hard wedges instead of bolsters, and down coverings three feet thick; while another whole people just round a geographical corner fiercely demand brass beds, springy mattresses, and blankets light as—as love. But nobody has ever satisfactorily answered that question, which may be far more important in solving the profound mystery of racial differences than it would seem."

"Why are *you* prudent and economical, and I reckless and extravagant?" inquired Terry.

"Because I come from the country that took over England, and you from the country that England took over," I explained. But Terry only laughed, being too busy to pick up the cudgels for his native land. "Probably that's also why I'm a chauffeur while you're an editor," he added, and Miss Destrey's little nose and long curve of dark eyelash, seen by me in profile, expressed the sympathy which one young soul in misfortune must feel for another.

"Now we're in Italy," he went on. "What I said is coming true already. Look at these carts crawling to meet us down the hill. The harness seems to be a mere collection of 'unconsidered trifles,' picked up accidently by the drivers; bits of leather, string and rope. And the road you see is strewn with loose stones, though a few metres further back it was so smooth one might dance on it. In dear, lazy Italy, steam-rollers are almost as unknown as dragons. In most districts, if one wants to mend a road, one dumps some stones on it, and trusts to luck and traffic to have them eventually ground in. But luckily our tyres are almost as trustworthy as the Bank of England, and we don't need to worry about the roads."

At the pink Italian custom house Terry got down and vanished within, to pay the deposit and receive certain documents without which we could not "circulate" on Italian soil. Far above our heads looked down the old, brown keep of the Grimaldis, once lords of all the azure coast; below us glittered Mentone, pink and blue and golden in the sun; beyond Monte Carlo sat throned, siren-like, upon her rock.

Terry had scarcely engaged the attention of the officials when the buzz of a motor, livelier and more nervous than our faithful "thrum, thrum," called to us to turn our heads; and there was Prince Dalmar-Kalm's brilliant car flying up the hill, even as we had wished to fly.

The Prince stopped his motor close to ours, to speak with the Countess sitting alone in it, and announced that he would have overtaken us long ago, had he not found himself obliged to pause for a talk with the ex-Empress Eugenie.

This announcement much impressed Mrs. Kidder, who doubtless realized more fully than before her good fortune in having such a distinguished personage for a travelling companion.

He stood leaning on the side of our luggage-wreathed vehicle, with an air of charming condescension. There was no need for him to hurry over the formalities of the *douane*, he said, for even if he were considerably behind us in starting, he would catch us up soon after we had reached La Mortola.

Thus beguiled, the half-hour occupied by the leisurely officials in providing us with papers and sealing the car with an important looking leaden seal, passed not too tediously for the ladies. Finally, the Prince saw us off, smiling a "turned-down smile" at our jog trot as we proceeded up that everlasting hill, which runs like a shelf along the face of the great grey cliff of rock.

Far below, azure waves draped the golden beach with blue and silver gauze and fringed it daintily with a foam of lace.

Then, at last, the steep ascent came to an end, with a curve of the road which plunged us down into a region of coolness and green shadow.

"Why, I don't think Italy's so shabby after all," exclaimed the Countess. "Just see that pretty little Maltese cross above the road, and that fine school-house —"

"Ah, but we're in Hanbury-land now," I said.

"Hanbury-land? I never heard of it. Is it a little independent principality like Monacoa? But how funny it should have an English-sounding name sandwiched in right here between Italy and France."

"The lord of the land is an Englishman, and a benevolent one, a sort of fairy god-father to the poor in all the country round," I explained. "You won't find Hanbury-land mentioned on the map; nevertheless it's very real, fortunately for its inhabitants; and here's the gate of the garden which leads to the royal palace. La Mortola is a great show place, for the public are allowed to go in on certain days. I forget if this is one of them, but perhaps they will let us see the garden, nevertheless. Shall I ask?"

It was in my mind that, if we stopped, we might miss the Prince as well as see the garden, so that we should be killing two birds with one stone, and I was glad when the Countess caught eagerly at the suggestion that we should beg for a glimpse of La Mortola, a place famed throughout Europe.

Permission was given; the big iron gates swung open to admit us. We entered, and a moment later were descending a long flight of stone steps to terraces far below the level of the road where the car stood waiting our return.

Had Aladdin rubbed his lamp in the days before his unfortunate misunderstanding with the Geni and demanded the most beautiful of gardens, the fulfilment of his wish could have taken no fairer form than this. Strange, tropical flowers, vivid as flame, burned in green recesses; water-sprites upset their caskets of pearls over rock-shelves into translucent pools where lilies lay asleep, dreaming of their own pale beauty. Long, green pergolas, starred with flowers, framed blue-veiled pictures of distant coast-line, and mediæval strongholds, coloured with the same burnt umber as the hills on which they stood, gloomed and glowed across a cobalt sea.

There is nothing that pleases the normal male more than to be able to point out objects worthy of interest or admiration to the female of his kind. Since time immemorial, have not landscape-pictures in books of travel been filled in, in the foreground, with the figures of men showing the scenery to women? Did any one ever see such a work of art representing a woman as indicating any point of view to a man? No doubt many could have done so; and the ladies in the pictures had probably noticed the objects in question before their male escorts pointed to them; but knowing the amiable weakness of the other sex, they politely refrained from saying, "Oh, we saw that *long* ago."

Thus did Terry and I, after the conventional traditions of our species, lead our little party through avenues of cypresses, to open rock-spaces, or among a waving sea of roses to battle-grounds of rare cacti, with writhing arms like octopi transformed into plants.

Here, peering down into a kind of dyke, paved with rough tesselation, we vied with each other in telling our charges that this was the old Roman road to Gaul, the Aurelian Way, over which Julius Cæsar, St. Catherine of Siena, Dante, and other great ones passed. Then we showed them one of Napoleon's old guns, covered with shells, as when it was fished out of the sea. We enlarged upon the fact that there was no tree, shrub, or blossom on the known face of the earth of which a specimen did not grow at La Mortola; and when we had wandered for an hour in the garden without seeing half there was to see, we climbed the long flight of steps again, congratulating ourselves— Terry and I—that we had played Dalmar- Kalm rather a neat trick. The crowd of villagers who had clustered round our car outside the entrance gates would screen it from the Prince as he flashed by, and he would go on and on, wondering how we had contrived to get so far ahead.

Our way would take us, after passing through Ventimiglia, up the Roya Valley which Terry had decided upon as a route because of its wild and unspoiled beauty, different from anything that our passengers could have seen in their brief experience of the Riviera. But as there were no inns which offered decent entertainment for man or automobile within reasonable distance, we were to lunch at Ventimiglia, and no arrangement had been made with Dalmar-Kalm concerning this halt. His confidence—perhaps well founded—in the superiority of his speed over ours had led him to believe that he could pause at our side for consultation whenever he wished.

Therefore, we had left Cap Martin without much discussion of plans. Mrs. Kidder was of opinion that we would find him waiting in front of the "best hotel in Ventimiglia," with an excellent luncheon ordered.

"The best hotel in Ventimiglia!" poor lady, she had an awakening before her. Not only was there no Prince, but there was no best hotel. Old Ventimiglia, in its huddled picturesqueness, must delight any man with eyes in his head; new Ventimiglia must disgust any man with a vacancy under his belt. As we sat in the shabby dining-room of a seventh-rate inn (where the flies set an example of attentiveness the waiters did not follow), pretending to eat macaroni hard as walking-sticks and veal reduced to *chiffons*, I feared the courage of our employers would fail. They could never, in all their well- ordered American lives, have known anything so abominable as this experience into which we had lured them, promising a pilgrimage of pleasure. But the charmingly dressed beings, who looked like birds of paradise alighted by mistake in a pigsty, made sport of the squalor which we had expected to evoke their rage.

"Dear me, I wish we'd brought some chewing gum," was Beechy's one sarcasm at the expense of the meal, and Maida and the Countess laughed merrily at everything, even the flies, which they thought did not know their own power as well as American flies.

"We've some *lovely* cakes and candy packed in that sweet tea-basket we bought at an English shop in Paris," said Mrs. Kidder; "but I suppose we'd better not get anything out to eat now, for fear of hurting the waiters' feelings. What do you think, Sir Ralph?"

"Personally, I should like nothing better than to hurt them," I replied severely, "but I'm thinking of myself. Cakes and candy on top of those walking-sticks! 'T were more difficult to build on such a foundation than to rear Venice on its piles and wattles.

"We'd better save what we have till later on," said Maida. "About four o'clock, perhaps we shall be glad to stop somewhere, and I can make tea. It will be fun having it in the automobile."

"There she goes now, revealing domestic virtues!" I thought ruefully. "It will be too much for Teddy to find her an all-round out- of-doors and indoors girl in one. He always said the combination didn't exist; that you had to put up with one or the other in a nice girl, and be jolly thankful for what you'd got."

But Terry did not seem to be meditating upon the pleasing trait just brought to light by his travelling companion. He remarked calmly that by tea-time we should doubtless have reached San Dalmazzo, a charming little mountain village with an old monastery turned into an inn; and then he audibly wondered what had become of the Prince.

"My! What a shame, I'd almost forgotten him!" exclaimed Mrs. Kidder. "He must have given us up in despair and gone on."

"Perhaps he's had a break-down," I suggested.

"What! with that wonderful car? He told me last night that nothing had ever happened to it yet. He must be miles ahead of us by now."

"Then this is his astral body," said Terry. "Clever of him to 'project' one for his car too. Never heard of its being done before."

Nor had I ever heard of an astral body who swore roundly at its chauffeur, which this apparition now stopping in front of the restaurant windows did. It called the unfortunate shape in leather by several strange and creditably, or perhaps discreditably, original names, but as this flow of eloquence was in German, it could not be appreciated by the ladies. Mrs. Kidder knew the languages not at all, and Miss Destrey and Beechy had remarked, when Dalmatia was proposed, that their knowledge was of the copy-book order.

So completely upset was the Prince, that on joining us he forgot to be sarcastic. Not a question, not a sneer as to our progress, not an apology for being late. He flung himself into a chair at the table, ordered the waiters about with truculence, and, having thus relieved his mind, began complaining of his bad luck.

An Austrian Prince, when cross and hungry, can be as undesirable a social companion as a Cockney cad, and the Countess's distinguished friend did not show to advantage in the scene which followed. Yes, there had been an accident. It was unheard of—abominable; entirely the fault of the chauffeur. Chauffeurs (and he looked bleakly at Terry) were without exception brutes—detestable brutes. You put up with them because you had to; that was all. The automobile had merely stopped. It must have been the simplest thing in the world for a professional to discover what was wrong; yet this animal, Joseph, could do nothing but poke his nose into the machinery and then shrug his hideous shoulders. Why yes, he had taken out the valves, of course, examined the sparkling plugs, and tested the coil. Any amateur could have done so much. It gave a good spark; there was no short circuit; yet the motor would not start, and the chauffeur was unable to give an explanation. Twice he had taken the car to pieces without result—absolutely to pieces. Then, and not till then, had the creature found wit enough to think of the carburetter. There was the trouble, and nowhere else. All that delay and misery had been caused by some grit which had penetrated into the carburetter and prevented the needle working. This it was to have a donkey instead of a chauffeur.

"But it didn't occur to you that it might be the carburetter," said Terry, taking advantage of a pause made by the arrival of the Prince's luncheon, which that gentleman attacked with ardour.

"Why should it?" haughtily inquired Dalmar-Kalm. "I am not engaged in that business. I pay other people to think for me. Besides, it is not with me as with you and your friend, who must be accustomed to accidents of all sorts on a low-powered car, somewhat out of date. But I am not used to having mine *en panne*. Never mind, it will not happen again. *Mon Dieu*, what a meal to set before ladies. I do not care for myself, but surely, Sir Ralph, it would have been easy to find a better place than this to give the ladies luncheon?"

"Sir Ralph and Mr. Barrymore wanted us to go to the railway-station," Miss Destrey defended us, "but we thought it would be dull, and preferred this, so our blood is on our own heads."

We finished gloomily with lukewarm coffee, which was so long on the way that the Countess thought we might as well wait for the "poor Prince." Then, when we were ready, came a violent shower, which meant more waiting, as the Countess did not agree cordially with her daughter's remark that to "drive in the rain would be good for the complexion."

When at last we were able to start it was after three, and we should have to make good speed if we were to arrive at San Dalmazzo even by late tea-time. Terry was on his mettle, however, and I guessed that he was anxious our first day should not end in failure.

Tooling out of Ventimiglia, that grim frontier town whose name has become synonymous to travellers with waiting and desperate resignation, we turned up by the side of the Roya, where the stream gushes seaward, through many channels, in a wide and pebbly bed. The shower just past, though brief, had been heavy enough to turn a thick layer of white dust into a greasy, grey paste of mud. On our left was a sudden drop into the rushing river, on the right a deep ditch, and the road between was as round-shouldered as a hunchback. Seeing this natural phenomenon, and feeling the slightly uncertain step of our fat tyres as they waddled through the pasty mud, the pleasant smile of the proud motor-proprietor which I had been wearing hardened upon my face. I didn't know as much about motors as our passengers supposed, but I did know what side-slip was, and I did not think that this was a nice place for the ladies to be initiated. There might easily be an accident, even with the best of drivers such as we had in Terry, and I was sure that he was having all he could do to keep on the crown of the road. At any moment, slowly as we were going, the heavily laden car might become skittish and begin to waltz, a feat which would certainly first surprise and then alarm the ladies, even if it had no more serious consequences.

It was while we were in this critical situation, which had not yet begun to dawn upon our passengers, that Dalmar-Kalm seized the opportunity of racing past us from behind, blowing a fanfarronade on his horn, to prove how much faster his car could go than ours. In the instant that he was abreast of us, our tonneau, which overhung the back axle further than is considered wise in the latest types of cars, swung outwards, with a slip of the tyre in the grey grease, and only by an inch which seemed a mere hair's breadth was Terry able to save us from a collision.

The Countess screamed, Beechy clung once more to my knee, and we all glared at the red car with the white canopy as it shot ruthlessly ahead. The Prince's tyres were strapped with spiked leather covers, which we could not carry as they would lose us too much speed; therefore the danger of side-slip was lessened for him, and he flew by without even knowing how near we had been to an accident. The anger painted on our ungoggled faces he doubtless attributed to jealousy, as he glanced back to wave a triumphant *au revoir* before flashing out of sight, round a bend of the road.

There is something very human, and particularly womanish, about a motor-car. The shock of the narrow escape we had just had seemed to have unsteadied the nerve of our brave Panhard for the moment. We were nearing a skew bridge, with an almost right-angled approach; and the strange resultant of the nicely balanced forces that control an automobile skating on "pneus" over slippery mud twisted us round, suddenly and without warning. Instantly, oilily, the car gyrated as on a pivot, and behold, we were facing down the valley instead of up. Terry could not had done it had he tried.

"Oh, my goodness!" quavered the Countess, in a collapse. "Am I dreaming, or has this happened? It seems as if I must be out of my wits!"

"It *has* happened," answered Terry, laughing reassuringly, but far from joyous within, I knew. "But it's nothing alarming. A little side-slip, that's all."

"A *little* side-slip!" she echoed. "Then may I be preserved from a big one. This automobile has turned its nose towards home again, of its own accord. Oh, Sir Ralph, I'm not sure I like motoring as much as I thought I would. I'm not sure the Hand of Providence didn't turn the car back."

"Nonsense, Mamma!" cried Beechy. "The other day the Hand of Providence was pointing out Sir Ralph's advertisement in the newspaper. It can't be always changing its mind, and you can't, either. We're all *alive*, anyhow, and that's something."

"Ah, but how long shall we be?" moaned her mother. "I don't want to be silly, but I didn't know that an automobile had the habits of a kangaroo and a crab, and a base-ball, and I'm afraid I shall never get used to them."

Terry explained that his car was not addicted to producing these sensational effects, and compared the difficulties it was now combatting with those which a skater might experience if the hard ice were covered an inch deep with soft soap. "We shall soon be out of this," he said, "for the road will be better higher up where the hill begins, and the rain has had a chance to drain away."

Cheered by these promises, the poor Countess behaved herself very well, though she looked as if she might burst an important blood-vessel, as Terry carefully turned his car on the slippery surface of the road's tortoise-back. I was not happy myself, for it would have been as "easy as falling off a log" for the automobile to leap gracefully into the Roya; but the brakes held nobly, and as Terry had said, there was better going round the next corner.

Here the mountains began to draw together, so that we were no longer travelling in a valley, but in a gorge. Deep shadow shut us in, as if we had left the warm, outer air and entered a dim castle, perpetually shuttered and austerely cold. Dark crags shaped themselves magnificently, and the scene was of such wild grandeur that even Beechy ceased to be flippant. We drove on in silence, listening to the battle song of the river as it fought its way on through the rocky chasm its own strength had hewn.

The road mounted continuously, with a gentle incline, weaving its grey thread round the blind face of the mountain, and suddenly, turning a shoulder of rock we came upon the Prince's car which we had fancied many kilometres in advance. The big red chariot was stationary, one wheel tilted into the ditch at the roadside, while Dalmar-Kalm and his melancholy chauffeur were straining to rescue it from its ignominious position.

Our Panhard had been going particularly well, as if to justify itself in its employers' eyes after its late slip from rectitude. "She" was taking the hill gaily, pretending not to know it from the level, and it did seem hard to play the part of good Samaritan to one marked by nature as a Levite. But—*noblesse oblige*, and—honour among chauffeurs.

Terry is as far from sainthood as I am, and I knew well that his bosom yearned to let Dalmar-Kalm stew in his own petrol. Nevertheless, he brought the car to anchor without a second's hesitation, drawing up alongside the humiliated red giant. Amid the exclamations of Mrs. Kidder, and the suppressed chuckles of the *enfante terrible*, we two men got out, with beautiful expressions on our faces and dawning haloes round our heads, to help our hated rival.

Did he thank us for not straining the quality of our mercy? His name and nature would not have been Dalmar-Kalm if he had. His first words at sight of the two ministering angels by his side were: "You must have brought me bad luck, I believe. Never have I had an accident with my car until to-day, but now all goes wrong. For the second time I am *en panne*. It is too much. This viper of a Joseph says we cannot go on."

Now we began to see why the Prince's chauffeur had acquired the countenance of a male Niobe. Wormlike resignation to utter misery was, we had judged, his prevailing characteristic; but hard work, ingratitude, and goodness knows how much abuse, caused the worm to turn and defend itself.

"How go on with a change-speed lever broken short off, close to the quadrant?" he shrilled out in French. "And it is His Highness who broke it, changing speed too quickly, a thing which I have constantly warned him against in driving. I cannot make a new lever here in a wilderness. I am not a magician."

"Nor a Félicité," I mumbled, convinced that, had my all- accomplished adjutant been a chauffeur instead of a cook, she would have been equal to beating up a trustworthy lever out of a slice of cake.

"Be silent, brigand!" roared the Prince, and I could hardly stifle a laugh, for Joseph is no higher than my ear. His shoulders slope; his legs are clothespins bound with leather; his eyes swim in tears, as our car's crankhead floats in an oil bath; and his hair is hung round his head like many separate rows of black pins, overlapping one another.

"We shall save time by getting your car out of the ditch, anyhow," suggested Terry; and putting our shoulders to it, all four, we succeeded after strenuous efforts in pushing and hauling the huge beast onto the road. I had had no idea that anything less in size than a railway engine could be so heavy.

There was no question but that the giant was helpless. Terry and Joseph peered into its inner workings, and the first verdict was confirmed. "There's an imperfection in the metal," said expert Terry. In his place, I fear I should not have been capable of such magnanimity. I should have let the whole blame rest upon my rival's reckless stupidity as a driver.

"It's plain you can do nothing with your car in that condition," he went on. "After all" (even Terry's generous spirit couldn't resist this one little dig), "it would have been well if I'd brought that coil of rope."

"Coil of rope? For what purpose?"

"To tow you to the nearest blacksmith's, where perhaps a new lever could be forged."

"This is not a time for joking. Twelve horses cannot drag twenty-four."

"They're plucky and willing. Shall they try? Here comes a cart, whose driver is wreathed in smiles. Labour exulting in the downfall of Capitol. But Labour looks good-natured." "Good morning," Terry hailed him in Italian. "Will you lend me a stout cord to tow this automobile?"

The Prince was silent. Even in his rage against Fate, against Joseph, and against us, he retained enough common sense to remember that 'tis well to choose the lesser of two evils.

The carter had a rope, and an obliging disposition. A few francs changed hands, and the Hare was yoked to the Tortoise. Yoked, figuratively speaking only, for it trailed ignominiously behind at a distance of fifteen yards, and when our little Panhard began bumbling up the hill with its great follower, it resembled nothing so much as a very small comet with a disproportionately big tail.

The motor, in starting, forged gallantly ahead for a yard or two, then, as it felt the unexpected weight dragging behind, it appeared surprised. It was, indeed, literally "taken aback" for an instant, but only for an instant. The brave little beast seemed to say to itself, "Well, they expect a good deal of me, but there are ladies on board, and I won't disappoint them."

"Félicité," I murmured. "She might have stood sponser to this car."

With another tug we began to make progress, slow but steady. Joseph, as the lighter weight, sat in his master's car, his hand on the steering-wheel, while the Prince tramped gloomily behind in the mud. Seeing how well the experiment was succeeding, however, he quickened his pace and ordered the chauffeur down. "I do not think that the difference in weight will be noticeable," he said, and as Joseph obediently jumped out the Prince sprang in, taking the wheel. Instantly the rope snapped, and the big red chariot would have run back had not Joseph jammed on the brake.

Terry stopped our car, and the ill-matched pair had to be united again, with a shorter rope. "Afraid you'll have to walk, Prince," said he, when he had finished helping Joseph, who was apparently on the brink of tears.

Dalmar-Kalm measured me with a glance. "Perhaps Sir Ralph would not object to steering my car?" he suggested. "Then Joseph could walk, and I could have Sir Ralph's place in the tonneau with the ladies, where a little extra weight would do no harm. Would that not be an excellent arrangement?"

"David left Goliath on the ground, and dragged away only his head," I remarked. "*We* are dragging Goliath; and I fear his head would be the last—er—feather. So sorry. Otherwise we should be delighted."

What the Prince said as the procession began to move slowly up-hill again, at a pace to keep time with the "Dead March in Saul," I don't pretend to know, but if his remarks matched his expression, I would not in any case have recorded them here.

VI

A CHAPTER OF PREDICAMENTS

On we went, and twilight was falling in this deep gorge, so evidently cut by the river for its own convenience, not for that of belated tourists. Here and there in the valley little rock towns stood up impressively, round and high on their eminences, like brown, stemless mushrooms. Each little group of ancient dwellings resembled to my mind a determined band of men standing back to back, shoulder to shoulder, defending their hearths and homes from the Saracens, and saying grimly, "Come on if you dare. We'll fight to the death, one and all of us."

At last, without further mishap, we arrived at a mean village marked Airole on Terry's map. It was a poverty-stricken place, through which, in happier circumstances, we should have passed without a glance, but—there, by the roadside was a blacksmith's forge, more welcome to our eyes than a castle double-starred by Baedeker.

Joseph's spleen reduced by the sight of his master tramping in the mud while he steered, the little chauffeur looked almost cheerful. He promised to have a new lever ready in half an hour, and so confident was he that he urged us to go on. But the Prince did not echo the suggestion, and Mrs. Kidder proposed that we should have tea while we waited.

Though it was she who gave birth to the idea, it would have been Miss Destrey who did all the work, had not Terry and I offered such help as men can give. He went in search of water to fill the shining kettle; I handed round biscuits and cakes, while the Prince looked on in the attitude of Napoleon watching the burning of Moscow.

We were as good as a circus to the inhabitants of Airole; nay, better, for our antics could be seen gratis. The entire population of the village, and apparently of several adjacent villages, collected round the two cars. They made the ring, and—we did the rest. We ate, we drank, and they were merry at our expense. The children wished also to eat at our expense, and when I translated (with amendments) a flattering comment on Mrs. Kidder's hair and complexion offered by an incipient Don Juan of five years, she insisted that all the spare pastry should be distributed among the juveniles. The division led to blows, and tears which had to be quenched with coppers; while into the mêlée broke a desolate cry from Joseph, announcing that his lever was a failure. The Prince strode off to the blacksmith's shop, forgetful that he held a teacup in one hand and an *éclair* in the other. With custard dropping onto the red-hot bar which Joseph hammered, he looked so forlorn a figure that Terry was moved to pity and joined the group at the forge. He soon discovered what Joseph might have known from the first, had he not lived solely in the moment, like most other chauffeurs. The village forge was not *assez bien outillée* for a finished lever to be produced; the Prince's car must remain a derelict, unless we towed it into port.

We started on again, in the same order as before and at the same pace, followed by all our village *protegés*, who commented frankly upon the plight of the Prince, and the personal appearance of the whole party. At length, however, our moving audience dwindled. A mile or two beyond Airole the last, most enterprising boy deserted us, and we thought ourselves alone in a twilight world. The white face of the moon peered through a cleft in the mountain, and our own shadows crawled after us, large and dark on the grey ribbon of the road. But there was another shadow which moved, a small drifting shadow over which we had no control. Sometimes it was by our side for an instant as we crept up the hill, dragging our incubus, then it would fall behind and vanish, only to reappear again, perhaps on the other side of the road.

"What *is* that tiny black thing that comes and goes?" asked Mrs. Kidder.

"Why," exclaimed Miss Destrey, "I do believe it's that forlorn little dog that was too timid to eat from my hand in the village. He must have followed all this time."

"Do see if it is the same dog, Prince," Beechy cried to the tall, dark figure completing the tail of our procession.

A yelp answered. "Yes, it is he," called the Prince. "A mangy little mongrel. I do not think he will trouble us any longer."

Then a surprising thing happened. The Vestal Virgin rose suddenly in the car. "You have *kicked* him!" she exclaimed, the gentleness burnt out of her pretty voice by a swift flame of anger. "Stop the car, Mr. Barrymore—quickly, please. I want to get down."

Never had that Panhard of Terry's checked its career in less space. Out jumped Maida, to my astonishment without a word of objection from her relatives. "I will not have that poor, timid little creature frightened and hurt," I heard her protesting as she ran back. "How *could* you, Prince!"

Now, though the girl was probably no more than a paid companion, she was lovely enough to make her good opinion of importance to the most inveterate fortune hunter, and as Miss Destrey called, "Here, doggie, doggie," in a voice to beguile a rhinoceros, Dalmar-Kalm pleaded that what he had done had been but for the animal's good. He had not injured the dog, he had merely encouraged it to run home before it was hopelessly lost. "I am not cruel, I assure you. My worst troubles have come from a warm heart. I hope you will believe me, Miss Destrey."

"I should be sorry to be your dog, or—your chauffeur," she answered. "He won't come back to be comforted, so I suppose after all we shall have to go on. But I shall dream of that poor little lonely, drifting thing to-night."

Hardly had she taken her seat, however, than there was the dog close to the car, timid, obsequious, winning, with his wisp of a head cocked on one side. We drove on, and he followed pertinaciously. Mildly adjured by the Countess to "go home, little dog," he came on the faster. Many adventures he had, such as a fall over a heap of stones and entanglement in a thorn-bush. But nothing discouraged the miniature motor maniac in the pursuit of his love, and we began to take him for granted so completely that after a while I, at least, forgot him. On we toiled with our burden, the moon showering silver into the dark mountain gorges, as if it were raining stars.

78

The further we burrowed into the fastnesses of the Roya, the more wild in its majestic beauty grew the valley, so famed in history and legend. The gorge had again become a mere gash in the rock, with room only for the road and the roaring river below. High overhead, standing up against the sky like a warning finger, towered the ancient stronghold of Piena, once guardian fortress of the valley; where the way curved, and crossed a high bridge spanning the torrent, we passed a tablet of gleaming bronze set against the rock wall, in commemoration of Masséna's victory in an early campaign of Napoleon's against Italy. Sometimes we rushed through tunnels, where the noise of the motor vibrated thunderously; sometimes we looked down over sublime precipices; but the road was always good now, and we had no longer to fear side-slip.

We met no one; nevertheless Terry got down and lit our lamps, Dalmar-Kalm making an unnecessary delay by insisting that Joseph should light his too. This was sheer vanity on the Prince's part. He could not bear to have his great Bleriots dark, while our humbler acetylene illumined the way for His Mightiness.

Suddenly we ran out of the bewildering lights and shadows, woven across our way by the moon, into the lights of a town; and two *douaniers* appeared in the road, holding up their hands for us to stop. Down jumped Terry to see why he should be challenged in this unexpected place, and the Prince joined him.

"Your papers, if you please," demanded the official.

Terry produced those which had been given us at the custom-house in Grimaldi.

"But these are Italian papers. Where are those for France?" asked the *douanier*.

"This is not France," said the Prince, before Terry could speak.

"It is Breil, and it is France," returned the man. "France for nine kilometres, until Fontan, where Italian territory begins again."

Terry laughed, rather ruefully. "Well," said he, "I have no French papers, but we paid a penny at the Pont St. Louis to leave France.

This car is French, and we ought not to pay anything to enter; nevertheless, I shall be delighted to hand you the same sum for the privilege of coming in again."

"Ah, you paid ten centimes? Then, if you have the receipt it may be possible to permit you to go on."

"Permit us to go on!" echoed Dalmar-Kalm angrily. "I should think so, indeed."

"I'm sorry, I took no receipt," said Terry. "I thought it an unnecessary formality."

"*No* formality is unnecessary, monsieur," said the servant of form. "I also am sorry, but in the circumstances you cannot enter French territory without a receipt for the ten centimes. As a man I believe implicitly that you paid the sum, as an official I am compelled to doubt your word."

Who but a Frenchman could have been so exquisitely pompous over a penny? I saw by Terry's face that he was far from considering the incident closed; but he had too much true Irish tact to try and get us through by storming.

"Let us consider," he began, "whether there is not some means of escape from this difficulty."

But Dalmar-Kalm was in no mood to temporize, or keep silent while others temporized. The lights of Breil showed that it was a town of comparative importance; it was past eight o'clock; and no doubt His Highness's temper was sharpened by a keen edge of hunger. That he—he should be stopped by a fussy official figure-head almost within smell of food, broke down the barrier of his self-restraint— never a formidable rampart, as we had cause to know. In a few loud and vigorous sentences he expressed a withering contempt for France, its institutions, its customs, and especially its custom-houses.

"If you'd mix up the Prince's initials, as you do Mr. Barrymore's sometimes, and call him Kalmar-Dalm, there'd be some excuse for it," Beechy Kidder murmured to the Countess.

80

"Hush, he'll hear!" implored the much-enduring lady, but there was small danger that His Highness would hear any expostulations save his own.

The functionary's eye grew dark, and Terry frowned. Had the *douanier* been insolent, my peppery Irishman would have been insolent too, perhaps, in the hope of cowering the man by truculence more swashbuckling than his own; but he had been as polite as his countrymen proverbially are, if not goaded out of their suavity. "Look here, Prince," said Terry, hanging onto his temper by a thread (for he also was hungry), "suppose you leave this matter to me. If you'll take the ladies to the best hotel in town, Moray and I will stop and see this thing through. We'll follow when we can."

Dalmar-Kalm snapped at the suggestion; our passengers saw that it was for the best, and yielded. As they moved away, a shadowy form hovered in their wake. It was the little black dog of Airole.

The Marquis of Innisfallen's first quarrel with his brother had been caused by Terry's youthful preference for an army instead of a diplomatic career. Now, could his cantankerous relative have seen my friend, he would once more have shaken his head over talents wasted. The oily eloquence which Terry lavished on that comparatively insignificant French *douanier* ought to have earned him a billet as first secretary to a Legation. He pictured the despair of the ladies if the power of France kept them prisoners at the frontier; he referred warmly to that country's reputation for chivalry; he offered to pay the usual deposit on a car entering France and receive it back again at Fontan. To this last suggestion the harassed official replied that technically his office was closed for the night, and that after eight o'clock he could not receive money or issue papers. Finally, therefore, Terry was reduced to appealing to the cleverness and resource of a true Frenchman.

It was a neat little fencing-match, which ended in the triumph of Great Britain. The functionary, treated like a gentleman by a gentleman, became anxious to accommodate, if he could do so "consistently with honour." He had an inspiration, and suggested that he would strain his duty by sending a messenger with us to Fontan, there to explain that we were merely *en passage*. Out of the crowd which had collected a loutish youth was chosen; a *pourboire* promised; and after many mutual politenesses we were permitted to *teuf-teuf* onto the sacred soil of France.

It is no more safe to judge a French country inn by its exterior, than the soul of Cyrano de Bergerac by his nose. The inn of Breil had not an engaging face, but it was animated by the spirit of a Brillat Savarin, by which we were provided with a wonderful dinner in numerous courses. We could not escape from it, lest we hurt the *amour-propre* of the cook, and it was late when we were ready for our last *sortie*.

"You will never reach San Dalmazzo to-night, towing that car," we were informed by the powers that were in the hotel. "The hills you have passed are as nothing to the hills yet to come. You will do well to spend the night with us, for if you try to get on, you will be all night upon the road."

Our passengers were asked to decide, and we expected a difference of opinion. We should have said that the two girls would have been for pushing on, and the Countess for stopping. But that plump lady had already conquered the tremors which, earlier in the day, had threatened to wreck our expedition at its outset.

"It's a funny thing," said she, "but I want to go on, just *on*, for the sake of *going*. I never felt like that before, travelling, not even in a Mann Boudoir car at home, which I guess is the most luxurious thing on wheels. I always wanted to *get* there, wherever 'there' was; but now I want to go on and on—I wouldn't care if it was to the end of the world, and I can't think why, unless it's the novelty of automobiling. But it can't be that, either, I suppose, for only a little while ago I was thinking that bed-ridden people weren't badly off, they were so *safe*."

We all laughed at this (even the Prince, whom plenty of champagne had put into a sentimental mood), and I suddenly found myself growing quite fond of the Countess, crowns and all.

After the heat of the *salle à manger*, the night out of doors appeared strangely white and cold, its purple depths drenched with moonlight, the high remoteness of its dome faintly scintillant with icy points of stars. An adventure seemed to lie before us. We turned wistfully to each other for the warmth of human companionship, and had not the Prince been trying to flirt with little Beechy unseen by Mamma, I should have felt kindly even to him. Even as it was, I consented to let him try sitting in his own car, and the rope, inured to suffering, had the consideration not to break.

We forged on, up, up the higher reaches of the Roya valley, so glorious in full moonlight that it struck us into silence. The mountains towering round us shaped themselves into castles and cathedrals of carved marble, their façades, grey by day, glittering white and polished under the magic of the moon. The wonderful crescent town of Saorge, hanging on the mountain-side, would alone have been worth coming this way to see if there had been nothing else. Veiled by the mystery of night, the old Ligurian stronghold appeared to be suspended between two rocky peaks, like a great white hammock for a sleeping goddess, and now and then we caught a jewelled sparkle from her rings.

They had not told an idle tale at the inn. The road, weary of going uphill on its knees, like a pilgrim, got suddenly upon its feet and we were on its back, with the Prince's chariot trailing after us. Nevertheless, our car did not falter, though the motor panted. Scarcely ever were we able to pass from the first speed to the second, but then (as Beechy remarked), considering all things, we ought to be thankful for any speed above that of a snail.

At Fontan—when he had vouched for us—we dismissed our *oaf*, with a light heart and a heavy pocket. Again, we were in Italy, a silent, sleeping Italy, drugged with moonlight, and dreaming troubled dreams of strangely contorted mountains. Then suddenly it waked, for the moon was sinking, and the charm had lost its potence. The dream-shapes vanished, and we were in a wide, dark basin, which might be green as emerald by day. A grey ghost in a long coat, with a rifle slung across his back, flitted into the road and startled the Countess by signing for us to stop.

"Oh, mercy! are we going to be held up?" she whispered. "I'd forgotten about the brigands."

"Only an Italian custom-house brigand," said Terry. "We've got to San Dalmazzo after all, and it isn't morning yet."

"Yes, but it is!" cried Beechy. "There's a clock striking twelve."

A few minutes later we were driving along a level in the direction of the monastery-hotel, which was said to be no more than a hundred metres beyond the village. I had often heard of this hostelry at the little mountain retreat of San Dalmazzo, loved and sought by Italians in the summer heat. The arched gateway in the wall was clearly monastic, and we felt sure that we had come to the right place, when Terry steered the car through the open portal and a kind of tunnel on the other side.

Before the door of a long, low building he stopped the motor. Its "thrum, thrum" stilled, the silence of the place was profound, and not a light gleamed anywhere.

Terry got down and rang. We all waited anxiously, for much as we had enjoyed the strange night drive, the day had been long, and the chill of the keen mountain air was in our blood. But nothing happened, and after a short pause Terry rang again. Silence was the only answer, and it seemed to give denial rather than consent.

Four times he rang, and by this time the Prince and I were at his back, striving to pierce the darkness behind the door which was half of glass. At last a greenish light gleamed dim as a glow-worm in the distance, and framed in it a figure was visible—the figure of a monk.

For an instant I was half inclined to believe him a ghost, haunting the scene of past activities, for one does not expect to have the door of an hotel opened by a monk. But ghosts have no traffic with keys and bolts; and it was the voice of a man still bound to flesh and blood who greeted us with a mild "Buona sera" which made the night seem young.

Terry responded and announced in his best Italian that we desired accommodation for the night.

"Ah, I see," exclaimed the monk. "You thought that this was still a hotel? I am sorry to disappoint you, but it ceased to be such only to-day. The house is now once more what it was originally—a monastery. It has been bought by the Order to which I belong."

"Isn't he going to take us in?" asked the Countess, dolefully.

"I'm afraid not," said Terry, "but I'll see what I can do."

Ah, that "seeing what he could do!" I knew it of old, for Terry's own brother is the only person I ever met who could resist him if he stooped to wheedle. Italian is a language which lends itself to wheedling, too; and though the good monk demurred at first, shook his head, and even flung up his hands with a despairing protest, he weakened at last, even as the *douanier* had weakened.

"He says if we'd come to-morrow, it would have been impossible to admit us," translated Terry for the ladies' benefit. "The lease is going to be signed then. Until that's done the house isn't actually a monastery, so he can strain a point and take us in, rather than the ladies should have to travel further so late at night. I don't suppose we shall find very luxurious accommodation, but—"

"It will be perfectly lovely," broke in Beechy, "and Maida, anyhow, will feel quite at home."

"He won't accept payment, that's the worst of it," said Terry, "for we shall make the poor man, who is all alone, a good deal of bother. Still, I shall offer something for the charities of his Order, and he can't refuse that."

We filed into the hall, lit only by the lantern in our host's hand, and "Kid, Kidder, and Kiddest," charmed with the adventure, were delightfully ready to be pleased with everything. We seemed to have walked nearly half a kilometre before we were shown into small, bare rooms, furnished only with necessaries, but spotlessly clean. Then beds had to be made and water brought. Every one worked except the Prince, and every one, with the same exception, forgot to be tired and ceased to be cold in the pleasure of the queer midnight picnic. We had not dared hope for anything to eat, but when our host proposed a meal of boiled eggs, bread, and wine, the good man was well-nigh startled by the enthusiastic acceptance of his guests.

A small room containing a table, and a pile of chairs against the wall, was chosen for the banquet. Terry and Maida laid the table with the dishes from the tea-basket, and a few more found in neighbouring cupboards. Beechy boiled the eggs while our host unearthed the wine; the Countess cut slices of hard, brown bread, and I added butter in little hillocks.

Then we ate and drank; and never was a meal so good. We seemed to have known each ether a long time, and already we had common jokes connected with our past—that past which had been the present this morning. It was after one o'clock when it occurred to us that it was bedtime; and as at last the three ladies flitted away down the dim corridor, Terry and I, watching them, saw that something flitted after.

It was the little black dog of Airole.

PART II

TOLD BY BEECHY KIDDER

VII

A CHAPTER OF CHILDISHNESS

When I waked up that morning in the old monastery at San Dalmazzo, if that's the way to call it, and especially to spell it, I really thought for a few minutes that I must be dreaming. "There's no good getting up," I thought, "for if I do I shall somnambulize, and maybe break my rather pleasing nose." Once, when I was a little girl, I fell downstairs when I was asleep, and made one of my front teeth come out. It was a front tooth, and Mamma had promised me five dollars if I'd have it pulled; so that was money in my pocket. But I haven't got any teeth to sell for five dollars now, and it's well to be careful. Accordingly I just lay still in that funny little iron bed, saying, "Beechy Kidder, is this *you?*"

Perhaps it was because of all those bewildering impressions the day before, or perhaps it was from having been so dead asleep that I felt exactly as if I were no relation to myself. Anyhow, that was the way I *did* feel, and I began to be awfully afraid I should wake up back in Denver months ago, before anything had happened, or seemed likely ever to happen.

When I thought of Mamma and myself, as we used to be, I grew almost sure that the things hadn't happened, because they didn't seem the kind of things that could possibly happen to us.

Why, I didn't even need to shut my eyes to see our Denver house, for it was so much more real than any other house I'd been in, or dreamed I'd been in since, and especially more real than that tiny, whitewashed room at the monastery with a green curtain of vines hanging over the window.

A square, stone house, with a piazza in front (only people out of America are so stupid, they don't know what I mean when I say "piazza"); about six feet of yard with some grass and flowers. Me at school; Mamma reading novels with one eye, and darning papa's stockings with the other. My goodness, what a different Mamma! When I thought of the difference, I was surer than ever that I must be dreaming her as she is now, and I had half a mind to go and peek into the next room to look, and risk falling down-stairs bang into realities and Denver.

Would she have smooth, straight dark hair with a few threads of grey, all streaked back flat to her head to please papa; or would she have lovely auburn waves done on a frame, with a curl draped over her forehead? Would her complexion be just as nice, comfortable, motherly sort of complexion, of no particular colour; or would it be pink and white like rose-leaves floating in cream? Would she have the kind of figure to fit the corsets you can pick up at any shop, ready made for fifty-nine and a half cents, and the dresses Miss Pettingill makes for ten dollars, with the front breadth shorter than the back? Or would she go in at the waist like an hour-glass and out like an hour-glass, to fit three hundred-franc stays in Paris, and dresses that would be tight for *me*?

Poor Mamma! I'd made lots of fun of her these last few months, if they were real months, I said to myself; and if more real months of that kind should come, I'd probably make lots of fun of her again. I am *like* that; I can't help it. I suppose it's what Papa used to call his "originality," and Mamma his "cantankerousness," coming out in me. But lying there in the narrow bed, with the dream-dawn fluttering little pale wings at the window, I seemed suddenly to understand how hard everything had been for her.

At some minutes, on some days, you *do* understand people with a queer kind of clearness, almost as if you had created them yourself— even people that you turn up your nose at, and think silly or uninteresting at other times, when your senses aren't sharpened in that magic sort of way. My "God-days," are what I call those strange days when I can sympathize with every one as if I'd known their *whole* history and all their troubles and thoughts and struggles, ever since they were born. I call them that, not to be irreverent, but because I suppose God *always* feels so; and the little spark of Him that's in every human being—even in a naughty, pert thing like me—comes out in us more on some days than on others, though only for a few minutes at a stretch even then.

Well, my spark burned up quite brightly for a little while in the dawn, as I was thinking of Mamma.

I don't suppose she could ever have been in love with Papa. I guess she must have married him because her parents were poor, or because she was too kind hearted to say no. Anyway, it must have been horrid for her to know that he was rich enough to let her do anything she liked, but wouldn't let her do anything nice, because he was a Consistent Democrat, and didn't believe in show or "tomfoolery."

I'm sure I couldn't explain what a Consistent Democrat really is; but Papa's idea of being it was to scorn "society people," not to have pretty clothes or many servants, to look plain and speak plainly, always to tell the whole truth, especially if you would hurt anybody's feelings by doing so, and not to spend much money except on uninteresting books

.

Mamma would have loved better than anything to be a society leader, and have her name appear often in the papers, like other ladies in Denver who, she used to tell me, didn't come from half as good family as she did. But Papa wouldn't let her go out much, and she didn't know any of the people she wanted to know—only quite common ones whose husbands kept stores or had other businesses which she didn't consider refined. I'm afraid I was never much comfort to poor Mamma either. That cantankerousness of mine which makes me see how funny people and things are, always came between us, and I expect it always will. I must have been born old.

Her only real pleasure was reading novels on the sly, all about smart society and the aristocracy, but especially English aristocracy. She simply revelled in such stories; and when Papa died suddenly without time to tie up his money so as to force Mamma to go on doing what *he* wanted, and not what *she* wanted, all the rest of her life, the first thing that occurred to her was how to make up for lost time.

"We'll travel in Europe for a year or two," she said to me, "and when we come back we'll just show Denver society people that we're *somebody*."

That was all she thought of in the beginning, but when we'd gone East to Chicago for a change, and were staying at a big hotel there, a new idea came into her head. Partly it was from seeing so many smart-looking young women having a good time every minute of their lives, and feeling what was the use of being free to enjoy herself at last, with plenty of money, when she was dowdy and not so very young any more? (I could tell just what was in her mind by the wistful way she looked at gorgeous ladies who had the air of owning the world, with a fence around it.) And partly it was seeing an advertisement in a newspaper.

Mamma didn't mention the advertisement to me at first. But when she'd been away one morning alone on a secret errand she stammered and fidgetted a little, and said she had something to explain to me. Then it all came out.

She'd been to call on a wonderful French madame who could make a woman of thirty-eight (that's Mamma's Bible age) look twenty-five, and she hoped I wouldn't lose respect for her as my mother or think her frivolous and horrid if she put herself into the madame's hands for a few weeks. I couldn't help laughing, but Mamma cried, and said that she'd never had a real good time since she was grown up. She did long to have one at last, very much, if only I'd let her do it in peace.

I stopped laughing and almost cried, myself; but I didn't let her see that I wanted to. Instead, I asked what would be the sense of *looking* twenty-five, anyhow, when everybody would know she *must* be more, with a daughter going on seventeen.

Mamma hadn't thought of that. She seemed years older than ever for a minute; and then she put her hand in mine. Hers was as cold as ice. "Would you mind going back a little, darling?" she asked. "It would be *so* kind and sweet of you, and it would make all the difference to me."

"Going back?" I repeated. "Whatever *do* you mean?"

It made her dreadfully nervous to explain, because she was afraid I'd poke fun at her, but she did get out the idea finally. "Going back" was to bring on my second childhood prematurely. Thirteen was a nice age, she thought, because many girls get their full growth then; and if I wasn't more than thirteen she could begin life over again at twenty-nine.

"What, let down my hair and wear my dresses short?" I asked.

She admitted that was what I'd have to do.

I thought for a whole minute, and at last I just couldn't bear to disappoint her. But all the same, I reminded myself, I might as well make a good bargain while I was about it.

"If I do what you want," said I, "you'll have to be mighty nice to me. I must be given my way about important things. If you ever refuse to do what I like, after I've done so much for you, I'll just turn up my hair and put on a long frock. Then everybody'll see how old I am."

She would have promised anything, I guess; and that very afternoon she gave me three lovely rings, and a ducky little bracelet-watch, when we were out shopping for short clothes and babyfied hats. Soon we moved away from that hotel to one on the north side, where nobody had seen us; and the first thing I knew, I was a little girl again.

It certainly was fun. To really appreciate being a child, you ought to have been grown up in another state of existence, and remember your sensations. It was something like that with me, and my life was almost as good as a play. I could say and do dreadfully naughty things, which would have been outrageous for a grown-up young lady of nearly seventeen. And *didn't* I do them all? I never missed a single chance, and I flatter myself that I haven't since.

The French madame made a real work of art of Mamma. The progress was lovely to watch. She kept herself shut up in her room all day, pretending to be an invalid, and drove out in a veil to the madame's. Then, when she was finished, we went right away from Chicago to New York, where we meant to stay for a while till we sailed for Europe.

Mamma hadn't been East before, since she was a girl of twenty, for that was when she married Papa, and he took her to live in Denver. We bought lots of beautiful things in New York, and Mamma enjoyed herself so much, being pretty and having people stare at her, that she was almost sick from excitement.

When we'd seen all the sights and were tired of shopping, she remembered that she'd got a niece staying in the country not far away, on the Hudson River. I'd heard Mamma speak of her sister, who, when seventeen, had married a Savant (whatever that is), and had gone to California soon afterwards, because she was delicate. But evidently the change hadn't done her much good, because she died when her baby was born. The Savant went on living, but he couldn't love his daughter properly, as she'd been the cause of her mother's death. Besides, he wasn't the kind of man to understand children, so when Madeleine was nine or ten, he sent her to a school—a very queer school. It was kept by a Sisterhood; not nuns exactly, because they were Protestants, but almost as good or as bad; and an elderly female cousin of the Savant's was the head of the institution.

There Madeleine Destrey had been ever since, though Mamma said she must be nineteen or twenty; and now her father was dead. That news had been sent to Mamma months before we left Denver, but as she and the Savant had written to each other only about once every five or six years, it hadn't affected her much. However, she thought it would be nice to go and see Madeleine, and I thought so too.

It was a short journey in the train, and the place where the Sisterhood live is perfectly lovely, the most beautiful I ever saw, with quantities of great trees on a flowery lawn sloping down to the river.

I was wondering what my cousin would be like—the only cousin I've got in the world; and though Mamma said she must be pretty, if she was anything like her mother, I didn't expect her to be half as pretty as she really is.

We surprised her as much as she did us, for naturally she expected Mamma to be like other aunts, which she isn't at all—now; and evidently she considered me a *curiosity*. But she was very sweet, and when she found Mamma didn't want to be called Aunt Kathryn, she tried hard always to "Kitty" her.

We only intended to spend the day, but it turned out that the time of our visit was rather critical for Maida. She was in the act of having her twentieth birthday; and it seemed that in her father's will he had "stipulated" (that's the word the cousin-Mother-Superior used) that his daughter should be sent to travel in Europe when she was twenty, for a whole year.

The reason of the stipulation was, that though he didn't care for Maida as most fathers care for their children, he was a very just man, and was afraid, after living so long in the Sisterhood his daughter might wish to join the Order, without knowing enough about the outside world to make up her mind whether it truly was her vocation for good and all. That was why she was to go to Europe; for when you're twenty-one you can become a novice in the Sisterhood, if you like.

The Mother Superior didn't really want Maida to go one bit. It was easy to see her anxiety to have the "dear child safe in the fold." But Maida wasn't to inherit a penny of her father's money if she didn't obey his will, which wouldn't suit the Sisterhood at all; so the Mother had to hustle round and think how to pack Maida off for the year.

When we happened to arrive on the scene, she thought we were like Moses's ram caught in the bushes. She told Mamma the whole story—(a ramrod of a lady with a white face, a white dress, and a long, floating white veil, she was) asking right out if we'd take Maida with us to Europe.

Mamma didn't like the idea of being chaperon for such a girl as Maida; but it was her own sister's daughter, and Mamma is as good- natured as a Mellin's Food Baby in a magazine, though she gets into little tempers sometimes. So she said, "Yes," and a fort-night later we all three sailed on a huge German steamer for Cherbourg. "At least, that's what we did in the 'dream,'" I reminded myself, when I had got so far in my thoughts, lying in the monastery bed. And by that time the light was so clear in the tiny white room, that there was no longer any doubt about it, I really was awake. I was dear little thirteen-year-old Beechy Kidder, who wasn't telling fibs about her age, because she *was* thirteen, and was it anybody's business if she were something more besides?

VIII

A CHAPTER OF PLAYING DOLLS

I looked at my bracelet-watch, which I had tucked under my pillow last night. It wasn't quite six o'clock, and we hadn't gone to bed till after one; but I knew I couldn't sleep any more, and life seemed so interesting that I thought I might as well get up to see what would come next.

The water-pitcher didn't hold much more than a quart, but I took the best bath I could, dressed, and decided to find out what the monastery grounds were like. We were not to be called till half-past seven, and it was arranged that we should start at nine, so there was an hour and a half to spare. I wondered whether I should wake Maida, and get her to go with me, but somehow I wasn't in the mood for Maida. I was afraid that, being in a monastery, she would be thinking of her precious Sisterhood and wanting to hurry back as fast as she could. She does mean to join when her year is up, I know, which is so silly of her, when the world's such a nice place; and it nearly gives me nervous prostration to hear her talk about it. Not that she often does; but it's bad enough to see it in her eyes.

Maida is a perfect dear, much too good for us, and she always knows the proper etiquetical thing to do when Mamma and I are wobbly; but she is such an edelweiss that I'm always being tempted to claw her down from her high white crags and then regretting it afterwards. Mamma gets cross with her too, when she's particularly exalted, but we both love her dearly; and we ought to, for she's always doing something sweet for us. Only she's a great deal too humble. I suppose it's the thing to be like that in a Sisterhood, but Mamma and I *aren't* a Sisterhood, and the sooner Maida realizes that there's such a place as the world, the better it will be for her.

So I didn't wake Maida, but went tiptoeing out into the long corridor, and got lost several times looking for the way out of doors.

95

At last I was in the garden, though, and it was very quaint and pretty, with unexpected nooks, old, moss-covered stone seats, and a sundial that you'd pay hundreds of dollars for in America. Staring up at the house I thought a window-shutter moved; but I didn't attach any importance to that until, after I'd crossed several small bridges and discovered a kind of island with the river rushing by on both sides, I saw Prince Dalmar-Kalm coming towards me.

I was sitting on a bench on the little green island, where I pretended to be gazing down at the water and not to see him till he was close by; for I was in hope that he wouldn't notice me in my grey dress among the trees. I don't believe the Prince's best friends would call him an early morning man. He's the kind that oughtn't to be out before lunch, and he goes especially well with gaslight or electricity. I felt sure he'd be unbearable before breakfast—either his breakfast or mine.

"It's a pity," I thought, "that I can't run down as rapidly from the age of thirteen to the age of one as I have from seventeen to thirteen. When the Prince found me. I should be sitting on the grass playing with dandelions and saying. 'Da, da?' which would disgust him so much that he'd stalk away and leave me in peace to grow up in time for breakfast."

But even a child must draw the line somewhere; and presently the Prince said "Good-morning" (so nicely that I thought he must have had a cracker or two in his pocket), asking if he might sit by me on the bench.

"I was just going in to wake Mamma," I replied, and I wondered whether, if I jumped up suddenly, his end of the bench would go down and tilt him into the river. It would have been fun to see His Highness become His Lowness, and to tell Sir Ralph Moray afterwards, but just as I was on the point of making a spring, he remarked that he had seen me come out, and followed for a particular reason. If I tumbled him into the water, I might never hear that reason; so seventeen-year-old curiosity overcame thirteen-year- old love of mischief, and I sat still.

"As you have only just come out, I don't see why you should be just going in, unless it is to get away from me," said the Prince, "and I should be sorry to think that, because you are such a dear little girl, and I am very fond of you."

"So was Papa," said I, with my best twelve-and-a-half-year-old expression.

"But I am not quite ancient enough to be your Papa," replied the Prince, "so you need not name us together like that."

"*Aren't* you?" I asked, with big eyes.

"Well, that depends on how old you are, my dear."

"I'm too old for you to call your dear, unless you *are* old enough to be my Papa," was the sage retort of Baby Beechy.

"I'm over thirty," said the Prince.

"Yes, I know," said I. "I found the Almanach de Gotha on the table of our hotel at Cap Martin, and you were in it."

"Naturally," said the Prince, but he got rather red, as people always do when they find out that you know just how far over thirty they've really gone. "But I'm not married," he went on, "therefore you cannot think of me as of your papa."

"I don't think of you much as anything," said I. "I'm too busy."

"Too busy! Doing what?"

"Playing dolls," I explained.

"I wish you were a little older," said the Prince, with a good imitation of a sigh. "Ah, *why* haven't you a few years more?"

"You might ask Mamma," I replied. "But then, if I had, *she* would have more too wouldn't she?"

"That would be a pity. She is charming as she is. She must have married when almost a child."

"Did you come out here at this time of the morning to ask me about Mamma's marriage?" I threw at him. "Because, if *that* was your reason, I'd rather go in to my dolls."

"No, no," protested the Prince, in a hurry. "I came to talk about yourself."

I began to feel an attack of giggles coming on, but I stopped them by holding my breath, as you do for hiccoughs, and thinking about Job, which, if you can do it soon and solemnly enough, is quite a good preventive. I knew now exactly why Prince Dalmar-Kalm had dashed on his clothes at sight of me and come into the garden on an empty stomach. He had thought, if he could get me all alone for half an hour (which he'd often tried to do and never succeeded) he could find out a lot of things that he would like to know. Perhaps he felt it was impossible for anybody to be as young as I seem, so that was what he wanted to find out about first. If I *wasn't*, he would flirt; if I *was*, he would merely pump.

There wasn't much time to decide on a "course of action," as Mamma's lawyer in Denver says; but I put on my thinking-cap and tied it tight under my chin for a minute. "There's more fun to be had in playing with him than with dolls," I said to myself, "if I set about it in the right way. But what *is* the right way? I can't be bothered having him for my doll, because he'd take up too much time. Shall I give him to Maida? No, I'll lend him to Mamma to play with, so long as she plays the way I want her to, and doesn't get in earnest."

"What are you anxious to say about me that can't wait till breakfast?" I asked.

"*Those men* will be at breakfast," said he. "They are in the position of your couriers, yet they put themselves forward, as if on an equality with me. I do not find that conducive to conversation."

"Mamma asked Maida yesterday whether it was better to be an Austrian prince, or an English baronet?" said I. "Sir Ralph Moray's a baronet."

"So he says," sneered the Prince.

"Oh, he is. Mamma looked him out in Burke the very day I found you were thirty-nine in the Almanach de Gotha."

"Anybody can be a baronet. That is nothing. It is a mere word."

"It's in three syllables, and 'prince' is only in one. Besides, Austrians are foreigners, and Englishmen aren't."

"Is that what Miss Destrey said to your Mamma?"

"No, because Mamma's a foreign Countess now, and it might have hurt her feelings. Maida said she felt more at home with a plain mister—like Mr. Barrymore, for instance; only he's far from plain."

"You consider him handsome?"

"Oh, yes, we all do."

"But I think you have not known him and Sir Ralph Moray for long. Your Mamma has not mentioned how she met them, but from one or two things that have been dropped, I feel sure they are in her employ—that she has hired them to take you about in their very inadequate car; is it not so?"

"I'll ask Mamma and tell you what she says, if you'd like me to," I replied.

"No, no, dear child, you are too literal. It is your one fault. And I find that you are all three too trusting of strangers. It is a beautiful quality, but it must not be carried too far. Will you not let me be your friend, Miss Beechy, and come to me for advice? I should be delighted to give it, for you know what an interest I take in all connected with you. There! Now you have heard what I followed you out especially to say. I hoped that this would be a chance to establish a confidential relationship between us. *Voulez-vous, ma chère petite?*"

"What kind of a relationship shall we establish, exactly?" I asked. "You say you don't want to be my Papa."

"If I were your Papa, I should be dead."

"If you were my brother, and the age you are now, Mamma might as well be dead."

"Ah, I would not be your brother on any consideration. Not even your step-brother; though some step-relationships are delightful. But your Mamma is too charming—you are *all* too charming, for my peace of mind. I do not know how I lived before I met you."

I thought that the money-lenders perhaps knew; but there are some things even little Beechy can't say.

"Your Mamma must have great responsibilities for so young a woman," he went on, while I pruned and prismed. "With her great fortune, and no one to guard her, she must often feel the weight of her burden too heavy for one pair of shoulders."

"One can always spend one's fortune, and so get rid of the burden, if it's too big," said I.

The Prince looked horrified. "Surely she is more wise than that?" he exclaimed.

"She hasn't spent it all yet, anyhow," I said.

"Are you not anxious lest, if your Mamma is extravagant, she may throw away your fortune as well as her own; or did your Papa think of that danger, and make you quite secure?"

"I guess I shall have a little something left, no matter what happens," I admitted.

"Then your Papa was thoughtful for you. But was he also jealous for himself? Had I been the husband of so fascinating a woman as your Mamma, I would have put into my will a clause that, if she married again, she must forfeit everything. But it may be that Americans do not hug their jealousy in the grave."

"I can't imagine poor Papa hugging anything," I said. "I never heard that he objected to Mamma marrying again. Anyhow, she's had several offers already."

"She should choose a man of title for her second husband," said the Prince, very pleased with the way the pump was working.

"Maybe she will," I answered.

He started slightly.

"It should be a title worth having," he said, "and a man fitted to bear it, not a paltry upstart whose father was perhaps a tradesman. You, Miss Beechy, must watch over your dear Mamma and rescue her from fortune hunters. I will help. And I will protect *you*, also. As for Miss Destrey, beautiful as she is, I feel that she is safe from unworthy persons who seek a woman only for her money. Her face is her fortune, *n'est-ce pas*?"

"Well, it's fortune enough for any girl," said I, thinking again of Job and all the other really solemn characters in the Old Testament as hard as ever I could.

The Prince sighed, genuinely this time, as if my answer had confirmed his worst suspicions. "He will be nice to Mamma, now," said little Beechy to big Beechy. "No more vacillating. He'll come straight to business." And promising myself some fun, I got up from the bench so cautiously that the poor river was cheated of a victim. "Now I *must* go in," I exclaimed. "*Good-bye*, Prince. Let me see; what are we to each other?"

"Confidants," he informed me. "You are to come to me with every difficulty. But one more word before we part, dear child. Be on your guard, and warn your Mamma to be on hers, with those two adventurers. Perhaps, also, you had better warn Miss Destrey. Who knows how unscrupulous the pair might be? And unfortunately, owing to the regrettable arrangements at present existing, I cannot always be at hand to watch over you all."

"Owing a little to your automobile too, maybe," said I. "By the way, what is its state of health?"

"There has been no room for the automobile in my thoughts," said the Prince, with a cooled-down step-fatherly smile. "But I have no doubt it will be in good marching order by the time it is wanted, as my chauffeur was to rise at four, knock up a mechanic at some shop in the village, and make the new change-speed lever which was broken yesterday. If you are determined to leave me so soon, I will console myself by finding Joseph and seeing how he is getting on."

We walked together towards the house, which had opened several of its green eyelids now, and at the mouth of a sort of stucco tunnel which led to the door there was Joseph himself—a piteous, dishevelled Joseph, looking as if birds had built nests on him and spiders had woven webs round him for years.

"Well," exclaimed the Prince with the air of one warding off a blow. "What has happened? Have you burnt my automobile, or are you always like this when you get up early?"

"I am not an incendiary, Your Highness," said Joseph, in his precise French, which it's easy to understand, because when he wishes to be dignified he speaks slowly. "I do not know what I am like, unless it is a wreck, in which case I resemble your automobile. As you left her last night, so she is now, and so she is likely to remain, unless the gentlemen of the other car will have the beneficence to pull her up a still further and more violent hill to the village of Tenda. There finds himself the only mechanic within fifty miles."

"I engaged *you* as a mechanic!" cried the Prince

. "But not as a workshop, Your Highness. That I am not and shall not be this side of Paradise. And it is a workshop that we must have."

"Do not let me keep you, Miss Beechy," said the Prince, "if you wish to go to your Mamma. This little difficulty will arrange itself."

I adore rows, and I should have liked to stay; but I couldn't think of any excuse, so I skipped into the house, and almost telescoped (as they say of railroad trains) with the nice monk, who was talking to Maida in the hall.

I supposed she was telling him about the Sisters, but she was quite indignant at the suggestion, and said she had been asking if we could have breakfast in the garden. The monk had given his consent, and she had intended to have everything arranged out doors, as a surprise, by the time we all came down.

"Aunt Kathryn is up; I've been doing her hair," explained Maida, "but we didn't hear a sound from your room, so we decided not to disturb you. What *have* you been about, you weird child?"

"Playing dolls," said I, and ran off to help Mamma put on her complexion.

But it was on already, all except the icing. I confessed the Prince to her, and she looked at me sharply. "Don't forget that you're a little girl now, Beechy," she reminded me. "What were you talking about?"

"You and my other dolls, Mamma," said I. "Even when I was seventeen I never flirted fasting."

"What did you say about me, dearest?"

"Oh, it was the Prince who said things about you. You can have him to play with, if you want to."

"Darling, you shouldn't talk of playing. This is a very serious consideration," said Mamma. "I never heard much about Austrians at home. Most foreigners there were Germans, which made one think of beer and sausages. I do wonder what standing an Austrian Prince would have in Denver? Should you suppose he would be preferred to—to persons of less exalted rank who were—who were not quite so *foreign*?"

"Do the Prince and Sir Ralph Moray intend to go over as samples?" I asked sweetly, but Mamma only simpered, and as a self-respecting child I cannot approve of a parent's simpering.

"I wish you wouldn't be silly, Beechy," she said. "It is a step, being a Countess, but it is not enough."

"You mean, the more crowns you have, the more crowns you want."

"I mean nothing of the sort," snapped Mamma, "but I have some ambition, otherwise what would have been the good of coming to

Europe? And if one gets opportunities, it would be sinful to neglect them. Only—one wants to be sure that one has taken the best."

"There they all three are, in the yard," I remarked, pointing out of the window at the Opportunities, who were discoursing earnestly with Joseph. "Of course, I'm too young *now* to judge of such matters, but if it was *I* who had to choose—"

"Well?"

"I'd toss up a penny, and whichever side came, I'd take—"

"Yes?"

"Mr. Barrymore."

"Mr. Barrymore! But he has no title! I might as well have stayed in America."

"I said that, because I think he'd be the hardest to get. The other two—"

"What about them?"

"Well, you don't need to decide between them yet. Just wait till we've travelled a little further, and see whether you come across anything better worth having."

"Oh, Beechy, I never know whether you're poking fun at me or not," sighed poor Mamma, so forlornly that I was sorry—for a whole minute—that I'd been born wicked; and I tied her tulle in a lovely bow at the back of her neck, to make up.

IX

A CHAPTER OF REVELATIONS

Maida really was the prettiest thing ever created, when I looked down at her from Mamma's window, as she arranged flowers and cups and saucers on the table which the monk had carried out for her, into the garden. He had quite a gallant air, in his innocent way, as if he were an old beau, instead of a monk, and his poor face seemed to fall when Mamma's untitled Opportunity—all unconscious that he was an Opportunity—saw Maida, left Joseph, and sprang to her assistance. But no wonder those two men, so different one from the other, found the same joy in waiting on her! The morning sun sprinkled gold on her hair, and made her fair skin look milky white, like pearl; then, when she would pass under the arbour of trees, the shadows threw a glimmering veil over her, and turned her into a mermaid deep down in the green light of the sea.

I don't believe our glorified chauffeur would have stopped talking motor talk and run about with dishes for Mamma or me as he did for Maida. And I wonder if one of us had adopted that little scarecrow of a black dog, whether he would have given it a bath in the fountain and dried it with his pocket-handkerchief?

That is often the way. If a girl has set her face against marriage and would rather be good to the poor than flirt, every man she's reluctantly forced to meet promptly falls in love with her, while all the thoroughly nice, normal female things like Mamma and me have to take a back seat.

By the way, Mamma and I are literally in the back seat on this automobile trip; but my name isn't Beechy Kidder if it's dull for any length of time.

However, this reflection is only a parenthesis in the midst of breakfast; for we all had breakfast together in the monastery garden and were as "gay as grigs." (N.B.—Some kind of animal for which Sir Ralph is responsible.)

The Prince was nice to the two "adventurers," because he didn't want them to repent their promise to tow his car up to Tenda; Maida was nice to everybody, because a monastery was next best to a convent; Mr. Barrymore was nice to her dog; Sir Ralph and the Prince were both nice to Mamma, and Breakfast (I spell it with a capital to make it more important) was nice to the poor little girl who would have had nobody to play with, if each one hadn't been a dancing doll of hers without realizing it.

The monk wouldn't charge us a cent for our board, so we had unconsciously been paying him a visit all the time, though paying nothing else, and the Prince had actually found fault with the coffee!

However, Sir Ralph gave him a donation for the charities of the house, which he accepted, so we could bid him good-bye without feeling like tramps who had stolen a lodging in somebody's barn.

As our automobile had to drag the Prince's, and it appeared that Tenda was less than three miles away, Maida and I decided to walk. Sir Ralph walked with us, and the Prince looked as if he would like to, but after our talk before breakfast, he naturally felt that his place was by the side of Mamma. She comes down two inches in common- sense walking shoes, so of course hills are not for her, now that she's trying to be as beautiful as she feels; but the Prince persuaded her to sit in the tonneau of his car, as it crawled up the steep white road behind Mr. Barrymore and the Panhard, so slowly that he could pace beside her. Sir Ralph talked to Maida, as we three trailed after the two motors, and I began to wonder if I hadn't been a little too strenuous in making the Prince entirely over to Mamma.

Not that I wanted him personally, but I did want some one to want me, so presently I pretended to be tired, and running after the toiling cars, asked Mr. Barrymore whether my weight would make much difference if I sat by him.

"No more than a feather," said he, with such a delightful smile that I wished myself back at seventeen again, so that he might not talk "down" to me in that condescending, uncomfortable way that grown-ups think themselves obliged to use when they're entertaining children. If he had only known it, I should have been quite equal to entertaining *him*; but I was a victim to my pigtails and six inches of black silk stocking.

"Do you like motoring?" he asked, conscientiously.

"Yes," said I. "And it *is* a fine day. And I would rather travel than go to school. And I admire Europe almost as much as America So you needn't bother about asking me those questions. You can begin right now with something you would really *like* to ask."

He laughed. "As you're so fastidious, I'd better consider a little," he said.

"Maybe it would save time if I should suggest some subjects," said I, "for I suppose we'll be at Tenda soon, even though the Prince's car is as big as a house, and this hill is as steep as the side of one. Would you like to ask me about Mamma's Past?"

"Good gracious, what do you take me for?" exclaimed Mr. Barrymore.

"I haven't decided yet," I replied, "though the Prince has talked to me quite a good deal about you."

"Has he, indeed? What does he know about me?" and our magnificent chauffeur turned suddenly so red under his nice dark skin, that I couldn't help wondering if, by any chance, the Prince were the least little bit right about his being an adventurer. I almost hoped he was, for it would make things so much more romantic. I felt like saying, "Don't mind me, my dear young sir. If you've anything to conceal about yourself, I shall like you all the better." But what I really did say was that the Prince seemed much more interested in people's Pasts than he—Mr. Barrymore—appeared to be.

"My future is more interesting to me than my own past, or any one else's," he retorted. But I thought that he looked a little troubled, as if he were racking his brain for what the Prince could have let out, and was too proud or obstinate to ask.

"You *are* selfish," I said. "Then there's no use my trying to make this ride pleasant for you, by telling you anecdotes of my past—or Maida's."

At this his profile changed. I can't say his "face" because he was steering a great deal more than was flattering to me, or necessary in going up hill. Would the fish bite at that last tempting morsel of bait? I wondered. The Prince would have snapped at it; but though Mr. Barrymore's title is only that of chauffeur, he is more of a gentleman in his little finger than the Prince in his whole body. He may be an adventurer, but anyhow he isn't the kind who pumps naughty little girls about their grown-up relations' affairs.

"I am only concerned with yours and Miss Destrey's present," he said after a minute.

"But the present so soon becomes the past, doesn't it? There's never more than just a minute of the present, really, if you come to look at it in that way, all the rest is past and future."

"Never mind," said Mr. Barrymore. "You've got more future than any of the party."

"And poor Maida has less."

He forgot about his old steering-wheel for part of a second, and gave me such a glance that I knew I had him on my hook this time.

"Why do you say that?" he asked, quite sharply.

"Oh, you *are* interested in somebody's future beside your own then?"

"Who could help being—in hers?"

"You look as if you thought I meant she was dying of a decline," said I. "It isn't quite as bad as that, but—well, beautiful as Maida is I wouldn't change places with her, unless I could change souls as well.

It would be a good deal better for Maida in *this* world if she could have mine, though just the opposite in the next."

"Such talk clouds the sunshine," said Mr. Barrymore, "even for a stranger like me, when you prophesy gloomy mysteries for one who deserves only happiness. You said something of the sort to Moray yesterday. He told me, but I was in hope that you had been joking."

"No," said I. "But I suppose Maida doesn't think the mysteries gloomy, or she wouldn't 'embrace' them—if that's the right word for it. Mamma and I imagined that coming to Europe would make her see differently perhaps, but it hadn't the last time I asked her. She thought Paris lots of fun, but all the same she was homesick for the stupid old convent where she was brought up, and which she is going to let *swallow* her up in a year."

"Good Heavens, how terrible!" exclaimed our chauffeur, looking tragically handsome. "Can nothing be done to save her? Couldn't you and your mother induce her to change her mind?"

"We've tried," said I. "She saw a lot of society in Paris and when we were at Cap Martin, but it gave her the sensation of having made a whole meal on candy. Mamma has the idea of being presented to your Queen Alexandra next spring, if she can manage it, and she told Maida that, if she'd tack on a little piece to her year of travel, *she* might be done too, at the same time. But Maida didn't seem to care particularly about it; and the society novels that Mamma loves don't interest her a bit. Her favourite authors are Shakspere and Thomas Hardy, and she reads Cooper and Sir Walter Scott. So what *can* you do with a girl like that?"

"There are other things in life besides society."

"Mamma doesn't think so. I guess we've both done all we can. I'm afraid poor Maida's doomed. But there's one comfort; she'll look perfectly beautiful in the white robe and veil that her Sisterhood wears."

Mr. Barrymore gave a sort of groan. "What a vocation for a girl like that!" he muttered, more to himself than to me, I imagine. "Something desperate ought to be done."

"*You* might try to influence her," I said. "Not that I think it's likely you *could*. But there's no harm in trying."

He didn't answer, but his face was as grave as if I had just invited him to a funeral, and as even Job couldn't have kept my features from playing (why shouldn't features play, if they can work?), I hastily sought the first excuse for laughter I could find lying about loose.

"Oh, how *funny!*" I exclaimed. "Ha, ha, ha, how *funny!*"

"What is funny?" drearily demanded our chauffeur.

"Why, that queer little grey-brown town we're coming to. It looks for all the world like an exhibition of patent beehives at a country fair."

"That is Tenda," volunteered Mr. Barrymore, still plunged in the depths of gloom. "Your unfortunate namesake, poor Beatrice di Tenda, would have been surprised to hear such a simile applied to her native town."

"Who was she?" I felt bound to inquire.

"I was telling Miss Destrey about her yesterday. She seemed interested. Miss Destrey is very fond of history, isn't she?"

"Yes. But I'm tired talking of her now. I want to hear about the other Beatrice. I suppose, if she was Italian, she was Bice too; but I'm sure her friends never made her rhyme with mice."

"Her husband made her rhyme with murder. Did you never hear of the opera of Beatrice di Tenda? Her story is one of the most romantic tragedies in history. Well, there she was born, and there she lived as a beautiful young woman in that old castle whose ruined tower soars so high above your collection of beehives. When she was in her gentle prime of beauty, the ferocious Duke Filippo Maria Visconti came riding here from Milan to court the sweetest lady of her day. She didn't care for him, of course, but young women of high rank had less choice in those times than they have in these, and that was the way all the mischief began. She did love somebody else, and the wicked Duke starved her to death in the tower of another old castle.

When we get to Pavia, which we shall pass on the way to Milan, I'll show you and Miss Destrey where your namesake lived when she was a duchess, and died when her duke would have her for a duchess no more, but wanted somebody else. Poor Beatrice, I wonder if her spirit has ever been present at the performance of the opera, and whether she approved."

"I hope she came with the man she loved, and sat in a box, and that the duke was down in—in—"

"The pit," said Mr. Barrymore, laughing, and giving a glance back over his shoulder for Maida and Sir Ralph, as he stopped the car in front of a machinist's place. "Here we are, Joseph," he called to the Prince's chauffeur, who was steering the broken car. "Now, how soon do you expect to finish your job?"

"With proper tools, it should be no more than an hour's work," said Joseph, jumping down.

"An hour? Why, I should have thought three would be more like it," exclaimed Mr. Barrymore.

"I am confident that I can do it in one all little hour," reiterated Joseph, and for once the Prince regarded him benignly.

"Whatever Joseph's faults, he is an excellent mechanician," said His Highness. "I did not intend to ask that you would wait, but if my car can be ready so soon, perhaps you will have pity upon me, Countess, and let me escort you to the castle while Joseph is working."

"Castle? I don't see any castle," returned Mamma, gazing around.

"What's left of it looks more like a walking-stick than a castle," said I, pointing up to the tall, tapering finger of broken stone that almost touched the clouds.

"Is Mamma's new property in Dalmatia as well perserved as that, Prince?"

"You have always a joke ready, little Miss Beechy." His lips smiled; but his eyes boxed my ears. Almost I felt them tingle; and suddenly I said to myself, "Good gracious, Beechy Kidder, what if your dolls should take to playing the game their own way, in spite of you, now you've set them going! Where would you be *then*, I'd like to know?" And a horrid creep ran down my spine, at the thought of Prince Dalmar-Kalm as a step-father. Maybe he would shut *me* up in a tower and starve me to death, as the wicked duke did with the other Beatrice; and it wouldn't comfort me a bit if some one wrote an opera about my sufferings. But if he thinks he'll really get Mamma, he little knows Me, that's all. We shall see what we shall see.

X

A CHAPTER OF THRILLS

The hotel at Tenda is apparently the one new thing in the town, and it is new enough to more than make up for the oldness of everything else. We went there to grumble because, after we had done the ruined castle (and it had done Mamma), Joseph's "all little" hour threatened to lengthen itself into at lest two of ordinary size.

Mr. Barrymore's eyebrows said, "I told you so," but his tongue said nothing, which was nice of it; and the Prince did all the complaining as we sat on perfectly new chairs, in a perfectly new parlour, with a smell of perfectly new plaster in the air, and plu-perfectly old newspapers on the table. According to him, Joseph was an absolutely unique villain, with a combination of deceit, treachery, procrastination, laziness, and stupidity mixed with low cunning, such as could not be paralleled in the history of motor-men; and it was finally Mr. Barrymore who defended the poor absent wretch.

"Really, you know," said he, "I don't think he's worse than other chauffeurs. Curiously enough, the whole tribe seems to be alike in several characteristics, and it would be an interesting study in motor lore to discover whether they've all—by a singular coincidence— been born with those peculiarities, whether they've been thrust upon them, or whether they've achieved them!"

"Joseph never achieved anything," broke in the Prince.

"That disposes of one point of view, then," went on Mr. Barrymore. "Anyhow, he's cut on an approved pattern. All the professional chauffeurs I ever met have been utterly unable to calculate time or provide for future emergencies. They're pessimists at the moment of an accident, and optimists afterwards—until they find out their mistakes by gloomy experience, which, however, seldom teaches them anything."

The Prince shrugged his shoulders in a superior way he has, and drawled, "Well, you are better qualified to judge the brotherhood, than the rest of us, at all events, my dear sir."

Mr. Barrymore got rather red, but he only laughed and answered, "Yes, that's why I spoke in Joseph's defence. A fellow-feeling makes us wondrous kind," while Maida looked as if she would like to set the new dog at His Highness

.

The fact is she has got into her head that our handsome chauffeur is very unfortunate; and when Maida is sorry for anybody or anything she'll stick by that creature — man, woman, or dog — through thick and thin. And funnier still, *he* is sorry for *her*. Well, it all comes into my game of dolls. But I'm not sure that I shan't fall in love with him myself, and want to keep him up my sleeve against the time when I'm seventeen again

. The hotel clock was so new that it hadn't learned to go yet; and I never saw people glance at their watches so much, even in the midst of a long sermon, as we did, sitting on those new chairs in that new parlour. At last Sir Ralph Moray proposed that we should have lunch; and we had it, with delicious trout as new as the dish on which they came frizzling to the table. While we were eating them Joseph was announced, and was ordered to report himself in the dining-room. He seemed quite cheerful — for him.

"I came to tell Your Highness that I shall be able to finish in time to start by four o'clock this afternoon," said he complacently.

Up sprang the Prince in a rage and began to shout French things which must have been shocking, for Sir Ralph and Mr. Barrymore both scowled at him till he superficially calmed down.

Joseph had either forgotten that he'd promised to be ready hours ago, or else he didn't see why we should attach the least importance to a tiny discrepancy like that.

In the midst of the argument, while the Prince's language got hot and his fish cold, Mr. Barrymore turned to Mamma and proposed that we should start directly after lunch, as most probably the Prince wouldn't get off till next morning.

The prospect of staying all night at Tenda, with nothing to do but sit on the new chairs till bed time, was too much even for Mamma's wish to please Titled Opportunity Number One. She nervously elected to go on with Titled Opportunity Number Two and his friend.

I thought that the Prince would be plunged in gloom by this decision, even if he didn't try to break it. To my surprise, however, he not only made no objection, but encouraged the idea. He wouldn't wish to sacrifice us on the altar of his misfortune, he said. We must go on, dine at Cuneo, and he would meet us at the hotel there, which he could easily do, as, when once his automobile was itself again, it would travel at more than twice the speed of ours. "Especially up hill," he added. "The landlord has told Joseph that beyond Tenda the ascent is stupendous, nothing less than Alpine. You will be obliged to travel at a snail's pace, even if you reach the top without every passenger walking up the hill, which mounts, curve after curve, for miles."

Poor Mamma's face fell several inches. She had had enough walking up hill for one day, as the Prince knew well, and no doubt he enjoyed the chance of disgusting her with motoring in other people's automobiles. But Mr. Barrymore's expression would have put spirit into a mock turtle. "I know what the gradients are," he said, "and what we can do. To show that I'm an exception which proves the rule I laid down for chauffeurs, I'm not making any experiments without counting the cost. I hope we shall get to Cuneo by tea-time, not dinner-time, and push on to Alessandria as a better stopping- place for the night."

"Very well. In any case I shall expect to catch you up at Cuneo," said the Prince, "and so, if you please, we will make a rendezvous at a certain hotel."

Baedeker was produced, a hotel was selected, and half an hour later His Highness was bidding us *au revoir*, as we settled ourselves in our luggage-wreathed car, to leave the town of Beatrice and the dominating, file-on-end shaped ruin.

We had all been up so early that it seemed as if the day were growing old, but really it was only one o'clock, for we'd lunched at twelve, and all the afternoon was before us in which to do, or not to do, our great climbing act.

Just to see how our gorgeous chauffeur would look, I asked if I mightn't sit on the front seat for a change, because my feet had gone to sleep in the tonneau yesterday. I half-expected that he would shuffle round for an excuse to keep Maida; but with an immovable face he said that was for the three ladies to arrange. Of course, Maida must have wanted to be in front, but she is so horribly unselfish that she glories in sacrificing herself, so she gave up as meekly as if she had been a lady's-maid, or a dormouse, and naturally I felt a little brute; but I usually do feel a brute with Maida; she's so much better than any one I ever saw that I can't help imposing on her, and neither can Mamma. It's a waste of good material being so awfully pretty as Maida, if you're never going to do anything for people to forgive.

Yesterday we had been too hot in our motor-coats till night came on. To-day, when we had left Tenda a little way below, we opened our shawl-straps and got out our fur stoles.

At first I thought that the Prince had only been trying to frighten us, and make us wish we were in a big car like his, for the road went curving up as gracefully and easily as a swan makes tracks in the water, and our automobile hummed cheerfully to itself, forging steadily up. It was so nice having nothing to drag that, by comparison with yesterday afternoon, we moved like a ship under full sail; but suddenly the road reared up on its hind feet and stood almost erect, as though it had been frightened by the huge snow- capped mountains that all at once crowded round us. An icy wind rushed down from the tops of the great white towers, as if with the swooping wings of a giant bird, and it took our car's breath away.

Instead of humming it began to pant, and I noticed the difference at once. If I'd been Maida, I should probably have been too polite to put questions about the thing's behaviour, for fear Mr. Barrymore might think I hadn't proper confidence in him; but being Beechy, with no convictions to live up to, I promptly asked if anything was the matter.

"The car's only trying to tell me that she can't manage to spurt up on third speed any more," said he. "I shall put on the second, and you'll hear what a relief it gives to the motor."

It certainly was as if the automobile had gulped down a stimulant, and revived in a second. But as we turned a shoulder of the mountain, coming in sight of a railroad depôt, a high embankment, and a monstrous wall of mountain with the sky for a ceiling, I couldn't help giving a little squeak.

"Is that a *road*?" I asked, pointing up to a network like a skein of silk twisted in a hundred zigzags across the face of the mountain from bottom to top. "Why, it's like the way up Jack's beanstalk. No sane automobile could do it."

"Some could," said Mr. Barrymore, "but I dare say it's lucky for us that ours hasn't got to. It's the old road, only used now to communicate with that desolate fortress you see on the top shelf of the mountain, standing up there on the sky-line like the ark on Ararat. All this country is tremendously fortified by both the French and Italians, in case they should ever come to loggerheads. Above us somewhere is a long tunnel burrowing into the *col*, and the new road runs through that instead of over the summit."

"Bump!" went the car, as he finished his explanation, and then we began to wade jerkily through a thick layer of loose stones that had been spread over the road like hard butter over stale bread.

"Le corse" (that is what our landlord had called the cruel wind sweeping down from the snow mountains) was hurling itself into our faces; our fat rubber tyres were bouncing over the stones like baseballs, and I'd never been so uncomfortable nor so perfectly happy in my life. I wished I were a cat, so that I could purr, for purring has always struck me as the most thorough way of expressing satisfaction. When other people are in automobiles, and

you are walking or jogging past with a pony, you glare and think what insufferable vehicles they are; but when you're spinning, or even jolting, along in one of them yourself, then you know that there's nothing else in the world as well worth doing. I made a remark like that to Mr. Barrymore, and he gave me such a friendly, appreciative look as he said, "Have you discovered all this already?" that I decided at once to eat my heart out with a vain love for him.

I haven't been really in love before since I was ten; so the sensation was quite exciting, like picking up a lovely jewel on the street, which you aren't sure won't be claimed by somebody else. I was trying to think what else I could say to fascinate him when the car lost its breath again, and—"r-r-retch" went in another speed.

"It's our 'first and last,'" said Mr. Barrymore. "Good old girl, she's going to do it all right, though there's many a twenty-four horse-power car that wouldn't rise to it. By Jove, this is a road—and a half. I believe, Ralph, that you and I had better jump off and ease her a bit."

Mamma squeaked, and begged our chauffeur not to leave us to go up by ourselves, or we should be over the awful precipice in an instant. But Mr. Barrymore explained that he wasn't deserting the ship; and he walked quickly along by the side of the car, through the bed of sharp stones, keeping his hand always on the steering-wheel like a pilot guiding a vessel among hidden rocks.

Maida would have been out too, in a flash, if Mr. Barrymore had let her, but he told us all to sit still, so we did, happy (judging the others by myself) in obeying him.

I hadn't supposed there could be such a road as this. If one hadn't had hot and cold creeps in one's toes for fear the "good old girl" would slide back down hill and vault into space with us in her lap, one would have been struck dumb with admiration of its magnificence. As a matter of fact, we were all three dumb as mutes, but it wasn't only admiration that paralysed my tongue or Mamma's, I know, whatever caused the phenomenon with Maida, who has no future worth clinging to.

As we toiled up, in spite of the stones that did their best to keep us back, we simply hung on the breathing of the motor, as Mamma used to on mine when I was small and indulged in croup. When she gasped, we gasped too; when she seemed to falter, we involuntarily strained as if the working of our muscles could aid hers. All our bodies sympathized with the efforts of her body, which she was making for our sakes, dragging us up, up, into wonderful white, shining spaces where it seemed that summer never had been and never would dare to come.

The twisted skein of silk we had looked up to was turning into a coil of rope now, stretched taut and sharp from zig to zag, and on from zag to zig again. Below, when we dared to look back and down, the coil of rope lay looser, curled on itself. The mountain-top crowned by the fort (which as Mr. Barrymore said, did certainly look like the ark on Ararat when all the rest of creation was swept off the globe) didn't appear so dimly remote now. We were coming almost into friendly relations with it, and with neighbouring mountains whose summits had seemed, a little while ago, as far away as Kingdom Come.

I began to feel at last as if I could speak without danger of giving the motor palpitation of the heart. "What are you thinking of, Maida?" I almost whispered.

"Oh!" she answered with a start, as if I'd waked her out of a dream. "I was thinking, what if, while we're still in this world we could see heaven, a far, shining city on a mountain-top like one of these. How much harder we would strive after worthiness if we *saw* the place always with our bodily eyes; how much harder we'd try; and how much less credit it would be for those who succeeded."

"What are *you* thinking of, Mamma?" I asked. "Did the big mountains give you a thought too?"

"Yes, they did," said she, "but I'm afraid it was more worldly than Maida's. I was saying to myself, the difference in being down far below, where we were, and high up as we are now, is like our old life in Denver and our life here." As she went on to expound her parable, she lowered her voice, so that Sir Ralph and Mr. Barrymore,

119

walking, couldn't catch a word. "In those days at home, it would have seemed as impossible that we could have princes and baronets and — and such people for our most *intimate* friends, as it looked a little while ago for us to get near that fort up there, or the mountain- tops. Yet we are, in — in every sense of the word, *getting there.*"

The thoughts which the mountains had put into Maida's golden head and Mamma's (now) auburn one were so characteristic of the heads themselves that I chuckled with glee, and our two men glanced round questioningly. But in accordance with Mamma's simile, to explain to them would have been like explaining to the mountains themselves.

By and by, though still going up, we were on snow level. Snow lay white as Maida's thoughts on either side of the steep road, but *le corse* had run shrieking farther down the mountain, and was not at home in its own high house. We were less cold than we had been; and when presently the worst of the zigzags were past and a great black tunnel- mouth in sight to show we'd reached the *col*, the sun was almost warm. A few moments more, and (on our second best speed, with all five on board) we had shot into that great black mouth.

I always thought that we had the longest and biggest of everything in our country, but I never heard of a tunnel like this in America.

It was the queerest thing to look into I ever saw.

 The lamps of our automobile which Mr. Barrymore had stopped to light before plunging in, showed us a long, long, straight passage cut through the mountain, with an oval roof arched like an egg. Except for a few yards ahead, where the way was lit up and the arch of close-set stones glimmered grey, the blackness would have been unbroken had it not been for the tunnel-lights. They went on and on in a sparkling line as far as our eyes could reach; and if the most famous whale in the world had had a spine made of diamonds, Jonah would have got much the same effect that we did as he wandered about in the dark trying to get his bearings.

It was only the most distant electric lamps that looked as if they were diamonds stuck close together along the roof. The near ones were balls of light under swaying umbrellas of ink-black shadow; and sometimes we would flash past great sharp stalactites, which were, as Maida said, like Titanesses' hatpins stuck through from the top of the mountain.

At first the tunnel road was inches thick with white dust; then, much to our surprise, we ran into a track of greasy mud which made our car waltz as it had in the Roya valley close to the precipice.

"It's the water filtering in through the holes your Titanesses' hatpins have made in their big pincushion," explained Mr. Barrymore, who had heard Maida make that remark. And the hateful creatures had so honeycombed the whole mountain over our heads, that Mamma and I put up umbrellas to save ourselves from being drenched.

"What a place this would be for an accident! Or—suppose we met something that *objected* to us!" Mamma shrieked, her voice all but drowned by the reverberation made by our motor in the hollow vault.

With that, as if her words had "conjured it from the vasty deep"—to use a quotation of Sir Ralph's—something appeared, and it did object to us very much.

It was a horse, and it gleamed like silver as our front lamp pointed it out to our startled eyes with a long, bright finger of light.

He was coming towards us, down the narrow, arched passage, walking on his hind legs, with some one in a cart behind him, standing up and hitting him on the head with a whip.

We were not really going very fast on account of the splashy mud; but what with the roaring echo of the motor, the dripping of water, the narrowness of the tunnel, the yapping of our little dog, the shouts of the man in the cart, and the strangeness of the picture ahead—just like a lighted disc on the screen of a magic lantern—it did seem as if everybody concerned must come to awful grief in about three seconds.

I don't know whether I screamed or not; though I know Mamma did; a deaf man would have known that. But the first thing I was really sure of was that Mr. Barrymore had not only stopped the car but the motor, had jumped down, and gone to the horse's head.

He said something quickly to the driver, which I couldn't understand, because it was in Italian; but the man didn't yell or whip the horse any more. Mr. Barrymore patted the poor beast, and talked to him, until he seemed tired of dancing about as if he were popcorn over a hot fire. Then, when he had quieted down, and remembered that his forefeet were given him to walk with and not to paw the air, Mr. Barrymore led him gently up to our automobile, patting his neck all the time. He snorted and quivered for a minute, then smelt of what Mr. Barrymore calls the "bonnet," with the funniest expression of disgust and curiosity.

I imagined the horse was thinking, "This is a very nasty thing, but it seems to belong to the nicest, kindest man I ever met, so perhaps it isn't as bad after all as I thought at first."

The driver's scowl turned to a smile, as he eventually drove by, we waiting till he had got safely past.

"I think that was real nice of you, Mr. Barrymore," said Mamma, as we went teuf-teufing on again.

She is always a little uneasy with him, because, though he's a friend of Sir Ralph Moray's, he's only a chauffeur, and she isn't quite sure whether she oughtn't to patronize him a little to keep up her dignity as a Countess. But it was a good sign that she should remember his name for once. As for me, I've given him one for use behind his back, which is to make up for his lack of a title, express his gorgeousness and define his profession all at the same time. It is "Chauffeulier," and I rather pride myself on it.

"It was only decent," he answered Mamma. "I love horses, and I've enough imagination to guess pretty well how one feels when he's called upon to face some unknown horror, with no sympathy from behind. It would have been sheer brutality not to stop motor and all for that poor white chap. He won't be as bad next time; and perhaps his master will have learned a little common sense too. All the same, that kind of adventure spells delay, and I hope this tunnel isn't infested with timid horses. Luckily, the line seems all clear ahead."

A few minutes more, and looking before and after, we could see far away two little oval pearls of daylight, one straight ahead, one straight behind. It was like having one's foresight as good as one's hindsight; which in real life, outside tunnels, would save a lot of disasters. Mr. Barrymore explained that we'd reached the apex of two slopes, and now we would be descending gradually.

It gave us a shock to burst out into the sunlight again by-and-by, but it was a glorious shock, with a thrill as the dazzling white mountains seemed to leap at our eyes.

If you speak of zigzags going up hill, oughtn't you to call them zagzigs going down? Anyway, there they were, hundreds of them apparently, looking something as a huge corkscrew might look if it had been laid on a railroad track for a train to flatten.

We began to fly down, faster and faster, the motor making no noise at all. At each turn of the corkscrew it seemed to me as if we must leap over into space, and I felt as if I had been struck by lightning; but always our chauffeur steered so as to give plenty of margin between our tyres and the edge of the precipice; and by-and-by I was thoroughly charged with electricity so that I ceased to be actually afraid. All I felt was that my soul was covered with a very thin, sensitive skin.

"Oh, Mr. Terrymore, for mercy's sake, for *heaven's* sake...!" wailed Mamma. "I don't feel *able* to die to-day."

"You shan't, if I can help it," answered Mr. Barrymore, without looking round; but as he never wears goggles, I could see his face plainly from my place by his side, and I thought it had rather an odd, stern expression. I wondered whether he were cross with Mamma for seeming to doubt his skill, or whether something else was the matter. But instead of fading away, the expression seemed to harden. He looked just as I should think a man might look if he were going to fight in a battle. I awfully wanted to ask if anything were wrong, but something mysterious—a kind of atmosphere around him, like a barrier I could feel but not see—wouldn't let me.

"I believe the thing is broken, somehow," I said to myself; and the thought was so awful, when I stared down at all those separate layers of precipice which we would have to risk before we reached human-level (if we ever reached it) that my heart pounded like a hammer in my side. It was a terrible sensation, yet I revelled in it with a kind of desperate joy; for everything depended on the eye, and nerve, and hand of this one man whom it was so thrilling to trust.

Each time we twisted round a corkscrew I gave a sigh of relief; for it was one less peril to pass on the way to safety.

"Do just stop for a moment and let us breathe," cried Mamma; and my suspicions were confirmed by Mr. Barrymore's answer, thrown over his shoulder. "It's best not, Countess," he said. "I'll explain afterwards."

Mamma is always ecstatic for an instant after any one has addressed her as "Countess," so she didn't insist, and only murmured to herself, "Oh, *why* did I leave my peaceful home?" in a minor wail which showed me that she wasn't really half as anxious as I was. But if she could have seen Mr. Barrymore's profile, and had the inspiration to read it as I did, she would probably have jumped out of the automobile in full flight. Whereupon, though she might have gained a crown to wear upon her forehead, all those on her brushes and powder-pots, and satchels and trunks, would have been wasted. Poor little Mamma!

We plunged down below the snow-line; we saw far beneath us a wide, green valley, where other people, the size of flies, were safe if not happy. We passed some barracks, where a lot of sturdy little mountain soldiers stopped bowling balls in a dull, stony square to watch us fly by. We frightened some mules; we almost made a horse faint away; but the Chauffeulier showed no desire to stop and let them admire our "bonnet" at close quarters.

The excitement of the drive, and my conviction that Mr. Barrymore was silently fighting some unseen danger for us all, filled me with a kind of intoxication. I could have screamed; but if I had, it wouldn't have been with cowardly fear. Partly, perhaps, the strange exhilaration came from the beauty of the world on which we were descending almost as if we were falling from the sky. I felt that I could have lovely thoughts about it—almost as poetical as Maida's— if only I had had time; but as it was, the ideas jostled each other in my mind like a crowd of people rushing to catch a train.

From behind, I could hear Maida's voice from moment to moment, as she talked to Mamma or Sir Ralph, innocently unsuspicious of any hidden danger.

"Isn't it all wonderful?" she was saying. "Day before yesterday we left riotous, tumultuous summer on the Riviera; found autumn in the Roya valley, chill and grim, though so magnificent; and came into winter snows this morning. Now we've dropped down into spring. It's like a fairy story I read once, about a girl whose cruel stepmother drove her from home penniless, and sent her into the mountains at dead of night, telling her never to come back unless she could bring an apronful of strawberries for her stepsister. The poor girl wandered on and on in the dark in a terrible storm, until at last she strayed to a wild mountain-top, where the twelve Months lived. Some were old men, wrapped in long cloaks; some were young and ardent; some were laughing boys. With a stroke of his staff, each Month could make what he would with the weather. Father January had but to wave his stick to cause the snow to fall; May, in pity for the girl's tears, created a rose garden, while his brother's snow- wreaths were melting; but it was June who finally understood what she wanted, and gave her a bed of fragrant strawberries. I feel as if *we* had wandered to the house of the Months, and they were waving their staffs to create miracles for us."

"It will be a miracle if we ever get out of the house of the Months and into one of our own," I said to myself, almost spitefully, for the talk in the tonneau did seem frivolous when I glanced up furtively at that tight-set mouth of Mr. Barrymore's. And after that, to look down from a frame of snow mountains through a pinky-white haze of plum, cherry, and pear blossoms to delicate green meadows sparkling with a thick gold-dust of dandelions, was for me like going out to be tried for my life in a frock made by a fairy.

I hardly breathed until the corkscrew uncurled itself at last and turned into an ordinary downhill road. Our car slackened speed, and finally, as we came upon the first long, level stretch, to my astonishment moved slower and more slowly until it stopped dead.

XI

A CHAPTER OF BRAKES AND WORMS

Mamma laughed one of those coquettish, twenty-five-year-old laughs that go with her auburn hair and her crowns.

"Well, have you decided to give us a chance to breathe, after all?" she asked. "I should say it was about time."

"I'm afraid you'll breathe maledictions when you hear what is the matter," said our Chauffeulier.

"Good gracious! what's happened?" exclaimed Mamma. "If the thing's going to explode, do let us get out and run."

"So far from exploding, she's likely to be silent for some time," Mr. Barrymore went on, jumping down and going to the automobile's head. "I'm awfully sorry. After the delays we've suffered, you won't think motoring is all it's painted, when I tell you that we're in for another."

"Why, what is it this time?" Mamma asked

.

"I'm not quite sure yet," said Mr. Barrymore, "but the chains are wrong for one thing, and I'm inclined to think there's some deep-seated trouble. I shall soon find out, but whatever it is, I hope you won't blame the car too much. She's a trump, really; but she had a big strain put upon her endurance yesterday and this morning. Dragging another car twice her size for thirty miles or more up a mountain pass isn't a joke for a twelve horse-power car."

Any one would think the automobile was his instead of Sir Ralph's by the pride he takes in it. Sir Ralph doesn't seem to care half as much; but then I don't believe he's a born sports-man like his friend. You can be a motor-car owner if you've got money enough; but I guess you have to be *born* a motor-car man.

127

"Well, this isn't exactly an ideal place for an accident," remarked Mamma, "as it seems to be miles from anywhere; but we ought to be thankful to Providence for not letting the break come up there on that awful mountain."

I saw a faint twinkle in Mr. Barrymore's eyes and a twitch of his lips, as he bent down over the machinery without answering a word, and I couldn't resist the temptation of letting him see that I was in his secret. There couldn't be any harm in it's coming out now.

"Thankful to Mr. Barrymore for bringing us safely down the 'awful mountain' when the break *had* come at the top," I corrected Mamma, with my chin in the air.

"Good Heavens, Beechy, what *do* you mean?" she gasped, while our Chauffeulier flashed me a quick look of surprise.

"Oh, only that the accident, whatever it was, happened soon after we came out of the tunnel, and if Mr. Barrymore'd stopped when you wanted him to, he couldn't have started again, for we were just running downhill with our own weight; and I knew it all the time," I explained airily.

"You're joking, Beechy, and I think it's horrid of you," said Mamma, looking as if she were going to cry.

"Am I joking, Mr. Barrymore?" I asked, turning to him.

"I had no idea that you guessed, and I don't see now how you did; but it's true that the accident happened up there," he admitted, and he looked so grave that I began to feel guilty for telling.

"Then it was only by a merciful dispensation that we weren't hurled over the precipice and dashed to pieces," exclaimed Mamma.

"That depends on one's definition of a merciful dispensation," said Mr. Barrymore. "From one point of view every breath we draw is a merciful dispensation, for we might easily choke to death at any instant. We were never for a single moment in danger. If I hadn't been sure of that, of course I would have stopped the car at any cost. As a matter of fact, when we began the descent I found that the hand-brake wouldn't act, and knew the chains had gone wrong. If I'd thought it was only that I could have put on our spare chains, but I believed there was more and worse, so I determined to get on as far towards civilization as I could before stopping the car."

"You brought us down those ghastly hills without a brake!" Mamma cried out, losing her temper. "And Sir Ralph called you careful! I can never trust you again."

I could have slapped her and myself too.

"Aunt Kathryn!" exclaimed Maida. Then I could have slapped her as well for interfering. It would serve her right if I married her off to the Prince.

The Chauffeulier looked for a second as if he were going to say "Very well, madam; do as you like about that." But Maida's little reproachful exclamation apparently poured balm upon his troubled soul.

"Not without a brake," he answered, with great patience and politeness, "but with one instead of two. If the foot-brake had burned, as possibly it might, the compression of the gas in the cylinder could have been made to act as a brake. The steering-gear was in perfect order, which was the most important consideration in the circumstances, and I felt that I was undertaking a responsibility which the car and I together were well able to carry out. But as I thought that amateurs were likely to be alarmed if they knew what had happened, I naturally kept my knowledge to myself."

"I saw that something was wrong by the set expression of your face," said I, "and I wasn't a bit afraid, because I felt, whatever it was, you'd bring us through all right. But I'm sorry I spoke now."

"You needn't be," said he. "I shouldn't have done so myself yet I wasn't silent for my own sake; and I should do the same if it had to be done over again."

But this didn't comfort me much, for I was sure that Maida wouldn't have spoken if she had been in my place. I don't know why I was sure, but I was.

"Whatever Barrymore does in connection with a motor-car, is always right, Countess," said Sir Ralph, "though in other walks of life I wouldn't vouch for him."

His funny way of saying this made us all laugh and Mamma picked up the good temper which she had lost in her first fright. She began to apologize, but Mr. Barrymore wouldn't let her; and the storm was soon forgotten in the interest with which we hung upon the Chauffeulier's explorations.

He peered into the mysterious inner workings of the machine, tapped some things, thumped others, and announced that one of the "cones of the countershaft" was broken

.

"There's no doubt that the undue strain yesterday and this morning weakened it," he said, coming up from the depths with a green smear on his noble brow. "What we've really to be thankful for is that it waited to snap until we'd got up all the hills. Now, though as the Countess says we seem to be miles from anywhere, we're actually within close touch of civilization. Unless I'm out in my calculations, we must be near a place called Limone, where, if there isn't much else, at least there's a station on the new railway line. All we've got to do is to find something to tow us, as we towed Dalmar- Kalm (a mere mule will answer as well as a motor) to that station, where we can put the car on the train and be at Cuneo in no time. The guide-books say that Cuneo's interesting, and anyhow there are hotels of sorts there — also machine tools, a forge, a lathe, and things of that kind which we can't carry about with us."

"What a splendid adventure!" exclaimed Maida. "I love it; don't you, Beechy?"

I answered that I entertained a wild passion for it; but all the same, I wished I'd mentioned it first.

This settled Mamma's attitude towards the situation. She saw that it was *young* to enter into the spirit of the adventure, so she took the cue from us and flung herself in with enthusiasm enough to make up for her crossness.

"Somebody must go on an exploring expedition for a mule," said Mr. Barrymore, "and as I'm the only one whose Italian is fairly fluent, I suppose I must be the somebody. Miss Destrey, would you care to go with me for the sake of a little exercise?"

In another minute I would have volunteered, but even thirteen-year-olds have too much pride to be the third that makes a crowd. Gooseberry jam is the only jam I don't like; so I kept still and let them go off together, chaperoned by the little black dog. Sir Ralph stood by the automobile talking to Mamma while I wandered aimlessly about, though I could tell by the corner of his eye that she didn't occupy his whole attention.

Just to see what would happen, I suddenly squatted down by the side of the road, about twenty yards away, and began to dig furiously with the point of my parasol. I hadn't been at work for three minutes when I was rewarded. "The Countess has sent me to ask what you are doing, Miss Beechy," announced a nice voice; and there was Sir Ralph peering over my shoulder.

"I'm looking for one of my poor relations," said I. "A worm. She's sent up word that she isn't in. But I don't believe it."

"I'm glad my rich relations aren't as prying as you are," said he. "I often send that message when it would be exceedingly inconvenient to have further inquiries pressed. Not to rich relations, though, for the very good reason that they don't bother about me or other poor worms, who have not my Félicité to defend them."

"Who's Félicité?" I asked, not sorry to keep Sir Ralph for my own sake or that of Mamma—who was probably taking advantage of his absence to put powder on her nose and pink stuff on her lips, by the aid of her chatelaine mirror.

"Who's Félicité? You might as well ask who is the Queen of England. Félicité is my cook—my housekeeper—my guide, philosopher and friend; my all."

"That dear, fat duck who brought us tea the day we were at your house?"

"I have two ducks. But Félicité was the one who brought you the tea. The other eats mice and fights the cat. Félicité doesn't eat mice, and fights me."

"I loved her."

"So do I. And I could love you for loving her."

"Perhaps you'd better not."

"Why? It's safe and allowable for men of my age to love little girls."

"I'm different from other little girls. You said so yourself. Besides what is your age?"

"Twenty-nine."

"You look about nineteen. Our Chauffeulier looks older than you do."

"Chauffeulier? Oh, I see, that's your name for Terry. It's rather smart."

"I call it a title, not a name," said I. "I thought he ought to have one, so I dubbed him that."

"He ought to be complimented."

"I mean him to be."

"Come now, tell me what name you've invented for me, Miss

Beechy."

I shook my head. "You've got a ready-made title. But you look too boyish to live up to it. The Chauffeulier would come up to my idea of a baronet better than you do."

"Oh, you don't have to be dignified really to be a baronet, you know. Terry—er—you mustn't mention to him that I told you; but he may be something a good deal bigger than a baronet one day."

"He's a good deal bigger than a baronet now," said I, laughing, and measuring Sir Ralph from head to foot. "But what may he be one day?"

"I mustn't say more. But if you're at all interested in him, that will be enough to fix your attention."

"What would be the good of fixing my attention on him, if that's what you mean," I inquired, "when he's got his attention fixed upon another?"

"Oh, you mustn't judge by appearances," said Sir Ralph hastily. "He likes you awfully; though, of course, as you're so young, he can't show it as he would to an older girl."

"I shall grow older," said I. "Even before we finish this trip I shall be a *little* older."

"Of course you will," Sir Ralph assured me soothingly. "By that time, Terry will, no doubt, have screwed up courage to show you how much he likes you."

"I shouldn't have thought he lacked courage," said I.

"Only where girls are concerned," explained Sir Ralph.

"He seems brave enough with my cousin Maida. It's Mamma and me he doesn't say much to, unless we speak to him first."

"You see he's horribly afraid of being thought a fortune-hunter. He's almost morbidly sensitive in that way."

"O-oh, I see," I echoed. "Is that the reason he's so stand-off with us—because he knows we're rich?"

"Yes. Otherwise he'd be delightful, just as he is with Miss Destrey, with whom he doesn't have to think of such things."

"You're fond of him, aren't you?" I asked, beginning again to dig for the worm; for Sir Ralph was squatting beside me now, watching the point of my parasol.

"Rather!" he exclaimed. "He's the finest fellow on earth. I should like to see him as happy as he deserves to be."

"But you don't want him to fall in love with Maida?"

"That's the last thing I should choose for either of them. Though it's early to talk of such contingencies, isn't it, as they've known each other—we've all known each other—only a few days?"

"It only takes a few minutes for the most important things to happen, such as being born and dying. *Why* should falling in love take more? It wouldn't with me."

"You're young to judge."

"Pooh, I've been in love several times. Now I come to think of it, I'm in love this moment—or almost. *Why* don't you want Mr. Barrymore to fall in love with my cousin?"

"It would be imprudent."

"Perhaps you're falling in love with her yourself."

"I shouldn't wonder."

"If you'll tell me whether you are or not, I'll tell you who it is I *think* I'm in love with."

"Well, I *could* be. Now for your secret."

"I give you leave to guess."

"Really?"

"And truly."

"Some one we've just been talking about?"

"'I could be.' Oh dear, I believe this worm *is* out after all."

"This is most interesting. I don't mean about the worm. Terry's in luck for once."

"But he thinks me a little girl."

"Little girls can be fascinating. Besides, I'll make it my business to remind him that little girls don't take long to grow up."

"Will you really? But you won't let him know about this talk?"

"Sooner would I be torn in two by wild motor-cars. These confidences are sacred."

"I'll say nice things about you to Maida," I volunteered.

He stared for a minute, and then laughed. "I should tell you not to if I weren't certain that all the nice things in the world might be said on that subject with no more effect upon Miss Destrey than a shower of rain has on my duck's back. You must try and help me not to fall in love with her."

"Why?" I asked.

"Because, for one reason, she'd never fall in love with me; and for another, I couldn't in any event afford to love her, any more than can my friend Terry Barrymore."

"Perhaps I'd better work her off on the Prince, and then you'd both be out of danger," said I.

"It would at least save me anxiety about my friend, though I should doubtless suffer in the process," replied Sir Ralph.

"I'll comfort you whenever I have time," I assured him

.

"Do," he entreated. "It will be a real charity. And in the meantime, I shan't be idle. I shall be working for you."

"Thank you ever so much," said I. "I should be glad if you'd report progress from time to time."

"I will," said he. "We'll keep each other up, won't we?"

"Be-echy!" shrieked Mamma. "I've been screaming to you for the last *twenty* minutes. Come here at once and tell me what you're doing. It's sure to be something naughty."

So we both came. But the only part that we mentioned was the worm.

XII

A CHAPTER OF HORRORS

It is wonderful how well it passes time to have a secret understanding with anybody; that is, if you're a girl, and the other person a man. Mr. Barrymore and Maida seemed hardly to have gone before they were back again; which pleased me very much. In attendance was a man with a mule—a grinning man; a ragged and reluctant mule; which was still more reluctant when it found out what it was expected to do. However, after a fine display of diplomacy on our Chauffeulier's part, and force on that of the mule's owner, the animal was finally hitched to the automobile with strong rope.

Mr. Barrymore had to sit in the driver's seat to steer, while the man led the mule, but we others decided to walk. Mamma's heels are not quite as high as her pride (when she's feeling pretty well), so she preferred to march on the road rather than endure the ignominy of being dragged into even the smallest of villages behind the meanest of beasts.

A train for Cuneo was due at Limone, it seemed, in an hour, and we could walk there in about half that time, Mr. Barrymore thought. He had made arrangements with the *capo di stazione*, as he called him, to have a truck in readiness. The automobile would be put on it, and the truck would be hitched to the train.

Maida and I were delighted with everything; and when Mamma grumbled a little, and said this sort of thing wasn't what she'd expected, we argued so powerfully that it was much more fun getting what you did not expect, than what you did, that we brought her round to our point of view, and set her laughing with the rest of us.

"After all, what does it matter, as long as we're all young together?" said she, at last; and then I knew that the poor dear was happy.

Sir Ralph considered Limone an ordinary Italian village, but it seemed fascinating to us. The fruit stalls, under overhanging balconies, looked as if piled with splendid jewels; rubies, amethysts and pearls, globes of gold, and silver, and coral, as big as those that Aladdin found in the wonderful cave. Dark girls with starry eyes and clouds of hair stood gossipping in old, carved doorways, or peered curiously down at us from oddly shaped windows; and they were so handsome that we liked them even when they doubled up with laughter at our procession, and called their lovers and brothers to laugh too.

Men and women ran out from dark recesses where they sold things, and from two-foot-wide alleys which the sun could never have even seen, staring at us, and saying "molta bella" as Maida passed. She really was very effective against the rich-coloured background — like a beautiful white bird that had strayed into the narrow village streets, with sunshine on its wings. But she didn't seem to realize that she was being looked at in a different way from the rest of us. "I suppose we're as great curiosities to them, as they are to us," she said, lingering to gaze at the gorgeous fruit, or some quaint Catholic emblems for sale in dingy windows, until Sir Ralph had to hurry her along lest we should miss the train.

We were in plenty of time, though; and at the railroad depôt (according to me), or the railway station (according to Sir Ralph and our Chauffeulier), the automobile had been got onto the truck before the train was signalled. Our tickets had been bought by Mr. Barrymore, who would pay for them all, as he said it was "his funeral," and we stood in a row on the platform, waiting, when the train boomed in.

As it slowed down, car after car passing us, Mamma gave a little scream and pointed. "Look, there's another automobile on a truck!" said she. "My goodness, if it isn't exactly like the Prince's!"

"And if that isn't exactly like the Prince!" echoed Sir Ralph, waving his hand at the window of a car next to the truck.

We all broke into a shout of ribald joy. Not even a saint could have helped it, I'm sure; for Maida is pretty near to a saint, and she was as bad as any of us.

The Prince's head popped back into the window, like a rabbit's into its hole; but in another second he must have realized that it was no use playing 'possum when there, within a dozen yards, was that big scarlet runner of his, as large as life, though not running for the moment. He quickly decided to make the best of things by turning the tables upon us, and pointing the finger of derision at our automobile, which by careening himself out of the window he could see on its truck.

Before the train had stopped, he was down on the platform, gallantly helping Mamma up the high step into the compartment where he had been sitting; so we all followed.

"You broke something, I see," His Highness remarked jovially, as if nothing had ever happened to him.

"It was you who broke it," said I, before either of our men could speak.

"But I mean something in your motor," he explained.

"Yes, its heart! The long agony of towing you up those miles of mountain was too much for it. But motors' hearts can be mended."

"So can young ladies', *n'est-ce pas*? Well, this is an odd meeting. I telegraphed you, Countess, to the hotel at Cuneo, where we arranged our rendezvous, in case you arrived before me, to say that I was on the way; but now we will all go there together. Since we parted I have had adventures. So, evidently, have you. Joseph's repairs were so unsatisfactory, owing to his own inefficiency and that of the machine shop, that I saw the best thing to do was to come on by train to Cuneo, where proper tools could be obtained. After some difficulty I found horses to tow me up to the railway terminus at Vievola, where I succeeded in getting a truck, and —*voila!*"

Whereupon Mamma poured a history of our exploits into the Prince's ears, exaggerating a little, but saying nothing detrimental to our Chauffeulier, who would perhaps not have cared or even heard if she had, for he was showing things to Maida through the window.

"We're in Piedmont now," he said. "How peaceful and pretty, and characteristically Italian it is, with the vines and chestnut trees and mulberries! Who would think, to see this richly cultivated plain, that it was once appropriately nicknamed 'the cockpit of Europe,' because of all the fighting that has gone on here between so many nations, ever since the dawn of civilization? It's just as hard to realize as to believe that the tiny rills trickling over pebbly river-beds which we pass can turn into mighty floods when they choose. When the snows melt on Monte Viso—that great, white, leaning tower against the sky—and on the other snow mountains, then is the time of danger in this land that the sun loves."

Mamma thought the train rather restful after an automobile, but I discouraged her in that opinion by saying that it sounded very old-fashioned, and she amended it by hurriedly remarking that, anyhow, she would soon be tired of resting and glad to get on again.

"That must be Cuneo, now," said Mr. Barrymore, pointing to a distant town which seemed to grow suddenly up out of the plain, very important, full of vivid colours, and modern looking after the strange, ancient villages we had passed on the way.

When we got out of the train Joseph was on the platform, more depressed than ever, but visibly brightening at sight of Mr. Barrymore, for whom he evidently cherishes a lively admiration; or else he regards him as a professional brother.

What happened to the two automobiles, I don't know, for we didn't stop to see. Sir Ralph had a hurried consultation with Mr. Barrymore, and then said that he would take us up to the hotel in a cab, with all our luggage.

There wasn't room for the Prince in our ramshackle old vehicle, and he took another, being apparently very anxious to arrive at the hotel before us. He spoke to his driver, who lashed the one poor nag so furiously that Maida cried out with rage, and they flashed past us, the horse galloping as if Black Care were on his back. But something

140

happened to the harness, and they were obliged to stop; so we got ahead, and reached the wide-arcaded square of the hotel first after all.

It was quite a grand-looking town, for a middle-sized one, but Mamma drew back hastily when she had taken a step into the hall of the hotel. "Oh, we can't stop here!" she exclaimed. "This must be the worst instead of the best."

With that several little men in greasy dress-coats, spotted shirts, and collars so low that you could see down their necks, sprang forward and bowed very humbly, like automata. "May I have the extreme honour of asking if it is her very high grace, Madame the Countess Dalmar and suite who felicitate our humble hotel with their presence?" inquired the fattest and spottiest in one long French breath.

Mamma drew herself up to her full height, which must be at least five feet three, heels included. I don't know exactly what it is to bridle, but I'm sure she did it. She also moistened her lips and smiled with both dimples.

"Wee, wee, jay swee Countess Dalmar," she admitted, leaving her suite to account for itself.

"Then I have here a telegram for madame," went on the man, giving her a folded paper which, with an air, he drew forth from an unspeakable pocket.

Mamma looked important enough for a princess, at least, as she accepted (I can't say took) the paper and opened it. "Oh, I might have known," she said, "it's that one the Prince sent this morning. But isn't it funny he telegraphs 'Automobile in grand condition, took hills like bird, shall make slight détour for pleasure, but will reach Cuneo almost as soon as your party. Dalmar-Kalm.' I don't understand, do you?"

"I understand why the Prince was willing to be left behind at Tenda, and why he wanted to get to this hotel first, anyhow," said I; and Sir Ralph and I were laughing like mad when his belated Highness appeared on the scene. Seeing Mamma with the telegram in her hand, he explained volubly that it had been sent before he decided to save time and wear and tear by coming on the train; but he was red, and stammery, and Sir Ralph looked almost sympathetic, which made me wonder whether *all* motor-men sometimes tell fibs.

After being received with so much appreciation, Mamma began to think that perhaps the hotel wasn't so dreadful after all; and when Sir Ralph gave his opinion that it would prove as good as any other, she said that we would stay.

"I should be sorry to hurt the people's feelings, as they seem such *nice* men," she sighed. "But—I suppose it will only be for coffee?"

"I'm sorely afraid it will be for dinner to-night and breakfast to-morrow morning too," replied Sir Ralph. "It's too bad that virtue such as ours should have such a reward. We did unto others as we would they should do unto us; and this is the consequence. Terry intends to work all night on the car, if he can get the mechanic to keep his shop going, and we may hope to start as early in the morning as you like."

"Perhaps Joseph may have mine ready to-night, in which case I can take the ladies on—" the Prince began, but Mamma was too overcome to hear him. Trying to look like a Countess at all costs, she allowed herself and us to be led, as lambs to the slaughter, up a flight of dirty stone stairs, to see the bedrooms.

"You will have our best, is it not, Madame la Comtesse?" inquired the man of the hotel, who seemed to be a cross between a manager and a head-waiter, and who swelled with politeness behind a shirt- front that resembled nothing so much as the ten of clubs. "Yes, I was sure of that, gracious madame. You and your suite may assure yourselves that you will be placed in our *chambres de luxe.*"

With this announcement, he threw open a door, and stood salaaming that we might file in before him.

Mamma pitched forward down a step, shrieked, tottered, saved herself by clawing the air, while Maida and I both pitched after her, falling into fits of laughter.

It couldn't have been colder in the spotty man's family vault, and I hope not as musty.

Maida flew to one of the two windows, set deep in the thickness of the wall, and darkened by the stone arcade outside. But apparently it was hermetically sealed, and so was the other which I attacked. The Ten of Clubs looked shocked when we implored him to open something—anything; and it was with reluctance that he unscrewed a window. "The ladies will be cold," he said. "It is not the weather for letting into the house the out of doors. We do that in the summer."

"Haven't these windows been opened since then?" gasped Maida.

"But no mademoiselle. Not to my knowledge."

"Make him show us other rooms, quick," said Mamma, who can't speak much more French than a cat, though she had a lesson from a handsome young gentleman every day at Cap Martin, at ten francs an hour.

"This is the only one that will accommodate the ladies," replied the Ten of Clubs. "The other that we have unoccupied must be for the gentlemen."

The idea of our two men and the Prince as room-mates was so excruciating that I suddenly felt equal to bearing any hardship; but Mamma hasn't the same sense of humour I have, and she said that she knew she was sickening for something, probably smallpox.

"Three of us in this room all night!" she wailed. "We shall never leave the hotel alive."

At this juncture Sir Ralph appeared at the door, peeping gingerly in at us, and looking the picture of misery.

"I'm so sorry for everything," he said. "Terry's down-stairs, and we both feel that we're awful sweeps, though we hope you won't think we are. He's going to interview the other hotels and see if he can find anything better, so don't decide till he comes back."

We three female waifs stood about and smelt things and imagined that we smelled still more things, while Sir Ralph exhausted himself in keeping up a conversation with the Ten of Clubs, as if all four of our lives depended upon it. The ordeal lasted only about ten minutes, though it seemed a year, and then Mr. Barrymore's tall form loomed in the dark doorway.

"There's nothing better," he announced desperately. "But you ladies can go on to Alessandria by train with Dalmar-Kalm, who'll be only too happy to take you."

"What, and desert Mr. Automobile-Micawber?" I cut in. "Never! We're none of us *infirm old women*, are we, Mamma, that we should mind roughing it, for once?"

"No-o," said Mamma. "It—I dare say it will be fun. And anyhow, we can have them make a fire here, so it will be less like picnicking in one's own grave."

The very thought of a fire was cheering, and we trooped off to the *salle à manger*, where it was understood that the Prince had gone to order coffee. Mr. Barrymore wouldn't stay, for he was anxious to get back to the motor, which he had left at a machinist's, and deserted only long enough to come and give us news. The "shop" was to keep open all night, and he would work there, making a new cone. Joseph, it seemed, was to work all night in another shop, and both automobiles were to be ready in the morning.

"But you will be horribly tired, driving through the day and working through the night," said Maida. "I for one would rather stop here to-morrow."

"It's nothing, thanks. I shall rather like it," replied the Chauffeulier. "Please don't worry about me." Then he gave us a smile and was off.

The coffee was so good that our spirits rose. We decided to unpack what we needed, and then, by way of passing the time before dinner, take a walk.

Strange to say, the Prince did not complain of his quarters, but, after we had for the second time refused his offer of an escort to

Alessandria, became somewhat taciturn. We left him in the *salle à manger*, Mamma heading the procession of three which trailed to our room. Maida and I lingered behind for a moment, to play with our first Italian cat, until a wild cry of "Fire!" from Mamma took us after her with a rush. A cloud of wood smoke beat us back, but Maida pushed bravely in, got a window open again, and, after all, there was nothing more exciting than a smoky chimney.

Sir Ralph, hearing the clamour, flew to the rescue, poured water from the pitcher into the ricketty three-legged stove, upset a good deal on himself and on the cemented floor (which looked like a slab of frozen sausage), and finally succeeded in putting out the fire, though not until both beds were covered with blacks.

By this time the Ten of Clubs, the Nine, the Eight, and all the little cards of the pack were dancing about us in a state bordering on frenzy, but Maida and Sir Ralph together eventually evolved a kind of unlovely order out of chaos, and everybody was told off to perform some task or other: one to sweep, one to dust, one to change the bedding.

In self-defence we hurried off for our walk, leaving the unpacking for later, and Sir Ralph proposed that we should find the machine shop where the Chauffeulier was working.

We asked the way of a good many people, all of whom gave us different directions, and at last arrived at a building which looked as if it might be the right place. But there was Joseph pounding and mumbling to himself, and no Mr. Barrymore.

In common humanity we stopped for a few words, and Joseph mistook our inch of sympathy for an ell. Almost with tears he told us the history of his day, and choked with rage at the prospect of the long task before him. "What is it to His Highness that I lose a night's sleep?" he demanded of a red-hot bar which he brandished at arm's length. "Less than nothing, since he will sleep, believing that all will be ready for him in the morning. But his dreams would be less calm if he knew what I know."

"What do you know, Joseph?" asked Sir Ralph, edging nearer to the door.

"That the water-power will be shut off at eleven o'clock, the lathes will no longer turn, and I can do nothing more till to-morrow morning at six, which means that we will not get away till noon."

"By Jove, that's a bad look-out for us, too," said Sir Ralph, when we had escaped from Joseph. "I suppose things will be the same at Terry's place. What a den for you to be delayed in! But I've an idea the Prince means to sneak quietly off to Alessandria, and will expect Joseph to meet him there to-morrow morning. My prophetic soul divined as much from his thoughtful air as we discussed our quarters."

It was almost dark when we found the other machine shop, at the end of a long straight road with a brook running down it, and trees walking beside it, straight and tall. It was a wonderful, luminous kind of darkness, though, that hadn't forgotten the sunset, and the white mountains were great banks of roses against a skyful of fading violets. But the minute we stepped inside the machine shop, which was lighted up by the red fire of a forge, night seemed suddenly to fall like a black curtain, shutting down outside the open door and windows.

Two or three men were moving about the place, weedy little fellows; and Mr. Barrymore was like a giant among them, a splendid giant, handsomer than ever in a workman's blouse of blue linen, open at the throat, and the sleeves rolled up to his elbows to show muscles that rippled under the skin like waves on a river.

That was what I thought, at least; but Sir Ralph apparently differed with me, for he said, "You do look a sweep. Isn't it about time you dropped work, and thought of making yourself respectable for dinner? Judging by appearances, that will take you several hours."

"I'm going to have a sandwich and some wine of the country here," answered the giant in the blue blouse. "Awfully good of you all to come and call on me. Would you like to see the new cone, as far as it's got?"

Of course we said "yes," and were shown a thing which looked as if it might be finished in ten minutes; but when Sir Ralph commented on it to that effect, Mr. Barrymore went into technical explanations concerning "cooling" and other details of which none of us understood anything except that it would be an "all night job."

"But you can't work without the water-wheel, I suppose?" said Sir Ralph. "And we've just heard from Joseph toiling away at a rival establishment, that the water is taken off at eleven."

"This water won't be. I'm paying extra for it. As a great concession I'm to have it all night. Joseph could have got it, too, if he'd had a little forethought."

"Joseph and forethought! Never. And what is more, I don't think he'd thank us for the information. He is rejoicing in the thought of an excuse for bed."

"That's the difference between a chauffeur and a Chauffeulier," I whispered to Maida.

"It's really very good of you to work so hard," said Mamma, condescending to the blue blouse.

"I never enjoyed anything more in my life," replied its wearer, with a quick glance towards Maida, which I intercepted. "The one drop of poison in my cup is the thought of your discomfort," he went on, to us all. "You must make them give you warming-pans anyhow, and be sure that the beds are dry."

"I should think they're more like swamps than beds," said Mamma. "We shall sit up rather than run any risk."

"Besides," I began, "there might be—"

"*Hush*, Beechy!" she indignantly cut me short.

"I was only going to say there might be—"

"You mustn't say it."

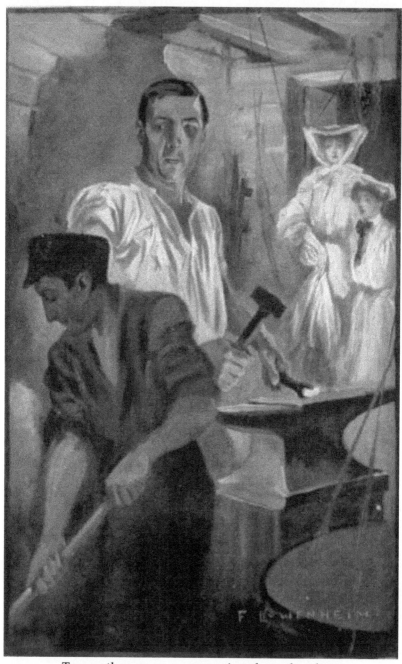

Two or three men were moving about the place

"Sofa birds."

"You naughty, dreadful child. I am astonished."

"Don't prig or vipe, Mamma. Sir Ralph, don't you think those are nice abbreviations? I made them up myself. 'Prig', be priggish. 'Vipe', be viperish. Mamma's not at all nice when she's either."

"I think you're all wonderfully good-natured," remarked Mr. Barrymore hastily. "You are the right sort of people for a motoring trip, and no other sort ought to undertake one. Only men and women of fairly venturesome dispositions, who revel in the unexpected, and love adventure, who can find fun in hardships, and keep happy in the midst of disappointments, should set out on such an expedition as this."

"In fact, *young* people like ourselves," added Mamma, beaming again.

"Yes, young in heart, if not in body. I hope to be still motoring when I'm eighty; but I shall feel a boy."

We left him hammering, and looking radiantly happy, which was more than we were as we wandered back to the arcaded town and our hotel; but we felt obliged to live up to the reputation Mr. Barrymore had just given us.

Somehow, the Ten of Clubs and his assistant cards (there were no chambermaids) had contrived to make a fire that didn't smoke, and the bed linen looked clean, though coarse. Dinner—which we ate with our feet on boards under the table, to keep them off the cold stone floor—was astonishingly good, and we quite enjoyed grating cheese into our soup on a funny little grater with which each one of us was supplied. We had a delicious red wine with a little sparkle in it, called Nebiolo, which Sir Ralph ordered because he thought we would like it; and when we had finished dining, Mamma felt so much encouraged that she spoke quite cheerfully of the coming night.

We went to our room early, as we were to start at eight next day, and try to get on to Pavia and Milan. We had said nothing to the Prince about the water-wheel, as it was not our affair to get Joseph into trouble with his master; and I'm afraid that all of us except Mamma derived a sinful amusement from the thought of His Highness's surprise in the morning, at Alessandria or elsewhere. Even Maida's eyes twinkled naughtily as he bade us "*au revoir*, till our start," kissing Mamma's hand, and saying nothing of his night plans.

"I wonder, if we *could* go to bed, after all?" soliloquized Mamma, looking wistfully at the hard pillows and the red-cased down coverlets, when we were in our room. "What was that Mr. Terrymore said about warming-pans? I should have thought they were obsolete, except to hang up on parlour walls."

"I should think nothing that was in use six hundred years ago, was obsolete in an Italian town like this," said I. "Anyhow, I'll ring and see."

I did ring, but nobody answered, of course, and I had to yell over the top of the stairs for five minutes, when the Ten of Clubs appeared, looking much injured, having evidently believed that he was rid of us for the night.

He almost wept in his earnest endeavours to assure us that the bedding was as dry and warm as the down on a swan's breast; but when Maida insisted on warming-pans, he admitted that they existed in the house.

We were sleepy, but having ordered warming-pans which might stalk in at any moment, we could not well begin to undress until they had been produced and manipulated. We waited an hour, until we were nodding in our chairs, and all started from a troubled doze at the sound of loud knocking at the door.

In the passage outside stood four sad-faced young men of the card tribe, bearing two large and extraordinary implements. One looked like a couple of kitchen chairs lashed together foot to foot, to make a cage, or frame, the space between being lined with sheets of metal. The other was a great copper dish with big enough holes pricked in the cover to show the red glow from a quantity of acrid smelling wood-ashes.

All four came into the room, solemn and silent, while we watched them, struck dumb with amazement.

They set down the things on the floor, turned open the larger bed of the two, which Mamma and I were to share, put in the huge frame, shoved the copper bowl inside it, as a cook would shove a dish into the oven, and replaced the covering. Then they stood and gravely waited for ten or fifteen minutes, till they thought that the dampness had been cooked out. We stood by also, momentarily expecting to see the bed break into flames; but nothing happened, except rather a nice, hot smell. At last, with one accord they flew at the blankets, turned them down, took out dish and frame, and repeated the same process with Maida's narrow bunk.

It took us nearly an hour afterwards to get ready for bed, but when we crept in at last it was like cuddling down in a hot bird's-nest, odorous of cooked moss.

In the daytime we hadn't noticed that the hotel was particularly noisy, though it apparently had most other vices; but ten o'clock seemed the hour when all the activities of the house and town began.

Church bells boomed; electric bells rang; myriads of heavy carts rolled through the stone-paved square; people sang, whistled, laughed, gossipped, quarrelled, and even danced in the street under our windows, while those in the hotel had apparently been advised by their physicians to run up and down stairs for hours without stopping, for the good of their livers.

It was a busy night for everybody, and my one consolation was in planning the dreadful tortures I would inflict on the whole population of Cuneo if I were King of Italy. I thought of some very original things, but the worst of it was, when I did finally fall asleep I dreamed that they were being tried on me

.

XIII

A CHAPTER OF WILD BEASTS

"The dear thing! How nice to see it again! I could kiss it," I heard Maida saying. Something was snorting dreadfully, too. I'm not sure which waked me. But I sleepily asked Maida what it was she could kiss.

"Why, the automobile, of course," she replied. "Now, Beechy, *don't* drop off again. It's down there in the courtyard. Can't you hear it calling? This is the third time I've tried to wake you up."

"Oh, I thought it was the Ten of Clubs roaring, while I dipped him repeatedly into boiling cod-liver oil," I murmured; but I jumped out of bed and dressed myself as if the house were on fire.

Mamma said that she had been up since six; and I knew why; she hadn't liked to make herself beautiful under the eyes of Maida, so exquisitely adorned by Nature. But she was fresh and gay as a cricket.

In the *salle à manger* were Sir Ralph and Mr. Barrymore, who had brought the motor from the machine shop. He looked as well tubbed and groomed as if he had had two hours for his toilet, instead of twenty minutes; and we laughed a great deal as we told our night adventures, feeling as if we'd been friends for months, if not years. It was much nicer without the Prince, I thought, though Mamma kept glancing at the door, and showed her disappointment on learning that he had stolen off to sleep at Alessandria. Joseph, it seemed, had telegraphed him this morning about the water-wheel, and the news that his automobile couldn't be ready till twelve or one o'clock.

As we thankfully turned our backs on Cuneo we realized why it had been given a name signifying "wedge," because of the two river torrents, the Stura and Gesso, that whittle the town to a point, one on either side. For a while we ran smoothly along a road on a high embankment, which reminded Sir Ralph and the Chauffeulier of the Loire; less beautiful though, they thought, despite the great wedding-ring of white mountains that girdled the country round.

By and by the mountains dwindled to hills, purple and blue in the distance, misty spring-green in the foreground; in place of the dandelions of yesterday we had a carpet of buttercups woven in gold on either side of the road. There was always the river, too; and, as Maida said, water brightens a landscape as a diamond brightens a ring.

The air was as warm now as on the Riviera but there was a tingle of youth and spring in it, while at Cap Martin it was already heavy with the perfume of summer flowers. And we had not to be sorry for poor people to-day, for there were no poverty-stricken villages. The country was rich, every inch cultivated, and there were comfortable farms with tall, important-looking gateways. But, then, Mr. Barrymore told us that it was no safer to judge an Italian farm by its gateway than an Italian village shop by the contents of its windows.

After a while, just as we might have begun to tire of the far-reaching plain, it broke into billows, each earthy wave crested by a ruined château, or a still thriving mediæval town. Bra was the finest, with a grand old red-brown castle towering high on a hill, and throwing a cool shadow all across the hot, white road below.

"We must stop in Asti, if it's but for ten minutes," said Sir Ralph.

"Why?" asked Maida, over her shoulder (she was sitting in the front seat again, where Mr. Barrymore had contrived to put her). "Do you mean on account of Vittorio Alfieri?"

"Who is he?" inquired Mamma; and I was wondering, too; but I hate to show that I don't know things Maida knows.

"Oh, he was a charming poet, born in Asti in the middle of the eighteenth century," said Maida. "I've read a lot about him, at—at home. He had one of the prettiest love stories in history. It is like an Anthony Hope romance. I thought, perhaps, Sir Ralph wanted us to see the house where he lived."

"I'm ashamed to say it was the Asti Spumante I was thinking of," confessed Sir Ralph. "It's a wine for children, but it might amuse you all to taste it on its native heath; and you could drink the health of Vittorio Alfieri—in a better world."

Mamma thought that proceeding rather too Popish for a professed Presbyterian; nevertheless, we decided to have the wine. We approached Asti by way of a massive gateway, which formed a part of the ancient fortifications of the city; and though we had seen several others rather like it since coming into Piedmont and Lombardy, it struck me with a sort of awe that I would have been ashamed to put into words, except on paper, for fear somebody might laugh. I suppose it's because I come from a country where we think houses aged at fifty, and antique at a hundred; but these old fortified towns and ruined castles frowning down from rocky heights give me the kind of eerie thrill one might have if one had just died and was being introduced to scenery and society on the fixed stars or planets.

At home it had always seemed so useless to know which was which, Guelfs or Ghibellines, when I was studying history, that I made no effort to fix them in my mind; but now, when I caught snatches of talk between Maida and the Chauffeulier, to whom the Guelfs and Ghibellines are still apparently as real as Republicans and Democrats were to Papa, I wished that I knew a little more about them. But how could I tell in those days that I would ever be darting about in a country where George Washington and Abraham Lincoln would seem more unreal than the Swabian Emperors, the Marquesses of Montferrat, and the Princes of Savoie ever did to me in Denver?

I envied Maida when I heard her say that the House of Savoie had been like Gœthe's star, "unhasting and unresting" in its absorption of other principalities, marquisates, counties, duchies, and provinces, which it had matched into one great mosaic, at last, making the kingdom of Italy. Mr. Barrymore loves Italy so much that he likes her for knowing these things, and I think I shall steal that book she bought at Nice, and is always reading—Hallam's "Middle Ages."

The effect of the grim old gateways, even upon me, is a little marred by the fact that from out of their shadows usually jump small blue-uniformed Octroi men like Jacks from a box. At Asti there was a particularly fussy one, who wouldn't take Mr. Barrymore's word that we'd nothing to declare, but poked and prodded at our hold-alls and bags, and even sniffed as if he suspected us of spirits, tobacco, or onions. He looked so comic as he did this that Maida laughed, which appeared to overwhelm him with remorse, as if an angel had had hysterics. He flushed, bowed, motioned for us to pass on, and we sailed into a wide, rather stately old street.

"Oh, look!" Maida cried out, pointing, and the Chauffeulier slowed down before a house with a marble tablet on it. It was almost a palace; and Mamma began to feel some respect for Vittorio Alfieri when she read on the slab of marble that he had been born there. "Why, he must have been a gentleman!" she exclaimed.

Maida and Mr. Barrymore laughed at that, and Sir Ralph said that evidently the Countess had a small opinion of poets.

"Another Countess loved Alfieri," remarked Mr. Barrymore; and when Mamma heard that, she made a note to buy his poems. But I don't believe she knew who the Countess of Albany was, though she was able to join feebly in the conversation about the Young Pretender.

We went into the house, and wandered about some cold, gloomy rooms, in one of which Vittorio had happened to be born. We saw his portrait, and a sonnet in his own handwriting, which Mr. Barrymore translated for Maida, and would for me, perhaps, only I was too proud to interrupt. Altogether I should have felt quite out of it if it hadn't been for Sir Ralph. After our talk about the worm and other things, he couldn't help guessing what my feelings were, and he did his best to make me forget my sorrow. He said that he didn't know anything about the Italian poets except the really necessary ones, such as Dante and Petrarch, and as little as possible of them. Then he asked about the American ones, and seemed interested in Walt Whitman and Eugene Field and James Whitcomb Riley, all of whom I can recite by the yard.

When we had scraped up every item of interest about Alfieri, as Papa used to scrape up butter for his bread rather than take a fresh bit, we spun on again to an old-fashioned hotel, where everybody rushed to meet us, bowing, and looked ready to cry when they found we didn't want rooms.

"Perhaps the Countess would absolve you from your vow of temperance, Terry, that you may have the exquisite delight of quaffing a little Asti Spumante," said Sir Ralph to Mr. Barrymore, when we were at a table in a large, cool dining-room.

"Why, of course," replied Mamma, and then opened her eyes wide when both men laughed, and Mr. Barrymore intimated that Sir Ralph's head would be improved by punching. Neither of them would take any of the wine when it came, though it looked fascinating, fizzling out of beautiful bottles decked with gold and silver foil, like champagne. It tasted like champagne too, so far as I could tell; but perhaps I'm not a judge, as there was never any wine except elderberry at home, and I've only had champagne twice since I've been the child of a Countess. The Asti was nice and sweet. I loved it, and so did Mamma, who said she would have it, torrents of it, at the next dinner party she gave. But when Sir Ralph hurried to tell her that it was cheap, she vacillated, worrying lest it shouldn't be worthy to go with her crowns.

I don't know whether it was the Spumante, or the sunshine, as golden as the wine, but I felt quite happy again when we drove out of Asti. I didn't care at all that I wasn't sitting beside Mr. Barrymore, though I thought that I probably should care again by and by. Mamma was happy, too, and Sir Ralph amused us by planning a book to be called "Motoring for Experts, by Experts." There were a good many Rules for Automobilists, such as:—

No. 1. Never believe you have got money enough with you when you start. Whatever you think will be right, be sure you will want exactly twice as much.

No. 2. Never suppose you have plenty of time, or plenty of room for your luggage. Never get up in the morning at the time your chauffeur (not Mr. Barrymore, but others) tells you he will have the car ready. Do not leave your bed till the automobile is under your window, and do not pack the things you have used for the night until the chauffeur has started your motor for the third time.

No. 3. All invalids, except those suffering from pessimism, may hope to be benefited by motoring; but pessimism in a mild form often becomes fatally exaggerated by experience with automobiles, especially in chauffeurs.

No. 4. Hoping that things which have begun to go wrong with a motor will mend, should be like an atheist's definition of faith: "believing what you know isn't true." If you *think* a bearing is hot, but hope against hope it 's only oil you smell, make up your mind that it *is* the bearing.

No. 5. Never dream that you'll get anywhere sooner than you thought you would, for it will always be later; or that a road may improve, for it is sure to grow worse; or that your chauffeur, or anyone you meet, knows anything about the country through which you are to pass, for every one will direct you the wrong way.

No. 6. If your chauffeur tells you that your car will be ready in an hour, it will be three, if not four; if he says that you can start on again that afternoon, it will be to-morrow before lunch.

No. 7. Put not your trust in Princes, nor in the motor-cars of Princes.

No. 8. Cultivate your bump of presence of mind, and the automobile will see that you have plenty of other bumps.

We hadn't got half to the end of the rules we had thought of, when things began to happen. The road, which had been splendid all the way to Asti and beyond, seemed suddenly to weary of virtue and turn eagerly to vice. It grew rutty and rough-tempered, and just because misfortunes never come singly, every creature we met took it into its head to regard us with horror. Fear of us spread like an epidemic through the animal kingdom of the neighbourhood. A horse drawing a wagon-load of earth turned tail, broke his harness as if it had been of cobweb instead of old rope, and sprang lightly as a gazelle with all four feet into another wagon just ahead. A donkey, ambling gently along the road, suddenly made for the opposite side, dragging his fruit-laden cart after him, and smashed our big acetylene lamp into a brass pancake before Mr. Barrymore could stop. Children bawled; women, old and young, ran screaming up embankments and tried to climb walls at the bare sight of us in the distance; old men shook their sticks; and for a climax we plunged deep into a tossing sea of cattle just outside Alessandria.

It was market day, the Chauffeulier explained hastily, over his shoulder, and the farmers and dealers who had bought creatures of any sort, were taking them away. As far as we could see through a floating cloud of dust, the long road looked like a picture of the animals' procession on their way to the ark. Our automobile might have stood for the ark, only it is to be hoped, for Noah's sake, after all he was doing for them, that the creatures behaved less rudely at sight of it, novelty though it must have been.

Great white, classic-looking oxen whose horns ought to have been wreathed with roses, but weren't, pawed the air, bellowing, or pranced down into ditches, pulling their new masters with them. Calves ran here and there like rabbits, while their mothers stood on their hind legs and pirouetted, their biscuit-coloured faces haggard with despair.

 Mamma said that never before had she given cows credit for such sensitive spirits, but perhaps it was only Italian ones which were like that, and if so she would not drink milk in Italy. She was very much frightened, too; and talking of an automobile supplying bumps, her grip on Sir Ralph's arm must have supplied a regular pattern of bruises, during the animal episode.

But worse than the terrified beasts were the ones that were not terrified. Those were the most stupidly stolid things on earth, or the most splendidly reckless, we couldn't tell which; we knew only that they were irritating enough to have made Job dance with rage, if he had had an automobile. What they did was to wheel round at the sound of our horn, plant themselves squarely in the centre of the road, and stand waiting to see what we were, or else to trot comfortably along, without even taking the trouble to glance over their shoulders. As the road was too narrow for us to pass on either side, with an enormous ox lolling insolently in the middle, refusing to budge an inch, or an absurd cow taking infinite pains to amble precisely in front of the motor's nose, we were frequently forced to crawl for ten or fifteen minutes at the pace of a snail, or to stop altogether and push a large beast out of the way.

By the time we got into Alessandria, with its mighty maze of fortifications, I was so weak from laughing that I giggled hysterically at sight of the Prince standing in the doorway of a hotel which we were sailing past. I pointed at him, as Maida had pointed at Vittorio Alfieri's tablet, and Mamma gave a welcome meant to drown my giggle. Mr. Barrymore stopped, and His Highness came to the side of the car.

"I was so sorry to miss you this morning," he said, "but after bidding you *au revoir* last evening, I suddenly remembered that I had a friend in Alessandria whom I had not seen for long, and it occurred to me that I would pay him a visit. After all, I might have saved myself the pain, as I found that he was away."

"At least you saved yourself the pain of a bad night," said I.

"Oh, that would have been nothing," he exclaimed. "Indeed, if there were hardships to be borne, I would have preferred to share them with you."

I don't know what would have happened at that moment if I'd met Maida's eyes, or Sir Ralph's eyes, or indeed, any eyes on the prowl; but all avoided mine.

The Prince was expecting, or said that he was expecting Joseph to arrive at any instant with the car. Then he would follow us, and as we planned to stop at Pavia and he did not, he would be in Milan before us. We had suffered so many delays at the hands, or rather the hoofs of our four-footed brethren, that we had no time to waste in compliments with irrelevant Princes, so we quickly sped on again as well as the uneven road would allow, leaving behind the big fortified town which Mr. Barrymore said had been built by the Lombard League (whatever that was) as a place of arms to defy the tyranny of the Emperors.

Though the road was poor, except in bits, and gave us all the bumps mentioned in Sir Ralph's rules, the country was lovely and loveable.

Grapes, mulberries, rice, and stuff called maize, which looked exactly like our American corn, grew together like a happy family of sisters, and from the hills dotted about, more thickly than Mamma's crowns on her toilet things, looked down old feudal castles as melancholy as the cypresses that stood beside them, like the sole friends of their adversity.

Of Tortona and Voghera I carried away only the ghost of an impression, for we darted through their long main streets, deserted in the noon-tide hour, and darted out again onto the straight white ribbon of road that was leading us across all Northern Italy. It was so dusty that Mamma, Maida, and I put on the motor-veils we had discarded after the first few hours of the trip till now; things made of pongee silk, with windows of talc over our eyes and little lace doors for our breath to pass through. It was fun when we would slacken speed in some town or village, to see how the young Italians tried to pry into the motor-masks' secrets and find out if we were pretty. How much more they would have stared at Maida than at her two grey-clad companions, if they had known! But behind the pongee and the talc, for once our features could flaunt themselves on an equality with hers. Even monks, brown of face and robe, gliding noiselessly through wide market places in the blue shadows of hoary campaniles, searched those talc windows of ours with a curiosity that was pathetic. Young officers, with great dark eyes and slender figures tightly buttoned-up in grey-blue uniforms, visibly preened themselves as the car with the three veiled ladies would sweep round a corner; and really I think there must be something rather alluring about a passing glance from a pair of eyes in a face that will always remain a mystery. If I were a man I believe I should find it so. Anyway, it's fun for a girl to guess how she would feel about things if she were a man. I suppose though, we 're generally wrong.

After we 'd frightened enough horses and other domestic animals to overstock the whole of Northern Italy and felt quite old in consequence (considerably over thirteen), a sweet peace fell suddenly upon us. We had passed the place where Napoleon's great battle was fought, and Voghera, where we might have stopped to see the baths but didn't, because we were all too hungry to be sincerely interested in anything absolutely unconnected with meals. Then

160

turning towards Pavia, we turned at the same moment into Arcadia. There were no more beasts in our path, unless it was a squirrel or two; there were no houses, no people; there was only quiet country, with a narrow but deliciously smooth road, colonies of chestnut and acacia trees, and tall growths of scented grasses and blossoming grain. It was more like a by-path through meadows than an important road leading to a great town, and Mr. Barrymore had begun to wonder aloud if he could possibly have made a mistake at some cross-way, when we spun round a corner, and saw before us a wide yellow river. It lay straight in front, and we had to pass to the other side on the oddest bridge I ever saw; just old grey planks laid close together on top of a long, long line of big black boats that moved up and down with a lazy motion as the golden water of the Po flowed underneath.

"This is a famous bridge," said the Chauffeulier; so Mamma hurried to get out her camera and take a picture, while we picked our way daintily over the wobbly boards at a foot pace; and another of the man at the far end, who made us pay toll—so much for each wheel, so much for each passenger. Maida never takes photographs. She says she likes better just to keep a picture-gallery in her brain. Mamma always takes them, but as she usually has three or four on the same film, making a jumble of Chicago street-cars with Italian faces, legs, and sun-dials, as intricate as an Irish stew, I don't see that in the end they will be much of an ornament to the journal of travel we're all keeping.

"This is where the Po and the Ticino meet, so we're near Pavia," Mr. Barrymore told us; and if our eyes brightened behind our masks, it wasn't so much with interest in his information, as at the thought of lunch. For we were to lunch at Pavia, before seeing the Certosa that Maida had been talking about for hours with the Chauffeulier; and before us, as we crossed the Ticino—bridged by a dear, old, arching, wooden-roofed thing supported with a hundred granite columns— bubbled and soared a group of grey domes and campaniles against a turquoise sky.

The roofed bridge, that seemed to be a lounging place and promenade, led into a stately city, which impressed me as a regular factory for turning out Italian history, so old it was, and so conscious, in a dignified kind of way, of its own impressiveness. I felt sure that, if I could only remember, I must have studied heaps of things about this place at school; and the town was full of students who were probably studying them, with more profit, now. They were very Italian, very good-looking, very young youths, indeed; and they were all so interested in us that it seemed ungrateful not to pay more attention to them than to their background. They grouped round our automobile with a crowd of less interesting people, when we had stopped before a hotel, and some of the students came so close in the hope of seeing what was behind the motor-veils, that Maida was embarrassed, and Mamma and I pretended to be.

XIV

A CHAPTER OF SUNSHINE AND SHADOW

Mamma's lunch was spoiled because, in pronouncing "campanile" for the first time, she rhymed it with the river Nile, and realized what she had done when some one else soon after inadvertently said it in the right way. She didn't get over this for a long time, so the landlord profited, and must have been pleased, as all the Italians at the table d'hôte took twice of everything. Those who were not officers were middle-aged men with fat smiles which made them look like what I call "drummers," and Sir Ralph wastes time in naming commercial travellers. He and Mr. Barrymore explained that, at all these quiet provincial hotels with their domed roofs and painted ceilings, their long tables and great flasks of wine hung in metal slings, more than half the customers come every day to eat steadily through cheap monthly subscriptions.

"They can live like fighting cocks for next to nothing," said Sir Ralph. "If *The Riviera Sun* ever suffers an eclipse, I shall probably end my days in a place like this, Pavia for choice, because then I can make my friends at home believe that I live here to worship the Certosa."

Now to make up for her slip about the campanile, Mamma began to talk about the Certosa as if it were an intimate friend of hers; but though she hurried to get out the word while Sir Ralph's pronunciation of it still echoed under the painted dome, her first syllable was shaped so much like a "Shirt" that I had to take a drink of water quickly. It is a funny thing, if people have no ear for music, and can't tell one tune from another, they don't seem to *hear* foreign words rightly, and so, when they speak, their pronunciation is like "Yankee Doodle" disguised as "God Save the King." It is that way with Mamma; but luckily for me, Papa had an Ear.

We had to pass through "Pavia of the Hundred Towers" after a look at the grand old Castello, and go out into Arcadian country again to reach the Certosa. Our way lay northward now instead of east, beside a canal bright as crystal, and blue as sapphire because it was a mirror for the sky. Then, we turned abruptly down a little side road, which looked as if it led nowhere in particular, and suddenly a wonderful thing loomed up before us.

I don't know much about churches, but there are some things which one is born knowing, I suppose; such as the difference between really great things and those that don't touch greatness. One wouldn't need to be told by a guide-book that the Certosa of Pavia is great—as great as anything ever made, perhaps. Even "little Beechy Kidder" felt that at first glance; and then—there was nothing to say. It was too beautiful to chatter about. But it did seem strange that so pure and lovely a building could have owed its existence to a crime. I had heard Mr. Barrymore telling Mamma that it was originally founded in thirteen hundred and something, by the first Duke of Milan with the view of taking off the attention of Heaven from a murder he had committed— quite in his own family—which got rid of his father-in-law, and all the father-in-law's sons and daughters at the same time. No wonder it took a whole Certosa to atone for it, with statues of the founder dotted about, presenting models of the church to the Virgin; or praying with clasped hands; or having his funeral procession in great pomp. But I didn't like his face; and judging from its expression, I shouldn't be surprised if he were glad the Certosa had been taken away from the monks to be made a national monument, so that more people could glorify him. It wasn't until I had seen a great many other things, however, that I made acquaintance with his Dukeship Gian Galeazzo Visconti (it is always easy to remember wicked peoples' names), for at first sight there was only the wonderful gateway, with a glimpse of the dazzling marble church, a splendid great dome, and some bewildering towers glittering in the sun.

Mr. Barrymore hired a youth to guard the automobile and the dog while we went in, strange figures for such a place, in our motoring get-up. I didn't know before what exquisite stuff terra-cotta could be, but had despised it in America as the thing cheap statuettes are made of. Now, when I saw it mellowed by centuries, combined with marble, and moulded into arches and cornices, and a thousand marvellous ornamentations, I made up my mind that I would never have a house of my own unless it could have terra-cotta window and door-frames, and chimneys, and everything else besides that could possibly be made of terra-cotta.

But the cloisters, great and small, were better than anything else; better than the façade; better than the marble church, with all the lovely little side chapels; better than anything I ever saw; and I walked about alone, pleased with myself because, in spite of my ignorance, I had enough sense of appreciation to be happy. Still, I wasn't sorry when Sir Ralph left Mamma listening with Maida, to things Mr. Barrymore was saying about moulded brick and terra- cotta architecture in North Italy, to join me.

"Terry says there's something in the world more beautiful than this," he remarked.

"I suppose he's thinking of Maida," said I.

"Not at all. Probably, if you could see into his mind you'd discover that he's wishing you hadn't wandered away from his orations. The thing which he considers more beautiful is the cloister of Monreale, at Palermo, in Sicily. But, then, this isn't the part of Italy Terry loves best. He won't begin to shine till he gets to Verona; and even Verona he calls only a charming inn where the world's great travellers have left mementoes of their passage, rather than a true Italian town stamped with the divine genius of Italy. When he's at Venice, he'll be at home. You'll like Terry in Venice."

"The question is, will he like *me* in Venice?" I asked, looking out of the corner of my eye at the tall Chauffeulier in his leather-coat, showing a heavenly white marble doorway to Maida, and Mamma.

"Of course he will. You mustn't be discouraged by his manner. If only he thought you were poor!"

"Shall I intimate to him that Maida is very rich?"

"No, no. I wouldn't deceive him about that. Let well alone. All will come right in time."

"Meanwhile, I suppose I must put up with you?"

"If you can. Unless I bore you. Would you rather I left you alone?"

"No-o. There's just enough of you to fill an aching void," said I, pertly. But he didn't seem to mind at all, and was very kind in telling about frescoes and things, although he calls himself ignorant. He has forgotten the boast in his advertisement perhaps, or he's trying to live up to it as well as he can when his chauffeur isn't available.

We stopped so long at the Certosa that the sun had gone far down the west as we walked through the beautiful, strange gateway to the roadside resting-place of our car.

Where crowds come from in the country is as mysterious as where pins and hairpins go to; but anyhow, there was a wide ring of people round the automobile, in which our hired caretaker sat gazing condescendingly on the throng. When we arrived on the scene, with our hands full of scents made and bottled by the banished monks, quaint pottery, and photographs of frescoes, general interest was transferred to us, but only for a moment. Even Maida's beauty failed as an attraction beside the starting-handle of the car, when the Chauffeulier turned it.

"Don't you see many motors here?" asked Sir Ralph of our deposed guard, and he shook his head. "Not one a month," he said, "though they say that some of the rich men in Milan use them. I do not know where they go."

Almost as he spoke a big one shot by, heading for Alessandria and — who knows but for Cuneo? When we came to think, it was the first we had seen since Ventimiglia, though on the French side of the Riviera the things had been a pest to everybody — who hadn't one.

As we started, the sinking sun turned a million tiny clouds floating up from behind the world into rose-pink marabout feathers, which by-and-by were silvered round their curly edges by a wonderful light kindled somewhere in the east. It grew brighter and brighter as the rose-coloured plumes first took fire down at the western horizon, and then burned to ruddy ashes. When half the sky was silver up came floating a huge pearl, glistening white, and flattened out of the perfect round on one side, like two or three of the biggest pearls on Mamma's long rope.

Even in America I never saw the sunset-glow so quickly quenched by a white torrent of moonlight. But on this night it was not white; it was soft and creamy, like mother-of-pearl. And as the opal gleam of the sky darkened to deep amethyst the stars came out clear and sparkling and curiously distinct one from the other, like great hanging lamps of silver, diamond-crusted.

All the world was bathed in this creamy light, while the sky scintillated with jewels like the flashing of a spangled fan, as we drove into the outskirts of Milan.

It had been lucky for us that there was a moon, as we had a crumpled brass waffle in the place of our big lamp; but the effect of the town lights, orange-yellow mingling with the white radiance pouring down from the sky, was wonderful and mysterious on arched gateways, on dark façades of tall buildings, on statues, on columns, on fountains. Coming in out of the country stillness, the noise and rush of the big city seemed appalling. Fierce electric trams dashed clanging and flashing in all directions, making a pandemonium worse than Chicago or the streets of Paris. Horses and carts darted across the glittering tracks under our noses, bicyclists spun between our car and lumbering hotel omnibuses, and hadn't an inch to spare. In the middle of one huge street was something that looked like a Roman ruin, with every shadow sharp as a point of jet in the confused blending of light. Brazen bells boomed, mellow chimes fluted, church clocks mingled their voices, each trying to tell the hour first; and to add to the bewildering effect of our entry, drivers and people on foot waved their arms, yelling wildly something I couldn't understand.

Mr. Barrymore understood, however, and only just in time to save an accident, for it seemed that we were on the wrong side of the road. Suddenly and arbitrarily it was the rule to keep on the left side instead of the right, and the Chauffeulier shot across before a tram, approaching at the speed of a train, could run us down.

"That's the worst of this part of Italy," I heard him shout over the din to Maida. "Any town that chooses makes a different rule for itself and its suburbs, and then expects strangers to know by instinct just where and when it changes."

It was like being shot out of a catapult from the Inferno straight to Paradise, as Sir Ralph said, when suddenly we saved ourselves from the hurly-burly, flashing into a noble square with room for a thousand street-cars and as many automobiles to browse together in peace and harmony.

A mass of glimmering white towers and pinnacles, the Cathedral rose, a miracle of beauty in the flood of moonlight that turned grey into white, old marble into snow, and gave to each of the myriad carvings the lace-like delicacy of frost-work.

"I wanted you to see the Duomo first by moonlight," said Mr. Barrymore, after we had sat still, gazing up for some moments, with even the car motionless and silent. "To-morrow morning you can come again for the detail, and spend as much time as you like inside, for I hope it won't take us many hours to run to Bellagio; but you will never forget to-night's impression."

"I shall never forget anything that has happened, or that we've seen on this trip," Maida answered, in a voice that told me how much she felt her words. But if she had anything more to say the motor impolitely drowned it, and we were whirled away again via pandemonium, to quite a grand hotel.

The first person we met in a big, square hall full of wicker chairs and tables, was Prince Dalmar-Kalm, in evening dress, looking as calm as if he had never heard of an automobile. He flung agreeable smiles at Maida and me, but his real welcome was for his "chère Comtesse," and she was delighted, poor dear, to be made much of at the expense of two girls, one a beauty.

"I arrived over an hour ago," he said, "very dusty, a little tired, a good deal hungry; but, of course, I would not have dreamed of dining without you."

"Did you get in on the car, or on the cars, this time?" I asked.

"But certainly in the car," said he, reproachfully. "Joseph met me at Alessandria early in the afternoon, and once started, we went as the wind goes—a splendid pace, without a single breakdown. I passed your automobile at Pavia, and thought of joining you at the Certosa, where you no doubt were at the time; but I decided that it would be more satisfactory to keep on and greet you here. I knew you would take my advice, as you promised, Comtesse, and come to this hotel, so I ventured to have my place laid at your table and order a few extras which I thought you would like. Have pity, I beg, on a starving man, and make yourselves ready in twenty minutes."

"But Mr. Barrymore can't join us then," Maida objected to Mamma, in a low voice. "He has the car to look after before he can dress, and after the good day he has given us wouldn't it be ungrateful to begin without him?"

"My dear girl, when all's said and done, he *is* the chauffeur," replied Mamma, at her worst under His Highness's influence. "It would be a pretty thing if we were to keep the Prince waiting for him. *You* can come down later if you like."

"Very well, I will," said Maida, very pink as to her cheeks and bright as to her eyes. I didn't think she would dare keep her word, for fear Mr. Barrymore might believe she cared too much about him; but just because he's poor and she imagines he is snubbed, she will do anything. Everybody except the Chauffeulier had been at table for a quarter of an hour, and hors d'œuvres and soup, and fish, had given place to beef, when Maida came in, dressed in white, and looking beautiful. As she appeared at one door Mr. Barrymore appeared at another, and was just in time to pull out her chair instead of letting the waiter do it.

The Chauffeulier, seeing we had ploughed through half the menu, wouldn't have bothered with soup or fish, but Maida insisted on having both, piping hot too, though she never cares what she eats; so the belated one got as good a dinner as anybody. Whether he realized that Maida had waited for him I don't know, but he was so unusually talkative and full of fun that I longed to "vipe" somebody, feeling as I did that his cheerfulness was due to Maida's kindness. Unfortunately there was no excuse for viping; but I suddenly thought how I could throw a little cold water. "Have you noticed, Mr. Barrymore," I asked, "that my cousin Maida never wears anything except black, or grey, or white?"

He looked at her. "Yes, I have noticed," he said, with an expression in his eyes which added that he'd noticed everything concerning her. "But then," he went on, "I haven't had time to see her whole wardrobe."

"If you had, it would be the same," said I. "It's a pity, I think, for blue and pink and pale green, and a lot of other things would be so becoming. But she's got an idea into her head that because, when she goes back home a few months from now, she will enter that old con—"

"Beechy, please!" broke in Maida, her face almost as pink as an American Beauty rose.

"Well you *are* going to, aren't you?" I flew out at her. "Or have you changed your mind—already?"

"I think you are very unkind," she said, in a low voice, turning white instead of red, and Mr. Barrymore bit his lip, looking as if he would rather shake me than eat his dinner. Then all at once I was dreadfully sorry for hurting Maida, partly because Mr. Barrymore glared, partly because she is an angel; but I would have died in agony sooner than say so, or show that I cared, though I had such a lump in my throat I could scarcely swallow. Of course everybody thought I had turned sulky, for I shrugged my shoulders and pouted, and didn't speak another word. By and by I really did begin to sulk, because if one puts on a certain expression of face, after a while one finds thoughts that match it stealing into one's mind. I grew so cross with myself and the whole party, that when Mamma said she was tired and headachy, and would go to our sitting-room if Maida didn't object, I determined that whatever happened those two shouldn't have the satisfaction of a *tête-à-tête*.

Every one had finished except Maida and the Chauffeulier, who had only got as far as the chicken and salad stage; and when Mamma proposed going, a look came over the Prince's face which I translated to myself as, *"Rien à faire ici."* Since our talk in the garden at San Dalmazzo, he has given himself no more trouble for Maida or me; all is for Mamma, at least, when she is present; so I wasn't surprised when he said that he had several telegrams to send off, and would excuse himself.

"But about to-morrow," he exclaimed, pausing when he had risen. "Shall you stop to see the Cathedral, and something of Milan by daylight, before going on to the Lake of Como?"

"Oh, yes," Maida answered. "Mr. Barrymore says we shall have plenty of time."

"He is quite right," replied the Prince so graciously that I instantly asked myself what little game he was playing now. "It is not far from here to Bellagio, where you intend to stop. You will go, of course, by way of the Brianza?" (This to the Chauffeulier.)

"I suppose we must," answered Mr. Barrymore. "I don't know anything at first-hand about the road, but at the garage they tell me motors occasionally do it. The gradients are steep according to the route-book, but unless there's something worse than meets the eye there, our car will get through all right."

"I have already driven over the whole length of that road," said the Prince. "Not *en automobile*, but, no doubt, what a couple of horses can do, your twelve horse-power car can do better. As for me, I have been in Milan many a time, and its sights are an old story. I will therefore go on early to-morrow morning, leaving your party to follow; for I have acquaintances who live in a charming villa near Bellagio—the Duke and Duchess of Gravellotti—and I wish to ask them as soon as possible to call on the Countess."

Mamma was delighted at the prospect of receiving a call from a real, live Duke and Duchess, so she shed rays of gratitude upon the Prince, and trotted out both her dimples.

"Come, Beechy," she said. "We'll go now, as Maida doesn't mind." "I

haven't finished my nuts and raisins, and I want some of those *marrons glacés* afterwards," said I. "I'll stay and eat them, and chaperon Maida. I guess she needs it more than you, Mamma, though you're both an awful responsibility for me."

That sent Mamma away with a vexed rustle of three separate layers of silk. The Prince walked after her, just far enough behind not to step on her train (he isn't the kind of man who would ever tear a woman's dress, though he might pull her reputation to pieces), and Maida, Mr. Barrymore, Sir Ralph, and I were left together.

Both men had jumped up when Mamma rose, but they sat down again when she had turned her back, the Chauffeulier (presumably) to finish his dinner, Sir Ralph to keep me in countenance. But there was no more gaiety. My douche of cold water had quenched Mr. Barrymore's Irish spirits, and Maida was depressed. I was the "spoil- sport;" but I "stuck it out," as Sir Ralph would have said, to the bitter end.

When we all streamed into the big hall there sat Mamma in a corner with the Prince, instead of having gone up-stairs to nurse her headache. What was worse, she was letting the man teach her to smoke a cigarette in imitation of some Russian ladies in another corner. They were puffing away as calmly as they breathed, because it was the same thing with them; but Mamma was far from calm. She was flirting with all her might, and feeling tremendously pretty and popular.

She didn't see me until I had stalked up behind her. "Mamma!" I said, in a tone of freezing virtue. "Four years ago, you spanked me for that. And if Papa were here now, what would *he* do to you?"

She started as if a mouse had sprung at her—and Mamma is dreadfully afraid of little innocent mice. Then she began to explain and apologize as if she had been thirteen, and I—well, I'll *say* twenty-nine.

I foresee that I am going to have trouble with Mamma.

PART III

TOLD BY THE COUNTESS

XV

A CHAPTER OF PITFALLS

A woman finds out a great many things about herself when she is automobiling. Or is it automobiling that makes new qualities grow? I'm not sure; but then I'm so different in many ways from what I used to be that I hardly know myself any more.

Beechy would tell me that it's all owing to Madame Rose-Blanche of Chicago; but it isn't really. She changed me on the outside; she couldn't change my disposition—except that one is happier when one's pretty than when one's a "trump," as the English ladies say.

But I used to hate being out-of-doors; it seemed such a waste of time. And when poor Mr. Kidder was alive, I often thought that if I could be free to do exactly as I liked for a month, I'd spend it lying on a sofa among a pile of cushions, with a big box of candy, and dozens of new English society novels. Yet now that I *am* free to do as I like, not for one month, but for all the time, I go gadding around the world at twenty or thirty miles an hour (they feel like twice as many) in an automobile.

However, it's just as if I had walked right into a novel myself, to be one of the heroines. I've read a good many novels with young widows for heroines; in fact, I prefer them, as it's so pleasant to put yourself in the heroine's place while you read, especially if you're interested in the hero.

In my novel that I've stepped into, there are three heroes if I count Mr. Barrymore, and I suppose I may (though he's only the chauffeur, as the Prince often reminds me), for Beechy says that Sir Ralph Moray tells her he comes from a very fine family.

At first I didn't know but Sir Ralph would be the real hero, for by an odd coincidence *he* is twenty-nine, which is my age—if it's true, as Madame says, that a woman has a right to count herself no older than she looks. Besides, I'm very partial to the English; and though I was a little disappointed, after seeing that advertisement of his, to learn that the "titled Englishman" owning a motor-car, was no higher than a baronet, I thought he might do. But somehow, though kind and attentive, he has never shown the same warm interest that Prince Dalmar-Kalm takes in me, and then it is so romantic that I should be buying an estate with one of the titles belonging to the Prince's family. I can't help feeling now that the Prince, and no one but the Prince, is *meant* for the hero of this story of which I am the heroine. After all, what title sounds so well for a woman as "Princess"? It might be royalty, and I'm sure it would be admired in Denver.

The change in me may be partly owing to the excitement of realizing that I'm in a grander sphere than any I have ever entered before, or dared hope to enter, and that this may be but a kind of ante-chamber to something still grander. Of course I might have gone on this trip in the Prince's automobile, if he had known in time that I had a fancy to try motoring, but perhaps it's better as it is. I like being independent, and it's just as well to have several men in the party, so that no one among them can think he's going to have everything his own way.

Who, that knew me a few years—or even a few months—ago, would have believed I could be perfectly happy sitting all day in a cramped position in an automobile, covered with dust or wet with sudden showers; tired, hungry, putting up with all sorts of discomforts by the way, and half the time frightened out of my wits by appalling precipices or terrific wild beasts? But happy I am, happier than I've ever been, though I keep asking myself, or Maida, or Beechy, "*Why* is it so nice?"

Maida says she doesn't know why, she only knows it is, and much more than nice. "The Quintessence of Joy-of-Life," that is what she has named the sensation; and as Maida uses it, it is sure to be all right, though I must admit that to me it sounds almost improper.

Then there is another thing which strikes me as queer about myself and the two girls since we've been travelling in an automobile. We used to be glad when a train journey was over, and thankful to arrive at almost any place, whether it was beautiful or not, but now we're always in a perfect fever to go on—on—on. We shoot into some marvellous old town, that we would once have thought worth coming hundreds of miles just to see; and instead of wanting to get out of the motor-car and wander about, visiting all the churches or museums or picture-galleries, we think what a pity to spoil the record of so many miles in so many hours. If we stop long of course it brings down the average, and that seems nothing less than a calamity, though why on earth we should care so much, or care at all (considering we have our whole future before us) is a mystery. Even Maida, who is so fond of history, and countries that have made history in dim old ages, feels this. She thinks there is a motoring microbe that gets into your blood, just as other microbes do, so that it's a disease, only instead of being disagreeable it's almost dangerously pleasant. You know you ought to pause and do justice to a place, says Maida, but the motoring microbe wriggles and writhes against the decision of your reason, and you have to use violent measures before you can dull it into a state of coma for a while.

Mr. Barrymore tries to explain this phenomenon by arguing that, of all modern means of getting about the world, motoring is in itself the most enjoyable. The mere journey is as good a part of your tour as any, if not better; and that's the reason why, according to him, you never have the same longing to "get there" or "stay there" (wherever "there" may be) that you have when you travel by train, or boat or carriage. It is the thrill of flying through the air at such a rate that intoxicates you and makes you feel you are conquering the world as you go. Perhaps he's right. But after all, reasons don't signify much. The principal thing is that you do feel so, and it is lovely.

I was so tired after that long day from Cuneo to Milan that I wouldn't get up to go and look at the cathedral. I'd seen it by moonlight, and it couldn't be better by day, so I just lay in bed, and made a comfortable toilet afterwards without hurrying, which was a nice change, and gave me time to use my electric face-roller.

When the girls came back, they were raving about magnificent statues, aisles, columns, windows, vistas, gargoyles, and saints' bodies in gorgeous shrines of silver. Beechy had apparently forgotten that she'd been vexed with me over night, and I was relieved, for she will *not* agree with me about the Prince, and I don't know what I should do if she really did carry out any of her threats. If she *should* put on the long frock she had before Mr. Kidder died (which she *says* she's got with her, locked up in her portmanteau), and should fix her hair on top of her head, that would be just about the end of my fun, once and for all. But she is such a dear girl at heart, in spite of the peculiarities which she has inherited from poor Simon, I can't think (if I manage her pretty well) that she would do anything to spoil my first real good time and hurt my feelings.

We had an early lunch, and started about one with such a crowd outside the hotel to see us go away, that we made up our minds there must be precious few automobiles in Milan, big and busy city as it is.

The whole party was so taken up with the Cathedral, that for a while they could talk of nothing but Gian Galeazzo Visconti (who seemed to have spent his life either in murdering his relations or founding churches), or marble from the valley of Tosa, or German architects who had made the building differ from any other in Italy, or the impulse Napoleon had given to work on the façade, or the view from the roof all the way to Como with the Apennines and lots of other mountains whose names I'd never heard; but presently as we got out into the suburbs the road began to be so awful that no one could talk rationally on any subject.

We three Americans weren't quite so disgusted as Sir Ralph and Mr. Barrymore seemed to be, for we are used to roads being pretty bad outside large cities; but the gentlemen were very cross, and exclaimed that it was a disgrace to Milan. Our poor automobile had

176

to go bumping and grinding along through heaps of sharp stones, more like the dry bed of a mountain torrent than a road; and my nerves were on edge when Mr. Barrymore told us not to be frightened if we heard an explosion like a shot, because it would only be one of the tyres bursting. No pretty little ladylike automobile, said he, could possibly hope to come through without breaking her bones; only fine, manly motor-cars, with noble masculine tyres, could wisely attempt the feat; but ours would be all right, even if a tyre did go, for the damage could be repaired inside half an hour.

Still, the thought of the possible explosion that might go off right under my ears at any instant kept me in a state of suspense for a long distance—about thirty kilometres, Mr. Barrymore said; and then the way improved so much that I settled down again. Even the scenery had been ugly up to that time, as if to match the road, but it began to change for the better at precisely the same moment.

The only interesting things we had seen so far were peasants playing bowls in the villages through which we passed (for it was a fête day) and the curious carts with wooden frames for awnings arched over them, which gave an effect as if the passengers were crowding inside the white ribs of some skeleton monster. Such pretty women and children were in the carts, too; the women like beautiful, dark madonnas with their soft eyes looking out from under graceful head-draperies of black cashmere, or blue or yellow silk, glorious in colour as the sun touched it.

They didn't seem to mind the bumping over the stones, though the carts were springless, but then, they had no hats lolloping over to one side, or stays to pinch in their waists and make them uncomfortable as I had, though—as Beechy says—my daytime motoring waist is *inches* bigger round than my evening waist.

I was glad when I could put my hat straight again, once for all, and have time to enjoy the scenery through which, as I told myself, the Prince must lately have passed on his car, perhaps thinking of me, as he had promised.

Behind us was the great plain in which Milan lies, and before us soared into the air a blue chain of mountains, looking mysterious and inaccessible in the far distance, though we were sweeping on towards them, charging down hill after hill into a more exquisite landscape than I could have imagined, enchantingly Italian, with dark old châteaux crowning eminences above fertile fields; pretty brown villages on hillsides clustering round graceful campaniles (a word I've practised lately with several other difficult ones); green- black cypresses (which Maida says seem like sharp notes in music); and wonderful, flat-topped trees that Mr. Barrymore calls umbrella pines.

We were now in a region known as the Brianza, which is, it appears, a summer resort for the Milanese, who come to escape the hot weather of the plains, and find the breezes that blow up from the lakes— breezes so celebrated for their health-giving qualities that nobody who lives in the Brianza can die under ninety. There were a great many inviting looking, quaint farmhouses, and big cottages scattered about, where the people from Milan are taken as lodgers.

I had forgotten my nervousness about the tyres, when suddenly a queer thing happened. There was a wild flapping and beating as if a big bird had got caught in the engine, while something strange and horrifying kept leaping up and down with every revolution of the wheels, like a huge black snake racing along with us and trying for a chance to pounce. It was so like a weird and horrid dream that I shrieked; but in a few seconds Mr. Barrymore had stopped the car. "We *are* in luck," said he.

"Why?" I asked. "Have we killed the Serpent-thing—whatever it is?"

Then he laughed. "The Serpent-thing is the outer covering of the tyre on one of our driving wheels," he explained. "And we're in luck because, after that ghastly road it isn't the tyre itself. This is nothing; I'll tear it off, and the good old tyre's so sound that we can go on with its skin off, until Bellagio, when I'll put on a new one before we start again. It has cracked the mud guard in its gyrations, though fortunately not enough to make it unsafe for the luggage."

In about three minutes we were teuf-teufing on once more; but we hadn't been going for ten minutes when, half-way up a hill, the motor gave a weary sigh, and moved languidly, as if it were very tired and discouraged, yet trying its best to obey. We were on the outskirts of a village called Erba, and the automobile crawled on until it saw a little inn, with a lot of peasants sitting in the cool shade of an arbour, drinking wine; there it stopped, which was wonderfully intelligent of it.

"The poor animal wants water after its hard work," said Mr. Barrymore; so he got down and asked a boy to bring some, ordering at the same time a siphon of fizzy lemonade for everybody. While we were sipping the cold, sweet stuff, Mr. Barrymore burst out laughing, and we all looked up to see what was the matter. There was that silly boy bringing a pint of water, in a *carafe*, to pour into the tank of the motor; and he seemed quite surprised and disgusted when he was told to go back and fetch about twenty litres more.

The automobile had thoughtfully slowed down in the one bit of shade there was; still it was tremendously hot, and we realized that it was only the motion of the car which had kept us from finding it out before. We should have been miserable if we hadn't changed our tailor motoring-costumes for the holland dresses and coats which we'd bought ready-made at the last moment, in Monte Carlo. In spite of them, however, we were glad when the water was in, and the motor-car's heart began to beat again. Then down went ours, for after a dozen throbs the comforting sound grew faint and presently stopped. "There's no proper explosion," Mr. Barrymore announced in a puzzled way. "I'm afraid the petrol I bought in Milan wasn't very good; the Italian never is as good as the French, though it's more expensive. But perhaps it's only 'tired.' I'll empty it out and put in some fresh."

He did, but the poor automobile was not revived by the change; and Mr. Barrymore began to peer about in the inner workings of the thing to see what had gone wrong. He examined the *bougie*, whatever that was, and cleaned the aspiration valve with petrol, all of which took time; and what with the heat, and the noise the peasants in the inn-garden made with their *boules*, I began to get the feeling that Beechy calls "caterpillars in the spine." Just when they were crawling up and down my marrow, however, Mr. Barrymore cried out, "Eureka! it's the pump."

This exclamation didn't convey much to me, but it was encouraging that he seemed pleased; and when he had adjusted the friction roller against a fly-wheel, or something queer and ticklish of that sort, we flew away from Erba at a splendid pace, as if the car had decided to let bygones be bygones.

We ran beautifully along a smooth and level road that was trying to make up for its evil past, by the side of a small but pretty lake, and it seemed as if our troubles were over at last. But the astonishment on the faces of the peasants who stared from doorways in a couple of very picturesque villages through which we drove, was ominous. Evidently they had scarcely ever seen a motor-car, for they glared at us as if we were antediluvian animals. Running out of the second village, Asso, we found ourselves climbing a road which was not only as steep as the side of a house, but so narrow that, if we had met anything, it couldn't possibly have passed us. The way was wild and eerie; we could not tell what might come beyond each corner, and we could see nothing but the roughly climbing road, with its embankments, except as we looked back and down into vast spaces of strange beauty, like fleeting scenes in dreams.

"I'm sure we must have come wrong. This can't be the way that the Prince meant," I said. "It's more like a track for goats than automobiles."

"We have come right according to directions," answered Mr. Barrymore, "but I must say, I rather wonder at the directions. According to Dalmar-Kalm's account, the road was fairly good. I can hardly think he risked this route for his own car."

"Is there another he could have taken?" inquired Sir Ralph.

"Yes. He could have driven along the lake as far as Varenna, and then sent his car across to Bellagio on one of the steamers."

"My prophetic soul, which I inherit from a long line of Scotch ancestors, tells me that's what he did," said Sir Ralph. Then he added in a lower voice, "It would be like him." But I heard, and wondered if, after all, he were a little jealous of the Prince?

"Whether he did or not, I'm glad *we* didn't," remarked Beechy. "This looks like being an adventure; and none of us are old enough to have outgrown our love of adventure, are we, Mamma?"

Of course, I had to say "no," though I'd been on the point of asking whether it wouldn't be possible for us to go back. We had just come into a ragged hamlet, and there was literally no more than room for us to scrape through between the poor stone houses which leaned over us on either side the steep, roughly cobbled road. Six inches less, and we would have been in danger of slicing off our mud- guards, upon which lay a lot of our luggage as if on shelves. My heart was in my mouth, and I said so to Beechy; but she only laughed, and replied pertly—even for her—that she hoped it was a good fit, or should she pat me on the back?

Instead of smoothing out to a level again, as I hoped against hope that it would, the road grew steeper with each quarter-mile, so steep that it seemed as if the car must take to running down hill backwards. But always it went forging steadily up on the strongest speed with a dependable, bumbling noise, never once faltering, though the Col di Tenda wasn't as steep a gradient as this. Certainly, after one's faith in the car has stopped wobbling, there was a kind of wild pleasure in the experience, especially in looking over one's shoulder at the valleys lying far below us, cut deep into the green heart of the mountain, as if they had been hollowed out of an emerald. Suddenly the road gave a twist, and instead of prancing in the air, lay down at the feet of a grim, grey town, as a dog lies down at the feet of his master.

Mr. Barrymore stopped to see if the motor had got hot or burst a blood-vessel or anything; but all was well, and when we had slipped on our thick coats, those who had got out to walk the steepest hills— Sir Ralph and Beechy—climbed in again. We had been a long time creeping up, longer than Mr. Barrymore had calculated, and the chill of evening was in the air. Besides, we were in the midst of the mountains now, and it was hard to realize that we had ever felt too hot. As we drove along the edge of ridge, a keen wind caught us. I shivered and felt as if there were no more thickness to me than a paper doll; but I shouldn't have dared to tell Beechy that, or she would have laughed, for I haven't got my weight down yet to less than a hundred and fifty pounds. There was a gnawing just under my new gold belt-buckle with the cat's-eyes on it, as if the cats had claws as well as eyes, and I remembered that it was ages since lunch. Maida and Beechy never appear to be hungry when they motor, though, so *I* wouldn't complain, for fear it might seem old and frumpy to think of such material things. But five minutes later being cold or hungry mattered as little as it would in a shipwreck.

The first thing that happened was a view—a view so unexpected and so superb that I gaped at it with my mouth open. So far away, so far below, that it was as if we looked down from a balloon sailing among the clouds, two lakes were set like sapphires in a double ring of mountains, whose greens and blues and purples were dimmed by a falling veil of twilight. But through the veil, white villas gleamed on the dark hillsides, like pearls that had fallen down the mountain- side, scattering as they fell; and above, in the great pale dome of the sky, a faint silver light pulsed and quivered, like the water-lights that one sees on the wall of a room near the river. It was a search-light sent out by the moon, which was *en panne* somewhere on its way up the horizon, Maida said; and it was she who put some of those other thoughts into my mind; but my head didn't hold any of them long at that time, because of the next thing that happened.

It was not a view; it was a plunge that we took down into the view.

We had come up one side of a house to get to this place on the roof, and now we began to slither down the other side, which was worse, a hundred times worse.

Who was it who said, "A horse, my kingdom for a horse?" I think it must have been Richard the Third in Shakspere's play, which I went to see once in Denver, at a matinée, and Mr. Kidder scolded me afterwards for wasting my time and his money. Well, I never sympathized with any one so much in life as I sympathized with that poor man (I mean Richard, not Mr. Kidder) at this moment. I knew just how he must have felt, though of course the circumstances were somewhat different, automobiles not having been invented in those days, and he being on the stage, with a battle going on behind the scenes, where it was cheaper to produce, I suppose.

But I would have given my money, and even my title, for a kind, gentle horse (the older the better) instead of a motor-car. A horse, at his worst, doesn't want to kill himself, while an automobile doesn't care what happens to it; and in these dreadful moments the only possible comfort would have been in sitting behind a thing with an instinct of self-preservation.

As it was, I sat with every muscle tense and a feeling as if my hair was standing up so straight on my head that every hairpin must fall out. But what was a hairpin more or less, or even a "transformation" a little awry, to a woman about to become a corpse? I held my breath, as if to let it go meant to lose it forever, while that automobile walked down the mountain exactly as a fly walks down a long expanse of wall-paper, making a short turn for every flower in the pattern.

There was a flower every other second in *our* pattern, which meant a sharp turn for the fly; and I could have slapped Mr. Barrymore for talking on, as if we weren't in peril enough to be prayed for in church, about the Lake of Como and the Lake of Lecco, and Bellagio (where we were going) on the promontory. Where we were going, indeed! Our only hope, clearly, was in heaven; though I should have liked just to see my new estate in Dalmatia first.

I had to let my breath go at last, and while snatching another, I managed to gasp that I would get out and walk. But that imp of a Beechy (who must, I sometimes think, be a changeling) hugged my arm and said that I wasn't to be "an old woman, like the Prince"; that this experience was too blissful to be spoiled by anybody's nerves, and no one was going to be hurt, not even the little dog from Airole.

"How do you know?" I panted.

"Oh, because I do. And besides, I put my faith in our Chauffeulier."

"You had better put your trust in Providence," I said severely.

"It hasn't come to *that* yet," was her flippant reply; and I shouldn't have been surprised if white bears had come out to devour her, for those mountain fastnesses looked capable of bears or worse.

"Don't forget this is the road the Prince recommended," Beechy went on. "It would be too unflattering to our vanity to think he could have wished to hurl us to our death, so it must be all right."

"He had forgotten what it was like," I said. But the idea did enter into my mind that perhaps he had thought if our car should break down we might be induced to continue our journey in his. And the suggestion of so strong a desire on his part to monopolize a certain member of our party wasn't wholly unpleasant. It gave me enough warmth round the heart to support life during the rest of the experience which Beechy considered so "blissful."

I will say for Mr. Barrymore that he drove carefully, keeping the brakes on all the time, and slowing down for one curve after another, so short and so sharp, that if our automobile had been much longer in the body the turn couldn't have been managed.

We had trusted to Mr. Barrymore's judgment about where we were to stop at Bellagio, for even Sir Ralph had never done more than pass through the place; and he had telegraphed for rooms at a hotel on a high promontory above the lake, once the château of a famous old Italian family. It is still called the villa Serbelloni, and Mr. Barrymore had described the view and the garden as being so exquisite, that he had excited our curiosity and interest. I always think, too, there is something fascinating, if you aren't very grand yourself (or haven't been till lately), about living in the same rooms where grand people have lived. You can say to yourself, "Here the Duchess ate her Dinner, here she danced, here she wrote her letters. In this garden she walked; her eyes looked upon this view," and so I was particularly attracted towards the Villa Serbelloni, even though Prince Dalmar-Kalm had suggested several reasons for our going to one of the hotels on the level of the lake. Of course I'd not confided these reflections either to Maida or Beechy, for even Maida is unsympathetic about some things, and thinks, or says that she thinks, it is horridly snobbish to care about titles. She told Beechy, in an argument they were having together, that she would just as soon

184

as not snub an English duke or marquise, just to show that there were *some* American girls who didn't come abroad to spend their money on buying a husband from the British aristocracy. She hasn't had a chance to prove her strength of mind in this way yet, for so far we have met only an English baronet; though I must admit that she's much nicer to Mr. Barrymore, who is nobody at all, than she is either to Sir Ralph Moray or the Prince.

When we seemed to be dangling midway between heaven and earth, and the sapphires that had been the lakes had turned into burnished silver mirrors, Mr. Barrymore drew our attention to a high point of land running out into the water, its shape sharply cut like a silhouette in black against the silver. "That is where we shall be in about half an hour more," said he, "for all those twinkling yellow stars mean the Villa Serbelloni."

I thought it much more probable that we would be at the bottom of Lake Como, having been previously dashed into pieces so small that no expert could sort them. But just as the moon had painted a line of glittering gold along the irregular edges of the purple mountains we did actually arrive on level ground close to the border of the lake. Then we had to mount again to the Villa Serbelloni, for there was no more direct way to it, connecting with the road by which we had come, and after we had wound up the side of the promontory for a little while we began to drink in a fragrance as divine as if we really had been killed and had gone straight to heaven.

It was quite a different fragrance from any I had ever known before in any garden; not so richly heavy as on the Riviera, though penetrating; as delicate, Maida said, as a Beethoven symphony, and as individual. I believe if I were to go blind, and somebody should lead me into the garden of the Villa Serbelloni without telling me where I was, I should know by that wonderful perfume. I can't imagine its being the same anywhere else.

At the sound of our motor several people came out to the door of the long, white, crescent-shaped building, and among them, to my great pleasure, was the Prince.

"How late you are!" he exclaimed, coming to help me out before Sir Ralph, or a very handsome young man who was the manager of the hotel, had time to do it. "I've been expecting you for the last two hours. Do you know that it's nearly nine o'clock? I began to be afraid something had happened."

"What a pity you didn't think of that in Milan!" snapped Beechy. "Did you get Mamma to make a will in your favour last night?"

"My dear young lady, what do you mean?" implored the poor Prince.

"I guess you'd know that without asking, if you'd come the way we have, instead of taking boats and things all over the place," giggled the impossible child, and then complained out aloud that I was pinching her.

Naturally, the Prince was too dignified to bandy words with a naughty little girl, so he didn't pursue the subject further, but began inquiring particulars of our adventures as we went into the house together.

"Do you know why I was especially anxious to arrive ahead of you?" he asked me, in a low voice.

"I think I remember your explaining last night," said I.

"Ah, but I didn't give my most important reasons. I kept them for your ears alone; and I hope you won't be displeased. Do you remember telling me something about to-morrow?"

I thought for a moment. "Do you mean that it will be my birthday?" I asked.

"I mean nothing else. Did you imagine that I would forget?"

To tell the truth, I hoped he had, for I'd only mentioned it on an impulse, to regret the words as soon as they were out. A woman who is—well, I'll say over twenty-eight—had, perhaps, better let "sleeping dogs lie" when it comes to talking about birthdays, especially if she has a daughter who doesn't sleep, and never lies when she's wanted to. However, out the news had popped about the

30th of April being my birthday, and the Prince would hardly believe that I was as much as twenty-nine, though, of course, there is Beechy, and I couldn't well have married younger than fifteen. I murmured something now about a birthday being of no consequence (I wish it weren't), but the Prince said that mine was of a great deal to him, and he had made exertions to arrive early and arrange a little surprise for me.

"I will say no more," he went on. "You will know the rest to- morrow; but the best, not until evening." I could think of nothing during dinner except what he had said, though it was so late, and I'd been so hungry. And afterwards, standing on the balcony outside my bedroom window looking down on a scene of fairy-like beauty, the wonderful white moonlight and thoughts of the Prince seemed to mingle together in my head, like some intoxicating draught. "Countess Dalmar, Princess Dalmar-Kalm," I kept saying over to myself, until the words wove themselves into a song in my brain, with the scent of the flowers for accompaniment.

The whole house seems to have absorbed the perfumes of the garden, as if they had soaked into the wood. The corridors, the bedrooms, the wardrobes, even the chests of drawers, have the same delicate fragrance. It scented my dreams and told me where we were when I waked in the morning, confused with sleep.

XVI

A CHAPTER OF ENCHANTMENT

A birthday *must* be happy spent in such an exquisite place, I told myself, when I'd got up and peeped out of the window upon a land of enchantment—even a birthday more advanced than one would choose. By morning light the lake was no longer sapphire, but had taken on a brilliant, opaque blue, like *lapis lazuli*. Umbrella pines were stretched in dark, jagged lines on an azure background. Black cypresses pointed warning fingers heavenward, rising tall and slim and solemn, out of a pink cloud of almond blossoms. The mountains towering round the lake, as if to protect its beauty with a kind of loving selfishness, had their green or rugged brown sides softened with a purplish glow like the bloom on a grape. And in the garden that flowed in waves of radiant colour from terrace to terrace, as water flows over a weir, roses and starry clematis, amethyst wistaria, rosy azalea, and a thousand lovely things I'd never seen before, mingled tints as in a mosaic of jewels.

I had lain awake in the night listening to a bird which I could almost have believed a fairy, and, though I'd never heard a nightingale, I wondered if he could be one. He said over and over again, through the white hours perfumed with roses and flooded with moonlight: "Do look, do look! Spirit, spirit, spirit!" And so, just in case he might have been calling me, I got up early to see what he had wanted me to see. Then I was gladder than ever that we had decided to spend at least that day and another night at Serbelloni, for one might journey to all four corners of the globe and not find another place so magically beautiful.

Although I was up so early, perhaps I spent a longer time over my toilet than the two girls do over theirs; and when I was ready neither Maida nor Beechy were in their rooms. I had opened my door to go down and look for them when I came face to face with a waiter carrying an enormous bouquet. It was for me, with a perfectly lovely poem written by the Prince. At least, it was in his handwriting, so I suppose it was by him, and it was full of pretty allusions to an "adorable woman," with praises for the gracious day that gave her to the world. I *was* pleased! It was like going back and being a young girl again, and I could have sung for joy, as the bird did last night.

The rest of the party were on an entrancing terrace, looking down over other flowery terraces upon the town of Bellagio, with its charming old campanile, and its grey roofs like a flock of doves clustering together on the border of the lake. The water was so clear and still that the big hotels and villas on the opposite shore seemed to have fallen in head down, and each little red-and-white canopied boat waiting for passengers at the quay had its double in the bright blue mirror. Clouds and mountains were all reflected too, and it seemed as if one might take one's choice between the real world and the dream world.

Maida and Beechy had already been for a walk with Sir Ralph and Mr. Barrymore, who had taken them up by a labyrinth of wooded paths to an old ruined castle which they described as crowning the head of the promontory. It had been built by the Romans, and in the Middle Ages was the stronghold of brigands, who captured beautiful ladies and terrorized the whole country. The girls were excited about some secret passages which they had found, leading down from the ruin to wonderful nooks screened on one side by trees and hanging over sheer abysses on the other. They wanted to show also an old chapel and a monks' burying ground which you had to reach by scrambling down a narrow stairway attached to the precipitous rocks, like a spider web. But I had on my white *suede* shoes with the Louis Quinze heels, which look so well with a white dress and dark blue silk stockings; besides, I began to want my breakfast, and it would have been impolite to disappear before I thanked the Prince, who might come out at any moment.

We had our coffee and rolls in a kind of bower close to the terrace; and afterwards I did walk along the level path, fenced in with a tangle of roses—pink, and white, and gold, and crimson—as far as a high shelf, cut into the face of the sheer cliff which plunges vertically down, down into the blue-green water. The Prince was my companion, and he (who has distinguished friends in the neighbourhood, which he has visited before) told me a strange story of the place. Once, he said, the Princes of Stanga were lords of the land here, and a certain daughter of the house was famous as the handsomest and cruellest Princess of her time. Despite her dreadful disposition, she had crowds of lovers, whom she used to invite to walk with her by moonlight, after a *tête-à-tête* supper. She would lead them to this very spot on which we stood, and just as she had lured them on to make a burning declaration of love she would give a laugh, and a sudden push, which hurled them to death in the lake far below. How different, judging from what I have read in the ladies' magazines, from the home-life of our dear Princesses of to-day! And how different from *my* habits, if I am asked to become, and do become, a Princess. I should have liked to throw out some delicate little suggestion of this sort, and perhaps would have found the right words, had not Beechy appeared at that moment with Sir Ralph. Then my whole attention was taken up, as it had been during breakfast, by tactfully staving off any allusion on the Prince's part to my birthday. All was in vain, however; he said something gallant, and I was quite as giddy for a few seconds as one of the wicked Princess's lovers, lest Beechy should be in an impish mood and throw out allusions to my age. But she was as good as a kitten, though she looked at me in a naughty way, and only said, "Would any one believe Mamma was twenty-nine to-day—if it weren't for Me?"

When we went indoors afterwards I gave her that ruby heart ring of mine that she likes.

All day long we were busy doing agreeable things. We lunched down by the lake shore, in the garden of a big hotel there, and afterwards were rowed across to Cadenabbia, in one of the canopied boats, to visit the Villa Carlotta in its wonderful terraced garden. I was delighted with the boat and the man who rowed us, in his white clothes and scarlet sash, but the Prince half-whispered in my ear that he was going to show me something better in the evening, when the time came for the "birthday surprise" about which I must please say nothing—not even to Beechy.

We had coffee at the most idyllic spot imaginable, which we reached by leaving the boat and mounting rather a steep path that went up beside a baby cascade. At the top was a shady terrace, with arbours of grape vines and roses, and a peasant's house, where the people live who waited upon us. We had thick cream for our coffee, and delicious stuff with raisins in it and sugar on top, which was neither bread nor cake. I wanted the recipe for it, but I didn't like to get any one to ask; and perhaps it wouldn't taste the same in Denver. Oh dear me, I begin to think there are lots of things that won't taste the same in Denver! But I *should* love better than anything to go back with a high title, and see what some of those society women, who turned up their noses at me when I was only Mrs. Simon Kidder, would do then. There isn't one who has a right to put crowns on her baggage or anywhere else, and I've got that already, whatever happens by and by.

We were rowed back to Bellagio again, and climbed up by a short cut to the Villa Serbelloni just in time to escape a storm on the lake. In a flower-draped cave above our favourite terrace, we sat in garden chairs and watched the effect, while Mr. Barrymore and Sir Ralph talked about Pliny, whose statue was nearby, and some strange old general of Napoleon's who lived for awhile at the Villa Serbolloni, and terrorized people who wanted him to pay his debts, by keeping fierce, hungry bloodhounds to patrol the place night and day.

When you are nicely sheltered, to watch rain falling in the distance, and marching like troops of grey ghosts along the sky, is something like watching other people's troubles comfortably, while you are happy yourself—though Maida would think that a selfish speech. Anyway, the effect of that storm was thrilling. First, Nature seemed to stop smiling and grow very grave as the shadows deepened among the mountains. Then, suddenly the thing happened which she had been expecting. A spurt of ink was flung across the sky and lake, leaving on the left a wall of blue, on the right an open door of gold. Black feathers drooped from the sky and trailed across the roughened water, to be blown away from sight as the storm passed from our lake to another; and when they had vanished, out came the sun again to shine through violet mists which bathed the mountain sides, and made their peaks seem to rise from a transparent sea.

We could not tear ourselves away until sunset; and by the time we had dressed for dinner, the rising moon had traced a path of silver from shore to shore, across the pansy-purple water, where the lights of Cadennabia were sending golden ladders down to the bottom of the lake.

I supposed that we would dine indoors, but the arbour where we had breakfasted was illuminated with coloured lanterns, which gleamed like rubies and emeralds and topazes among the dark tree branches, and the trails of roses and wistaria. "This is part of my surprise," said the Prince. "I have arranged this in honour of your birthday, dear Countess. No, don't thank me. Is it not my greatest pleasure to think of you?"

Perhaps it was because I was in a mood to be pleased with everything, but it did seem as if I had never tasted such a dinner as that was. We had every delicacy in and out of season, a fruit salad which is a specialty of the house, made of strawberries, fresh figs, cherries, pineapples, and almonds; and when I thought that all the surprise was over, along the terrace came a procession of green, blue and rose-coloured lights, as if fairies were flitting among the trees. But the fairies turned out to be waiters, bringing illuminated ices in fantastic shapes, and a birthday cake for me lighted with twenty- nine tiny wax candles.

All had been thought of by the Prince; and if there had been any doubt in my mind before, I now saw that he really loved me for myself alone. When everybody had wished me good wishes, blowing out the candles as they wished, we left the table to stroll about in the moonlight, and the Prince and I got separated from the others. "Ah, but this isn't all," he broke in, when I was trying to tell him how much I appreciated what he had done. "The best, I hope, is to come, if you will trust yourself to me for a little while."

I was ready to do so for any length of time, and when he had sent to the house for my wrap, and was leading me down a sloping path which I hadn't seen before, my curiosity bubbled like a tea-kettle beginning to boil.

"We are going to the little harbour on the Lecco side," he explained, "and there—you shall see what you shall see."

"Are you planning to run away with me?" I asked, laughing.

"Perhaps," said he, "and as fast as if we were in my automobile, though we shall travel by water."

I couldn't think what he meant, until we arrived at the harbour of which he had spoken. There, among two or three canopied row- boats was one as different as a swan is from geese. It had no canopy; and as the Prince brought me down to the quay, a man who had been sitting in the boat jumped up and touched his cap, which was shaped like a chauffeur's. And sure enough it was a chauffeur's, for this was a motor-boat, which had been lent by friends to Prince Dalmar-Kalm, especially for him to take me on the lake by moonlight.

He told me that he had hurried to Bellagio on purpose to borrow it, and if we did not leave too early to-morrow the people would call on me—distinguished people, who would delight in doing honour to the "American Countess."

Those were his very words; and he was so kind that I hadn't the heart to let him see I was frightened to go out in the motor-boat. I should have been far happier in a slow, comfortable old row-boat; and when I found that the Prince intended to leave the chauffeur behind, and manage the thing himself, my heart felt as if it had melted and begun to trickle down between my ribs. It did seem hard, just as I had got used to a motor-car, to have this new experience thrust upon me, all unprepared. Often I had thought what noble sentiments one ought to utter while driving in an automobile, considering that, at any moment your next words might be your last! but as we shot away from that little quay, out into the cold white path of the moon, I felt that to save my life I couldn't have uttered any sentiments at all.

The Prince, however, appeared to be happy, and to have perfect confidence in himself, in spite of the water looking twice as wet as it had looked in the afternoon. This motor was of the same make as that in his car, he said; it was by his advice that his friends had bought it, therefore he understood it very well, and where would I like to go?

"Anywhere," I answered, as pleasantly as a woman can, whose heart has just turned to water.

"If I could but flatter myself that you meant anywhere with *me*!" he exclaimed. "To me, also, our destination is indifferent, provided that I am with you and have you to myself, undisturbed by others not worthy to approach you. Do you know, Countess, this is the first time you have ever been alone with me, for more than a few moments?"

"It's only been a few minutes now," I faltered, for the sake of something to say.

"Ah, but it will be many minutes before I give you up," said he, "unless you are cruel."

My heart began to beat fast, for his manner made me guess that something special was coming, and though I had often thought such a moment might arrive, and decided, or almost decided, how I would act, when it was actually at hand it seemed more tremendous than I had supposed.

"You must try to keep me in good humour, then," said I; but though the moon was beautifully romantic, and I felt he was looking at me with his whole soul in his eyes, I couldn't help keeping one of mine glued on the steering gear, or whatever one ought to call it, and wondering whether he was paying as much attention to it as he was to me.

"I am more anxious to please you than anything else in the world; you must have seen that long ago," he went on, moving closer. I gave a little bound, because the boat was certainly going in zigzags, and he was so near that by accident I jogged his elbow. With that, the boat darted off to the left, at twice the rate it had been going. I screamed under my breath, as Beechy says, and caught hold of the seat with both hands. The Prince did something in a hurry to the machinery, and suddenly the engine was as still as death. The boat went on for a few yards, as if by its own impetus, and then began to float helplessly.

"I've stopped the motor by mistake," he explained. "I will start it again soon, but let us remain as we are for the present. It is so delicious to rock quietly on the little waves with you beside me, and the rest of the world far away."

"Oh, but the waves aren't so very little," I said. "The water hasn't smoothed down since the storm. It's awfully nice and poetic, but don't you think it would be still nicer if you just steered?"

"I cannot steer the boat unless the motor is working," he replied. "But there is no danger of our being run down at this time. The moon lights the water with a great white lamp."

"Yes, but look at that big, dark cloud," said I, pointing up. "It will be putting out the light of the lamp in about five minutes. And—and I *do* see things moving on the water. When the moon is obscured, we *might* have a collision."

The Prince looked up and saw the cloud too. "Very well," he said. "I will start the motor at once on one condition—that you do not ask me to take you home for an hour, at least."

"I promise that," I answered, quite shyly.

Instantly he set to work at the motor; but it wouldn't start. The Prince did a great many things, and even lighted dozens of matches, to see what was the matter, but not a throb would the engine give.

"I am afraid," he announced at last, in a voice that tried not to sound cross, "I'm afraid the sparking-plug is broken."

"Well?" said I, "What then? Shall we be drowned?"

"Not at all," he reassured me, taking my hand. "We shall only drift about until some one comes to our rescue, as unfortunately there are no oars on board. If I thought you were not unhappy, I could rejoice in the accident."

I let him keep my hand, but I couldn't feel as happy as I ought, to be polite. "It's—it's very interesting," I stammered, "but they don't know where we are, and they'll never think to search the lake for us!"

"The chauffeur will come to see what is wrong if I do not get the boat back by a little after midnight," said the Prince

.

"A little after midnight!" I echoed. "But that would be awful! What would they think? And oh, see, the cloud's over the moon! Ugh, how dark it is. We shall certainly be run down. Couldn't we call for help?"

"We are a long way already from the shore," said the Prince; "and besides it is not dignified to shout. By and by some one will come. Meanwhile, let us enjoy ourselves. Dear Countess, I confess I brought you here to-night—your birthday night—for a purpose. Will you listen while I tell you what it is?"

"Sh! Wait one minute. Aren't those voices in the distance, and don't you see something big and dark bearing down upon us?"

"They exist but in your imagination," answered the Prince; "Or is it only that you wish to put me off?"

"Oh, no; I wouldn't be so rude," said I. "Please excuse me." But I was on pins and needles, trying to keep an eye in every direction at once (as if I'd had a headlight in my face) and to make the most of my situation at the same time.

"Then I will no longer strain my patience," cried the Prince in a warm voice. "Dearest Countess, I am at your feet."

And so he was, for he went right down on his knees in the bottom of the boat, kneeling on my dress so that I couldn't have stirred an inch if I'd wanted to, which I didn't; for I meant to accept him. He had had only my right hand, but now he seized the left, too, and began to kiss, first one, and then the other, as if I'd been a queen.

This was the first time a man had ever gone down on his knees to me, for the Prince is the only foreign gentleman I ever knew, and Mr. Kidder proposed in a buggy. Afraid as I was of a collision, I was enjoying myself very much, when suddenly a horrid thing happened. A great white light pounced upon us like a hawk on a chicken, and focussed on us as if we were a tableau. It was so bright, shining all over us and into our eyes, that it made everything else except just the Prince and me, and our boat, look black, as if it were raining ink. And we were so taken aback with surprise, that for an instant or two we kept our position exactly as if we were sitting for our photographs, the Prince kneeling at my feet and kissing my hands, I bending down my face over his head.

I never experienced such a moment in my life, and the thought flashed into my head that it was Simon's ghost come to forbid my second marriage. This idea was so frightful, that it was actually a relief to hear a vulgar shout of laughter coming from the other end of the light, wherever that was.

The Prince recovered before I did, and jerked himself up to a sitting posture on the seat, exclaiming something in German, which I am afraid was swearing.

"Those Italian ruffians of the *douane*, with their disgusting search-light!" he sputtered in English when he was recovering himself a little. "But do not derange yourself, Countess. They have seen that we are not smugglers, which is one advantage, because they will not trouble us any more."

All this time the light was in our faces, and the hateful customs people could see every feature, down to the shortest eyelash. When they did turn the horrid white stream in another direction, I felt as weak as if the search-light had been a stream of cold water.

I tried not to be hysterical, but I couldn't help crying and laughing alternately, especially when the Prince would have taken my hands and begun all over again.

A great white light pounced upon us like a hawk on a chicken

"'Ware the light!" I gasped, as nervous as a cat that hears a mouse in the wall. And though I really did want the Prince to propose to me, and was anxious to say that I would be his princess, in the circumstances I was as thankful as I was astonished to hear Beechy's voice calling to me across the water.

In five minutes more a row-boat containing all the members of our party came alongside, and the lights in our bow and theirs showed us their faces, though the moon was still hiding her face in her hands with a pair of black gloves on.

"We *thought* you'd gone down to the lake," said Beechy, "so I persuaded the others to come too; but we never dreamed you were in a motor-boat, or whereabouts you were, till we *saw* you."

I felt myself get as red as fire; though, when one comes to think of it, I am my own mistress, and Beechy can't keep me from doing anything that I've made up my mind to do.

"This boat belongs to a friend of the Prince's," I explained. "We were trying it when it broke down, and he has been examining the motor."

"So I noticed," remarked Beechy. "I guess you're a little near- sighted, aren't you, Prince?"

He did not answer her, but explained to Mr. Barrymore the cause of the accident, and asked to be towed into harbour.

Of course, my evening was spoiled. I tried to laugh it off and say how Providential it was they had come to our rescue; but though I kept telling myself every minute that there was no need for me to mind Beechy, I dreaded meeting her alone. However, the evil moment wouldn't be put off forever, and she came along the balcony from her window to mine when I had shut myself up in my bedroom.

I expected her to fly out at me, but her manner was the same as usual.

"Want me to undo your frock behind, Mamma?" she asked.

Then, when she had got me half unhooked: "Tell me what the Prince said when he proposed."

"He didn't propose," said I.

"If he didn't I shall ask Sir Ralph to call him out. He'd no business kissing your hands unless he'd proposed."

I was surprised at this attitude. But it made me feel confidential. "He hadn't had a chance," I volunteered. "He was just going to, when the search-light—"

"—Searched. Lucky for you the interruption came at the right moment."

"Why? I thought—"

"Because it saved you the pain of refusing him."

"But, Beechy darling, I don't think I was going to refuse him."

"Don't you? Well, I do. I'm sure of it."

"Dearest, if you wouldn't look at me in that square-chinned way! It's so like your poor Papa."

"I'm Papa's daughter. But I don't intend to be Prince Dalmar-Kalm's step-daughter."

I began to cry a little. "Why do you always try to thwart me when I want to be happy?" I asked.

"That isn't fair to say. Look at my short dress and my hair in pigtails. There's proof enough of what I'm ready to do to make you happy. I let you be a Countess, and you may be a Princess if you can *buy* the title, but no Princes on this ranch!"

My blood was up, and I determined to fight. "Beechy," I exclaimed. "I guess I've a right to do as I like, and I *will*. It's for your good as well as mine, for me to marry a title, and I'm *going* to. I shall say 'yes' when the Prince proposes."

"He won't propose," said she, suddenly as cool as if she had been in a refrigerator.

"He will, the minute I give him the opportunity, and I shall to-morrow; I don't care what you do."

"I bet he won't. I'll bet you a good deal. Anything you like, except the long dress I've got in my trunk, and the package of hairpins in my grip."

"What makes you think he won't?" I asked, worried by her manner, which was odd.

"I know he won't."

"You know the Prince will never propose to me?"

She nodded.

I flew at her, and took her by the shoulders, as if she'd been seven instead of — her present age.

"You cruel girl!" I exclaimed. "You're going to tell him how old I am, and — and a lot of hateful things."

"No, I'm not, and for a good reason. It wouldn't change his mind. So long as your banking account's all right, he wouldn't care if you were Methusaleh. I shan't tell him anything about you. I shan't mention your name. But he won't propose."

"What *are* you going to do?" I stammered.

"That's my secret."

"Oh, you have got something in your head?"

She nodded again. "And up my sleeve."

"You will poison his mind."

"No, I won't. I shall only — play dolls."

And she went on unfastening my waist.

PART IV

TOLD BY MAIDA DESTREY

XVII

A CHAPTER OF MOTOR MANIA

What becomes of the beautiful army of days marching away from us into the past? The wonderful days, each one differing from all the others: some shining in our memory, in glory of purple and gold, that we saw only as they passed, with the setting of the sun; some smiling back at us, in their pale spring dress of green and rose; some weeping in grey; but all moving at the same pace along the same road? The strange days that have given us everything they had to give, and yet have taken from us little pieces of our souls. Where do the days go? There must be some splendid world where, when they have passed down to the end of the long road, they all live together like queens, waited upon by those black slaves, the nights that have followed them like their shadows, holding up their robes.

I've had this thought in my mind often since I have been flashing across Europe in an automobile, grudging each day that slipped from me and would not stay a moment longer because I loved it. I wish I knew the way to the land where the days that have passed live; for when those that are to come seem cold to me, I would like to go and pay the old ones a visit. How well I would know their faces, and how glad I would be to see them again in their own world!

Well, perhaps, even though I can never find the way there, I can see the days' portraits painted in rows in the picture gallery of a house I own. It isn't a very big house yet, but at least one new room is being built onto it every year, and lately it has grown faster than ever before, though the architecture has improved. Fancy my being a householder! But I am, and so is everybody. We all have the House of our Past, of which we alone have a key, and whenever we wish, we can steal softly, secretly in, by dim passages, to enter rooms sealed to the whole world except ourselves.

I have been making the picture gallery in mine, since I left America; but the pictures I care for most have been put up since I began motoring.

I suppose some very rich natures can be rich without travel, for they are born with caskets already full of jewels; but ordinary folk have empty caskets if they keep them shut up always in one safe, and I begin to see that mine were but poor things. I keep them wide open now, and every day, every hour, a beautiful new pearl or diamond drops in.

It seems strange to remember how reluctant I was to come away. I thought there could be nothing more beautiful, more satisfying to eyes and heart, than my home. The white, colonial house set back from the broad Hudson River among locust trees and tall, rustling maples; the sloping lawn, with the beds of geranium and verbena; the garden with its dear, old-fashioned flowers—holly-hocks, sweet- williams, bleeding-hearts, grass pinks, and yellow roses; the grey- green hills across the water; that picture stood to me for all that was ideal on earth. And then, the Sisters, with their soft ways and soft voices, their white robes and pale blue, floating veils; how their gracious figures blended with and accentuated the peaceful charm of the scene, shut away from the storms of this world throughout their lives!

I was partly right, for of its kind there could be nothing more beautiful than that picture, but my mistake was in the narrow- minded wish to let one suffice. I rejoice now in every new one I have hung up, and shall rejoice all the more when I am back again myself—just one of those white figures that flit across the old canvas.

Yes, I shall be one of those figures, of course. The Mother has always told me it was my true vocation; that peace and leisure for reflection and concentration of mind were the greatest earthly blessings a woman could have. Ever since, as a very small girl, I longed for the day when I should be allowed to wear one of those pretty, trailing, white cashmere dresses and long, pale blue veils, I have looked forward to joining the Sisterhood of good women who alone have ever given me love and the protection of home.

Nothing has happened to change my intentions, and they are *not* changed. Only, I'm not homesick any more, as I used to be in the feverish Paris days, or even on the Riviera, when we did very little but rush back and forth between Monte Carlo and Cap Martin, with Prince Dalmar-Kalm and his friends.

I shall go home and carry out the plans I've had for all these years, but—I shall live—live—live—every single minute till the time comes for my good-bye to the world

. I should have liked to stay a month at Bellagio (with the wonderful garden of Serbelloni to explore from end to end), instead of the two days that we did stop; still, the moment our start was arranged, I was perfectly happy at the thought of being in the car again.

There was a discussion as to how we should begin the journey to Lecco and Desenzano, where we were to sleep one night, for our difficulty lay in the fact that there's but one road on which you can drive away from the wooded, wedge-like promontory which Bellagio pushes out into the lake; the steep, narrow road up to Civenna and down again to Canzo and Asso, by which we had come. As our car had done the climb and descent so well, Mr. Barrymore wanted to do it again, perhaps with a wicked desire to force the Prince into accompanying us or seeming timid about the capabilities of his automobile. But when Aunt Kathryn discovered how easy the alternative was (simply to put the car on a steamer as far as Varenna, then running along a good road from there southward to Lecco), she said that Mr. Barrymore's way would be tempting Providence, with whose designs, I must say she appears to have an intimate acquaintance. Heaven had spared us the first time, she argued, but now if we deliberately flew in its face, it would certainly not be considerate on a second occasion.

I was ready so much earlier on the last morning than Aunt Kathryn or Beechy, that I ordered coffee and rolls for myself alone on the terrace; and they had just appeared when Mr. Barrymore came out. He was going presently to see to the car, so naturally we had breakfast together, with an addition of some exquisite wild strawberries, gleaming like *cabouchon* rubies under a froth of whipped cream. It was only eight o'clock, when we finished, and he said there would be time for one last stroll through the divinest garden in Italy, if I cared for it. Of course I did care, so we walked together up the rose-bordered path from the sweet-smelling flower- zone to the pine-belt that culminates in the pirates' castle. While we stood looking down over the three arms of the lake in their glittering blue sleeves, a voice spoke behind us: "Ah, Miss Destrey, I've found you at last. Your cousin asked me to look for you and bring you back as soon as possible. You are urgently wanted for something, though what was not confided to me."

The Prince used to be troublesome when he first attached himself to our party. If ever he happened to meet me in the big hall or the garden of the hotel at Cap Martin, when neither Aunt Kathryn nor Beechy was with me, he always made some pretext to talk and pay me stupid compliments, though he would flee if my relations came in sight. After the trip began, however, his manner was suddenly different, and he showed no more desire for my society than I for his; therefore I was surprised by an equally sudden change this morning. It was hardly to be defined in words, but it was very noticeable. Even his way of looking at me was not the same. At Cap Martin it used to be rather bold, as if I were the kind of person who ought to be flattered by any attention from a Prince Dalmar-Kalm. Later, if he glanced at me at all, it was with an odd expression, as if he wished me to regret something, I really couldn't imagine what. But now there was a sort of reverence in his gaze and manner, as if I were a queen and he were one of my courtiers. As I'm not a queen, and wouldn't care to have him for a courtier if I were, I wasn't pleased when he attempted to keep at my side going down by the narrow path up which Mr. Barrymore and I had walked together. He didn't precisely thrust Mr. Barrymore out of the way, but seemed to take it for granted, as it were by right of his rank, that it was for him, not the others to walk beside me.

I resented this, for to my mind it is horribly caddish for a person to snub another not his equal in fortune; and as Mr. Barrymore never pushes himself forward when people behave as if he were their inferior, I determined to show unmistakably which man I valued more. Consequently, when the Prince persisted in keeping at my shoulder, I turned and talked over it to Mr. Barrymore following behind. But on the terrace level with the hotel he had to leave us, for the automobile was to be shipped on board a cargo-boat that sailed for Varenna some time before ours.

"Why are you always unkind to me? Have I been so unfortunate as to vex you in any way?" asked the Prince, when we were alone.

"I am neither kind nor unkind," I replied in a practical, dry sort of tone. "I am going in now to see why they want me."

"Please don't be in such a hurry," said the Prince. "Perhaps I made Miss Beechy's message too urgent, for I had seen you with the chauffeur, and I could not bear that you should be alone with him."

"It is stupid to speak of Mr. Barrymore as the chauffeur," I exclaimed in a rage. "And it's not your affair Prince, to concern yourself with my actions."

With that I darted into the long corridor that opens from the terrace, and left him furiously tugging at his moustache.

"Did you send the Prince to call me in, Beechy?" I asked, after I had tapped at her door.

"I happened to see the Prince and have a little talk with him in the garden a few minutes ago," said she, "and I told him if he saw you he might say we'd be glad if you'd come. Mamma's in such a stew finishing her packing, and it would be nice if you'd help shut the dressing-bag."

Aunt Kathryn hadn't been herself, it seemed to me, during our two days at Bellagio. This morning she had a headache, and though I'd hoped that she would walk down to the boat with the Prince, she decided to take the hotel omnibus, so I was pestered with him once more. Beechy and Sir Ralph were having an argument of some sort (in which I heard that funny nickname "the Chauffeulier" occur several times), and as Mr. Barrymore had gone ahead with the car and our luggage, the Prince kept with me all the way through the terraced garden, then down the quaint street of steps past the bright- coloured silk-shops, to the crowded little quay. I should have thought that after my last words he would have avoided me, but apparently he hadn't understood that he was being snubbed. He even put himself out to be nice to the black dog from Airole, which is my shadow now, and detests the Prince as openly as he secretly detests it.

It was scarcely half an hour's sail to Varenna, and ten minutes after landing there, we were in the car, bowling smoothly along a charming road close by the side of Lecco, the eastern arm of the triple lake of Como.

For a time we ran opposite the promontory of Bellagio, with the white crescent of the Villa Serbelloni conspicuous on the darkly wooded hillside. Near us was an electric railway which burrowed into tunnels, as did our own road now and then, to save itself from extinction in a wall of rock. As we went on, we found the scenery of Lecco more wild and rugged than that of Como with its many villas, each one of which might have been Claude Melnotte's. Villages were sparsely scattered on the sides of high, sheer mountains which reared their bared shoulders up to a sky of pure ultramarine, but Lecco itself was big and not picturesque, taking an air of up-to-date importance from the railway station which connects this magic land with the rest of Italy.

"I shouldn't care to stop in this town," said Beechy, when Mr. Barrymore slowed down before an imposing glass-fronted hotel with gorgeous ornamentations of iron and a wonderful gateway. "After what we've come from, Lecco *does* look unromantic and prosaic, though I daresay this hotel is nice and will give us a good lunch."

"Nevertheless it's the *Promessi Sposi* country," answered Mr. Barrymore.

"What's that?" asked Beechy and Aunt Kathryn together. But I knew; for in the garret at home there's an old, old copy of "The

Betrothed," which is Manzoni's *I Promessi Sposi* in English, and I found and read it when I was a small girl. It was very long, and perhaps I should find it a little dull now though I hope not, for I loved it then, reading in delicious secrecy and stealth, because the Sisterhood doesn't allow youthful pupils to batten on love stories, no matter how old-fashioned. I hadn't thought of the book for years; but evidently its story had been lying all this time carefully put away in a parcel, gathering dust on some forgotten shelf in my brain, for down it tumbled at the mention of the name. As Mr. Barrymore explained to Aunt Kathryn that this was the country of *I Promessi Sposi* because the scenes of Manzoni's romance had been laid in the neighbourhood, I could see as plainly as if they lay before my eyes the quaint woodcuts representing the beautiful heroine, Lucia, her lover, Renzo, and the wicked Prince Innominato.

Nevertheless I took some credit to myself for remembering the old book so well, and fancied that there weren't many other travellers nowadays who would have it. But pride usually goes before a fall, as hard-hearted nurses tell vain little girls who have come to grief in their prettiest dresses; and at lunch it appeared that the humblest, most youthful waiter at Lecco knew more about the classic romance of the country than I did. Indeed, not a character in the book that wasn't well represented in a picture on the wall or a painted post- card, and all seemed at least as real to the people of Lecco as any of their modern fellow-citizens.

The landlord was so shocked at the idea of our going on without driving a few kilometres to Acquate, the village where Renzo and Lucia had lived, and visiting the wayside shrine where Don Roderigo accosted Lucia, that Aunt Kathryn was fired with a desire to go, though the Prince (who had come the same way we had) would have dissuaded her by saying there was nothing worth seeing. "I believe you don't approve of stories about wicked Princes like Innominato," said Beechy, "and that's why you don't want us to go. You're afraid we'll get suspicious if we know too much about them." After that speech the Prince didn't object any more, and even went with us in his car, when we had rounded off our lunch with the Robiolo cheese of the country.

It was a short drive to Lucia's village; we could have walked in less than an hour, but that wouldn't have pleased Aunt Kathryn. Appropriately, we passed a statue of Manzoni on the way—a delightful Manzoni seated comfortably on a monument (with sculptured medallions from scenes in his books) almost within sight of the road to Acquate, and quite within sight of Monte Resegno, where the castle of wicked Innominato still stands. Then no sooner had we turned into the narrow road leading up to the little mountain hamlet than our intentions became the property of every passer-by, every peasant, every worker from the wire factories.

"*I Promessi Sposi*," they would say to each other in a matter-of-course way, with an accompanying nod that settled our destination without a loophole of doubt.

In Acquate itself, a tiny but picturesque old village (draped with wistaria from end to end, as if it were *en fête*), everything was reminiscent and commemorative of the romance that had made its fame. Here was Via Cristoforo; there Via Renzo; while naturally Via Lucia led us up to the ancient grey *osteria* where the virtuous heroine was born and lived. We went in, of course, and Sir Ralph ordered red wine of the country, to give us an excuse to sit and stare at the coloured lithographs and statuettes of the lovers, and to peep into the really beautiful old kitchen with the ruddy gleams of copper in its dusky shadows, its bright bits of painted china, its pretty window and huge fireplace.

On a shelf close by the fire sat a cat, and I attempted to stroke it, for it looked old enough and important enough to have belonged to Lucia herself. But I might have known that it would not suffer my caresses, for it's nearly always so with foreign cats and dogs, I find. The lack of confidence in their own attractions which they show is as pathetic as that of a neglected wife; they never seem to think of themselves as pets.

Aunt Kathryn would persist in talking of Innominato as "Abominato" (which was after all more appropriate), and the generous display of Lucia's charms in the pictures caused her basely to doubt that most virtuous maiden's genuine merit. "If the girl hadn't worn such dresses, they wouldn't have painted her in them,"

209

she argued. "If she *did* wear them, she was a minx who got no more than she might have expected, prancing about lonely mountain roads in such shameless things. And I don't want a piece of wood from the shutter of her bedroom to take away with me. I should be mortified to tell any ladies in Denver what it was; and what's the good of carting souvenirs of your travels around with you, if you can't tell people about them?"

We got back to our lakeside hotel sooner than we had thought, and the landlord prayed us to see one more of Lecco's great sights. "It is not as if I asked you to go out of your way to look at some fine old ruin or a beautiful view," he pleaded. "You have seen many such on your journey, and you will see many more; but this thing to which I would send you is unique. There is nothing like it anywhere else in the world; and to go will take you five minutes."

This excited Aunt Kathryn's curiosity, but when she heard that "it" was only a wonderful model of the cathedral at Milan, exact in every smallest detail and made by one man, she thought that she would seize the opportunity of lying down while the others went, and be fresh for our start, in an hour's time.

The idea of a model in wood of such a masterpiece as the Milan Cathedral didn't particularly recommend itself to me; but when we had arrived at a curiosity shop, and been ushered into a huge inner room, I suddenly changed my mind, for what I saw there was wonderful—as wonderful in its way as the great Cathedral itself.

It was the father of the man who showed us the model, and owned the shop, who had made the miniature *duomo*. His name was Giacomo Mattarelli, and he was an extraordinary genius, worthy of a tomb in the Cathedral to the worship of whose beauty he devoted twenty years of his life and sacrificed those which remained.

The story of his self-appointed task struck me as being as marvellous as the task's result, which stood there in the dim room, perfect in proportion and delicately wrought as ivory carved by Chinese experts. I don't know what the others thought, but the tale as told by the artist's son was for me full of pathos and beautiful sentiment.

The man had been a cabinet-maker by trade, but he had money and could gratify his craving for art. The glory of the Milan Cathedral, seen once, became an obsession for him, and he went again and again. At last the idea grew in his mind to express his homage in a perfect copy of the great church which, as he said, "held his heart." There was no train between Milan and Lecco in his day (1840), and he used to walk all those miles to make drawings of the Cathedral. At first he meant to do the work in iron, but iron was too heavy; then he began casting plates in copper, but they were hollow behind, and he could not get the effect he wanted, so after several wasted months he began again with olive wood. Often he would work all night; and no trouble was too much for his inexhaustible patience. Each statue, each gargoyle was copied, first in a drawing, then with the carving tools, and no hand but that of the artist ever touched the work. At the end of twenty-two years it was completed; not a detail missing inside or out; and then when all was done the modeller went blind.

Now his son had lighted up the model for us to see, and I was almost aghast at the thought of the incredible labour it had meant—literally a labour of love, for the artist had given his eyes and his best years to his adoration of the beautiful. And the whole thing seemed the more of a marvel when I remembered how Mr. Barrymore had called Milan Cathedral the most highly ornamented building in the world. Nowhere else, he said, existed a church so smothered with carving. Every point, every niche has its statue. There, in the model, one could find each one. Through magnifying glasses the little carved faces (hardly larger, some of them, than a pin's head) looked at one with the same expression as the original, and not a mistake had been made in a fold of drapery. Each sculptured capital, each column, each decorative altar of the interior had been carved with loving fidelity. All that, in the vast Cathedral had taken centuries and many generations of men to plan and finish, this one infinitely patient man had copied in miniature in twenty-two years. It would have been worth visiting the town to see the model alone, even if we had turned miles out of our path.

To go from there to Desenzano by way of Bergamo and Brescia was to go from lake to lake—Lecco to Garda; and the road was beautiful. Castles and ancient monasteries had throned themselves on hills to

211

look down on little villages cringing at their august feet. Along the horizon stretched a serrated line of pure white mountains, sharply chiselled in marble, while a thick carpet of wild flowers, blue and gold, had been cut apart to let our road pass through. It was a biscuit-coloured road, smooth as uncut velvet, and fringed on either side with a white spray of heavenly-fragrant acacia, like our locust- trees at home. Rustic fences and low hedges defining rich green meadows, were inter-laced with wild roses, pink and white, and plaited with pale gold honeysuckle, a magnet for armies of flitting butterflies. Every big farmhouse, every tiny cottage was curtained with wistaria and heavy-headed roses. Wagons passed us laden with new-mown hay and crimson sorrel; and we had one odd adventure, which might have been dangerous, but was only poetic.

A horse drawing some kind of vehicle, piled high with fragrant clover, took it into his head just as were side by side, that it was his duty to punish his mechanical rival for existing. Calculating his distance nicely, he gave a bound, flung the cart against our car, and upset half his load of clover on our heads. What he did afterwards we had no means of knowing, for we were temporarily extinguished.

It was the strangest sensation I ever had, being suddenly overwhelmed by a soft, yet heavy wave of something that was like a ton of perfumed feathers.

Instantly the car stopped, for Mr. Barrymore, buried as he was, didn't forget to put on the brakes. Then I felt that he was excavating me, and almost before I knew what had swallowed me up I was emerging from green and pink billows of clover, laughing, gasping, half-dazed, but wholly delighted. "You're not drowned?" he asked quickly.

"No, I can swim," I answered, and set myself promptly to help him and Sir Ralph rescue Beechy and Aunt Kathryn, which was rather like looking for needles in a haystack.

By the time we had all got our breath and wiped the clover out of our eyes, horse and cart had vanished comet-like into the horizon, leaving a green trail behind. We bailed out the car and started gaily on once more, but presently our speed slackened. Without a sigh the automobile stopped precisely in the middle of the road, and gently, though firmly, refused to go on again.

When Mr. Barrymore saw that this was more than a passing whim, he called Sir Ralph to the rescue, Beechy and I jumped out, and the car was pushed to one side. Then, with all of us standing round, he proceeded to search for the mischief. Apparently nothing was wrong. The engine was cool; the pump generously inclined, and fat yellow fireflies flew out of the sparking-plugs when they were tested. Then Mr. Barrymore remembered the cause of the Prince's first accident, and looked at the carburetter; but there was not so much as a speck of dust. For a while he continued to poke, and prod, and hammer, Sir Ralph offering humorous advice, and pretending to be sure that, if his housekeeper Félicité were on the spot, the car would start for her in an instant. The mystery only thickened, however, and to make matters worse the Prince, who had been proudly spinning on ahead, came tearing back to see what had happened. Though he pretended to be sympathetic, he was visibly overjoyed at our misfortune, which turned the tables upon us for once, and his suggestions were enough to wreck the valvular system of a motor-car; not to mention the nervous system of a distracted chauffeur.

"Perhaps the petrol's dead," said Mr. Barrymore, paying no heed to the Prince's ideas. He opened a new tin and was about to empty its contents into the reservoir, when he uttered an exclamation. "By Jove! Just look at that, Miss Destrey!" he said; and I couldn't help feeling flattered that he should appeal to me on a subject I didn't know anything about.

He was peering at the small round air-hole leading down to the reservoir, so I peered too, and in spite of my ignorance I saw what he meant. The hole was entirely stopped up with the body of a pinkish-grey caterpillar, and Mr. Barrymore explained that the poor car had simply stopped because it couldn't breathe. No air had been able to reach the petrol in the reservoir, and therefore no spirit had trickled through to the carburetter.

We had been delayed for more than half an hour by a mere worm, which had probably arrived with the clover; but when the automobile could fill her lungs again she started on at a great pace. We passed a wonderful old riverside town, that had one of the most remarkable churches we had seen yet; and by-and-by a fine city, set like a tiara on the forehead of a distant hill, seemed to spring up, peer at us from its eminence, and then dip down out of sight among other hills which made a dark foreground against white mountains.

It was Bergamo; and not once did we see it again until we were almost in the place, when it deigned to show itself once more—an old, old city on a height, a newer city extended at its feet in a plain.

"This town is packed full of interesting things," said Mr. Barrymore. "I stayed here two days once, at a nice old-fashioned hotel with domed, painted ceilings, marble walls and mahogany mantle-pieces which would have delighted you. And even then I hadn't half time for the two or three really fine churches, and the Academy, where there are some Bellinis, a Palma Vecchio, and a lot of splendid Old Masters. Bergamo claims Tasso, perhaps you remember, because his father was born here; and Harlequin, you know, was supposed to be a Bergamese."

"Oughtn't we to stop and see the pictures?" I asked.

"We ought. But one never does stop where one ought to, motoring. Besides, you'll see the best work of the same artists at Venice and as we want to reach Desenzano for dinner we had better push on."

We did push on but not far. Unless the main road runs straight into a town and out of it again it is often difficult to discover the exit from Italian cities like those through which we passed, and Mr. Barrymore seemed always reluctant to inquire. When I remarked on this once, thinking it simpler to ask a question of some one in the street rather than take a false turn, he answered that automobilists never asked the way; they found it. "I can't explain," he went on, "but I believe other men who drive cars share the same peculiarity with me; I never ask help from a passer-by if I can possibly fish out the way for myself. It isn't rational of course. Sometimes I could save a détour if I would stop and ask; but I prefer to plunge on and make a mistake rather than admit that a mere man on legs can teach me anything I don't know. It seems somehow to degrade the automobile."

The argument was too subtle for me, not being an automobilist; and on trying to get out of Bergamo, Mr. Barrymore made one of his little détours. The road twisted; and instead of finding the one towards Brescia it happened that we went down a broad way which looked like a high road, but happened to be only a *cul de sac* leading to the railway station. We were annoyed for a minute, but we were to rejoice in the next.

Seeing his error, Mr. Barrymore had just turned the car and was circling round, when two men stepped into the middle of the road and held up their hands. They appeared so suddenly that they made me start. They were very tall and very grave, dressed alike, in long black coats buttoned to their chins, black gloves, and high black hats. Each carried an oaken staff.

"They're mutes," said Sir Ralph as Mr. Barrymore put on the brake. "They've come to warn us that there's going to be a funeral, and we must clear out for the procession."

The pair looked so sepulchral, I thought he must be right, though I'd never seen any "funeral mutes." But Mr. Barrymore answered in a low voice, "No, they're policemen. I wonder what's up?" Then, aloud, he addressed the melancholy black beanpoles; but to my surprise, instead of using his fluent Italian to lubricate the strained situation, he spoke in English.

"Good day. Do you want something with me?"

Of course they didn't understand. How could they have been expected to? But they did not look astonished. Their black coats were too tight round their necks for them to change expression easily. One began to explain his object or intention, with gentle patience, in soft Italian—so soft that I could have burst out laughing at the thought of the contrast between him and a New York policeman.

Now almost my whole knowledge of Italian has been gained since Aunt Kathryn decided to take this trip, for then I immediately bought a phrase-book, a grammar, and "Doctor Antonio" translated into the native tongue of hero and author, all of which I've diligently studied every evening. Mr. Barrymore, on the contrary, speaks perfectly. I believe he could even think in Italian if he liked; nevertheless *I* could understand a great deal that the thin giant said, while *he* apparently was hopelessly puzzled.

Even without an accompaniment of words, the policeman's pantomime was so expressive, I fancy I should have guessed his meaning. With the grieved dignity of a father taking to task an erring child, he taxed us with having damaged a cart and injured a horse, causing it to run away. He pointed to the distance. With an arching gesture he illustrated a mound of hay (or clover?) rising from the vehicle; with a quick outward thrust of hands and widespread fingers he pictured the alarm and frantic rush of the horse; he showed us the creature running, then falling, then limping as if hurt; he touched his knees to indicate the place of the wound. What could the most elementary intelligence need more to comprehend? Certainly it was enough for the crowd collected about us; but it was not enough for Mr. Barrymore, who is an Irishman, and cleverer about everything than any man I ever met. He sat still, with an absolutely vacant though conscientious look on his face, as if he were trying hard to snatch at an idea, but hadn't succeeded. When the policeman finished, Mr. Barrymore sadly shook his head. "I wonder what you mean?" he murmured mildly in English.

The Italian retold the story, his companion throwing a word into a pause now and then. Both patient men articulated with such careful nicety that the syllables fell from their mouths like clear-cut crystals. But Mr. Barrymore shook his head again; then, suddenly, with a joyous smile he seized a pocket-book from inside his coat. From this he tore out an important-looking document stamped with a red seal, and pointed from it to a lithographed signature at the foot.

"Foreign Secretary; Lansdowne—Lord Lansdowne," he repeated. "Inglese. Inglese and Italiani sempre amici. Yes?" His smile embraced not only the long-suffering policemen but the crowd, who nodded their heads and laughed. Having made this effect, Mr. Barrymore whipped out another impressive paper, which I could see was his *permis de Conduire* from the Department of Mines in Nice.

He pointed to the official stamp on this document, and with the childlike pride of one who stammers a few words of a foreign tongue, he exclaimed, "Nizza. Nizza la bella." With this, he looked the giants so full and kindly in the face, and seemed to be so greatly enjoying himself, that every one laughed again, and two young men cheered, appearing to be rather ashamed of themselves afterwards. Then, as if every requirement must at last be satisfied, he made as if to go on. But the conscientious comrades, though evidently faint and discouraged, hadn't yet given up hope or played their last card, despite the yards of English red tape with which those two stamped papers had fed their appetite for officialism.

The taller of the pair laid his black glove on our mud-guard, cracked by the flapping tyre days ago, and to be mended (I'd heard Mr. Barrymore say) at the garage in Mestre. With such dramatic gestures as only the Latin races command, he attempted to prove that the mud-guard must have been broken in the collision near Bergamo, of which his mind was full

.

At last our Chauffeulier comprehended something. He jumped out of the throbbing car, and in his turn went through a pantomime. From a drawer under the seat he produced the rubber skin that had come off our tyre, showed how it fitted on, how it had become detached, and how it had lashed the mud-guard as we moved. Everybody, including the policemen, displayed the liveliest interest in this performance. The instant it was over, Mr. Barrymore took his place again, coiled up the rubber snake, and this time without asking leave, but with a low bow to the representatives of local law, drove the car smartly back into the town. What could the thwarted giants do after such an experience but stand looking after us and make the best of things?

"It was our salvation that we'd lost our way and were driving towards Bergamo instead of out," said the conqueror triumphantly. "You see, they thought probably they'd got hold of the wrong car, as the accused one had been coming from Lecco. What with that impression, and their despair at my idiocy, they were ready to give us the benefit of the doubt and save their faces. Otherwise, though we were innocent and the driver of the cart merely 'trying it on,' we might have been hung up here for ten days."

"Oh, could they have hung us?" gasped Aunt Kathryn. "What a dreadful thing Italian law must be."

Then we all laughed so much that she was vexed, and when Beechy called her a "stupid little Mamma," snapped back that anyhow she wasn't stupid enough to forget her Italian—if she knew any—just when it was needed.

She is too sweet-tempered to be cross for long, however, and the way towards Brescia was so charming that she forgot her annoyance. Though the surface was not so good as it had been, it was not too bad; and our noble tyres, which had borne so much, seemed to spurn the slight irregularities. With every twenty yards we had a new view, as if the landscape slowly turned, to assume different patterns like the pieces in a kaleidoscope. On our left the mountains appeared to march on with us always, white and majestic, with strange, violet shadows floating mysteriously.

Set back from the roadside, behind rich meadows rippling with gold and silver grain, were huge farmhouses, with an air of dignity born of self-respect and venerable age. We had pretty garden glimpses, too, and once in a while passed a fine mansion, good enough to call itself a château so long as there were no real ones in the neighbourhood. Often chestnut-trees in full glory of white blossom, as if blazing with fairy candles, lined our way for miles. There was snow of hawthorne too—"May," our two men called it—and ranks of little feathery white trees, such as I knew no name for, looking like a procession of brides, or young girls going to their first communion. Then, to brighten the white land with colour, there were clumps of lilac, clouds of rose-pink apple blossoms, blue streaks that meant beds of violets, and a yellow fire of iris rising straight and bright as flame along the edges of green, roadside streams.

Just as we came into a splendid old Italian town, thunder began to growl like a lion hiding in the mountains. A few drops of rain splashed on our motor-hoods, and a sudden chill wind gathered up the sweet country scents into one bouquet to fling at us.

"Here we are at Brescia. Shall we stop for the storm and have tea?" asked Mr. Barrymore.

Aunt Kathryn said "yes" at once, for she doesn't like getting wet, and can't bear to have the rain spray on her face, though I love it. So we drove quickly through streets, each one of which made a picture with its old brown palaces, its stone steps with pretty women chatting in groups under red umbrellas, its quaint bridge flung across the river, or its pergola of vines. Past a magnificent cathedral we went as the bells rang for vespers, and children, young girls, old black-shawled women, smart soldiers, and gallant-looking, tall officers answered their call. Thus we arrived at a quaint hotel, with a garden on the river's edge; and under a thick arbour of chestnut- trees (impervious to floods) we drank coffee and ate heart-shaped cakes, while the thunder played wild music for us on a vast cathedral organ in the sky.

"No wonder the soldiers are smart and the officers fine," said the Chauffeulier, in answer to a remark of mine which Beechy echoed. "Brescia deserves them more than most towns of Italy, for you know she has always been famous for the military genius and courage of her men, and once she was second only to Milan in importance. Venice — whose vassal she was—had a right to be proud of her. The history of the great siege, wherein Bayard got the wound which he thought would be mortal, is as interesting as a novel. 'The Escape of Tartaglia' and 'The Generosity of Bayard' are bits that make you want to shout aloud."

"And yet we'll pass on, and see nothing, except those panorama-like glimpses," I sighed. "Oh motoring, motoring, and motor maniacs!"

"How often one has that half-pleasant, half-regretful feeling about things or people one flashes by on the road," soliloquized Sir Ralph, pleasantly resigned to the pain of parting. I have it continually, especially about some of the beautiful, dark-eyed girls I see, and leave behind before I've fairly catalogued their features. I say to myself, "Lovely flower of beauty, wasted in the dust of the roadside. Alas! I leave you for ever. What is to be your fate? Will you grow old soon, under your peasant-burdens and cares? How sad it is that I shall never know your history."

"It wouldn't be a bit interesting," said Beechy. "But I suppose that theory won't comfort you any more than it did Maida the other day, when she tried too late to save a fly from dying in some honey, and I consoled her by saying it probably wasn't at all a nice fly, if one had known it."

"No, it doesn't console me," Sir Ralph complained. "Still, there's a certain thrill in the thought of bursting like a thunderbolt into the midst of other people's tragedies, comedies, or romances, just catching a fleeting glimpse of their possibilities and tearing on again. But there are some creatures we meet that I'm glad to lose sight of. Not those who glare anarchically, unconsciously betraying their outlook on life; not the poor slow old people who blunder in the way, and stare vacantly up at our fiery chariot—so strange a development of the world for them; not the dogs that yelp, and are furious if we don't realize that they're frightening us. No, but the horrid little jeering boys, who run beside the car at their best speed when we're forging up perpendicular hills on *our* lowest. These are the creatures I would wipe out of existence with one fierce wish, if I had it in me. To think that they—*they*—should have the power to humiliate us. I don't get back my self-respect till we're on a level, or my *joie de vivre* until we're shooting downhill, and can hold our own with a forty horse-power motor, to say nothing of a one-horse, Italian village boy."

"What a revelation of vindictiveness, where one would least expect it!" exclaimed Mr. Barrymore. "But the rain's over. Shall we go on?" And we all agreed eagerly, as we probably should in Paradise, if it were a question of motoring.

XVIII

A CHAPTER ACCORDING TO SHAKSPERE

"Another Cuneo!" groaned Aunt Kathryn, at sight of the hotel in the steep little town of Desenzano, on Lake Garda; but later she apologized to the quaint court-yard for her misunderstanding, and was more than tolerant of her vast bedroom draped with yellow satin, and opening on an arboured terrace worthy even of a Countess Dalmar.

For miles our way towards Verona next morning was pink and white with chestnut bloom. Even the shadows seemed warmly pink under the long unbroken arch of flowering trees. Far away, behind the green netting of their branches, we caught blue flashes of lake and mountain peaks of amethyst, while Beechy wished for a dozen noses dotted about here and there at convenient intervals on her body, so that she might make the most of the perfumed air. "But you would want them all cut off when you got to the nearest town," remarked Aunt Kathryn.

Ever since Brescia, the road had been so smooth and well kept that it was as if we had come into a different country; but Mr. Barrymore said it was because we were now under the jurisdiction of Venice— Venice, as rich and practical as romantic. And I had to repeat the name over and over in my mind—Verona and Padua too—to make myself believe that we were actually so near.

Horses were better trained in this district, and "knew a motor when they saw it." Even a drove of sheep (near the wonderful fortress of Peschiera with its coiled python of a river) seemed comparatively indifferent as they surged round us in a foaming wave of wool. But then, sheep have no facial expression. All other four-footed things show emotion by a change of countenance, just as human beings do— more, because they don't conceal their feelings—but sheep look as if they wore foolishly smiling masks. Even when, as their ranks closed in around the automobile, we broke a chain with a pretty little tinkling noise, and some of the sheep tripped up on it, they did nothing but smile and merely mention "ba-a" in an indifferent, absent-minded way.

"If you only *knew* how much nicer you are with mint sauce!" Beechy taunted them, as we swept round a corner and were in the labyrinth of the fortress, which was, our men told us, part of the once famous quadrilateral that made trouble for Italy in '48.

"There's something pathetic about old, obsolete forts as grand as Peschiera," Mr. Barrymore said to me. "So much thought and money spent, the best military science of the day employed to make a stronghold as feeble against modern arms as a fort of cards. Such a fortress seems like an aged warrior, past his fighting days, or an old hunting dog, as keen on the chase as ever, poor fellow, but too old to move from before the fire, where he can only lie and dream of past triumphs."

"I was thinking almost exactly the same!" I exclaimed, and I liked Mr. Barrymore all the better; for it draws you nearer to a person when you find that your thoughts resemble each other in shape and colour. Oddly enough, it's often so with Mr. Barrymore and me; which is the reason it's so agreeable to have the place beside him when he drives.

No more than half a dozen miles from Peschiera we saw the Tower of San Martino, raised on the great battlefield of Solferino. By this time we had left the lake behind; but we had exchanged the low, amethyst mountains for tall white ones, glorious pinnacles of snow which were the higher Austrian Alps. Everything was impressive on this road to Verona, even the farmhouses, of an entirely different character from those of the "yesterday country;" and then, at last, we came in sight of Verona herself, lying low within a charmed circle of protecting hills, on which castles and white villas looked down from among cypresses and rose-pink almond trees.

I was glad that the gateway by which we entered Verona was the finest through which we had passed, for though Mr. Barrymore called the town "an inn for the great travellers of history," it was more for me. It was the home of romance; for was it not Juliet's home and Romeo's?

That gateway, and the splendid old crenellated bridge of dark red brick (toning deliciously with the clear, beryl-green of the swift-rushing Adda) made a noble, preface for the city. And then, each old, old street into which we turned was a new joy. What lessons for modern architects in those time-softened brick façades, with the moulded arches of terra-cotta framing the green open-work of the shutters!

I began to feel a sense of exaltation, as if I had listened to an anthem played by a master hand on a cathedral organ. I couldn't have told any one, but I happened to glance at Mr. Barrymore, and he at me, just as he had driven into the *piazza* where Dante's house looks down over the tombs of the Scaligers. Then he smiled, and said, "Yes, I know. I always feel like that, too, when I come here—but even more in Venice."

"How *am* I feeling?" I asked, smiling with him.

"Oh, a little bit as if your soul had got out of your body and taken a bath in a mountain spring, after you'd been staggering up some of the steep paths of life in the dust and sun. Isn't that it?"

"Yes. Thank you," I answered. And we seemed to understand each other so well that I was almost frightened.

"I want all these streets for mine," said Beechy, in a chattering mood. "Oh, and especially the market-place, with that strange old fountain, and the booths under the red umbrellas like scarlet mushrooms. Mamma, have you got money enough to buy them for me, and have them packed up in a big box with dried moss, like the toy villages, and expressed to Denver?"

"Speaking of dried moss, all these lovely old churches and palaces and monuments look as if history had covered them with a kind of delicate lichen," I said, more to Mr. Barrymore than to Beechy. "And it enhances their beauty, as the lace of a bride's veil enhances the beauty of her face."

"Or a nun's veil," cut in Beechy. I wonder why she says things like that so often lately? Well, perhaps it's best that I should be reminded of my vocation, but it gives me a cold, desolate feeling for a minute, and seems to throw a constraint upon us all.

We had made the Chauffeulier stop three or four times in every street to look at some beautiful bit; a gate of flexible iron-work that even Ruskin must have admired, the doorway of a church, the wonderful windows of a faded palace; but suddenly I felt ready to go to the hotel, where we were to stop for the night, that we might do our sight-seeing slowly.

It was a delightful hotel, itself once a palace, and to be there was to be "in the picture," in such a place as Verona. The Prince had arrived before us, as his motor is retrieving its reputation, and we all lunched together, making plans for the afternoon.

As usual, he was *blasé*—so different from Mr. Barrymore, who has seen the best things in Italy as often as Prince Dalmar-Kalm has, yet never tires; indeed, finds something new each time.

The Prince began by announcing that Verona bored him. But one could always go to sleep.

"That's what I mean to do," said Aunt Kathryn, who generally takes her cue from him. "I consider that I've seen Verona now, and I shall lie down this afternoon. Perhaps later I shall write a few letters in the hall."

I was unkind enough to fancy this a hint for the Prince, but perhaps I wronged her. And anyway, why should she not give him hints if she likes? He has been very attentive to her, although for the last few days I don't think they have been quite so much in "each others' pockets" (as Beechy calls it) as before.

A little attention was needed by the automobile, it appeared—such as a tightening up of chains, and a couple of lost grease-cups to replace; therefore Mr. Barrymore's time would be filled up without any sight-seeing. But Sir Ralph offered to take Beechy and me anywhere we liked to go. I was very glad that the Prince said nothing about accompanying us, for somehow I'd been afraid he would.

We consulted guide-books until we were bewildered, but in the midst of confusion I held fast to two things. We had seen Romeo's house, towering picturesquely behind the Scaligers' tombs; but I wanted to see where Juliet had lived, and where she had been buried.

"The Prince says it's all nonsense," exclaimed Aunt Kathryn. "If there was a slight foundation for the story in a great family scandal here about Shakspere's time, anyhow there's none for the houses or the tomb—"

Beechy stopped her ears. "You're *real mean*," she said, "you and the Prince both. It's just as bad as when you thought it your duty to tell me there was no Santa Claus. But I don't care; there *is*. I shall believe it when I'm *seventeen*; and I believe in the Romeo and Juliet houses too."

But when we were in the street of Juliet's house—she and Sir Ralph and I—Beechy pouted. Standing with her hands behind her, her long braids of hair dangling half-way down her short skirt as she threw back her head to gaze up, she looked incredibly modern and American. "There were no tourists' agencies in those days," she remarked, regretfully, "so I suppose Shakspere *had* to trust to hearsay, and somebody must have told him a big tarradiddle. I guess Juliet was really on a visit to an aunt in the country when she first met Romeo, for fancy a girl in her senses yelling down from that balcony up at the top of a tall house to *any* lover, let alone a secret one? Besides, there wouldn't have been enough rope in Verona to make the ladder for Romeo to climb up."

After this speech, I decided that, fond as I really am of her, I could *not* visit Juliet's tomb in Beechy's society. I gave no hint of my intentions, but after an exquisite hour (which nobody could spoil) in that most adorable of churches, San Zenone, and another in Sant' Anastasia, I slipped away while Beechy and Sir Ralph were picking out the details of St. Peter's life on the panels of a marvellous pilaster.

We had had a cab by the hour; and when they should discover my absence, they would take it for granted that I had got tired and gone home. They would then proceed to carry out their programme of sight-seeing very happily without me, for Beechy amuses Sir Ralph immensely, child as she is, and she makes no secret of taking pleasure in his society. She teases him, and he likes it; he draws her out, and her wit brightens in the process.

I hurried off when their backs were turned. Not far away I found a prowling cab, and told the man to drive me to Juliet's tomb. He stared, as if in surprise, for I suppose girls of our class don't go about much alone in Italian towns; but he condescended to accept me as a fare. However, to show his disapproval maybe, he rattled me through streets old and beautiful, ugly and modern (why should most modern things be ugly, even in Italy?) at a tremendous pace. At last he stopped before a high, blank wall, in a most dismal region, apparently the outskirts of the town. I would hardly believe that he had brought me to the right place, but he reassured me. In the distance another cab was approaching, probably on the same errand. I rang a bell, and a gate was opened by a nice-looking woman, who knew well what I wanted without my telling, and she spoke so clearly that I was able to understand much of what she said. Instead of feeling that the romance of visiting Juliet's burial-place was destroyed by traversing the great open square of the communal stables, where an annual horse show is held, I was conscious of a strange charm in the unsuitable surroundings. It was like coming upon a beautiful white pearl in a battered old oyster-shell, to pass through this narrow gateway at the far end of a dusty square, and find myself face to face with a glimmering tomb in a quiet cloister.

The strong contrast between the sordid exterior and this dainty, hidden interior was nothing less than dramatic. The lights and shadows played softly at hide-and-seek, like dumb children, over the grass, among the pillars of the little cloister, over the tomb itself. I was thankful to be alone, troubled by no fellow-tourists, safe from little Beechy's too comical fancies, free to be as sentimental as I liked. And I liked to be very sentimental indeed.

I stood by the tomb, feeling almost like a mourner, when a voice made me start. "Is it Juliet's spirit?" asked Prince Dalmar-Kalm.

I would rather it had been any one else. "How odd that you should come here!" I exclaimed, while my face must have shown that the surprise was not too pleasant.

"It is not at all odd. You are here," answered the Prince. "You said at *déjeuner* that you were coming, if you had to come alone. *Eh bien?* I saw Miss Beechy and Sir Ralph Moray driving together, deep in Baedeker. My heart told me where you were; and I arrive to find you looking like Juliet come to life again. Perhaps it is so indeed. Perhaps you were Juliet in another incarnation. Yes, I feel sure you were. And I was Romeo."

"I'm sure you were not," I replied; but I could not help laughing at his stagey manner, though I was more annoyed than ever now, and annoyed with myself too. "I particularly wished to be alone here, or I wouldn't have slipped away from Beechy and Sir Ralph, so—"

"And I particularly wished to be alone here with you, or I wouldn't have followed when you *had* slipped away from them," he broke in. "Oh, Miss Destrey—my Madeleine, you must listen to me. There could be no place in the world more appropriate to the tale of a man's love for a woman than this, where a man and woman died for love of one another."

"I thought you called all this 'nonsense'?" I cut him short. "No, Prince, neither here nor anywhere must you speak of love to me, for I don't love you, and never could."

"I know that you mean to shut yourself away from the world," he interrupted me again. "But you shall not. It would be sacrilege. You— the most beautiful, the most womanly girl in the world—to—"

"No more, please!" I cried. "It doesn't matter what my future is to be, for you will not be in it. I—"

"I must be in it. I adore you. I can't give you up. Haven't you seen from the first how I loved you?"

"I *thought* I saw you liked trying to flirt when no one was looking. That sounds rather horrid, but—it's the truth."

"You misjudged me cruelly. Have you no human ambition? I could place you among the highest in any land. With me, your beauty should shine as it never could in your own country. Is it nothing to you that I can make you a Princess?"

"Less than nothing," I answered, "though perhaps it would be pretty of me to thank you for wanting to make me one. So I do thank you; and I'll thank you still more if you will go now, and leave me to my thoughts."

"I cannot go till I have made you understand how I love you, how indispensable you are to me," he persisted. And I grew really angry; for he had no right to persecute me, when I had refused him.

"Very well, then, *I* shall go," I said, and would have passed him, but he seized my hand and held it fast.

It was this moment that Mr. Barrymore chose for paying his respects to Juliet's tomb; and I blushed as I have never blushed in my life, I think—blushed till the tears smarted in my eyes. I was afraid he would believe that I'd been letting Prince Dalmar-Kalm make love to me. But there was nothing to say, unless I were willing to have a scene, and that would have been hateful. Nor was there anything to do except the obvious thing, snatch my hand away; and that might seem to be only because some one had come. But how I should have loved to box the Prince's ears! I never dreamed that I had such a temper. I suppose, though, there must be something of the fishwife in every woman— something that comes boiling up to the surface once in a while, and makes *noblesse oblige* hard to remember.

The one relief to my feelings in this situation was given by my queer little new pet—the wisp of a black doggie I've named Airole, after the village where he grew. I'd brought him into the cloister in my arms hidden under a cape, because he had conceived a suspicious dislike of the cabman. Now he said all the things to the Prince that I wanted to say, and more, and would have snapped, if the Prince had not retired his hand in time.

The process of quieting Airole gave me the chance to make up my mind what I should do next. If I went away, I couldn't prevent Prince Dalmar-Kalm from going with me, and Mr. Barrymore would have a right to imagine that I wished to continue the interrupted scene. If I stayed it was open for him to fancy that I wanted to be with *him*; but between two evils one chooses the less; besides, a nice thing about Mr. Barrymore is that, notwithstanding his good looks and cleverness, he's not conceited—not conceited enough, I sometimes think, for he lets people misunderstand his position and often seems more amused than angry at a snub.

Acting on my quick decision, I said, "Oh, I'm glad you've come. You know so much about Verona. Please talk to me of this place—only don't say it isn't authentic, for that would be a jarring note."

"I'm afraid I don't care enough whether things are authentic or not," he answered, both of us ignoring the Prince. "You know, in my country, legend and history are a good deal mixed, which makes for romance. Besides, I'm inclined to believe in stories that have been handed down from generation to generation—told by grandfathers to their grandchildren, and so on through the centuries till they've reached us. When they're investigated by the cold light of reason, at least they can seldom be disproved."

I agreed, and the conversation went on, deliberately excluding the Prince. Each minute I said to myself, "Surely he'll go." But he did not. He stayed while Mr. Barrymore and I discussed the genius of Shakspere, chiming in now and then as if nothing had happened, and remaining until we were ready to go.

At the cab there was another crisis. I hadn't yet entirely realized the Prince's stupendous capacity for what Beechy would put into one short, sharp word "Cheek." But I fully appreciated it when he calmly manifested his intention of getting into my cab, as if we had come together.

Something had to be done instantly, or it would be too late.

Leaning from my seat so that the Prince had to wait with his foot on the step, I exclaimed, "Oh! Mr. Barrymore, won't you let me give you a lift? Prince Dalmar-Kalm has his own cab, and I'm alone in this."

"Thanks very much, I shall be delighted," said the Chauffeulier.

Even the Prince's audacity wasn't equal to the situation created by these tactics. He retired, hat in hand, looking so furious that I could hardly help laughing. Mr. Barrymore got in beside me, and we drove off leaving the Prince with nobody but his own cabman to vent his rage on.

I rather hoped, for a minute, that Mr. Barrymore would say something which would give me the chance for a vague word or two of explanation; but he didn't. He simply talked of indifferent things, telling me how the work on the car was finished, and how he had had time after all to wander among his favourite bits of Verona. And then, in a flash of understanding, I saw how much more tactful and manly it was in him not to mention the Prince.

XIX

A CHAPTER OF PALACES AND PRINCES

What a pity clocks don't realize the interesting work they do in the making of history, as they go on ticking out moments which never before have been and never will be again! It would be such a reward for their patience; and I should like my watch to know how often I've thanked it lately for the splendid moments it has given me.

Some of those I had in Verona (no thanks to the Prince!) have really helped to develop my soul, and it used to need developing badly, poor dear; I see that now, though I didn't then. I never thought much about the development of souls, except that one must try hard to be good and do one's duty. But now I begin dimly to see many things, as if I caught glimpses of them, far away, and high up on some of the snowy mountain-tops we pass.

Must one live through several incarnations, I wonder, for true development? Are some people great-minded because they have gone through many such phases, and are the wondrous geniuses of the world — such as Shakspere — the most developed of all? Then the poor commonplace or stupid people, who never have any real thoughts of their own, are they the undeveloped souls who haven't had their chance yet? If they are, how kind those who have gone further ought to be to them, and what generous allowances they ought to make, instead of being impatient, and pleased with themselves because they are cleverer.

I think I should like to send whole colonies of those poor "beginners" to Italy to live for a while, because it might give them a step up for their next phase. As for myself, I'm going further every day, almost as fast, I hope, as the automobile goes.

"She," as the Chauffeulier affectionately calls her, went especially fast and well the morning we swept out of Verona. There was an entrancing smell of Italy in the air. There is no other way to describe it—it is that and nothing else

. As long as Verona was still within sight, I kept looking back, just as you drink something delicious down to the last drop, when you know there can be no dregs. Only to see how the town lay at the foot of the mountains of the north, was to understand its powers of defence, and its importance to the dynasties and princes of the past. With Mr. Barrymore's help, I could trace one line of fortification after another, from the earliest Roman, through Charlemagne and the Scaligers, down to the modern Austrian.

No wonder that Verona was the first halting-place for the tribes of Germans, pouring down from their cold forests in the north to cross the Alps and rejoice in the sunshine of Italy! For Verona's nearness to the north and her striking difference to the north impressed me sharply, as a black line of shadow is cut out by the sun. Up a gap in the dark barrier of mountains I gazed where Mr. Barrymore pointed, towards the great Brenner Pass, leading straight to Innsbruck through Tyrol. How close the northern nations lay, yet in the warm Italian brightness how far away they seemed.

But soon Verona disappeared, and we were speeding along a level road with far-off purple peaks upon our left, and away in front some floating blue shapes which it thrilled me to hear were actually the Euganean Hills. The Chauffeulier set them to music by quoting from Shelley's "Lines Written in Dejection in the Euganean Hills" —a sweet old-fashioned title of other days, and words so beautiful that for a moment I was depressed in sympathy—though I couldn't help feeling that I should be happy in the Euganean Hills. They called across the plain with siren voices, asking me to come and explore their fastnesses of blue and gold, but Aunt Kathryn couldn't understand why. "They're not half so imposing as lots of mountains we've passed," she said. "And anyway, I think the beauty of mountains is overestimated. What are they to admire so much, anyhow, when you think of it, more than flat places? They are only great lumps at best."

"Well," replied Sir Ralph, "if it comes to that, what's the sea but a big wet thing?"

"And what are people but a kind of superior ant, and the grandest palaces but big anthills?" Beechy chimed in. "I've often thought, supposing there were—well, Things, between gods and men, living here somewhere, invisible to us as we are to lots of little creatures, what kind of an idea *would* They get of us and our ways? They'd be always spying on us, of course, and making scientific observations, as we do on insects. I used to believe in Them, and be awfully afraid, when I was younger, because I used to think all the accidents and bad things that happened might be due to Their experiments. You see They'd be wondering why we did certain things; why lots of us all run to one place—like Venice, or any show city—instead of going to another nest of anthills; or why we all crowded into one anthill (like a church or theatre) at a particular time. So a theatre-fire would be when They'd touched the anthill with one of their cigars, to make the ants run out. Or a volcano would have an eruption because They'd poked the mountain with a great pin to see what would happen. Or when we're cut or hurt in any way, it's because They've marked us to know one from the other, as we run about. I do hope They're not thinking about *us* now, or They'll drop something and smash the automobile."

"Oh, don't, Beechy! You make my blood run cold!" cried Aunt Kathryn. "Do let's talk of something else quickly. How gracefully the vines are trained here, draped along those rows of trees in the meadows. It's much prettier than ordinary vineyards. You might imagine fairies playing tag under these arbours."

"Or fauns chasing nymphs," said Sir Ralph. "No doubt they did a few years ago and caught them too."

"I'm glad they don't now," replied Aunt Kathryn, "or this would be no fit place for ladies to motor."

But I wasn't glad, for the whole country was one wide background for a pre-Raphaelite picture, and the mountains to which Aunt Kathryn had applied so insulting a simile were even grander in size and nobler in shape than before. We had seen many old châteaux (though never a surfeit), but the best of all had been reserved for to-day. Far away on our left, as we drove towards Padua, it rose above the little town that crawled to the foot of the castle's hill to beg protection; and it was exactly like a city painted by Mantegna or Carpaccio, Mr. Barrymore said. Up the hill ran the noblest and biggest wall that an Old Master's imagination could have conceived. Many men might walk on it abreast; and at every few yards it bristled with sturdy watch-towers, not ruined, but looking as ready to defy the enemy to-day as they were six hundred years ago. The culmination was the castle itself, so magnificently proportioned, so worthily proud of its place, that it seemed as if the spirit of the Middle Ages were there embodied, gazing down in haughty resignation upon a new world it did not even wish to understand.

The name of the castle was Soave; but when I heard that nothing startling enough to please me had happened there, I wouldn't know its history, for my fancy was equal to inventing one more thrilling. There was plentiful sensation, though, in the stories the Chauffeulier could tell of Napoleon's battles and adventures in this neighbourhood. I listened to them eagerly, especially to that which covered his falling into a marsh while fighting the Austrians, and standing there, unable to get out, while the battle of Arcole raged around him. We were at the point of the rescue and the victory of the French, when we arrived at another gateway, another octroi, another city, to enter which was like driving straight into an old, old picture

. In a long street of palaces, all with an elusive family resemblance to one another, we paused for consultation. This was Vicenza, the birthplace and beloved town of Palladio; these palaces with fronts crusted with bas relief; these Corinthian pillars, these Arabesque balconies, these porticoes that might have been stolen from Greek temples, all had been designed by Palladio the Great. And the beautiful buildings seemed to say pensively, like lovely court ladies whose day is past, "We are not what we were. Time has changed and broken us, it is true; but even so we are worth seeing."

It was that view which our Chauffeulier urged, but Aunt Kathryn was for going on without a stop, until Sir Ralph said, "It's not patriotic of you to pass by. Palladio built your Capitol at Washington, and all the fine old colonial houses you admire so much in the East."

"Dear me, did he?" exclaimed Aunt Kathryn. "Why, I never heard of him."

"Moray doesn't mean his words to be taken undiluted," said Mr. Barrymore. "If it hadn't been for Palladio, there would have been no Inigo Jones and no Christopher Wren, therefore if you'd had a Capitol at all, it wouldn't be what it is now. And to understand the colonial architecture of America, you have to go back to Palladio."

"Well, here we are at him," sighed Aunt Kathryn. "But I hope we won't have to get *out*?"

Mr. Barrymore laughed. "The Middle Ages revisited, *en automobile*! However, I'll do my best as showman in the circumstances."

So he drove us into a splendid square, where Palladio was at his grandest with characteristic façades, galleries, and stately colonnades. Then, slowly, through the street of palaces and out into the open country once more—a rich country of grain-fields (looking always as if an unseen hand softly stroked their silver hair) and of hills swelling into a mountainous horizon. There was a bright little flower-bordered canal too, and I've grown fond of canals since the neighbourhood of Milan, finding them as companionable as rivers, if more tame. Indeed, they seem like rivers that have gone to live in town, where they've learned to be a bit stilted and mechanical in manner.

The farmhouses, standing but a short distance back from the level of the road, were manorial in a queer way; two or three of them, exquisite old things, their great roofed balconies covered with ivy and blossoming creepers. The women we met were pretty, too—so pretty often that, as Sir Ralph said, it wouldn't have been safe for them to walk out in the feudal ages, as they would promptly have been kidnapped by the nearest seignior. We might have guessed that we were not far out from Venice by the gorgeous Titian hair of the peasant children playing by the wayside, or a copper coil twisted above a girl's dark eyes.

"How long a time shall we spend in Padua, Countess?" asked the Chauffeulier as we came within sight of a gateway, some domes and campanili.

"Oh, don't let's make up our mind till we get there," replied Aunt Kathryn comfortably.

"But we are there," said he. "In another minute the little men of the *dazio* will be tapping our bags as a doctor taps his patient's lungs."

Padua! Each time that we actually arrived in one of these wonderful old places, it was an electric shock for me. I had to shake myself, mentally, to make it seem true. But if it was like a dream to enter the place of Petruchio's love story, what would it be by-and-by—oh, a very quick-coming by-and-by—to see Venice? I hardly dared let my thoughts go on to that moment for fear they should get lost in it, and refuse to come back. Sufficient for the day was the Padua thereof.

Not so beautiful as Verona, still the learned and dignified old city had a curiously individual charm of its own, which I felt instantly. I loved the painted palaces, especially those where most of the paint had worn off, leaving but a lovely face, or some folds of a velvet robe, or a cardinal's hat to hint its story to the imagination. The old arcaded streets were asleep, and grass sprouted among the cobbles. Where they followed the river we had glimpses of gardens and arbours backed with roses, or an almond tree—like a rosy bride leaning on a soldier-lover's neck—peeped at us, side by side with a dark ilex, over a high brick wall.

"How long *ought* we to stay in Padua?" Aunt Kathryn deigned to ask, as if in delayed answer to the Chauffeulier's question, when he helped her out of the car at the Stella d'Oro, where we were to lunch.

"A week," said Mr. Barrymore, his eyes twinkling.

Her face fell, and he took pity.

"If we weren't motor maniacs," he went on. "In that case we would have come here on a solemn pilgrimage to do full justice to the adorable Giotto, to the two best churches—not to be surpassed anywhere—and the dozen and one other things worth seeing. But as

236

we are mad we shall be able to 'do' Padua, and satisfy our consciences though not our hearts, in three hours. My one consolation in this deplorable course, lies in the thought that it will make it possible to give you your first sight of Venice between sunset and moonrise."

Beechy clapped her hands, and my heart gave a throb. Somehow, my eyes happened to meet Mr. Barrymore's. But I must not get into the habit of letting them do that, when I'm feeling anything deeply. I can't think why it seems so natural to turn to him, as if I'd known him always; but then we have *all* got to be great friends on this trip, and know each other better than if we'd been meeting in an ordinary way for a year. All except the Prince. I leave him out of that statement, as I would leave him out of everything concerning me nearly, if I could. I believe that *none* of us know him, or what is in his mind. But sometimes there's a look in his eyes if one glances up suddenly, which would almost frighten one, if it were not silly and melodramatic. That is the only way in which he has troubled me since the horrid little incident at Juliet's tomb — with these occasional, strange looks; and as he wrote me a note of apology for his bad conduct then, I ought to forgive and forget.

The hotel where we lunched was not in a quaint riverside street, but in a square so modern it was hard to realize for the moment that we were in the oldest city of Northern Italy, dating from before Roman days. However, the Stella d'Oro was old enough to satisfy us, and I should have been delighted with the nice Italian dishes Mr. Barrymore knew so well how to order, if I hadn't been longing to rush off with a bit of bread in my hand, not to waste a Paduan moment on so dull a deed as eating.

It was only twelve when we arrived, and before one we were out of the huge, cool dining-room, and in the May sunlight again. The Prince was with us; had been just ahead of us, or just behind us, all through the journey from Verona. But I thought by keeping close to Aunt Kathryn and Beechy there would be no danger that he would trouble me. Unfortunately, the pattern of our progress arranged itself a little differently from my plan.

All was simple enough in the churches, which we visited first, not to give them time to close up for their afternoon siesta. Mr. Barrymore was of the party, and we all listened to him—the Prince because he must, we others because we wished—while he ransacked his memory for bits of Paduan history, legend or romance. He showed us the Giottos (which he had done well to call adorable) at the Madonna of the Arena; he took us to pay our respects to St. Anthony of Padua (that dear, obliging Saint who gives himself so much trouble over the lost property of perfect strangers) in his extraordinary and well-deserved Basilica of bubbly domes and lovely cloisters. He guided us to Santa Giustina, where I would stop at the top of the steps, to pet two glorious old red marble beasts which had crouched there for four centuries. One of them—the redder of the two—had been all that time wrestling with an infinitesimal St. George whom he ought to have polished off in a few hours; while the other—the one with an unspeakable beard under his chin and teeth like the gearing of our automobile—had been engaged for the same period in eating a poor little curly lion.

The inside of the church—too strongly recommended by Baedeker to commend itself to me—made me feel as if I had eaten a lemon water-ice before dinner, on a freezing cold day; and it was there that the Chauffeulier departed to get ready the motor-car. There it was, too, that the pattern disarranged itself.

When we had finished looking at a splendid Paolo Veronese, we hurried out into the Prato della Valle (which has changed its name to something else not half so pretty, though more patriotic), and Sir Ralph took Beechy away, so that Aunt Kathryn and I were left to the Prince. He hardly talked to her at all, which hurt her feelings so much that she turned suddenly round, and said she must speak to Beechy.

I could have cried, for the piazza was so beautiful that I wanted some one congenial with me, to whom I could exclaim about it. It was girdled by a belt of clear water, with four stone bridges and a double wall on which stood a goodly company of noble gentlemen. There was the history of Padua's greatness perpetuated in marble— charming personages, one and all, if you could believe their statues, and it would have seemed treacherous not to. Each stood to be admired or revered in the attitude most expressive of his profession: Galileo pointing up, graceful, spiritual, enthusiastic; a famous bishop blessing his flock; some great poet dreaming over a book—his own, perhaps, just finished; and so on, all along the happy circle of writers, priests, scientists, soldiers, artists. I felt as if I wanted to know them— those faithful friends of all who love greatness, resting now in each others' excellent society, their sole reflection those in the watery mirror.

But Prince Dalmar-Kalm thought himself of importance even in this king's garden. "Did you get my letter?" he asked. "And do you forgive me?" he said. "And will you trust me, and not be unkind, now that I've promised to think of you only as a friend?" he persisted.

I didn't see why he should look upon me even as a friend; but a cat may look at a king, if it doesn't fly up and scratch; so why not a prince at an American girl? To save argument and not to be unchristian, I pledged myself to some kind of superficial compact almost before I knew. When it was done, it would have been too complicated to undo again; and so I let it go.

XX

A CHAPTER IN FAIRYLAND

"Nobody can ever quite know Venice who goes by rail from Padua," said the Chauffeulier to me, when we had started in the car. "The sixteen miles of road between the two places is a link in Venetian history, and you'll understand what I mean without any explanation as you pass along."

This made me post my wits at the windows of my eyes, and tell them not to dare sleep for an instant, lest I should disappoint expectations. But, after all, the meaning I had to understand was not subtle, though it was interesting.

The way was practically one long street of time-worn palaces and handsome villas which had once been the summer retreats of the rich Venetians; and I guessed it without being told. I guessed, too, that the owners came no more or seldom; that they were not so rich as they had been, or that, because of railways and automobiles, it was easier and more amusing to go further afield. But what I didn't know without telling was that the proprietors had been accustomed, in the good old leisurely days, to step into their gondolas in front of their own palaces in Venice and come up the Brenta to their summer homes without setting foot to ground.

If I hadn't been told, too, that the Brenta was a river big in Venetian history if not in size, I should have taken it for one of my favourite canals, with its slow traffic of lazy barges, and its hundred canals crossing it with long green arms that stretched north and south to the horizon. But at Stra I must have respected it in any case; and it was near Stra, also, that we passed the most important palace of any on that strange, flat road. The very garden wall told that here was a house which must have loomed large in historic eyes, and through magnificent gateways we caught flashing glimpses of a noble building in a neglected park.

"It belonged to the Pisani, a famous family of Venice," said the Chauffeulier as we sailed by. "But Napoleon took it—as he took so many other good things in this part of the world—and gave it to his stepson Eugène Beauharnais."

"I've never thought about Napoleon in connection with Venice, somehow," I said.

"But you will, when your gondola takes you under the huge palace where he lived," he answered.

"Talking of gondolas, I forgot to tell you what a nice plan the Prince has for us," said Aunt Kathryn, with the air of breaking news. "As soon as I mentioned at what time you had arranged to leave Padua, he said he would telegraph to some dear friends of his at Venice, the Conte and Contessa Corramini, to send their beautiful gondola to meet us at Mestre (wherever that is) so that we needn't go into Venice by train across the bridge. Isn't that lovely of him?"

No one would have answered if it hadn't been for Mr. Barrymore. He said that it was a very good plan indeed, and would be pleasanter for us than the one he had made, which he'd meant for a surprise. He had telegraphed from Padua to the Hotel Britannia, where we would stay, ordering gondolas to the tram-way station in Mestre to save our sneaking into Venice by the back-door. Now those gondolas would do very well for our luggage, while the party of five made the journey more luxuriously.

"Party of six, you mean, unless the Prince has had an accident," amended Beechy.

"No; for I shan't be with you. I must drive the car to the garage at Mestre, and see that she's all right. Moray'll be with you to arrange everything at the Britannia, which you'll find one of the nicest places in the world, and I'll come when I can. Now, here's the turning for Mestre, and you must look for something interesting on the sky-line to the right, before long."

I couldn't help being disappointed, because I'd wanted the Chauffeulier to be with us when I saw Venice first; but I couldn't say that; and I'm afraid he thought, as everybody was silent, that nobody cared.

There was nothing to show the turning to Mestre, except a small tablet that we might easily have missed; and the road was laughably narrow, running along a causeway with a deep ditch on either hand. Aunt Kathryn was so afraid that a horse would come round one of the sharp bends walking on its hind legs, that she was miserable, but I trusted Mr. Barrymore and enjoyed the country—real country now, with no more palaces, villas, or beautiful arcaded farmhouses.

The distance was hidden by long, waving grasses, over which the blue line of the Corinthian Alps seemed to hover like a cloud. There was a pungent smell of salt and of seaweed in the air, that meant the nearness of the lagoon—and Venice. Then, suddenly, the "something" Mr. Barrymore had told us to look for, grew out of the horizon—dim and mysterious, yet not to be mistaken; hyacinth-blue streaks that were pinnacles and campanili, bubbles that were domes, floating between the gold of the sunset and the grey-green of the tall grass, for no water was visible yet.

"Venice!" I whispered; but though Beechy and Aunt Kathryn each cried: "Oh, there it is! *I* saw it first!" they were so absorbed in a discussion as to what the Prince's friends ought to be called, and they soon lost interest in the vision.

"Conte! It's like Condy's Fluid!" said Beechy. "I won't call him 'Conte.' I should laugh in his face. If plain Count isn't good enough for him, and Countess for her, I shall just say 'You'—so there!"

Soon we saw a great star-shaped fortress as we ran into a town, which was Mestre; and at the same time we lost shadow-Venice. Passing a charming villa set back behind an avenue of cypresses and plane trees that gave an effect of dappling moonlight even in full day, some one in the tall gateway waved his hand.

"By Jove, it's Leo Bari, the artist!" exclaimed Sir Ralph. "I forgot his people lived here. I know him well; he comes to the Riviera to paint. Do slow down, Terry."

So "Terry" slowed down, and a handsome, slim young man ran up, greeting Sir Ralph gaily in English. He was introduced to us, and his sister, a lovely Italian girl with Titian hair, was invited to leave the becoming background of the gateway to make our acquaintance.

They were interested in the details of our tour, especially when they heard that, after a week in Venice, we were going into Dalmatia.

"Why, I'm going down to Ragusa to paint," said he. "I've been before, but this time I take my sister Beatrice. She paints too. We go by the Austrian Lloyd to-morrow. Perhaps we see you there?"

"Have you ever been down as far as Cattaro?" asked Aunt Kathryn, from whose tongue the names of Dalmatian towns fall trippingly, since she "acquired" a castle and a title there.

"Oh, yes, and to Montenegro," replied the artist.

"And do you remember the houses of the neighbourhood?" went on Aunt Kathryn.

"It is already but two years I was there, so a house would have to be young for me not to remember," replied the young man, unconscious of the funny little twist of his English.

"I am thinking of a very old house; Slosh—er—the Castle of Hrvoya. Have you seen it?"

"Ah, that old ruin!" exclaimed the artist. "I seen it, yes. But there is not more much Schloss Hrvoya to see, only the rock for it to stand."

Poor Aunt Kathryn! I was sorry for her. But she bore the blow well, and, after all, it's the title, not the castle for which she cares most—that, and the right to smear everything with crowns.

"Perhaps I'll ask you to paint Hrvoya for me some day," she said. But afterwards, when we had bidden the handsome brother and sister *au revoir*, she remarked that she was afraid Mr. Bari hadn't an artistic eye.

The good-byes said, we swept through the picturesque town to make up for lost time, and presently encountered a little electric tram running seaward on a causeway. We followed over a grass-grown road, and suddenly found Venice again, so near that we could actually distinguish one building from another. Beyond a broad stretch of water the dream city floated on the sea.

"Look; I did this for *you*, so that you would go into Venice in a way worthy of yourself," the Prince murmured in my ear, when the car had stopped, joining his which was waiting. He waved his hand towards a wonderful gondola, with a gesture such as Aladdin's Genie might have used to indicate the magic palace. The glossy black coat of the swan-like thing brought out the full value of the rich gold ornaments. A long piece of drapery trailed into the water behind, and two gondoliers, like bronze statues dressed in dark blue, crimson, and white, stood up tall and erect against a background of golden sea and sky.

They helped us in, hat in hand; and not the Chauffeulier's absence nor the Prince's presence could spoil for me the experience that followed.

Sunk deep in springy cushions, I half sat, half lay, while the bronze statues swayed against the gold, softly plying their long oars, and wafting me—*me*—to Venice.

I felt as if I were moving from the wings of a vast theatre onto the stage to play a heroine's part. Evening bells, chanting a paen to the sunset, floated across the wide water faint as spirit-chimes, and they were the *leitmotif* for my entrance.

"What a shame to be in motoring things!" I said to Beechy. "Women should have special gondola dresses; I see that already—a different one each day. I should like to have a deep crimson gown and a pale green one—lilac too, perhaps, and sunrise-pink, all made picturesquely, not in any stiff modern way."

"The costume of your Sisterhood would be pretty in a gondola," Beechy answered. And again that coldness fell upon me which I always feel at a reminder, intentional or unintentional, of the future. But the chill was gone in a moment—lost in the luminous air, which had a strange brilliancy, as if reflected from a stupendous mirror. I had never seen anything even remotely resembling it before. It was as though we were living inside a great opal, like flies in amber. And it seemed that in a world so wonderful everything one did, or looked, or thought, ought to be wonderful too, lest it should be out of tune with all surrounding beauty.

Sea and sky were of one colour, except that the sea appeared to be on fire underneath its glassy surface. The violet sky was strewn with blown rose-petals and golden feathers; the tiny waves were of violet ruffled with rose and gold, and spattered with jewelled sparks which might be flashes from a Doge's vanished ring.

In the distance, sails of big ships were beaten into gold leaf by the sinking sun; and nearer, there were other sails bright as flowers—a sea picture-gallery of Madonnas, of arrow-wounded hearts, of martyred saints, or bright-robed earthly ladies.

We were rowing straight into the sunset, straight into fairy-land, and I knew it; but—what would happen when the rose-and-golden glory had swallowed us up?

The sparkle of the water and air got into my blood, and I felt that it must be sparkling too, like champagne. I was more alive than I had ever been when I was on earth; for of course this was not earth—this Venice to which I was going.

No other road but this water-road could have consoled me for the thought that there would be no more motoring for a week. And clearly it was a road of which it was necessary for the gondoliers to know every oar-length; for it was defined by stakes, standing up out of the lagoon singly, or gathered into clusters like giant bunches of asparagus.

Turning my back to the arched railway bridge, which accompanied us too far, I looked only at sky and water, and at Venice rising from the sea.

The tide was running out, the Prince said (among other chatterings, while I wished everybody woven in a magic spell of silence) and the gondola made swift progress, rocking lightly like a shell, over the bright ripples of the lagoon.

The nearer we drew to Venice the more like a vision of enchantment did the city seem. Not a sound came to us, for the music of the bells had died. All was still as in a dream—for in dreams, does one ever hear a sound? I think I never have. And now the gold had faded from the clouds, leaving them pink and violet, transparent as gauze, through which the rising moon sifted silver dust. How could the others talk? I did not understand.

Aunt Kathryn was saying, "If I hire a gondolier, I want to get a singer." As if he were a sewing-machine, or a canary-bird! And Beechy was complaining that she felt "very funny;" she believed the motion of the gondola was making her seasick, just as she used to be in her cradle, when she was too young to protest except by a howl.

It was a relief to my feelings when we turned out of the wide lagoon into a canal, for then they did at least speak of the scene around them, asking questions about the tall palaces that walled us in; who lived here; who lived there; what was the name or history of that?

The odour of seaweed was more pungent, and there was a smell of water mingling with it too; something like fresh cucumbers, and the roots of flowers when they have just been pulled out of the earth. I could not have believed that water could have such clearness and at the same time hold so many colours, as the water in this, my first canal of Venice. It was like a greenish mirror, full of lights, and wavering reflected tints from the crumbling palaces whose old bricks, mellow pink, gold, and purple, showed like veins through the skin of peeling stucco. Down underneath the shining mirror, one could see the old marble steps, leading up to the shut mystery of water gates. There were shimmering gleams of pearly white and ivory yellow, under beardy trails of moss old as the marble out of which it grew. And over high walls, delicate branches of acacia and tamarisk beckoned us, above low-hung drapery of wistaria, that dropped purple tassels to the lapping water's edge.

So we wound through one narrow, palace-walled Rio after another, until Venice began to seem like a jewelled net, with its carved precious stones intricately strung on threads of silver; and then suddenly, to my surprise, we burst into a great canal.

I saw a bridge, which I knew from many pictures must be the Rialto, but there was no disappointment, no flatness in the impression of having seen this all before, for not the greatest genius who ever lived could paint Venice at her every day best. Palace after palace; and by-and-by a church with a front carved in ivory by the growing moonlight, thrown up against a background of rose.

"Palladio, it must be!" I cried.

"Yes; it's San Georgio Maggiore, Terry Barrymore's favourite church in Venice," said Sir Ralph, who had been almost as silent as I. "And here we are at the Hotel Britannia."

"Why, it has a garden!" exclaimed Aunt Kathryn. "I never thought of a garden in Venice."

"There are several of the loveliest in Italy," replied Sir Ralph. "But the Britannia's the only hotel that has one."

"My friend's palazzo has a courtyard garden with a wonderful old marble well-head, and beautiful statues," said the Prince. "He and his wife are coming to call on you to-morrow, and you will have the opportunity of thanking them for their gondola. Also, they will probably invite you to leave the hotel, and visit them during the rest of your stay, as they are very hospitable."

"I'll wager you won't want to leave the Britannia, once you are settled there," said Sir Ralph quickly. "It's the most comfortable hotel in Venice, and Terry and I have wired for rooms with balconies overlooking the Grand Canal, and the garden. There isn't a palace going that I would forsake the Britannia for."

By this time the gondola had slipped between some tall red posts, and brought us to the steps of the hotel. I was glad that they were marble steps and that the house had once been a palace, otherwise I should not have felt I was making the most of Venice.

If I live to be a hundred (one of the Sisters is close on eighty) I shall never forget that first night in the City of the Sea

.

It was good to see Mr. Barrymore back again for dinner in the big red and gold, brightly frescoed dining-room; and it was he who suggested that we should have coffee in the garden, at a table on a balcony built over the water, and then go out in gondolas.

We hired three; and as there are only two absolutely delightful seats in a gondola, I was trembling lest the Prince should fall to my unlucky lot, when Aunt Kathryn called to him, "Oh, do sit with me, please. I want to ask about your friends who are coming to see us." So of course he went to her, and Sir Ralph jumped in with Beechy; therefore the Chauffeulier was obliged to be nice to me, whether he liked or not. We all kept close together, and soon the three gondolas, following many others, grouped round a lighted music-barge like a pyramid of illuminated fruit floating on the canal.

Either the voices were sweet, or they had the effect of being sweet in the moonlight on the water; but the airs they sang got strangely tangled with the songs in other barges, so that I longed to unwind one skein of tunes from another, and wasn't sorry to steal away into the silence at last

We were not the only ones who flitted. The black forms of gondolas moved soundlessly hither and thither on the surface of the dark lagoon, their single lights like stars in the blue darkness.

Far away twinkled the lamps of the Lido, where Byron and Shelley used to ride on the lonely sands. Near-by, on the Piazzetta where the twin columns towered against the silver sky, white bunches of lights glimmered like magic night-blooming flowers, with bright roots trailing deep down into the river.

We talked of the countless great ones of the world who had lived and died in Venice, and loved it well; of Byron, who slept in Marino Faliero's dreadful cell before he wrote his tragedy; of Browning, whose funeral had passed in solemn state of gondolas down the Grand Canal; of Wagner, who found inspiration in this sea and sky, and died looking upon them from his window in the Palazzo Vendramin. But through our talk I could hear Aunt Kathryn in her gondola close by, saying how like the Doge's palace was to a big bird-cage she once had; and the Prince was continually turning his head to see if we were near, which was disturbing. We had nothing to say that all the world might not have heard, yet instinctively we spoke almost in whispers, the Chauffeulier and I, not to miss a gurgle of the water nor the dip of an oar, which in the soft darkness made the light flutter of a bird bathing.

I remembered suddenly how Sir Ralph had said one day, "You'll like Terry in Venice." I did like Terry in Venice; and I liked him better than ever at the moment of our return to the hotel, for there began a little adventure of which he became the hero.

As I stepped out of the gondola there was a flash and a splash. "Oh my gold bag!" I exclaimed. "Your present, Aunt Kathryn. It's in the canal; I shall never see it again."

"Yes, you will," said Mr. Barrymore. "I—"

"If there was much money in it, you had better have a professional diver come early to-morrow morning from the Arsenal," the Prince broke in.

"I know an amateur diver who will get back the bag to-night—now, within the next half-hour I hope," went on the Chauffeulier.

"Indeed? Where do you propose to find him at this time?" asked the Prince.

"I shall find him inside the hotel, and have him out here, ready for work in ten minutes," said Mr. Barrymore.

"What fun!" exclaimed Beechy. "We'll wait here in the moonlight and see him dive. It will be lovely."

Mr. Barrymore was gone before she finished.

It was nearly eleven o'clock. The music-barges had gone; the hotel garden was deserted, and scarcely a moving star of light glided over the canal. Our three gondolas, drawn up like carriages at the marble steps of the Britannia, where the water lapped and gurgled, awaited the great event. The Prince pooh-poohed the idea that Mr. Barrymore could find a diver, or that, if he did, the bag could be retrieved in such an amateurish way. But I had learned that when our

Chauffeulier said a thing could be done, it *would* be done, and I confidently expected to see him returning accompanied by some obviously aquatic creature.

What I did see however, was a great surprise. Something moved in the garden, under the curtain of creepers that draped the nearest overhanging balcony. Then a tall, marble statue, "come alive," vaulted over the iron railing and dropped into the lagoon.

It didn't seem at all strange that a marble statue should "come alive" in Venice; but what did seem odd was that it should exactly resemble Mr. Barrymore, feature for feature, inch for inch.

"Hullo, Terry, I didn't know you meant to do that!" exclaimed Sir Ralph. "You *are* a lightning change artist."

For it was the Chauffeulier, in a bathing suit which he must have hurriedly borrowed from one of the landlord's tall young sons, and he was swimming by the side of my gondola.

"I meant nothing else," laughed the statue in the water, the moon shining into his eyes and on his noble white throat as he swam. "Now, Miss Destrey, show me exactly how you stood when you dropped your bag, and I think I can promise that you shall have it again in a few minutes."

"If I'd dreamed of this I wouldn't have let you do it," I said.

"Why not? I'm awfully happy, and the water feels like warm silk. Is this where you dropped it? Look out for a little splash, please. I'm going down."

With that he disappeared under the canal, and stayed down so long that I began to be frightened. It seemed impossible that any human being could hold his breath for so many minutes; but just as my anxiety reached boiling point, up he came, dripping, laughing, his short hair in wet rings on his forehead, and in his hand, triumphantly held up, the gold bag.

"I knew where to grope for it, and I felt it almost the first thing," he said. "Please forgive my wet fingers."

"Why, there's something red on the gold. It's blood!" I stammered, forgetting to thank him.

"Is there? What a bore! But it's nothing. I grazed the skin of my hands a little, grubbing about among the stones down there, that's all."

"It's a great deal," I said. "I can't bear to think you've been hurt for me."

"Why, I don't even feel it," said the Chauffeulier. "It's the bag that suffers. But you can have it washed."

Yes, I could have it washed. Yet, somehow, it would seem almost sacrilegious. I made up my mind without saying a word, that I would not have the bag washed. I would keep it exactly as it was, put sacredly away in some box, in memory of this night.

XXI

A CHAPTER OF STRANGE SPELLS

"Never since Anne Boleyn has a woman so lost her head over a man with a title as Mamma over Prince Dalmar-Kalm," said Beechy, after our week at Venice was half spent. And I wished that, in fair exchange, he would lose his over Aunt Kathryn instead of wasting time on me, and casting his shadow on beautiful days.

Roses and lilies appeared on my writing-desk; they were from him. Specimens of Venetian sweets (crystallized fruits stuck on sticks, like fat martyrs) adorned large platters on the table by the window — gifts from the Prince. If I admired the little gargoylish sea-horses, or the foolish shell ornaments at the Lido, I was sure to find some when I came home. And the man hinted in whispers that the attentions of the Comte and Contessa were for me.

All this was annoying though he put it on the grounds of friendship; and I didn't like the Corraminis, although their influence opened doors that would otherwise have been closed. Through them we saw the Comte de Bardi's wonderful Japanese collection of the Palazzo Vendramin, the finest in the world; through them we had glimpses of the treasures in more than one old palace; they gave us a picnic dinner in their lighted gondola, on the lagoon, with many elaborate courses cooked in chafing-dishes, which the gondoliers served. They took us to Chioggia on their steam yacht which—it seemed—they must let half the year to afford the use of it the other half.

The "County" (as Aunt Kathryn pronounces him) must have been handsome before his good looks were ravaged by smallpox. As it is, Beechy compares his dark face to a "plum cake, from which somebody has picked out all the plums;" and the black eyes, deep set in this scarred mask, gaze out of it with sinister effect. Yet his manner is perfect, witty, and gracious. He speaks English fluently, and might be of any age between thirty-five and fifty. As for the Contessa, she has the profile of a Boadicea (with which I could never feel thoroughly at home if it were mine) and the walk of a bewitched table, so stout she is, and so square. Her principal efforts at conversation with me were in praise of Prince Dalmar-Kalm, so I scarcely appreciated them. Indeed, the Corraminis repelled me, and I was glad to spare all their distinguished society to Aunt Kathryn.

Each day in Venice (not counting the hours spent with them and the Prince) was more wonderful, it seemed, than the day before.

First among my pictures was San Marco, which I went out to see alone early in the morning, but met Mr. Barrymore as I inquired my way. I could have wished for that, though I wouldn't have dreamed of asking him to take me. As we went through the narrow streets of charming shops, we played at not thinking of what was to come. Then, Mr. Barrymore said suddenly, "Now you may look." So I did look, and there it was, the wonder of wonders, more like a stupendous crown of jewels than a church. Like a queen's diadem, it gleamed in the grey-white Piazza, under the burning azure dome of the sky.

"Oh, we've found the key of the rainbow, and come close to it!" I cried. "What a marvel! Can human beings really have made it, or did it make itself as gems form in the rocks, and coral under the sea?"

"The cornice does look as if it were the spray of the sea, tossing up precious stones from buried treasures beneath the waves," he answered. "But you're right. We've got the key of the rainbow, and we can go in."

I walked beside him, awe-struck, as if I were passing under a spell. There could be no other building so beautiful in the world, and it was harder than ever to realize that man had created it. The golden mosaic of the domed roof, arching above the purple-brown of the alabaster walls, was like sunrise boiling over the massed clouds of a dark horizon. Light seemed generated by the glitter of that mosaic; and the small white windows of the dome gained such luminous blues and pale gold glints, from sky without and opal gleams within, that they were changed to stars. The pavement was opaline, too, with a thousand elusive tints and jewelled colours, waving like the sea. It was all I could do not to touch Mr. Barrymore's arm or hand for sympathy.

We didn't speak as we passed out. I was almost glad when the spell was broken by the striking of the great, blue clock opposite San Marco, and the slow procession of the life-size mechanical figures which only open their secret door on fête days, such as this chanced to be.

Watching the stiff saints go through their genuflexions put me in a good mood for an introduction to the pigeons, which I longed to have for friends—strange little stately ruffling things, almost as mechanical in their strut as the figures of the clock; so metallic, too, in their lustre, that I could have believed them made of painted iron.

Some wore short grey Eton jackets, with white blouses showing behind; these were the ladies, and their faces were as different as possible from those of their lovers. So were the dainty little coral feet, for alas! the masculine shoes were the pinker and prettier; and the males, even the baby ones, were absurdly like English judges in wigs and gowns.

It was charming to watch the developments of pigeon love-stories on that blue-and-gold day, which was my first in the Grand Piazza of San Marco. How the lady would patter away, and pretend she didn't know that a rising young judge had his eye upon her! But she would pause and feign to examine a grain of corn, which I or some one else had thrown, just long enough to give him a chance of preening his feathers before her, spreading out his tail, and generally cataloguing his perfections. She would pretend that this demonstration had no effect upon her heart, that she'd seen a dozen pigeons within an hour handsomer than he; but the instant a rival belle chanced (only it wasn't chance really) to hop that way and offer outrageous inducements to flirtation, she decided that, after all, he was worth having—and, alas! sometimes decided too late.

That same afternoon Mr. Barrymore took me to the little church of San Giorgio degli Schiavoni to see the exquisite Carpaccios, because he was of opinion that Aunt Kathryn and Beechy would prefer to go shopping. Yet, after all, who should appear there but Beechy and Sir Ralph!

Beechy thought the dragon a delightful beast, with a remarkable eye for the picturesque, judging from the way in which he had arranged the remains of his victims; and she was sorry for him, dragged into the market-place, so pitifully shrunken, beaten, and mortified was he. She wanted to live in all the mediæval castles of the picture- backgrounds, and was of opinion that the basilisk's real intentions had been misunderstood by the general public of his day. "I should love to have such a comic, trotty beast to lead about in Central Park," said she. "Why the octopi that the people cook and sell in the streets here now, are ever so much horrider. One might run away from them, if you like. Loathsome creatures! I do draw the line at an animal whose face you can't tell from its—er—waist. And only think of *eating* them! I'd a good deal rather eat a basilisk."

Beechy was also convinced—before she crossed the Bridge of Sighs— that many people, especially Americans, would pay large sums or even commit crimes, in order to be put in prison at Venice. "Such a lovely situation," she argued, "and lots of historical associations too." But afterwards, when she had seen where Marino Faliero lay, and the young Foscari, she was inclined to change her mind. "Still," she said, "it would be an experience; and if you couldn't afford to stop at a hotel, it might be worth trying, if you didn't have to do anything very bad, and were sure of getting a cell on the canal."

Neither Beechy nor Aunt Kathryn cared much for the churches or the pictures, so they and Sir Ralph bargained for Venetian point or the lace of Burano, or went to the glass makers', or had tea at the Lido with the Corraminis, while Mr. Barrymore took me to the Frari, the Miracoli, and other churches that he loved best, or wandered with me among the glorious company of artists at the Accademia, and in the Doges' Palace. But Beechy did join in my admiration and respect (mingled with a kind of wondering pity) for the noble army of marble lions in Venice.

Oh, those poor, splendid lions! How sad they look, how bitter is the expression of their ponderous faces. Especially am I haunted by the left-hand lion in the Piazza degli Lioni, hard by San Marco. What can have happened to him, that he should be so despairing? Whatever it was, he has never got over it, but has concentrated his whole being in one, eight-century-long howl ever since. He is the most impressive of the tribe; but there are many others, big and little, all gloomy, sitting about in Piazzas, or exposed for sale in shops, or squatting on the railings of balconies. When I think of that fair city in the sea, I shall often want to run back and try to comfort some of those lions.

Beechy was with me in this; and as for Aunt Kathryn, even the flattering attentions of the Corraminis did not please her more than our experience at the antiquaries', which we owed to Mr. Barrymore.

We hadn't been in Venice for twenty-four hours before we saw that the Chauffeulier knew the place almost as if he had been born there. He was even well up in the queer, soft Venetian *patois*, with hardly a consonant left in it, so well up that he announced himself capable of bandying words and measuring swords with the curiosity-shop keepers, if we liked to "collect anything."

At first Aunt Kathryn thought that she wouldn't bother; there would be too much trouble with the custom house at home; but, when Beechy happened to say what a rare thing a marble well-head or a garden statue five hundred years old would be considered in Denver, she weakened, and fell.

The idea popped into Beechy's head just as our gondola (it was towards the end of our week in Venice) was gliding by a beautiful, shabby old palace in a side canal.

A canopy of grape-vines, heavy with hanging clusters of emeralds and here and there an amethyst, shadowed a carved water-gate. Under the jade-green water gleamed the yellow marble of the steps, waving with seaweed like mermaids' hair; and in the dim interior behind the open doors there were vague gleams of gilded chairs, pale glints of statuary, and rich streaks of colour made by priests' vestments or old altar hangings.

"I don't believe even Mrs. Potter Adriance has got anything like this in her house, though they call it so elegant," remarked Beechy.

That speech was to Aunt Kathryn what valerian is to a pussy cat; for Mrs. Potter Adriance (as I've often heard since I made acquaintance with my relations) is the leader of Denver society, and is supposed once to have said with a certain emphasis: "*Who* are the Kidders?"

"Perhaps I'll just step in and see what they've got here," said Aunt Kathryn.

"It isn't a cheap place," replied Mr. Barrymore. "This man knows how to charge. If you want any marbles, he has some fine ones; but for other things I'll take you somewhere else, where I promise you shall be amused and not cheated."

"I think our yard at home is big enough for two or three statues; and a marble well-head and a sundial would be lovely," exclaimed Aunt Kathryn.

"We'll look at some," said Mr. Barrymore, motioning to the gondolier. "But now, unless you're to pay six times what everything's worth, you must put yourselves in my hands. Remember, you don't care to glance either at statues, well-heads, or sun-dials."

"But that's what we're here for!" cried Aunt Kathryn.

 "Ah, but the man mustn't guess that for the world! We appear to be searching for—let's say, mirrors; but not finding the kind we want, we *may* deign to look at a few marbles as we pass. We don't fancy the fellow's stock; still, the things aren't bad; we may decide to save ourselves the trouble of going further. Whatever you do, don't mention a price, even in English. Appear bored and indifferent, never pleased or anxious. When I ask if you're willing to pay so and so, drawl out 'no' or 'yes' without the slightest change of expression."

As we landed on the wet marble steps and passed into the region of gilded gleams and pearly glints, our hearts began to beat with suppressed excitement, as if we were secret plotters, scheming to carry through some nefarious design.

Immediately on entering, I caught sight of two marble baby lions sitting on their haunches side by side on the floor with ferocious expressions on their little carved faces.

"I must have those for myself," I murmured to Mr. Barrymore in a painfully monotonous voice, as we passed along a narrow aisle between groves of magnificent antique furniture. "They appeal to me. Fate means us for each other."

But at this moment an agreeable and well-dressed Italian was bowing before us. He was the proprietor of the antiques, and he looked more like a philanthropic millionaire than a person with whom we could haggle over prices. Without glancing at my lions (I knew they were mine; and wanted them to know it) or Aunt Kathryn's statues and well-heads, Mr. Barrymore announced that he would glance about at paintings of old Venice. What had Signore Ripollo of that sort? Nothing at present? Dear me, what a pity! Lacquered Japanese temples, then? What, none of those? Very disappointing. Well, we must be going. Hm! not a bad well-head, that one with the procession of the Bucentaur in *bas relief*. Too obviously repaired; still, if Signore Ripollo would take three hundred lire for it, the thing might be worth picking up. And that little pair of lions. Perhaps the ladies might think them good enough to keep a door open with, if they didn't exceed fifteen lire each.

Signore Ripollo looked shocked, but laughed politely. He knew Mr. Barrymore, and had greeted him on our entrance as an old acquaintance, though, in his exaggerated Italian way, he gave the Chauffeulier a title more exalted than Beechy had bestowed.

"Milord will always have his joke; the well-head is two thousand lire; the lions fifty each," I thought I understood him to remark.

But not at all. Milord was not joking. Would the Signore sell the things for the price mentioned—yes or no?

The philanthropic millionaire showed now that he was hurt. Why did not Milord ask him to give away the whole contents of his shop?

After this the argument began to move at express speed, and I would have lost track of everything had it not been for the gestures, like danger signals, all along the way. Mr. Barrymore laughed; Signore Ripollo passed from injured dignity to indignation, then to passion; and there we sat on early Renaissance chairs, our outward selves icily regular, splendidly null, our features as hard as those of the stone lions, our bodies in much the same attitudes, on our uncomfortable seats. But inwardly we felt like Torturers of the Inquisition, and I knew by Aunt Kathryn's breathing that she could hardly help exclaiming, "Oh, *do* pay the poor man whatever he asks for everything."

"Will you give five hundred lire for the well-head?" Mr. Barrymore finally demanded, with a reminder of past warnings in his eye.

"Yes," answered Aunt Kathryn languidly, her hands clenched under a lace boa.

"And will you give twenty lire each for the lions? They are very good." (This to me, drawlingly.)

"Ye-es," I returned, without moving a muscle.

The offers were submitted to Signore Ripollo, who received them with princely scorn, as I had felt sure he would, and my heart sank as I saw my lions vanishing in the smoke of his just wrath.

"Come, we will go; the Signore is not reasonable," said Mr. Barrymore.

We all rose obediently, but our anguish was almost past hiding.

"I can't and won't live without the lions," I remarked in the tone of one who says it is a fine day.

"I will *not* leave this place without that well-head, the statue of Neptune, and the yellow marble sundial," said Aunt Kathryn in a casual tone which masked a breaking heart.

Nevertheless, Mr. Barrymore continued to lead us towards the door. He bowed to Signore Ripollo; and by this time we were at the steps of the water-gate. The gondoliers were ready. Driven to desperation we were about to protest, when the Italian, with the air of a falsely accused Doge haled to execution, stopped us. "Have your way, milord, as you always do," he groaned. "I paid twice more for these beautiful things than you give me, but—so be it. They are yours."

True to our instructions we dared not betray our feelings; but when the business had actually been arranged, and our gondola had borne us away from the much-injured antiquary, Aunt Kathryn broke out at the Chauffeulier.

"How *could* you?" she exclaimed. "I never was so sick in my life. That poor man! You've made us rob him. I shall never be able to hold up my head again."

"On the contrary, he's delighted," said Mr. Barrymore jauntily. "If we'd given him what he asked he would have despised us. Now we've earned his respect."

"Well, I never!" gasped Aunt Kathryn inelegantly, forgetful for the moment that she was a Countess. "I suppose I can be happy, then?"

"You can, without a qualm," said Mr. Barrymore.

"Where's that other place you spoke of?" she inquired, half-ashamed. "There's a—a kind of excitement in this sort of thing, isn't there? I feel as if it might grow on me."

"We'll go to Beppo's," replied the Chauffeulier, laughing.

Beppo was a very different man from Signore Ripollo, nor had he a palace with a water-gate to show his wares. We left the gondola, and walked up a dark and narrow rioterrà with coquettish, black-shawled grisettes chatting at glowing fruit-stalls and macaroni shops. There, at a barred iron door, Mr. Barrymore pulled a rope which rang a jangling bell. After a long interval, a little, bent old man in a shabby coat and patched trousers appeared against a background of mysterious brown shadow. Into this shadow we plunged, following him, to be led through a labyrinth of queer passages and up dark stairways to the top of the old, old house. There, in the strangest room I ever saw, we were greeted by a small brown woman, as shabby as her husband, and a supernaturally clever black cat.

A grated window set high up and deep in the discoloured wall, allowed a few rays of yellow sunlight to fall revealingly upon a motley collection of antiquities. Empire chairs were piled upon Louis Quinze writing-desks. Tables of every known period formed a leaning tower in one corner. Rich Persian rugs draped huge Florentine mirrors; priests' vestments trailed from half-open chests of drawers. Brass candlesticks and old Venetian glass were huddled away in inlaid cabinets, and half-hidden with old illuminated breviaries and pinned rolls of lace.

A kind of madness seized Aunt Kathryn. She must have thought of Mrs. Potter Adriance, for suddenly she wanted everything she saw, and said so, *sotto voce*, to Mr. Barrymore.

Then the bargaining began. And there was nothing Dog-like about Beppo. He laughed high-keyed, sardonic laughter; he scolded, he quavered, he pleaded, he was finally choked with sobs; while as for his wife, she, poor little wisplike body, early succumbed to whatever is Venetian for nervous prostration.

Surely the Chauffeulier could not bear the strain of this agonizing scene? Our consciences heavy with brass candlesticks and Marquise sofas, we stood looking on, appalled at his callousness. Beppo and Susanna cried weakly that this would be their ruin, that we were wringing the last drops of blood from their hearts, we cruel rich ones, and in common humanity I would have intervened had the pair not suddenly and unexpectedly wreathed their withered countenances with smiles.

"What has happened? Are you giving them what they wanted?" I asked breathlessly; for long ago I had lost track of the conversation.

"No; I promised them twenty lire over my first offer for that whole lot," said Mr. Barrymore, indicating a heap of miscellaneous articles reaching half-way to the ceiling, for which, altogether, Beppo had demanded two thousand lire, and our offer had been seven hundred.

I could have prayed the poor old peoples' forgiveness, but to my astonishment, as we went out they beamed with pleasure and thanked us ardently for our generosity.

"Is it sarcasm?" I whispered.

"No, it's pure delight," said Mr. Barrymore. "They've done the best day's work of the season, and they don't mind our knowing it—now it's over."

"Human nature is strange," I reflected.

"Especially in antiquarians," he replied.

But we arrived at the hotel feeling weak, and were thankful for tea.

XXII

A CHAPTER BEYOND THE MOTOR ZONE

We all felt when we had said good-bye to Venice that we had a definite object in view, and there was to be no more pleasant dawdling. It was ho for Schloss Hrvoya! Aunt Kathryn had suddenly discovered that she was impatient to see the ancient root from which blossomed her cherished title, and nothing must delay her by the way.

I should have wondered at her change of mood, and at the Prince's new enthusiasm for the Dalmatian trip—which, until our arrival in Venice, he'd tried to discourage—but Beechy explained frankly as usual. It seemed that Count Corramini (said by Prince Dalmar-Kalm to possess vast funds of legal knowledge) had intimated that the Countess Dalmar-Kalm was not rightfully a Countess until every penny was paid for the estate carrying the title. That same day, without waiting to be asked, she had given the Prince a cheque for the remaining half of the money. Now if she finds scarce one stone left upon another at Schloss Hrvoya, she can't cry off her bargain, so it's easy to understand why the Prince is no longer anxious. Exactly why he should seem so eager to get us to our destination is more of a puzzle; but perhaps, as Beechy thinks, it's because he hopes to influence Aunt Kathryn to rebuild. And certainly he has influenced her in some way, for she could hardly wait to leave Venice at the last.

We went as we had come, by water, for we wouldn't condescend to the railway; and at the landing-place for Mestre our grey automobile stood waiting for us, so well-cared for and polished that it might just have come from the makers, instead of having charged at full tilt "up the airy mountains and down the rushy glens" of half Europe.

It was goddess-like to be in the car again, yet I regretted Venice as I've regretted no other place I ever saw. Even when there, it seemed too beautiful to be real, but when we lost sight of its fair towers and domes, in bowling northward along a level road, I grew sadly convinced that Venice was a fairy dream.

We saw nothing to console us for what we had lost (though the scenery had a soft and melancholy charm) until we came to old fortified Treviso, with its park, and the green river Dante knew, circling its high walls.

At Conegliano—where Cima lived—we ran into the town between its guardian statues, gave a glance at the splendid old castle which must have given the gentle painter many an inspiration, and then turned eastward. There was a shorter way, but the route-book of the Italian Touring Club which the Chauffeulier pinned his faith to in emergencies, showed that the surface of the other road was not so good. Udine tried to copy Venice in miniature, and I loved it for its ambition; but what interested me the most was to hear from Mr. Barrymore how, on the spot where its castle stands, Attila watched the burning of Aquileia. That seemed to take me down to the roots of Venetian history; and I could picture the panic-stricken fugitives flying to the lagoons, and beginning to raise the wattled huts which have culminated in the queen city of the sea. From Udine we went southward; and at the Austrian custom house, across the frontier, we had to unroll yards of red tape before we were allowed to pass. Almost at once, when we were over the border, the scenery, the architecture, and even the people's faces, changed; not gradually, but with extraordinary abruptness, or so it seemed to me.

Just before dark we sailed into a great, busy town, with a surprising number of enormous, absolutely useless-looking buildings. It was Trieste, Austria's biggest port; and the Prince, who had kept near us for the hundred and thirty miles from Venice, began to wear an air of pride in his own country. He wanted us to admire the fine streets and shops, and made us notice how everywhere were to be seen Greek, Russian, Polish, French, German, Italian, and even English names. "That proves what a great trade we do, and how all the world comes to us," he said.

Our hotel was close to the quay, and there were a thousand things of interest to watch from the windows when we got up next morning, as there always are in places where the world "goes down to the sea in ships."

At breakfast there was a discussion as to our route, which, owing to suggestions and counter-suggestions from the Prince, hadn't been decided. The Chauffeulier wanted to run through Istria and show us Capodistria (another copy of Venice), Rovigno, and Pola, which he said had not only a splendid Roman amphitheatre, but many other sights worth making a détour for. I was fired by his description, for what I've seen of Northern Italy has stimulated my love for history and the architecture of the ancients; but Prince Dalmar-Kalm persuaded Aunt Kathryn that, as the neighbourhood of Cattaro is our goal, it would be a waste of time to linger on the threshold of Dalmatia.

"Why, a little while ago you thought it stupid to go into Dalmatia at all," said Beechy. "You warned us we'd have trouble about petrol, about roads, about hotels, about everything."

"I have been talking since with Corramini," replied the Prince unruffled. "He has motored through the country we are going to, and I see from his accounts, that the journey is more feasible than I had thought, knowing the way as I did, only from a yacht."

"Funny he should be more familiar with the country than you, as you've got a castle there," Beechy soliloquized aloud.

"I make no secret that I have never lived at Hrvoya," the Prince answered. "Neither I, nor my father before me. The house where I was born is at Abbazzia. That is why I want you to go that way. It is no longer mine; but I should like you to see it, since you cannot at present see Schloss Kalm, near Vienna."

"You seem so fond of selling your houses, why don't you offer Mamma the one near Vienna, if it's the best?" persisted naughty Beechy.

"I could not sell it if I would," smiled the Prince, who for some reason is almost always good-natured now. "And if I offer it to a lady, she must be the Princess Dalmar-Kalm."

I felt that a glance was thrown to me with these words, but I looked only at my plate.

The conversation ended by the Prince getting his way, as he had made Aunt Kathryn think it *her* way: and we gave up Istria. Soon after ten we were *en route* for Abbazzia—close to Fiume—slanting along the neck of the Istrian peninsula by a smooth and well-made road that showed the Austrians were good at highways.

It was but thirty miles from sea to sea, and so sweetly did the car run, so little were we troubled by cantankerous creatures of any sort, that we descended from high land and before twelve o'clock ran into as perfect a little watering place as can exist on earth.

Aunt Kathryn was prepared to like Abbazzia before she saw it, because it was the scene of Prince Dalmar-Kalm's birth, and also because she'd been told it was the favourite resort of Austrian aristocracy. I hadn't listened much, because I had clung to the idea of visiting historic Pola; but Abbazzia captured me at first glance.

Everywhere was beauty and peace. The Adriatic spread itself pure and clean as a field of spring flowers, and as full of delicate changing colour. Away on a remote horizon—remote as all trouble and worry seemed, in this fair spot—hovered islands, opaline and shimmering, like a mirage. Nearer rose a stretch of green hills, travelling by the seashore until they fell back for Fiume, a white town veiled with a light mist of smoke.

But for Abbazzia itself, it seemed the most unconventional pleasure place I ever knew. Instead of a smart "parade" all along the rocky indentations which jutted into or receded from the sea, ran a winding rustic path, tiny blue waves crinkling on one side; on the other, fragrant groves of laurel, olives, magnolias, and shady chestnut-trees.

We walked there, after lunching at quite a grand hotel, which, the Prince told Aunt Kathryn, was full of "crowned heads" in winter and earlier spring. Nowhere else have I seen the beauty of sea and shore so exquisitely mingled as on this path overhanging the Adriatic, nor have I smelled more heavenly smells, even at Bellagio.

There was the salt of the sea, the rank flavour of seaweed, mingled with the sharp fragrance of ferns, of young grass, of budding trees, and all sweet, woodsy things.

Along the whole length of the gay, quaint town, ran the beautiful path, winding often like a twisted ribbon, but never leaving the sea. Behind it, above and beyond, was the unspoiled forest only broken enough for the cutting of shaded streets, and the building of charming houses, their fronts half windows and the other half balconies.

The dark rocks starred with flowers to the water's edge, looked as if there had been a snow-storm of gulls, while the air was full of their wistful cries, and the singing of merry land birds that tried to cheer them.

Each house by the sea (the one where Prince Dalmar-Kalm first saw the light, among others) had its own bathing place, and pretty young girls laughed and splashed in the clear water. Up above, in the town, were public gardens, many hotels, theatres, and fascinating shops displaying embroideries and jewelry from Bosnia, which made me feel the nearness of the East as I hadn't felt it before, even in Venice.

We could not tear ourselves away in the afternoon, but spent hours in a canopied boat, dined in the hotel garden, and bathed in the creamy sea by late moonlight, the Chauffeulier giving me a lesson in swimming. Aunt Kathryn grudged the time, but we overruled her, and atoned by promising to go on each day after this to the bitter end, whatever that might be.

Next morning, by way of many hills and much fine scenery we travelled towards a land beyond the motor zone. Though the roads were good enough, if steep sometimes, judging by the manners of animals four-legged and two-legged, automobiles were unknown. Only children were not surprised at us; but then, children aren't easily surprised by new things, I've noticed. They have had so few experiences to found impressions on, that I suppose they would think a fiery chariot nothing extraordinary, much less a motor-car. The costumes began to change from ordinary European dress to something with a hint of the barbaric in it. Here and there we would see a coarse-featured face as dark as that of a Mongolian, or would hear a few curious words which the Chauffeulier said were Slavic. The biting, alkaline names of the small Dalmatian towns through which we ran seemed to shrivel our tongues and dry up our systems. There was much thick, white dust, and, to the surprise of the amateurs of the party, we once or twice had "side slip" in it.

How we hated the "mended" roads with their beds of stone, though near rivers they were not so bad, as the pebbles instead of being sharp were naturally rounded. But Aunt Kathryn wouldn't hear a word against the country, which was *her* country now. Once, when the cylinders refused to work, for some reason best known to themselves or the evil spirits that haunt them, we were "hung up" for twenty minutes, and surrounded with strange, dark children from a neighbouring hamlet, Aunt Kathryn insisted on giving each a coin of some sort, and received grinning acknowledgments with the air of a crowned queen. "I daresay I shall have tenants and retainers like these people," said she, with a wave of her hand.

For a part of our journey down the narrow strip of strange coast, we had on one side a range of stony mountains; on the other, only a little way across the sea, lay desolate islands rising in tiers of pink rock out of the milk-white Adriatic. But before long we lost the sea and the lonely islands; for at a place named Segna our road turned inland and climbed a high mountain—the Velebit—at whose feet we had been travelling

As we were trying to make a run of more than a hundred and twenty-five miles—a good deal for a heavily-loaded car of twelve horse-power—the Chauffeulier kept the automobile constantly going "for all she was worth." He had planned that we should spend the night at the sea-coast town of Zara—that place so inextricably tangled up in Venetian history—for there we might find a hotel fit to stop at.

About midday we lunched at a mean town called Gospic, and vast was the upheaval that our advent caused.

As we drove in, looking right and left for the cleanest inn, every able-bodied person under seventy and several considerably over ran to follow, their figures swarming after us as a tail follows a comet. At the door of our chosen lunching-place they surged round the car, pressing against us, and even plucking at our dresses as we pushed through into the house. Spray from this human wave tossed into the passage and eating-room in our wake, until the burly innkeeper, his large wife, and two solid handmaidens swept it out by sheer weight.

Mr. Barrymore was afraid to leave the car, lest it should be damaged, so he sat in it, eating bread and cheese with imperturbable good humour, though every mouthful he took was watched down his throat by a hundred eager eyes.

The landlord waited upon us himself, and could speak German and Italian as well as his own Croatian or Slavish dialect. We were surprised at the goodness of the luncheon, and Sir Ralph was surprised at the cheapness of the bill. "It will be different when they've turned this coast into the Austrian Riviera, as they 're trying to do," he said.

When we appeared at the door again, ready to go on, there fell a heavy silence on the Chauffeulier's audience. Not only had they had the entertainment of watching him feed, but had observed with fearful awe the replenishing of the petrol and water-tanks and examination of the lubricators. Now they had the extra pleasure of seeing us put on our motor-masks and take our places. When all was ready Mr. Barrymore seized the starting handle, and gave it the one vigorous twist which wakes the engine when it is napping. But almost for the first time the motor was refractory. The handle recoiled so violently and unexpectedly that the Chauffeulier staggered back and trod on the toes of the fat man of the crowd, while at the same time there burst from the inner being of the car a loud report. At this sign of the motor's power and rebellion against him whom it should have obeyed, the audience uttered cries, scattering right and left, so as to leave a large ring round the automobile which before had not had room to breathe.

"Misfire, that's all," said Mr. Barrymore, laughing and showing his nice white teeth in a comforting way he has when anything alarming has happened. Next instant the motor was docile as a lamb; the engine began to purr; the Chauffeulier jumped to his seat, and, followed by a vast sigh from the crowd, we darted away at thirty miles an hour.

The rest of the day was a changing dream of strange impressions, which made Aunt Kathryn feel as if Denver were at least a million miles away. We climbed once more up to the heights of the Velebit, seeing from among the dark, giant pines which draped it in mourning, the great forests of Croatia, Lika, and Krabava, with their conical mountains, and far off the chains of Bosnia. Then, at a bound, we leaped into sight of the Adriatic again and sped down innumerable *lacets* overlooking the beautiful land-locked sea of Novigrad, to tumble at last upon the little town of Obrovazzo. Thence we flew on, over an undulating road, towards Dalmatia's capital, Zara.

Just as anachronistic electric lights had shown us the way through curiously Italian streets, with beautifully ornamented windows, past a noble Corinthian column and out onto a broad space by the sea, without a warning sigh the automobile stopped.

"Our last drop of petrol!" exclaimed Mr. Barrymore. "Lucky it didn't give out before, as I began to be afraid it might, owing to the hills."

"By Jove! this doesn't look the sort of town to buy food and drink for motors!" remarked Sir Ralph ruefully.

The Chauffeulier laughed. "Ours won't starve," said he. "I thought you knew I'd ordered tins of petrol to meet us at every big town, for fear of trouble. It will come down by boat, and I shall find the Zara lot waiting for me at the Austrian Lloyd's storehouse. You'd have remembered that arrangement if your wits hadn't been wool-gathering a bit lately."

"I wonder if they have?" soliloquized Sir Ralph. "Well, here we are within three yards of a hotel which, if I've any brains left, is the very one you selected from Baedeker."

We all got out as if we had stopped on purpose, and the hotel which Fate and our Chauffeulier had chosen proved very fair, though too modern to be in the picture.

If the automobile had flashed us to Mars things could hardly have been more unfamiliar to our eyes than when we walked out next morning to find ourselves in the midst of a great fête.

Flags were everywhere: in arched windows, rich with sculptured stone; flying over the great gates of the city; festooned in the charming little houses with fountain courts surrounded by columns. The peasants of the country round had flocked to town for the holiday. Dark, velvet-eyed girls in short dresses of bright-coloured silk heavy with gold embroidery, their hair hidden by white head- dresses flashing with sequins, and tall men in long frock coats of dark crimson or yellow, were exactly like a stage crowd in some wonderful theatre; while handsome Austrian officers wearing graceful blue cloaks draped over one shoulder, might have been operatic heroes.

There was strange music in the streets, and a religious procession, which we followed for some time on our way to the maraschino factory which Mr. Barrymore said we must see. Of course, some monks had invented the liqueur, as they always do, but perhaps the cherries which grow only among those mountains, and can't be exported, had as much to do with the original success of the liqueur as the existence of the recipe.

If Aunt Kathryn had listened to Mr. Barrymore and me we would have gone from Zara inland to a place called Knin, to visit the cataract of Krka, described as a combination of Niagara and the Rhine Falls. But she said that the very sound of the names would make a cat want to sneeze, and she was sure she would take her death of cold there. So the proposal fell to the ground, and we kept to the coast route, the shortest way of getting to Ragusa and Cattaro.

When we had climbed out of Zara by the old post road, begun by Venice and finished by Austria, our way lay among the famous cherry-trees which have made Zara rich. There were miles of undulating country and fields of wheat, interspersed with vines and almond trees which mingled with the cherries. The pastures where sheep and goats grazed were blue and pink with violets and anemones; here and there was an old watch-tower, put up against the Turks; and the rich peasants drove in quaint flat chaises, which looked as if the occupants were sitting in large pancakes.

With a motor it was not far to Sebenico, which called itself modestly a "little Genoa;" and it was so pretty, lying by the sea, with its narrowest streets climbing up a hill to an ancient fortress, that I should have loved to linger, but Aunt Kathryn was for pushing on; and, of course, it is her trip, so her wishes must be obeyed when they can't be directed into other channels. We stopped only long enough for an omelette, and passed on after a mere glimpse of close-huddled houses (with three heads for every window, staring at the motor) and a cathedral with an exquisite doorway. Then we were out of the town, spinning on through the wild, unreal-looking country towards Spalato.

"What new ground for honeymooners!" exclaimed Sir Ralph, enchanted with everything, in his half-boyish, half-cynical way. "I shall recommend it in *The Riviera Sun* for a wedding trip *en automobile*. Shouldn't you like to do it, Miss Beechy—dawdling, not scorching?"

"I think when I get married," Beechy replied judicially, "I shan't want to *go* anywhere. I shall just *stay* somewhere for a change."

"It's early to decide," remarked Sir Ralph.

"I don't know. It's always well to be prepared," said Beechy, with the enigmatical look she sometimes puts on, which (in spite of her ankle-short dresses and knee-long tails of hair) makes her appear at least sixteen.

Beyond Sebenico the Dalmatian landscape frowned upon us, but we liked its savage mood. The road, winding inland, was walled with mountains which might have struck a chill to the heart of Childe Roland on his way to find the Dark Tower. On a rocky shoulder here and there crouched a sinister little hamlet, like a black cat huddling into the neck of a witch. Sometimes, among the stony pastures where discouraged goats browsed discontentedly, we would spy a human inhabitant of one of those savage haunts—a shepherd in a costume more strange than picturesque, with a plait of hair almost as long as

Beechy's, hanging down his back—a sullen, Mongolian-faced being, who stared or scowled as we flew by, his ragged dog too startled by the rush of the motor even to bark, frozen into an attitude of angry amazement at his master's feet. One evidence only of modern civilization did we see—the railway from Sebenico to Spalato, the first we had come near in Dalmatia; and we congratulated ourselves that we were travelling by automobile instead. No tunnels to shut out some wonderful view, just as our eyes had focussed on it, no black smoke, no stuffy air, no need to think of time tables!

When at last we sighted the Adriatic again, a surprise awaited us. The land of desolation lay behind; beyond, a land of beauty and full summer. We ran beside an azure sea, transparent as gauze, fringing a tropical strand; and so came into the little town of Trau, which might have been under a spell of sleep since mediæval days. Its walls and gates, its ornate houses, its fort and Sanmicheli tower, all set like a mosaic of jewels in a ring of myrtles, oleanders, and laurels, delighted our eyes; and the farther we went on the way to Spalato, keeping always by the glittering sea, the more beautiful grew the scene. The walls along our road were well-nigh hidden with agaves and rosemary. Cacti leered impudently at us; palms and pomegranates made the breeze on our faces whisper of the south and the east. Not a place we passed that I would not have loved to spend a month in, studying in the carved stones of churches and ruined castles the history of Venetian rule, or the wild romance of Turkish raids.

Spalato we reached at sunset, as the little waves which creamed against the pink rocks were splashed with crimson; and Spalato was by far the most imposing place Dalmatia had shown us yet. As in Italy, the ancient and modern towns held themselves apart from one another, as if there could be no sympathy between the two, though the new houses were pushing and would have encroached now and then if they could. We stayed all night; and by getting up at sunrise Beechy and I, with Mr. Barrymore and Sir Ralph, had time for a glimpse of Diocletian's palace, grand in ruinous desolation.

Still we went on beside the sea, and from Spalato to Almissa— sheltered under high rocks at the mouth of a river, was a splendid run leading us by the territory of an ancient peasant republic— Poljica; one of those odd little self-governing communities, like San Marino, which have flourished through troubled centuries under the very noses of great powers. Poljica had had its Jeanne d'Arc, who performed wondrous feats of valour in wars against the Turks, and I bought a charming little statuette of her.

At Almissa we bade good-bye to the blue water for a while to run by the banks of the Cetina, a big and beautiful river; for the range of the Biokovo Hills had got between us and the sea; but we threaded our way out to it again, after switchbacking up and down an undulating road close to the frontier of Herzegovina; and at the end of a wonderful day descended upon a harbour in an almost land-locked basin of water. It was Gravosa, the port of Ragusa, still hidden by an intervening tongue of land. It was a gay scene by the quay, where native coasting ships were unloading their queer cargoes. Dark-faced porters in rags carried on their shoulders enormous burdens; men in loose knickerbockers, embroidered shirts, and funny little turbans lounged about, and stared at us as if they were every-day people and we extraordinary. And the setting for the lively picture was the deeply-indented bay, surrounded with quaintly pretty houses among vineyards and olive groves, which climbed terrace after terrace to a mountainous horse-shoe, hemming in the port.

All this we saw in the moment or two that we halted by the quay, before turning up the road to Ragusa. It was a mile-long road, and like a pleasure garden all the way, with the whiteness of wild lilies flung like snow drifts against dark cedars, and trails of marvellous roses, strangely tinted with all shades of red and yellow from the palest to the deepest, clambering among the branches of umbrella pines. There were villas, too, with pergolas, and two or three dignified old houses of curious architecture, of which we had a flashing glimpse through doorways in enormous walls.

We bounded up the saddle of a hill, then down again, and so came to a charming hotel, white, with green verandahs, set in a park that was half a garden. We were to spend the night and go on next day, after seeing the town; but the Chauffeulier said that we should not see it to the same advantage by morning light as in this poetic flush of sunset. So after greeting Signore Bari and his sister, who were painting in the park, we drove on, through a crowded *place* where music played, crossed a moat, and were swallowed by the long shadow of the city gate, black with a twisted draping of ancient ivy.

A throng of loungers, theatrically picturesque, fell back in astonishment to give us passage, and a moment later we were caught in a double row of fortifications with a sharp and difficult turn through a second gate. It was almost like a trap for a motor-car, but we got out, and sprang at the same instant into the main street of a town that might have been built to please the fancy of some artist-tyrant.

"It's a delicious mixture of Carcassonne and Verona set down by the sea, with something of Venice thrown in, isn't it?" said Mr. Barrymore: and I thought that part of the description fitted, though I had to be told about splendid, fortified Carcassonne with its towering walls and bastions, before I fully understood the simile.

"Yes, a Verona and Venice certainly," I answered, "with a sunny coast like that of the French Riviera, and inhabited by people of the Far East."

I think one might search the world over in vain to find just such another fascinating street as that broad street of Ragusa, with its exquisitely proportioned buildings that gave one a sense of gladness, the extraordinary great fountain, the miniature palace of the Doges, the noble churches and the colourful shops brilliant with strange, embroidered costumes exposed for sale, Eastern jewelry, and quaint, ferocious-looking weapons. And then, the queer signs over the shops, how they added to the bewildering effect of unreality! Many of the letters were more like hooks and eyes, buckles and bent pins, than respectable members of an alphabet, even a foreign one. And the people who sold, and the people who bought, were more wonderful than the shops themselves.

There were a few ordinary Europeans, though it was past the season now; and plenty of handsome young Austrian officers in striking uniforms, pale blue and bright green; but the crowd was an embroidered, sequined, crimson and silver, gold and azure crowd, with here and there a sheepskin coat, the brown habit of a monk, and the black veil of a nun.

Through half-open doorways we peeped into courtyards where fountains flashed a diamond spray, all pink with sunset, between arcaded columns. We saw the cathedral planted on the site of the chapel where Richard Cœur de Lion worshipped; then, wheeling at the end of the street, we returned as we had come while the rose- pink air was full of chiming church bells and cries of gulls, whose circling wings were stained with sunset colour.

Altogether this day had been one of the best days of my life. So good a day, that it had made me sad; for I thought as I leaned on the rail of my balcony after dinner, there could not be many days so radiant in my life to come. Many thoughts came to me there, in the scented darkness, and they were all tinged with a vague melancholy.

There was no moon, but the high dome of the sky was crusted with stars, that flashed like an intricate embroidery of diamonds on velvet. From the garden the scent of lilies came up with the warm breeze, so poignant-sweet that it struck at my heart, and made it beat, beat with a strange tremor in the beating that was like vague apprehension, and a kind of joy as strange and as inexplicable.

Far away in the *place* some one was singing a wild, barbaric air, with a wonderful voice that had in its *timbre* the same quality the lilies had in their fragrance. For some reason that I didn't understand, my whole spirit was in a turmoil, yet nothing had happened. What was the matter? What did it mean? I couldn't tell. But I wanted to be happy. I wanted something from life that it had never given, never would give, perhaps. There was a voice down below in the garden— Mr. Barrymore talking to Sir Ralph. I listened for an instant, every nerve tingling as if it were a telegraph wire over which a question had been sent, and an answer was coming. The voice died away. Suddenly my eyes were full of tears; and surprised and frightened, I turned quickly to go in through my open window, but something caught my dress and drew me back.

"Maida!" said another voice, which I knew almost as well as that other I had heard—and lost.

Prince Dalmar-Kalm had come out of a window onto a balcony next mine, and leaning over the railing had snatched at a fold of my gown.

"Let me go, please," I said. "And that name is not for you."

"Don't say that," he whispered, holding me fast, so that I could not move. "It must be for me. *You* must be for me. You shall. I can't live without you."

His words jarred so upon my mood that I could have struck him.

"If you don't let me go, I'll cry out," I said, in a tone as low as his, but quivering with anger. "I would be nothing to you if you were the last man in the world."

"Very well. I *will* be the last man in your world. Then—we shall see," he answered; and dropped my dress.

In another instant, I was in my room and had fastened the shutters. But the words rang in my ears, like a bell that has tolled too loud.

XXIII

A CHAPTER OF KIDNAPPING

Beechy was ill next morning; nothing serious; but the Prince, it seemed, had brought her in the evening a box of some rich Turkish confection; and though she doesn't care for the man, she couldn't resist the sweet stuff. So she had eaten, only a little, she said; but the box contradicted her, and the poor child kept her bed.

Aunt Kathryn and I were with her until eleven o'clock. Then she was sleepy, and told us to go away. So we went, and took a drive to the pretty harbour of Gravosa, with Mr. Barrymore and Sir Ralph in the motor, unaccompanied by the Prince, whose car was said to be somehow disabled.

We expected, if Beechy were well, to get on next day; but the Chauffeulier was troubled about the road between Ragusa and Cattaro—and no proper "route-book" existing for that part of the world, unexplored by motors, he could find out surprisingly little from any one. Prince Dalmar-Kalm was as ignorant as others, or appeared to be, although this was his own land; and so it seemed doubtful what would be our next adventure.

The spin was a very short one, for the day was hot, and we didn't care to leave Beechy long alone. But when we came back she was asleep still; and I was getting rid of my holland motor-coat in my own room when Aunt Kathryn tapped at the door. "Don't take off your things," she said, "but come out again—that's a dear—for a drive to Gravosa."

"We've just come back from Gravosa," I answered, surprised.

"Yes, but we didn't see the most interesting thing there. You know the yacht standing out at a little distance in the harbour, that I said looked like the Corraminis'? Well, it is the Corraminis'. The Prince wants us to drive with him—not on the automobile, for it isn't mended yet, but in a cab, and go on board the yacht for lunch with the County and Contessa."

"Oh, you'd better go without me," I said.

Aunt Kathryn pouted like a child. "I can't," she objected. "The Prince *says* I can't, for it would be misunderstood here if a lady drove out alone with a gentleman. Do come."

"I suppose I shall have to, then," I answered ungraciously, for I hated going. At the last minute little Airole darted after me, and to save the trouble of going back I caught him up in my arms. I was rewarded for the sacrifice I had made by being let alone during the drive. The Prince was all devotion to Aunt Kathryn, and scarcely spoke a word to me.

At the harbour there was a little boat sent out from the Corraminis' "Arethusa" to fetch us, so it was evident that we had been expected and this was not an impromptu idea of the Prince's.

On board the yacht, which we had visited once or twice in Venice, Count Corramini met us, his scarred face smiling a welcome.

"I am more than sorry that my wife is suddenly indisposed," he said, in his careful English. "She is subject to terrible headaches, but she sends messages and begs that Countess Dalmar will take the head of the table in her absence."

We lunched almost at once, and as it was a simple meal, finished soon. Coffee was served on deck under the awning, and its shadow was so cool, the air so fresh on the water, and the harbour so lovely that I was growing contented, when suddenly I grew conscious of a throb, throb of the "Arethusa's" heart.

"Why, we're moving!" I exclaimed.

"A short excursion the Prince and I have arranged for a little surprise," explained Count Corramini. "We hoped it might amuse you. You do not object, Countess?"

"I think it will be lovely, this hot afternoon," said Aunt Kathryn, who was radiant with childish pleasure in the exclusive attentions of the two men.

"But poor little Beechy!" I protested.

"Probably she will sleep till late, as she couldn't lunch," said Aunt Kathryn comfortably. "And if she wakes, the 'other Beatrice' as she calls Signorina Bari, will sit with her. She offered to, you know."

I raised no further objection to the plan, as evidently Aunt Kathryn was enjoying herself. But when we had steamed out of the Bay of Ombla, far away from Ragusa's towering fortifications, and on for more than an hour, I ventured to suggest to Count Corramini that it was time to turn back. "We shan't get to the hotel till after three, as it is," I said, glancing at my watch.

"Let us consult the Countess," he replied. "Here she comes now."

Aunt Kathryn and the Prince had left us twenty minutes before, to stroll up and down the deck, and had been leaning over the rail for some time, talking in low voices, but with great earnestness. As the Count answered me, they had moved and were coming slowly in our direction, Aunt Kathryn looking excited, as if the Prince had been saying something strange.

"Don't you think we ought to go back to Beechy?" I asked, as she came nearer.

She sat down in the deck chair without replying for a moment, and then she said, in an odd, quavering tone, "Maida, I've just heard a thing from the Prince, that I'll have to talk to you about. County, can I take her into the sallong?"

The Count jumped up. "It is for Dalmar-Kalm and me to go, if you wish to speak with Mees Destrey alone," he exclaimed. And laying his hand on the Prince's shoulder, the two men walked away together.

My only thought was that Prince Dalmar-Kalm must have told Aunt Kathryn of my refusal and asked her to "use her influence." But her first words showed me that I was mistaken.

"I'm very angry with the Prince, but I can't help thinking what he's done is romantic. He and the County have *kidnapped* us."

"What do you mean?" I exclaimed.

"Oh, you needn't look so horrified. They're only taking us to Cattaro by yacht instead of our going by automobile, that's all."

"All?" I echoed. "It's the most impudent thing I ever heard of. Didn't you tell him that you wouldn't go, that you —"

"Well, I'd like to know what good my saying *'Wouldn't'* could do? I can't stop the yacht."

"It's Count Corramini's yacht, not the Prince's," I said, "and whatever else they may be, they're gentlemen, at least by birth. They can't run off with us like this against our wills."

Aunt Kathryn actually chuckled. "Well, they *have,* anyhow," she retorted. "And the Prince says, if only we knew what the road to Cattaro was like, I'd thank instead of scolding him."

"Nonsense!" I exclaimed. "We must go back. What's to become of Beechy left alone in Ragusa ill, with nobody but Mr. Barrymore and Sir Ralph to look after her? It's monstrous!"

"Yes, of course," said Aunt Kathryn, more meekly. "But Signorina Bari's there. It isn't so dreadful, Maida. Beechy isn't *very* sick. She'll be well to-morrow, and when they find we're gone, which they can't till late this afternoon, they won't waste time motoring down; they'll take a ship which leaves Ragusa in the morning for Cattaro. The Prince says they're sure to. We'll all meet by to-morrow noon, and meanwhile I guess there's nothing for us to do but make the best of the joke they've played on us. Anyway, it's an exciting adventure, and you like ad—"

"You call it a joke!" I cried. "I call it something very different. Let me speak to the Prince."

281

I sprang up, forgetting poor Airole asleep on my lap, but Aunt Kathryn scrambled out of her low chair also, and snatched my dress. "No, I'm not going to have you insult him," she exclaimed. "You shan't talk to him without me. He's *my* friend, not yours, and if I choose to consider this wild trick he's playing more a—a compliment than anything else, why, it won't hurt you. As for Beechy, she's *my* child, not yours."

This silenced me for the moment, but only until the men appeared. "Are we forgiven?" asked the Prince.

"Maida's very angry, and so am I, of course," replied Aunt Kathryn, bridling, and showing both dimples.

"Dear ladies," pleaded the Count, "I wouldn't have consented to help this mad friend of mine, if he hadn't assured me that you were too much under the influence of your rather reckless chauffeur, who would probably break your bones and his companion's car, in his obstinate determination to go down to Cattaro by motor."

"Why, lately the Prince has been encouraging it!" I interrupted.

"Ah, you have misunderstood him. A wilful fool must have his way; that was what he thought of your gentleman chauffeur, no doubt. This will give the self-willed young man an excuse to take the boat to Cattaro to-morrow. You will have a run on Dalmar-Kalm's motor (which he has put on board on purpose) this afternoon from Cattaro to Schloss Hrvoya. It will not be serious for Miss Beechy. You can wire, and get her answer that Signorina Bari is playing nurse and chaperon very nicely."

"You must understand, Miss Destrey, as I have made the Countess understand already," put in Prince Dalmar-Kalm, "that I only chose this course because I knew it would be useless trying to dissuade Mr. Chauffeur Barrymore from attempting the trip by road; but this will effectually stop him."

"You are very, very naughty, Prince," chattered Aunt Kathryn; and I was so angry with her for her frivolity and vanity that I should hardly have dared to speak, even if words hadn't failed me.

"At least, we have thought of your comfort," said Count Corramini. "There are two cabins ready for your occupation, with everything you will need for the toilet, so that you can sleep in peace after your trip to Hrvoya."

"I must protest," I said, just able to control my voice. "I think this an abominable act, not worthy of gentlemen. Knowing that one of us feels so strongly, Count, won't you order your yacht to turn back to Ragusa?"

He bowed his head, and shrugged his eyebrows. "If I had not given my word to my friend," he murmured. "For to-day "Arethusa" is his."

"I believe he's bribed you!" the words sprang from my lips, without my meaning to speak them; but they hit their mark as if I had taken close aim. The scarred features flushed so painfully that they seemed to swell; and with the lightning that darted from under the black thundercloud of his brows, the man was hideous. He bit his lip to keep back an angry answer, and Aunt Kathryn screamed at me, "Maida! I'm *ashamed* of you. You'd better go to your cabin and not come out till you're in a—a more *ladylike* frame of mind."

I took her at her word and walked sharply away with Airole trotting at my heels.

There were six cabins on "Arethusa", as I knew, because I had been shown them all. I knew also which was Count Corramini's, which his wife's, which her maid's, and which were reserved for guests. Now I walked into one of the spare cabins, of which the door stood open, and whether it was meant for me or for Aunt Kathryn I wasn't in a mood to care.

Various toilet things had been ostentatiously laid out, and there was a bunch of roses in a glass, which in my anger I could have tossed out of the window; but I hate people who are cruel to flowers almost as much as those who are cruel to animals, and the poor roses were the only inoffensive things on board.

"Oh, Airole," I said, "she takes it as a *compliment*! Well—well—*well!*"

My own reflections and the emphasis of Airole's tiny tail suddenly brought my anger down from boiling point to a bubbly simmer; and I went on, thrashing the matter out in a conversation with the dog until the funny side of the thing came uppermost. There was a *distinctly* funny side, seen from several points of view, but I didn't intend to let anybody know that I saw it. I made up my mind to stay in the cabin indefinitely; but it was not necessary to the maintenance of dignity that I should refrain from enjoying as much of the scenery as the porthole framed in a picture. Accordingly I knelt on the bed, looking out, too excited to tire of the strained position.

We had passed a long tongue of land, beaten upon by white rollers of surf, that seemed as if they strove to overwhelm the old forts set far above their reach. A rocky island too, rising darkly out of a golden sea; and then we entered the mouth of a wonderful bay, like the pictures of Norwegian fords. As we steamed on, past a little town protected by a great square-towered, fortified castle, high on a precipitous rock, I guessed by the formation of the bay, which Mr. Barrymore had shown me on a map, that we were in the famous Bocche di Cattaro.

"Yes," I told myself, "that must be Castelnuovo. Mr. Barrymore said the bay was like the Lake of Lucerne, with its starfish arms. This can't be anything else."

The yacht glided under the bows of two huge warships, with officers in white, on awninged decks, and steamed into a long canal-like stretch of water, only to wind out again presently into a second mountain-ringed bay. So we went from one to another, passing several pretty towns, one beautiful one which I took to be Perasto, if I remembered the name aright, and two exquisite islands floating like swans on the shining water, illuminated by the afternoon sun. Then, at last we were slowing down within close touch of as strange a seaside place as could be in the world. Close to the water's edge it crept, but climbed high on the rocks behind the houses of the foreground, with a dark belt of ancient wall circling the lower town and upper town, and finishing at the top with fortifications marvellous enough for a dream. In the near background were green hills; but beyond, towered desolate grey mountains crowned with dazzling snow, and on their rugged faces was scored a tracery of white lines seemingly scratched in the rock. I knew that they must mean the twistings of a road, up and up to the junction of mountain and sky, but the wall of grey rock looked so sheer, so nearly perpendicular, that it was impossible to imagine horses, or even automobiles mounting there.

In my interest and wonder as to whether we had arrived at Cattaro already I had forgotten my injuries for the moment, until I was reminded of them by Aunt Kathryn's voice.

"It's Cattaro," she called through the door. "Let me in, please. I've something to say."

I slipped back the bolt and she came in hurriedly, as if she were afraid of being kept out after all.

"See here, Maida," she said, "to save time the Prince is having his motor put on shore the minute we get in to the quay, and he'll drive us up to Schloss Hrvoya this afternoon. It's only four o'clock, and he says, though it's away up in the mountains and we'll be two hours getting there, we shall run down in half the time, so we shall be back soon after seven and can dine on board. It's quite appropriate that I should be with the Prince, whose ancestral home it was, when I look on Hrvoya first. He's fully persuaded me of that. I think the whole thing's most dramatic, and I do hope you won't spoil it by being disagreeable any longer."

"I think you're the—the *unwisest* woman I ever saw!" I couldn't help exclaiming.

"Well, I think *you're* very rude. I do believe you're jealous of me with the Prince. That's *his* idea, anyway, though he'd be vexed if he thought I'd told you, and I wouldn't if you hadn't aggravated me. Oh dear, you do make me so nervous and miserable! *Will* you come to Schloss Hrvoya or will you not?"

I thought very quickly for a few seconds before answering. Perhaps it would be better to go than to stay on "Arethusa" without Aunt Kathryn, especially as I had now made Count Corramini my enemy. Mr. Barrymore and Sir Ralph and Beechy couldn't arrive at Cattaro by ship till to-morrow, even if they found out what had become of us, and followed at the earliest opportunity without waiting to hear. No, there was nothing to keep me on the yacht, or in the town of Cattaro, and hateful as the whole expedition was, it would be better to cling to Aunt Kathryn than be anywhere else alone in a strange place, among people whose language I neither spoke nor understood.

"Yes, I will come," I said.

"Arethusa" touched the quay as I spoke, and there was a great bustle on deck, no doubt landing the Prince's motor, which had stood concealed on the forward deck under an enormous tarpaulin.

Aunt Kathryn, triumphant, hurried off to get ready, and I began slowly to follow her example.

XXIV

A CHAPTER ON PUTTING TRUST IN PRINCES

When I had put on my hat and coat, which I'd taken off in the cabin, I went on deck with Airole tucked under my arm, expecting to find Aunt Kathryn, as I had not made haste. She was not there, but on shore close to the quay stood the automobile, which had been put off in a kind of sling; and on the front seat was the familiar, plump figure in its long, light brown coat, and the mushroom-like mask with the talc window.

I had not brought my mask, but evidently Aunt Kathryn must have had hers stuffed into one of the big pockets of her coat, as she often did. The Prince stood talking to her, and seeing that all was ready I crossed the gang-plank and walked quickly to the car.

Aunt Kathryn neither spoke to me nor turned her head, which scarcely surprised me, considering the bad terms we were upon, for the first time in all the months of our acquaintance.

The Prince "hoped that I wouldn't mind sitting in the tonneau," and explained a pile of rugs on the seat opposite mine by saying that it would grow chilly as we ascended into the mountains, and he did not wish his passengers to suffer.

"Where's Joseph?" I asked, addressing him for the first time since taking him to task on deck.

"I left him in Ragusa," replied the Prince. "He will not be needed." With this, the tonneau door was shut, the car started, and we bounded away. A few men and women, in very interesting, Eastern costumes, quite different from anything we had seen yet, watched our progress in silence and with imperturbable faces, dark and proud.

Angry as I still was with Prince Dalmar-Kalm for the trick he had so impudently played upon us, and the part forced upon me for Aunt

Kathryn's sake, I could not be blind to the beauty of this strange world, or suppress all joy in it.

Cattaro seemed to lie plastered against a tremendous wall of sheer rock rising behind the ringed town and its fortress; and I saw, soon after starting, that we must be bound for the mountain with the silken skein of road, which I had gazed at in wonder from my porthole. We had not long left Cattaro, when our way began to mount in long zigzags, doubling back again and again upon itself. Presently we could look down upon the town, prone at the foot of its fortified hill on the very edge of the sea, which as we climbed, assumed the shape and colour of a great shimmering blue silk sleeve.

Mountains towered all around us, mountains in every direction as far as the eye could reach, many crowned by low, green forts, connected with the lower world by the lacings of thread-like roads.

Still we mounted, the car going well and the Prince driving in silence. Though the gradient was steep—sometimes so steep as to be terrible for horses—we seemed to travel so fast that it was surprising to find ourselves apparently no nearer the mountain-tops than when we started. Though we gazed down so far that all things on the sea level had shrunk into nothingness, and the big warship we had seen in coming was no larger than a beetle, we gazed still farther up to the line where sky and mountain met. And always, there were the grey-white, zigzag lines scored on the face of the sheer rock.

I longed for some one to talk with, some one sympathetic to exclaim to; in fact, I wished I were driving up this magnificent, this appalling road, beside the Chauffeulier instead of in Prince Dalmar-Kalm's tonneau. I wondered that Aunt Kathryn—usually so impulsive—could restrain herself here, and expected at any moment to have her turn to me, our differences forgotten. But no, she neither moved nor spoke, and I realized how angry she must be with me, to visit her vexation upon herself, and the Prince also.

I had thought the Col di Tenda wonderful, and the way down to Bellagio over the mountains still more thrilling; but here, they were dwarfed into utter insignificance. I could have imagined nothing like this feat of engineering, nothing so wild, so majestic as the ever-changing views from these incredible heights.

My respect for Schloss Hrvoya and its environment increased with every ascending mile; but the distance was proving itself so great that I did not see how it would be possible for the Prince to keep his promise, and get us back to Cattaro before eight. And we had left summer warmth as far behind as the level which it enriched with tropical flowers. The Prince suggested to Aunt Kathryn that she should wrap round her a shawl-like rug, and though I hated to follow his advice or take any favours from him, I decided that it would be foolish to make myself a martyr. So I, too, swaddled myself in woolly folds, and was thankful.

Now the windings of the Bocche di Cattaro revealed themselves completely. The bay was no longer a silk sleeve; but a vast star, seemingly cut out of a *lapis lazuli*, was set mosaic-like in the midst of green and blue-grey mountains that soared up from it—up, up, in shapes strange as a goblin's dream. Then, the azure star vanished, and rocky heights shut away the view of the distant sea. Vegetation grew sparse. At last we had reached the desolate and stony top of the mountain-range which a little while ago had touched the sky. Clouds like huge white swans swam in the blue air below us, where we could look down from some sheer precipice. But where was Schloss Hrvoya? And would Aunt Kathryn never speak to me?

Almost as if he read my thoughts, Prince Dalmar-Kalm turned his head, checking the speed of the motor. "Don't be discouraged," he said, cheerfully. "We shall be going down now, for a time, instead of up; and shortly we shall be at our journey's end."

"But soon it will be twilight," I answered. "Do you know, it is after six, and you said we would be back in Cattaro before eight. That's impossible now; and I'm afraid that there won't be much daylight for Aunt Kathryn to have a first look at her castle."

"It will be more imposing by twilight," replied the Prince; and though my words had been a bid for notice from Aunt Kathryn, she made no sign of having heard.

Once more Prince Dalmar-Kalm turned his attention to driving, and, as he had prophesied, we began to plunge down heights almost as tremendous as those we had climbed. The road, though splendidly engineered, was covered with loose, sharp stones; and the surging mountain-tops on every side were like the tossing waves of a desolate sea, turned to stone in some fierce spasm of nature. Then, in the midst of this petrified ocean, we flashed through a tiny village, and my hopes of reaching Schloss Hrvoya before nightfall brightened.

From the little group of low, stone buildings, men who must have sprung from a race of giants, rushed out in answer to the voice of our motor. I had never seen such wonderful men, unless, perhaps, Mr. Barrymore might be like them, if dressed as they were. Not one of the splendid band was under six feet in height, and many were much taller. On their handsome, close-cropped heads they wore gold-braided turbans over one ear. Their long coats, falling to the knee, were of green, or red, or white, open to show waistcoats crusted with gold embroidery. Round their slim waists were wound voluminous sashes stuck full of sheathed knives and huge pistols. Some had richly ornamented leather boots reaching half way up their long, straight legs, while others wore white leggings, with knitted stockings pulled up over them.

In a moment these gorgeous giants and their mean village were gone for us; but our road took us past persons walking towards the town; men, young and old, tall, beautiful boys, and white-clad women driving sheep, who knitted their husbands' stockings as they walked.

Here and there in a deep pit among the tumbled grey rocks would be a little vivid green dell, with a fairy ring of cultivated vegetation. This would be guarded, perhaps, by a hut of stone, almost savage in the crudeness of its construction. It was as if the proud people of this remote, mountain world, wishing to owe their all to their own country, nothing to outsiders, had preferred to make their houses with their own hands out of their own rocks, hewing the walls and roofing them with thatch from grass grown in their own pastures.

Impressed, almost terrified by the loneliness of this desolate land of giants, lit fiercely now by the lurid glow of sunset, I searched the distance for some towering hill crowned by a castle which might be Hrvoya. But there were no castles, even ruined castles, in this region of high rocks and lonely huts, and the red horizon was hemmed coldly in by a range of ghostly, snow-clad mountains.

"What mountains are those, far away?" I could not resist asking.

"They are the mountains of Albania," the Prince answered.

"Why, but that sounds as if we were at the end of the world!" I cried, startled.

He laughed over his shoulder. "And I am the last man in it! What did I say to you yesterday?"

This reminder brought back the anger I was forgetting in my need of human fellowship, and I did not speak again, but hugged little Airole the closer, nestled under the warm rug.

At the end of a long, straight road that stretched before us I could see a single, pale yellow light suddenly flash up in the twilight like a lonely primrose, and farther on a little knot of other lights blossomed in the dusk.

"We shall be there now in a few minutes," I was saying to myself, when suddenly I was startled by a loud report like a pistol-shot. Aunt Kathryn gave a shriek which was quite hoarse and unlike her natural voice, but I was silent, holding Airole trembling and barking under my arm.

The car swerved sharply, and my side of the tonneau seemed to settle down. I was sure that an invisible person must have shot at us, and wished sincerely that the Prince would drive on instead of slacking pace. But he stopped the engine, exclaiming in an angry voice, "A tyre burst! Thousand furies, why couldn't it have waited twenty minutes more?"

"Is it serious?" I asked; for we had never had this experience before, on any of the rough roads we had travelled.

"No," he answered shortly, "not serious, but annoying. We can crawl on for a little way. I was a fool to stop the motor; did it without thinking. Now I shall have the trouble of starting again."

Grumbling thus, he got out; but the motor wouldn't start. The engine was as sullenly silent as Aunt Kathryn. For ten minutes, perhaps, the Prince tried this device and that—no doubt missing Joseph; but at last he gave up in despair. "It is no use," he groaned. "I am spending myself for nothing. If you will sit quietly here for a few moments, I will go ahead to that house where the light is, to see if I can get you ladies taken in, and the car hauled into a place where I can work at it."

"What language do they speak here?" I asked, a chill of desolation upon me.

"Slavic," he answered. "But I can talk it a little. I shall get on, and you will see me again almost at once."

So saying, he was off, and I was alone with the statue of Aunt Kathryn.

At first I thought that, whatever happened, I wouldn't be the one to begin a conversation, but the silence and deepening darkness were too much for my nerves. "Oh, Aunt Kathryn, don't let's be cross to each other any longer," I pleaded. "I'm tired of it, aren't you? And oh, what wouldn't I give to be back in sweet Ragusa with Beechy and—and the others!"

Still not a word. It seemed incredible that she could bear malice so; but there was no cure for it. If she would not be softened by that plea of mine, nothing I could say would melt her. I should have liked to cry, for it was so lonely here, and so dreadful to be estranged from one's only friend. But that would have been too childish, and I took what comfort I could from Airole's tiny presence.

A quarter of an hour passed, perhaps, and then the Prince came back accompanied by a man so huge that the tall Austrian seemed a boy beside him. They looked at the car, communicating by gestures, and then the Prince said, if we would walk to the house the woman there would receive us, while he and his companion pushed the automobile into a shed which the man had.

I made no further attempt to extract a relenting word from Aunt Kathryn, as we tramped side by side along the road. Reaching a two-storied stone box of a house, she dropped behind at the doorway, leaving me to confront a hard-faced woman in a white jacket, with a graceful head-dress half-hiding her black hair. In one hand she had a partly finished stocking with knitting-needles in it; in the other she held a candle in a quaintly made iron candlestick. Something she said to us in a strange, but rather soft-sounding language, of which I couldn't understand one syllable; but seeing my hopelessly blank expression she smiled, nodded, and motioned us to cross the threshold.

The room was bare, with a floor of pounded earth. There was a wooden table in it, a few shelves, and a long bench; but beyond was a more attractive interior, for in an inner apartment she had lighted a fire of sticks on a rude hearth.

I stood aside to let Aunt Kathryn pass in before me, which she did without a word. We both stood before the fire, holding out gloved hands to the meagre blaze, while little Airole ran about, whimpering and examining everything with unconcealed disapproval.

I had just time to notice how oddly shabby Aunt Kathryn's gloves were, and to wonder if she didn't intend to take off the "mushroom" (the talc window of which the firelight transformed into a pane of red glass), when Prince Dalmar-Kalm appeared. Without asking permission he walked in, and looking at Aunt Kathryn, said in French, "You may go, Victorine."

I stared, as bewildered as if the unfamiliar scene were turning to a dream; but as the cloaked and mushroomed figure reached the door, the spell broke.

I took a step after it, exclaiming, "Aunt Kathryn—Kittie!"

The door shut almost in my face. "That is not your Aunt Kathryn," said the Prince, in a voice which, though low, vibrated with excitement. "It is one of the Contessa Corramini's servants, chosen to

293

play this part because her figure is enough like your aunt's to resemble it closely in a motor-coat. All that is of your aunt is that coat, the hat, the mask of silk. You must hear the truth now, for it is time, and know what you have to face."

"I don't understand you," I stammered weakly. It was more than ever as if I were in a dream. I actually told myself that I would wake up in bed at the Hotel Imperial in Ragusa. And oh, how I wished that I would wake soon!

"I will *make* you understand," went on the Prince. "You know — you've known for many days — how I love you. You have forced me to do this thing, because you were obstinate, and would not give me yourself, though I could not live without you. Because I could not, I have done this. It was planned as long ago as Venice. I confided all to Corramini, though not to his wife, and he promised to help me because he is in money difficulties, and I agreed to do something for him. But if you had been kind last night in Ragusa, when I gave you one more chance to repent, you might have been spared this. It was only to happen if all else failed."

"Still I don't understand," I said slowly.

"Then your brain is not as quick as usual, my dear one. I hoped Miss Beechy would be ill to-day, for she was the one I feared. There was a little medicine in that pink, Turkish stuff — not to hurt her much, but enough for my purpose. If I could, I would have got rid of the aunt, too; only she was needed as the cat's-paw. You would never have come without her. Contessa Corramini knows nothing of this, though she has a suspicion that something mysterious goes on. She was not on the 'Arethusa.' At this moment she is in Venice. Victorine was the one woman beside yourself and the aunt on the yacht, and Victorine has been well paid for the part she plays. She took the aunt's coat and hat and mask out of the cabin, when the lady was on deck with Corramini and me, wrapped in a becoming blue cloak with a hood, left on board by Contessa Corramini. While the aunt was looking everywhere for her missing things, you joined the masked lady in the car. Now, we are farther from Schloss Hrvoya than from Cattaro. You are in Montenegro, where I have brought

294

you because the Austrian Consul is my friend, and he will marry us."

"He will not!" I cried, choking and breathless.

"He must. It is the only thing for you, now. Let me show you the situation, in case you do not yet understand all. Your aunt is far away. She will be enraged with you, and believe you to blame for the humiliating trick played on her. Never will she forgive you. If there is a scandal, she will do her best to spread it. I know women well. Don't you remember, 'Hell hath no fury like a woman scorned?' There will be others, too. Victorine will tell a dramatic tale to the Contessa Corramini, and Corramini will gossip at his clubs in Venice, Rome, Florence, Paris, where many of your rich compatriots are members. The rights of the story will never quite be known, but it will leak out that you came to Montenegro with me alone, and spent many hours. The only safeguard is to make it an elopement, and that safeguard I offer you, with my heart and all that is mine. You must leave this place as the Princess Dalmar-Kalm, or it would be better for your future that you should never leave it. See, I am the last man in your world now, and it is necessary that you take me."

"I didn't know," I answered in the dream, "that men like you existed out of novels or stage plays. That is why I failed to understand at first. I was giving you the benefit of the doubt. But I understand now. Let me go—"

He laughed. "No! And if I did, what good would it do you? It is night; you are many miles from anywhere, in the wildest mountains of Europe. You do not speak one word of the language, or any one in this land a word of yours. Practically, you are alone in the world with me. Even your wretched little dog is not here to snarl. His curiosity took him outside, and he cannot get back through the keyhole of the door, small as he is. Presently the Consul will be at this house. I had meant to go to his had it not been for the accident, but I will send for him. He is my very good friend. He will do what I ask."

"But if I do not consent?" I flung at him.

"You will have to consent," he said; "and soon you will see that for yourself."

PART V

TOLD BY TERENCE BARRYMORE

XXV

A CHAPTER OF CHASING

I wondered why the ladies didn't come to lunch, for the last thing they had said when we brought them back in the motor was, "We shall see you again at half-past twelve."

Ralph and Bari and his sister and I, waited for a quarter of an hour; then we sat down, for the Signorina thought they might have changed their minds and be lunching with the little invalid. But at half-past one, while we were still at the table, a message came from Miss Beechy. She had waked up from her nap, "sent her compliments," and would be glad to know when her Mamma and cousin would return to her.

That took the Signorina flying to the bedroom, and there was an interval of some suspense for Ralph and me; for the absence of the ladies, with this new light thrown upon it, began to appear a little strange.

The Italian girl was away for an age, it seemed, and we knew the instant we saw her, that she was not the bearer of reassuring news. Her pretty face looked worried and excited.

"The Countess and Miss Destrey have not been up-stairs," she announced in her native tongue. "The little Bicé has been awake for an hour, wondering why they never came. Will you make inquiries of the landlord?"

I lost not a moment in obeying this request; and even before I got my answer, I seemed to know that Dalmar-Kalm would be mixed up in the affair. The ladies had driven away with His Highness in a hired cab not many minutes after we had brought them to the hotel door with the motor.

On the face of it, it looked ridiculous to fear mischief, yet I was uneasy. If I had not worshipped Her so much—but then, there had ceased to be any "if" in it long ago. I had very little hope that she could ever be got to care, even if I could reconcile it with common decency to ask a girl to think of a stony-broke beggar like me. But in some moods I was mad to try my luck, when I reflected on what she had before her if I— or some other brute of a man—didn't snatch her from it. But whether or no she were ever to be more to me than a goddess, the bare thought of trouble or harm coming to her was enough to drive me out of my wits.

While I was smoking two cigarettes a minute on the verandah, and asking myself whether I should be Paddy the Fool to track her down, with her aunt and the Prince, Signorina Bari (who had run up to Beechy with the latest developments) came out to us. "Sir Ralph," said she, "little Miss Kidder says she must see you, in a great hurry. She has something important to tell, that she can't tell to any one else; so she has got up, and is on the sofa in a dressing-gown, in the Countess's private sitting-room."

Ralph looked surprised, but not displeased, and was away twenty minutes.

"Miss Beechy wants us to find out where Dalmar-Kalm has taken her mother and Miss Destrey," said he, when he returned from the interview.

The order was welcome. Nothing was known at the hotel concerning the destination of the Prince and his companions in the cab, so I hurried to get the car, and Ralph and I drove off together, meaning to make inquiries in the town.

"Did Miss Beechy's mysterious communication have anything to do with her cousin? "I couldn't resist asking Ralph, who sat beside me, in that blessed seat sacred so long to the One Woman.

"Yes, it had," he replied discreetly.

"And with Dalmar-Kalm?"

"Distinctly with Dalmar-Kalm."

That sent some blood up behind my eyes, and I saw Ragusa red, instead of pink.

"By Jove, you've got to tell me what she did say, now!" I exclaimed.

"Can't, my dear chap. It's a promise—after a confidence. But I don't mind letting out this much. It seems Miss Beechy has been playing dolls with us, as she calls it, on this trip, without any of us suspecting it—or at least seeing the game in its full extent. Owing to her manipulation of her puppets, there's the dickens to pay, and she thinks she has reason to know that Dalmar-Kalm had better not be allowed to take a long excursion with Miss Destrey, even chaperoned by our dear, wise Countess."

"Good Heavens!" I jerked out. "What do you mean?"

"I don't exactly know myself. Things mayn't be as serious as the little girl thinks in her present remorseful mood, no doubt intensified by her late illness. 'When the devil was sick, the devil a monk would be,' you know—and the rest of it. Still, we're safe in finding out where the party has gone and taking steps accordingly."

"There's Joseph, mooning about with his hands in his pockets, like a lost soul," I exclaimed.

"*Have* lost souls pockets?"

"Shut up. I'm going to catechize him. He rather likes me, and has several times relieved his mind on the subject of his master, by spitting venom to his brother chauffeur until I refused to listen."

With this I stopped the car in front of the gaudy shop which had attracted the dismal little Joseph.

"Is your car mended already?" I asked him in French.

"It was not broken, Monsieur."

"Really. I understood the Prince to say it was."

299

"I know not what he said. Is there anything that His Highness would not say, if it pleased him? But so far from the car being injured, I was kept up most of the night by his command, putting it in the best order, looking to every nut, seeing that the grease-cups were filled, and everything as fine as though to try for first prize in a show. This morning did I get a moment's sleep? On the contrary, I must drive the automobile at eight o'clock, before any one was up, down to the harbour, and with much trouble put it on the yacht of the Conte Corramini, which had come into this port, the saints alone know why."

"I should say the saints had little to do with the affair," remarked Ralph, but I cut him short.

"What then?" I asked.

"Then it must be covered up, His Highness said, in case of rain—though the sky was as dry as my throat—till you could not tell the automobile from a haystack, on the forward deck where it had been placed."

"And after that?"

"After that I know nothing, except that His Highness condescended to remark that he would go away for a trip to-day, and I was to wait for him until I heard further. That will be soon, for when it comes to real work on the car it breaks his heart. He can drive, but apart from that he knows no more of the automobile than does the little black dog adopted by the beautiful mademoiselle."

"I suppose you'll get a wire to-morrow at latest," said I. "Well, *au revoir*. We're turning here."

"Going to the harbour?" Ralph asked, dryly, and I nodded.

I am afraid that we did the mile to Gravosa in a good deal less than the legal limit, but luckily no one was the worse for it, and there were no policemen about.

At Gravosa we found some men on the quay who could talk Italian, and in five minutes I knew for certain what I had suspected. A white yacht answering the description I gave of "Arethusa," had sent a boat before noon to meet a cab bringing to the port two ladies and a gentleman. The Signore were in long brownish coats and close hats. One was stout, with much colour; the other, a young girl, transcendently beautiful.

"That impudent fellow has whisked them off to Cattaro, to see his beastly ancestral ruin," suggested Ralph. "That's what he's done. He's probably chuckling now with savage glee to think that willy- nilly Countess Kidder-Dalmar can't get out of her bargain."

"I don't believe they would willingly have left the little girl lying there ill, to say nothing of leaving us in the lurch without a word," said I. "Ralph, there's something pretty devilish under this, or I'll eat my hat."

"Well, I should expect to see you devouring it, if—I hadn't heard Beechy's confess—if she hadn't told me some things," Ralph amended his sentence.

"I'm hanged if I won't give chase!" I exclaimed.

"How can you? You were saying at lunch that so far as you'd been able to fog it out, there wasn't more than the ghost of a road after Castelnuovo on to Cattaro; and it's to Cattaro one must go for the ancestral ruin."

"If there's a ghost of a road, it will do for me and this motor," I said. "What does it matter if we're both smashed, if only we get there first?"

"Men and motors don't get far when they're smashed. You'll have to wait till to-morrow morning, when we can all go flying down by the Austrian Lloyd, if the truants don't turn up in the meantime."

"Wait till to-morrow morning? My name isn't Terence Barrymore if I do that, or if I wait one minute longer than it will take me to go back where I came, and load up with petrol enough to see me through this job for good or evil."

"You'll start off at once, without finding out any more—and road or no road?"

"There's no more to find out this side of Cattaro, unless I'm far out of my reckoning; and if there's no road after Castelnuovo, I'll—I'll get through somehow, never fear."

"I don't fear much, when you set your jaw that way, my son. I suppose you'll just give me time to make my will, and—er—say good-bye to Miss Beechy?"

"You're not going, Ralph. I must travel light, for speed; I don't want an unnecessary ounce of weight on board that car to-day, for she's got to show her paces as she never did before. You must stop behind, and instead of saying good-bye, try to cheer Miss Beechy."

"Well, needs must, when *somebody* drives," mumbled Ralph. But he did not look very dismal.

I made no preparations, save to fill up with petrol and put all the spare *bidons* sent by the Austrian Lloyd in the tonneau. I was in flannels, as the day was not to be a motoring day, and I wouldn't have delayed even long enough to fetch my big coat, if I hadn't suddenly thought that I might be glad of it for Her. Ralph saw me off, making me promise to wire from Cattaro—if I ever got there!— as soon as there was news for Beechy of her mother and cousin.

Once out on the open road I gave the old car her head, and she bounded along like an India rubber ball, curtseying to undulations, spinning round curves along the sea coast, and past quaint old towns which I thought of only as obstacles.

Often when you wish your car to show what she can do, she puts on the air of a spoiled child and shames you. But to-day it was as if the motor knew what I wanted, and was straining every nerve to help me get it. In a time that was short even to my impatience, she and I did the thirty-odd miles to Castelnuovo. A few questions there as to the feasibility of trying to reach Cattaro by road, brought no information definite enough to make the experiment worth the risk of failure. At best there would be many rough miles to cover, in rounding the numerous arms of that great starfish, the Bocche di Cattaro, and no boat of the Austrian Lloyd or Hungarian Croatian lines was available to-day, even if shipping the motor in that way wouldn't have involved endless red tape, delay and bother. Nevertheless, with a simmering inspiration in my mind, I steered the car down a narrow road that led to the harbour, a crowd pattering after me which, no doubt, was very picturesque if I had been in the mood to observe it. But my eyes were open for one thing only, and at the port under the high walls of the fortresses that leap to the sky, I knew that I had found it.

A good-sized fishing boat with a painted sail aflap against the mast, lay alongside the quay. Beside it stood gossiping two fine sailor-men, heroically tall, with features cut in bronze. At the thrum of the motor and clatter of the crowd they turned to stare, and I drove straight at them, but in order not to give them a fright stopped short a good five yards away.

The proud men of these parts are not easily scared, and all that these two did was to take their black pipes out of their mouths. Not a word of Slavic have I to bless myself with, but I tumbled out Italian sentences, and they understood, as I was pretty sure they would. What I asked was, would they take me and my motor in their boat, immediately, on the instant, to Cattaro? One grinned; the other shook his head; but he hadn't wagged it from left to right before I pulled a handful of Austrian gold and silver out of my pockets, which were luckily well-filled with the hard-earned money of my chauffeurhood.

The man who had grinned, grinned wider; the man who had shaken his head did not shake it again. I bargained just enough to please them with the notion that they were plucking me; and five minutes later we three were hauling a few planks scattered on the quay, to form a gangway to the boat.

As for the fascinated crowd, not a man Jack of them but was at my service, after the display of coin which no bright eye had missed. In no time we had our gangway laid on to the gunwale, and a couple of sloping planks to roll the motor on board. The next thing was for me to jump into the car and begin to drive gently ahead, directing the sailors with nods and becks to steady her by grasping the spokes of her wheels. Thus we got her into the boat, none the worse for the ordeal; then, picking up a rope, I was about to make her fast when professional spirit woke in my two hosts, and taking the rope from me they lashed the car as none but seamen can.

While one stalwart fellow poled the boat off from the quay, his mate hoisted the yard that carried the triangular sail. A following wind, which had been detestable on the dusty road, gave us good speed on our errand; the broad-bowed old boat made creaking progress, a shower of silver foam hissing from her cutwater.

My furious energy had been contagious, and perhaps, seeing my desire for haste, the fishers hoped to earn something further from the madman's gratitude. All they could do to urge their craft they did.

In other circumstances—say with Her by my side—I should have been filled with enthusiasm for the Bocche di Cattaro and its scenery, for never had I seen anything quite like it; but now I grudged each screen of rock that stopped the breeze, each winding of the water.

From the narrow opening where the Adriatic rushes into Cattaro at the hidden end of the great sheet of lakes, can't be more than fifteen miles as the crow flies; but so does the course twist that it is much longer for mere wingless things, going by water. How I wished for a motor-boat! But we did not do badly in the big fishing smack. I feared at last that in the straits the wind might die, but instead it blew as through a funnel. We were swept finely up the narrow channel, and so into the last lake with Cattaro and its high fort at the end of it; and my heart gave a bound as I saw "Arethusa" lying anchored at the quay.

We had more trouble in landing the motor than in getting her aboard, but the thing was done at last; more coins changed hands, and there was the car on shore with another crowd round her. I engaged one of my bronzed fishermen to stand guard lest mischief should be done, and stalked off to the yacht; but before I reached her I was met by Corramini himself, all smiles and graciousness.

"I heard your motor," said he, "and guessed your mission. You have come, of course, to see the ladies?"

"Yes," said I, not troubling to waste words on him. "Miss Kidder is anxious."

"Ah, then did they not leave word? I suppose there wasn't time, as I understand the excursion was planned in a hurry. I don't know the details. It has only been my duty, as my pleasure, to act as host. Dalmar-Kalm desired to show the ladies Schloss Hrvoya, and brought his automobile on board for that purpose. He started almost as soon as we arrived here, well before five o'clock, and should have been back some time ago, according to his calculation. But I suppose it was a temptation to linger, or else there has been trouble with the motor. Unfortunately the chauffeur was left at Ragusa, as my friend is inclined to be a little vain of his driving. But I doubt his powers as an engineer, and have been somewhat anxious for the past half hour."

"It is after seven o'clock," I said.

"Yes. I was dining when I heard your motor. I would ask you on board to have something, but I see by your face that you have it in mind to run to the rescue; and perhaps it would be kind as well as wise. Do you know how to reach Schloss Hrvoya?"

"I have seen it on the map," I replied, "and can easily find it, no doubt, by inquiries."

"Or you may meet the other automobile *en route*. Well, your coming is a relief to my mind. I shall be glad to hear on your return that all is well."

"Thanks," said I rather stiffly, for the man's personality was repellent to me, and in Venice I'd heard some stories, not very nice ones, concerning his career. He is of good family, is tolerated by society for his dead father's sake and his wife's, but once or twice a crash has nearly come, so the whisper runs about the clubs.

Not trusting his fluent affability, I hesitated whether to believe him and start, or to say I would accept his suggestion to go on board, in order that I might have a look round "Arethusa" before committing myself to anything. As I stood in doubt I was hailed from the deck of the yacht, and there, to my surprise, stood our Countess, showing dishevelment even in the distance and twilight.

"Oh, Mr. Terrymore, is that *you*?" she cried to me.

I gave the Corramini a look, as I shouted in reply, but he shrugged his shoulders. "I had no time to mention yet that the Countess was not of the party for Schloss Hrvoya," said he, "for thereby hangs a tale, as your great poet says, and it would have taken too long to tell; but now I suppose she must delay you. It is a pity."

I had no answer for him. It was clear that, whatever had occurred, it had been his object to deceive me, and hustle me quickly away from the dangerous neighbourhood of the yacht before I could find out that the Countess, at all events, was still on board. But chance had thwarted him, and he was making the best of it with characteristic cleverness, saving his own skin.

Bareheaded, her wondrous auburn hair disordered, her face blurred with half-dried tears, the poor woman met me half-way, skipping across the gangway on to the now almost deserted quay.

"Something awful's happened," she gasped.

"What?" I asked, a sudden tightness in my throat

.

"That's the worst of it. I don't know. And the County doesn't know."

"Tell me as well as you can."

"Why, we came here on purpose for the Prince to take me to Slosh Hrvoya. He wanted it so much. Maida had to be along, because it would have made talk if he and I'd come alone; but her being with us wasn't of any importance to *him*, he told me so himself. Well, when his automobile was landed just where we're standing now, I told Maida to get ready and went to my cabin to get ready myself, but my things were all gone—my hat and coat, and motor-mask and everything. I thought, I could have left them in the sallong, though I was sure I hadn't; but I hurried to look. They weren't there, and I ran back to Maida's door, thinking it just possible, to play me a trick—as she was cross—she might have hidden my things while I was on deck. But she'd gone off and the things were nowhere. At that minute I heard a noise like a motor, and looked out of my porthole, but already it was out of sight from there, and I got up on deck again only in time to catch sight of the Prince's automobile flashing away at about a mile a minute."

"Miss Destrey was in the car?"

"Of course. She was sitting in the tonneau; and it looked as if there was some one beside the Prince; but Maida was in the way, so I couldn't make sure, and while I was dodging my head about, trying to see, the automobile disappeared. Did you ever know anything so horrid? I'm furious, and I don't know what the Prince must be thinking of me."

I was aghast at this unexpected point of view, but her next words enlightened me. "It's Maida's fault, I know that, though I don't see how she managed the thing. She was wild with me because I stood up for the Prince carrying us off like this, and I suppose she just thought she'd punish me by somehow cheating me out of the pleasure I'd been looking forward to. I can't think of anything else, and neither can the County. He says Maida probably told the Prince that at the last minute I'd refused to go with him; otherwise he never would have driven off with her and left me like that."

I saw that it would be a simple waste of time to argue with her, and didn't attempt it. "I'm going to look for them," I said.

"Oh, *do* take me with you."

I thought for a second or two. The Countess isn't exactly a featherweight, and speed was an object; but protection for Miss Destrey was a still greater consideration, and it might be well for her to have even this foolish little woman's companionship. "Certainly," I replied. "I shall be very glad."

Wraps of some sort for her head and body were borrowed on board the yacht, Corramini showing himself kind and helpful, and with but a few minutes' delay for the lady's preparations, and lighting the lamps, we were ready to start.

My mind was on the rack of doubt and distraction, but though I trusted Corramini not at all, I couldn't see why the most likely way to choose for the chase might not be the road to Hrvoya. Dalmar- Kalm must be more or less familiar with the neighbourhood, and might have acquaintances along the route who would help him. Corramini was watching the start, so I took the direction which, from some previous poring over local maps, I knew must lead towards Dalmar-Kalm's ruinous inheritance. This I did, lest he might have some means of communicating with his friend; but once out of his sight, I slowed down, and addressed every one I met, in Italian. Had a motor-car been seen driving this way during the afternoon? Several persons stared blankly, and did not brighten to intelligence when Italian was exchanged for faulty German; but we had not gone far when we caught up with a ricketty cab, whose driver was evidently dawdling homeward to shelter for the night. His pitch was, perhaps, near the quay, and if so he might be the very man I wanted.

I hailed him, and fortunately he had a little Italian, and more French, of which he was innocently vain.

"I have seen an automobile," said he, "but it was not coming this way. There cannot have been another, for till to-day we have seen no such thing since Prince Jaimé de Bourbon drove here and up to Montenegro, which made a great excitement for every one some years ago. And this one to-day has also gone to Montenegro."

I asked him to describe the vehicle, and not only did he give it all the characteristics of the Prince's car, but said that he had seen it slung on shore from a white yacht, which ended all doubt upon the motor's identity, unless by any chance he had been bribed by Dalmar-Kalm to mislead inquirers. This seemed a far-fetched supposition; but why should Montenegro be chosen as a destination? I asked this question aloud, half to myself, half to the Countess, and after a fashion she answered it from the tonneau.

"Dear me, I can't think why on earth they should go there; but I believe I *do* remember the Prince once saying, ever so long ago when we first talked of driving down into Dalmatia, that he had a friend in Montenegro—an Austrian Consul, though I don't know in what city there."

"There's only one—the capital, Cettinje," I said mechanically, and my thoughts leaped ahead to the place I named.

"The scoundrel!" I muttered under my breath.

"Who, the Austrian Consul?"

"No. For all I know, he may be a splendid fellow and probably is; he would never do the thing. But that beast might hope it."

"What beast—what thing—hope what?"

"I beg your pardon, Countess. I was talking to myself. Nothing that you would care to hear repeated."

XXVI

A CHAPTER OF HIGH DIPLOMACY

I had heard travellers speak, and had read in books, of that mighty feat of engineering the road to Montenegro; but even so I was not prepared for the thrilling grandeur of that night drive in the mountains.

With a carriage and two horses, counting halts for rests we must have been seven good hours on the way to Cettinje; but my little twelve horse-power car worked with me heart and soul (I shall always believe now that she's got something of the sort, packed away in her engine), and we reached the lonely Montenegrin frontier, near the mountain-top, in not much over an hour after our start. I caught the glimmer of the white stones that mark the dividing line between Austrian ground and the brave little Principality, and knew what they must mean. Twenty minutes more saw us at the highest point of the stupendous road; and dipping for a flight downward, we arrived not long after in the cup-like plain where the first Montenegrin village showed a few lights. I stopped at a small inn, ordered brandy for the Countess (who was half dead with cold or terror of our wild race beside precipices) and inquired of the German-speaking landlord about the Prince's car.

Yes, a big red automobile had rushed by, much to the surprise of everyone, about an hour ago. No doubt it was bound for Cettinje; but there had been no news of it since.

We flashed on without waiting for further parley. It was a long way yet, but the car devoured the road as if she were starving. At last we saw a single light to the left, and then a bunch of lights huddled together in a mountain-ringed plain, half a mile or so beyond. To my annoyance I had to slacken speed for a flock of belated and bewildered sheep, just as we were nearing the first light, but in a moment we would have shot ahead again, had not my attention been caught by the sharp yelping of a little dog

It was not the defiant yap of an enemy to motors, but rather a glad welcome; and the thin shred of sound was curiously familiar. Instead of putting on speed, I stopped dead in the middle of the road.

"Whist! Airole, is that you?" I called.

In an instant a tiny black form was making wild springs at the car, trying to get in. It was Airole and no other.

"This is where they are," I said. "In that house, yonder. If it hadn't been for the dog, we'd have gone on, and —" It wasn't worth while to finish.

I drove to the side and stopped the engine. The Countess would go with me, of course, and it was better that she should; for she was the girl's aunt, and this was the pass her foolishness had brought her to.

Airole pattered before us, leaping at the shut door of a rough, two-story house of dark stone. I knocked; no one came, and I pounded again. If there had been no answer that time, I meant to try and break the door in with my shoulder, which has had some experience as a battering ram and perhaps those inside guessed at my intentions, for there followed a scrambling sound. A bolt was slipped back, and then a tall Montenegrin, belted and armed with knife and big revolver, blocked up the doorway.

I tried him in Italian. No use; he jabbered protests in Slavic, with a wife peeping curiously over his shoulder, as the Countess peeped over mine. Finally, to save time and somebody's blood, perhaps, I offered an Austrian note and it proved a passport. They let us go in; and entering, I heard Miss Destrey's voice raised in fear or anger, behind another closed door.

Then most of the blood in my body seemed to spring to my head, and I have no very distinct recollection of anything more, till I found that I had done to that second door what I'd meant to do to the first, and that Maida had run straight into my arms.

"My darling!" I heard myself exclaiming. I know that I held her tight against my heart for an instant, saying, "Thank Heaven!" that she seemed to have been mine for all the past and must belong to me for all the future. I know that she was sobbing a little, that she clung to me; and that then, remembering the man and what was owing him, I put her away to begin his punishment.

"You unspeakable ruffian!" I threw the words at him, and threw myself at the same time. I think we struggled for a few moments, but I am younger than he, as well as bigger, so it was not much credit to my prowess that I soon had my hand twisted in his collar and was shaking him as if he'd been a rat

.

It was the Countess who stopped the fun, by hurling herself between us, quite like the heroine of old-fashioned melodrama. "Oh, for my sake, for *my* sake!" she was wailing. "It wasn't his fault. Wait and let him have the chance to explain."

One more shake I gave, and threw him off, so that he staggered back against the wall.

"He threatened to shoot me at last," cried Maida.

"Shall I kill him?" I asked.

"No," she said trembling. "Let him go. You are here. I am safe."

The man stood and glared at us like an animal at bay. I saw his eyes dart from Maida to me, from me to the Countess, and rest on her as if begging something. And his hunted instinct was right. If there were hope left for him anywhere, it was with her

"Don't believe anything they say of me," he panted, dry-lipped. "Corramini tricked me by sending his wife's servant in your place, dressed in your things, wearing your motor-mask. She wouldn't speak. I didn't know the truth till I got here. I thought it was you I had run away with to Montenegro, hoping I might persuade you to marry me, when you were out of the way of your daughter, who hates me, and would ruin me with you if she could. I would have left Miss Destrey behind, if I could have hoped you'd come without her. Imagine my feelings when I found out I'd lost you! If I have frightened her it was in my blind rage against her and every one concerned in the trick. As for your chauffeur, he is not worth fighting, and as I am a gentleman, I do not even return the blows of one who is not—especially before ladies."

"Aunt Kathryn, you must not believe his falsehoods," cried Maida. "If you do—if you let yourself care for him—he will spoil your life."

The Countess petulantly stopped her ears. "I won't listen to you," was her answer. "I knew there had been trickery of some sort, and you may as well save your breath, for whatever you say I will believe nothing against the man I love."

With that she took her fingers from her ears, and held out both hands to Dalmar-Kalm. He ran to take them, and pressed his lips ardently first upon one, then the other plump cushion of dimpled satin.

Disgusted with this exhibition of a woman's folly, while I pitied it, I could look no more, but turned to Maida.

"Will you let me take you away?" was all that my lips said, but my eyes said more, in memory of that first moment of our meeting, which was, please God, to influence our whole future—hers and mine.

"Yes," she answered."But—I can't leave here without Aunt Kathryn."

"You must go with Miss Destrey, Countess," I insisted. "Whatever you may decide later in regard to Prince Dalmar-Kalm, in any case you must go with your niece and me to stop at an hotel in Cettinje, for the night."

The man would not let go her hand. "Promise me you will not leave Montenegro till you are my wife," he begged. "If you do, I feel I shall lose you for ever."

"I'll do my best," faltered the lady, as a lady should, I suppose, who feels herself a heroine of romance. I could almost have respected that scoundrel for his diplomacy. His motto was, "Get what you want, or if you can't, take what you can;" and he was living up to it, playing up to it before an audience as no other man I ever saw could or would. He didn't seem to care what we thought of him, now that he was gaining his point. But when fatty degeneration of the soul sets in, there is room for little real pride in a man's breast.

"You will not allow yourself to be prejudiced against me?" he went on.

"Never," vowed the Countess. "No one had better try it."

"I will not try after to-night, if what I have to tell doesn't change your mind," said Maida. "But, just this once —"

"No — no!"

"Very well then, I will say nothing except —"

"Be careful!"

"Oh," and the girl turned imploringly to me, "take us somewhere, so that I can talk to her alone."

"There's said to be a good enough hotel in Cettinje. I'll take you both there," I ventured.

"Come and see me early — early, Prince," said the Countess.

"Yes. But I am not 'Prince' to you now. I am 'Otto.'"

"Otto, then."

So I got them away, leaving the man behind, to his own devices, and at the door I had the joy of wrapping Maida in my big coat. How glad I was that I had brought it! I drove them to a hotel in the *place* at the end of the long main street, and when the Countess had hurried ostentatiously off to her room, that no nefarious attempts might be made upon her resolution. She and I stood for a moment hand in hand, in the dim hall.

"You are mine?" I asked. "Are

you sure you want me?"

"I've been sure of that—too sure for my peace of mind since the first day I saw your dear face—the loveliest on earth. But I never thought to have you. I never thought that I would have a right to ask, for I'm poor—horribly poor."

"Oh, as if that mattered!"

"I know it doesn't now, for this that's happened has given us to each other. I'll work hard and make money. Nothing can part us—I couldn't bear it. But it seems too good to be true. Is it possible you care for me?"

"I think I've cared—ever since the first few days. I'd never guessed that I would meet a man like you. But oh, I did not mean to marry *any* man."

"I know, darling. I know what you'd planned. I lay awake nights over it, wondering if, beggar as I was, I couldn't snatch you from that cold future. But I shouldn't have thought I had the right if this thunderbolt hadn't struck me."

"As Aunt Kathryn—poor Aunt Kathryn!—is always saying, 'It must have been meant.' I never promised that—that I would join the Sisters, you know. I suppose this is why my father would have me go abroad when I came of age. He was afraid I might make up my mind before I had—found my heart."

"Have you found it now—for sure?"

"No. I—I've *lost* it."

"Angel! But you've got mine instead. You won't mind marrying a beggar and being a beggaress?"

The adorable creature laughed. "I shall love it," she said. There was no one in the hall except Airole, and the shadows were asleep—so I kissed her: and knew why I had been born. I'd often wondered, but I never will again.

315

We had a fierce tussle with the Countess to prevent her stopping in Montenegro and marrying her Prince there and then, as soon as might be. The truth was, and she owned it, that she was afraid to face Beechy till she had been made irrevocably a Princess. But finally we prevailed, almost by force, and tore the poor lady from her lover, who protested that he would follow, were it to the world's end. I believed he would, too, for he had threatened to be the last man in Maida's world; the Countess was now the last woman in his, and he would hold on to her and her money as a drowning man grasps at a substantial spar.

I shall never forget that drive down from the mountain land where a King rode to fetch a fairy bride

.

At Cattaro we took the fishing boat which had carried me yesterday; and I think the sailor-men realized, when they saw what I had brought back, that I wasn't a madman after all.

Then the spin from Castelnuovo to Ragusa that I had taken in such a different mood fifteen hours before. And at Ragusa, Beechy, still pale and shaken, springing up from her sofa to meet Maida and me as we opened the door.

Ralph sprang up too, and his chair had been drawn so close to her sofa that the rush of her white wrapper—or whatever it was—upset it.

"Where's Mamma?" came the first question, as was natural.

"She's gone to her room, and we're to talk to you before she sees you," said Maida. "Oh Beechy, you must be good to her; she's miserable."

Then we told the story, preparing Beechy for her mother's decision, and I expected hysterics. But she neither laughed nor cried. She only sat still, looking curiously guilty and meek.

"Isn't it dreadful? But I couldn't do anything," said Maida. "He is a wicked man—you don't know yet how wicked. He got me up to Montenegro by a horrid pretence, and when I wouldn't promise to marry him at once he tried arguments for about an hour, then locked the door of a room in the house where we were because his motor broke down, and threatened to shoot me. I don't know if he really would. Perhaps not. But anyway, Mr. Barrymore saved me. He came just then and burst the door open."

"It's all my fault from beginning to end!" broke out Beechy, tragically. "I confessed to Sir Ralph yesterday, when I was only worried for fear something might happen, but now it *has* happened, I'll confess to you, too. I got afraid Mamma would really marry the Prince—oh, but that wasn't the way it began! Just for fun, long ago, when we first started, I let him pump me—it was great fun *then*— and told him how rich Mamma was, and would be, even if she married again. I thought it would be such larks to watch his game, and so it was for a while, till I was in an awful stew for fear I'd gone too far and couldn't stop things. I was ready then to do something desperate rather than find myself saddled with *that* Prince for my step-father. So I sacrificed you."

"I don't see—" Maida began; but Beechy cut her short.

"Why, when we went to that Sisterhood of yours, I overheard the Mother Superior, or whatever you call her, confiding to Mamma that you were a tremendous heiress, that you didn't quite know how rich you were yourself, and wouldn't be told till you were safely back from Europe. It was a secret, and I hadn't any business to know. But I let it out to the Prince, when I was in such a state about him and Mamma, in Bellagio. He *went* for you at once, as I knew he would— but what's the matter, Mr. Barrymore? It isn't for you to be angry with me. It's for Maida."

"I'm not angry with you, but with myself," I said. And then for a minute I forgot Ralph and Beechy, and remembered only Maida. "Don't think I knew," I said. "If I had, I wouldn't—"

"Oh, don't say you wouldn't. I love to feel you *had* to," the Angel cried. "I hold you to your word, oh, with all my heart in my right to you. Beechy, your Chauffeulier and I—are engaged."

"There!" the child exclaimed, with a look at Ralph I couldn't fathom. "Didn't I tell you so?"

"Well, it doesn't matter *now*, does it?" was his retort. "How shall I feel if you don't wish Miss Destrey your best wishes?"

"Oh, I do, I do," exclaimed the strange child. "And I congratulate the Chauffeulier. But he must do some congratulating too. I'm going to put up my hair, come out in a long dress, and be engaged to Sir Ralph."

Maida's great eyes were greater than ever. "Beechy!" she protested. "You aren't fourteen!"

"No, I know I'm not; but I'm seventeen. And when I told Ralph that, he proposed at once. You see he's been my father confessor ever since we've been on this trip, so he knows all that's best and worst of me; and I do think we shall have real fun when we're married. I told Mamma I'd have no Princes on *my* ranch, and I won't. But if she's fool enough to take that man, after all, she and I can visit each other's ranches after this, and we'll be all right. Mine's going to be in England or Scotland in summer, and in winter I'm to live with Félicité and the duck. Oh, I shall be happy, and so will Ralph, I hope. But I never thought a good democrat like Papa's daughter would go and marry a man with a title."

"A mere baronet. It needn't go against the grain much," remarked Sir Ralph. "Think how much worse it is for your poor cousin!"

"Why?"

"To marry a 'real live lord,' who will some day be a marquis."

"Oh!" exclaimed Beechy. "She who said she would like to teach other American girls a lesson."

"I didn't know," Maida faltered.

"What?" asked Ralph. "You didn't tell her?"

"I forgot all about it," I said. "But Maida, dearest, it doesn't matter. I—"

"Nothing matters but you," she said.

"And you," I added.

THE END

Good Fiction Worth Reading.

A series of romances containing several of the old favorites in the field of historical fiction, replete with powerful romances of love and diplomacy that excel in thrilling and absorbing interest.

WINDSOR CASTLE. A Historical Romance of the Reign of Henry VIII. Catharine of Aragon and Anne Boleyn. By Wm. Harrison Ainsworth. Cloth, 12mo. with four illustrations by George Cruikshank. Price, $1.00.

"Windsor Castle" is the story of Henry VIII., Catharine, and Anne Boleyn. "Bluff King Hal," although a well-loved monarch, was none too good a one in many ways. Of all his selfishness and unwarrantable acts, none was more discreditable than his divorce from Catharine, and his marriage to the beautiful Anne Boleyn. The King's love was as brief as it was vehement. Jane Seymour, waiting maid on the Queen, attracted him, and Anne Boleyn was forced to the block to make room for her successor. This romance is one of extreme interest to all readers.

HORSESHOE ROBINSON. A tale of the Tory Ascendency in South Carolina in 1780. By John P. Kennedy. Cloth, 12mo. with four illustrations by J. Watson Davis. Price, $1.00.

Among the old favorites in the field of what is known as historical fiction, there are none which appeal to a larger number of Americans than Horseshoe Robinson, and this because it is the only story which depicts with fidelity to the facts the heroic efforts of the colonists in South Carolina to defend their homes against the brutal oppression of the British under such leaders as Cornwallis and Tarleton.

The reader is charmed with the story of love which forms the thread of the tale, and then impressed with the wealth of detail concerning those times. The picture of the manifold sufferings of the people, is never overdrawn, but painted faithfully and honestly by one who spared neither time nor labor in his efforts to present in this charming love story all that price in blood and tears which the Carolinians paid as their share in the winning of the republic.

Take it all in all, "Horseshoe Robinson" is a work which should be found on every book-shelf, not only because it is a most entertaining story, but because of the wealth of valuable information concerning the colonists which it contains. That it has been brought out once more, well illustrated, is something which will give pleasure to thousands who have long desired an opportunity to read the story again, and to the many who have tried vainly in these latter days to procure a copy that they might read it for the first time.

THE PEARL OF ORR'S ISLAND. A story of the Coast of Maine. By Harriet Beecher Stowe. Cloth, 12mo. Illustrated. Price, $1.00.

Written prior to 1862, the "Pearl of Orr's Island" is ever new; a book filled with delicate fancies, such as seemingly array themselves anew each time one reads them. One sees the "sea like an unbroken mirror all around the pine-girt, lonely shores of Orr's Island," and straightway comes "the heavy, hollow moan of the surf on the beach, like the wild, angry howl of some savage animal."

Who can read of the beginning of that sweet life, named Mara, which came into this world under the very shadow of the Death angel's wings, without having an intense desire to know how the premature bud blossomed? Again and again one lingers over the descriptions of the character of that baby boy Moses, who came through the tempest, amid the angry billows, pillowed on his dead mother's breast.

There is no more faithful portrayal of New England life than that which Mrs. Stowe gives in "The Pearl of Orr's Island."

GUY FAWKES. A Romance of the Gunpowder Treason. By Wm. Harrison Ainsworth. Cloth, 12mo. with four illustrations by George Cruikshank. Price, $1.00.

The "Gunpowder Plot" was a modest attempt to blow up Parliament, the King and his Counsellors. James of Scotland, then King of England, was weak-minded and extravagant. He hit upon the efficient scheme of extorting money from the people by imposing taxes on the Catholics. In their natural resentment to this extortion, a handful of bold spirits concluded to overthrow the government. Finally the plotters were arrested, and the King put to torture Guy Fawkes and the other prisoners with royal vigor. A very intense love story runs through the entire romance.

THE SPIRIT OF THE BORDER. A Romance of the Early Settlers in the Ohio Valley. By Zane Grey. Cloth, 12mo. with four illustrations by J. Watson Davis. Price, $1.00.

A book rather out of the ordinary is this "Spirit of the Border." The main thread of the story has to do with the work of the Moravian missionaries in the Ohio Valley. Incidentally the reader is given details of the frontier life of those hardy pioneers who broke the wilderness for the planting of this great nation. Chief among these, as a matter of course, is Lewis Wetzel, one of the most peculiar, and at the same time the most admirable of all the brave men who spent their lives battling with the savage foe, that others might dwell in comparative security.

Details of the establishment and destruction of the Moravian "Village of Peace" are given at some length, and with minute description. The efforts to Christianize the Indians are described as they never have been before, and the author has depicted the characters of the leaders of the several Indian tribes with great care, which of itself will be of interest to the student.

By no means least among the charms of the story are the vivid word-pictures of the thrilling adventures, and the intense paintings of the beauties of nature, as seen in the almost unbroken forests.

It is the spirit of the frontier which is described, and one can by it, perhaps, the better understand why men, and women, too, willingly braved every privation and danger that the westward progress of the star of empire might be the more certain and rapid. A love story, simple and tender, runs through the book.

RICHELIEU. A tale of France in the reign of King Louis XIII. By G. P. R. James. Cloth, 12mo. with four illustrations by J. Watson Davis. Price, $1.00.

In 1829 Mr. James published his first romance, "Richelieu," and was recognized at once as one of the masters of the craft.

In this book he laid the story during those later days of the great cardinal's life, when his power was beginning to wane, but while it was yet sufficiently strong to permit now and then of volcanic outbursts which overwhelmed foes and carried friends to the topmost wave of prosperity. One of the most striking portions of the story is that of Cinq Mar's conspiracy; the method of conducting criminal cases, and the political trickery resorted to by royal favorites, affording a better insight into the statecraft of that day than can be had even by an exhaustive study of history. It is a powerful romance of love and diplomacy, and in point of thrilling and absorbing interest has never been excelled.

DARNLEY. A Romance of the times of Henry VIII. and Cardinal Wolsey. By G. P. R. James. Cloth, 12mo. with four illustrations by J. Watson Davis. Price, $1.00.

In point of publication, "Darnley" is that work by Mr. James which follows "Richelieu," and, if rumor can be credited, it was owing to the advice and insistence of our own Washington Irving that we are indebted primarily for the story, the young author questioning whether he could properly paint the differences in the characters of the two great cardinals. And it is not surprising that James should have hesitated; he had been eminently successful in giving to the world the portrait of Richelieu as a man, and by attempting a similar task with Wolsey as the theme, was much like tempting fortune. Irving insisted that "Darnley" came naturally in sequence, and this opinion being supported by Sir Walter Scott, the author set about the work.

As a historical romance "Darnley" is a book that can be taken up pleasurably again and again, for there is about it that subtle charm which those who are strangers to the works of G. P. R. James have claimed was only to be imparted by Dumas.

If there was nothing more about the work to attract especial attention, the account of the meetings of the kings on the historic "field of the cloth of gold" would entitle the story to the most favorable consideration of every reader.

There is really but little pure romance in this story, for the author has taken care to having entertained the tender passion one for another, and he succeeds in making such lovers as all the world must love.

CAPTAIN BRAND, OF THE SCHOONER CENTIPEDE. By Lieut. Henry A. Wise, U.S.N. (Harry Gringo). Cloth, 12mo. with four illustrations by J. Watson Davis. Price, $1.00.

The re-publication of this story will please those lovers of sea yarns who delight in so much of the salty flavor of the ocean as can come through the medium of a printed page, for never has a story of the sea and those "who go down in ships" been written by one more familiar with the scenes depicted.

The one book of this gifted author which is best remembered, and which will be read with pleasure for many years to come, is "Captain Brand," who, as the author states on his title page, was a "pirate of eminence in the West Indies." As a sea story pure and simple, "Captain Brand" has never been excelled, and as a story of piratical life, told without the usual embellishments of blood and thunder, it has no equal.

NICK OF THE WOODS. A story of the Early Settlers of Kentucky. By Robert Montgomery Bird. Cloth, 12mo. with four illustrations by J. Watson Davis. Price, $1.00.

This most popular novel and thrilling story of early frontier life in Kentucky was originally published in the year 1837. The novel, long out of print, had in its day a phenomenal sale, for its realistic presentation of Indian and frontier life in the early days of settlement in the South, narrated in the tale with all the art of a practiced writer. A very charming love romance runs through the story. This new and tasteful edition of "Nick of the Woods" will be certain to make many new admirers for this enchanting story from Dr. Bird's clever and versatile pen.

A COLONIAL FREE-LANCE. A story of American Colonial Times. By Chauncey C. Hotchkiss. Cloth, 12mo. with four illustrations by J. Watson Davis. Price, $1.00.

A book that appeals to Americans as a vivid picture of Revolutionary scenes. The story is a strong one, a thrilling one. It causes the true American to flush with excitement, to devour chapter after chapter, until the eyes smart, and it fairly smokes with patriotism. The love story is a singularly charming idyl.

THE TOWER OF LONDON. A Historical Romance of the Times of Lady Jane Grey and Mary Tudor. By Wm. Harrison Ainsworth. Cloth, 12mo. with four illustrations by George Cruikshank. Price, $1.00.

This romance of the "Tower of London" depicts the Tower as palace, prison and fortress, with many historical associations. The era is the middle of the sixteenth century.

The story is divided into two parts, one dealing with Lady Jane Grey, and the other with Mary Tudor as Queen, introducing other notable characters of the era. Throughout the story holds the interest of the reader in the midst of intrigue and conspiracy, extending considerably over a half a century.

IN DEFIANCE OF THE KING. A Romance of the American Revolution. By Chauncey C. Hotchkiss. Cloth, 12mo. with four illustrations by J. Watson Davis. Price, $1.00.

Mr. Hotchkiss has etched in burning words a story of Yankee bravery, and true love that thrills from beginning to end, with the spirit of the Revolution. The heart beats quickly, and we feel ourselves taking a part in the exciting scenes described. His whole story is so absorbing that you will sit up far into the night to finish it. As a love romance it is charming.

GARTHOWEN. A story of a Welsh Homestead. By Allen Raine. Cloth, 12mo. with four illustrations by J. Watson Davis. Price, $1.00.

"This is a little idyl of humble life and enduring love, laid bare before us, very real and pure, which in its telling shows us some strong points of Welsh character—the pride, the hasty temper, the quick dying out of wrath.... We call this a well-written story, interesting alike through its romance and its glimpses into another life than ours. A delightful and clever picture of Welsh village life. The result is excellent."—Detroit Free Press.

MIFANWY. The story of a Welsh Singer. By Allan Raine. Cloth, 12mo. with four illustrations by J. Watson Davis. Price, $1.00.

"This is a love story, simple, tender and pretty as one would care to read. The action throughout is brisk and pleasing; the characters, it is apparent at once, are as true to life as though the author had known them all personally. Simple in all its situations, the story is worked up in that touching and quaint strain which never grows wearisome, no matter how often the lights and shadows of love are introduced. It rings true, and does not tax the imagination."—Boston Herald.

Lightning Source UK Ltd.
Milton Keynes UK
UKHW010631200821
389174UK00001B/39